The Rise of Ren Crown

Anne Zoelle

Copyright © 2015 Anne Zoelle

All rights reserved.

ISBN-13: 978-0-9858613-1-5

ISBN-10: 0985861312

This is a work of fiction. Names, characters, places, and incidents are the product of the author's imagination or are used fictitiously. Any resemblance to actual events, locales, or persons, living or dead, is purely coincidental.

Books in the Series:

The Awakening of Ren Crown
The Protection of Ren Crown
The Rise of Ren Crown

DEDICATION

To Matt, S, Mom, and Dad.

CONTENTS

		Page
1	Aftermath	1
2	Tests That Lead to Ruin	14
3	The Status of Threats	24
4	Roommates Forever	33
5	Explanations and Confessions	40
6	Of Those Most Hated	51
7	Choosing a Path	60
8	Relationships with Thorns	66
9	Counseling in a Sea of Grief	79
10	Bellacia Bailey	87
11	Words We Dare	93
12	A Delinquency of Plans	98
13	Reconnection	110
14	In Memory of the Fallen	120
15	Shadows in the Night	124
16	The Midlands	132
17	Negotiations with a Bad Hand	146
18	Shadows on My Soul	158
19	Connections of the Desired and Undesired Kind	171

20	Nightmares and Consequences	180
21	Kaine's Revenge	188
22	Waking in the Same World	196
23	Justice Squad	200
24	Dog Day Afternoon	204
25	Civilized Couch Warfare	212
26	Promises of Bloodshed	222
27	Cafeteria Blunders	230
28	Justice, the gift that keeps giving	239
29	Deadlines	248
30	Rally to Assign	254
31	Deals of Discussion	259
32	Two Devils and a Bag of Popcorn	265
33	Planning for Fire	273
34	Daughter of the Enemy	277
35	Apologies	281
36	Spells and Plots	284
37	In Between	293
38	Fighting in Two Places	298
39	Department of Justice	302
40	Friday Night Lights	308
41	Tattoos and Memories	311
42	The Enemy of My Enemy	315

43	The Third Layer	324
44	Approaching Doom	331
45	Golden Storm	337
46	Chaos	343
47	Excelsine United	355
	About the Author	359

ACKNOWLEDGMENTS

Special thanks to Maureen, Matt, Barbara, and Poppy.

And to S.

Chapter One

AFTERMATH

CAMPUS WAS IN total disarray. Carnage was visible as far as the eye could see.

All students—even those bruised and blood-splattered—were assembled at Top Circle, for a mandatory assembly directed by Administration Magic that had targeted every human life-form capable of movement on the top eighteen levels of the mountain. Only medical students with a Level Six clearance or above, and the severely injured, were exempt from the assemblage.

Non-students had been quickly shuffled to a field on the Second Circle, and the professors had gone there to suss out any remaining assailants.

Officials of all stripes argued fiercely behind a silencing field at the front edge of our shell-shocked student body.

I touched my elbow and the connection threads that had gone hazy. Constantine was in a bed somewhere, half dead.

And others...? I gripped the discarded scarf tightly in my hand, and clutched at the dwindling magic within it—a dwindling tie to its owner.

Others were lost.

A cold gust of wind swept over the grass on which we stood, followed by a warmer breeze. The weather enchantments were finally re-engaging, hiding the bitter cold reality of six thousand feet and the tragedy that we had all just experienced. The terrorists had turned off the regulatory enchantments along with the rest of the Administration Magic before they attacked.

Like the last time I had been thrust into the middle of the entire campus population on Top Circle, there were no dragons chirping and blowing fire on the breeze, and there were no mages performing silly or extraordinary enchantments. Only the weather enchantments steadily restarting provided any sense of normalcy.

Chapter One

Sobs could be heard—wild moor-like calls in the otherwise stifling verbal silence. Several students were frantically wielding cleansing enchantments and clothing spells with their diminished magic reserves, frenetically flipping from one outfit to another, trying to stave off panic attacks or grief by stripping it physically from their skin.

But most students stood silently, fiercely at the ready—wearing their injuries and grime like badges, grieving their losses, wearing the garments of battle with steely determination in their gazes.

Hard gazes focused on our group, and on me. Questioning. Demanding answers.

Olivia's scarf burned in my hand. The link to Olivia was slipping further away the longer I was held here, inactive.

We had only been standing on Top Campus for five minutes, waiting for whatever decision was being made by those engaged in the vehement, silent arguments occurring on the steps, but for me it was four and a half too many. Community Magic recharges would kick in soon, but the residual magic in my dorm room would give me a faster return. Impatiently, I stepped forward, but something grabbed my ankle, jerking me to an abrupt, stilted stop, my foot pulled harshly back to the ground.

Panicked, I jerked my foot upward. A vine, reaching upward from the dirt, wrapped my ankle.

The vine squeezed warningly and I froze in the act of yanking. The vine relaxed and slid upward to form another coil.

It took me a moment to identify the magic in the vine as Alexander Dare's. It took me a moment more to relax. The vine wound around my skin further, pulling free of the ground with a snap, and settling beneath my jeans.

I looked up to see Dare, the peak of physical perfection, leaning with forced casualness against a pillar on the steps of the cafeteria. He was staring at me, and when my gaze met his, he shook his head slowly. The vine mirrored the movement with a slow squeeze.

Beside me, Will jerked in shock, touching just below his ear as mages sometimes did when they were talking via frequency.

"He... He said you will stay put and wait for the coming spectacle to end," Will whispered to me. "Or you will end up in a cell." Will shook his head. "It was far more cryptic and terse than that, but that was the meaning. How did he get my frequency?"

No need for Will to specify who 'he' was. Dare, speaking lowly to his cousin and uncle near him on the steps, was no longer looking in our direction, but his forced, casual stance hadn't changed.

"Don't reply and don't access any other communication," Mike said, lips barely moving. "Nothing is truly secure right now."

* Aftermath *

Neph and Will tightened their positions around me, along with Mike, Delia, Patrick, Asafa, and the other members of Plan Fifty-two. Neph's fingers touched my right wrist. Relaxing magic pulsed through the connection, but my internal system couldn't absorb it in the usual way—my magic was sluggish and broken.

"They can't do anything to you while you are enrolled at Excelsine," Will whispered. "It's a safe haven still. They would have to get you kicked out first."

Enrolled at Excelsine? I gripped the bag on my shoulder—Justice Toad was toasted somewhere inside after croaking his throat out when the Administration Magic had reactivated on campus. There was every chance that I had been summarily expelled through the sheer overload of offenses committed by, and through, me.

The officials, who had been silently arguing had finally agreed on something. A signal was given and a unit of Department stooges frog-marched the remaining members of the Peacekeepers' Troop toward the Administration Building. Dare exchanged a look with his uncle, then Julian Dare strode in after them. The remaining officials followed in their wake.

"To the Truth Stone," Will murmured, shuddering.

Marsgrove held the door for a group of Department officials, including the truly scary one from the projection at the battlefield. Marsgrove then turned to face the crowd.

"*No one moves*," he said, painful consequences promised in every steely word. The words were addressed to the student body, but he looked right at me as he said them.

I touched the new cuff on my wrist—control cuff number four. Marsgrove had brushed roughly past me and clamped it on when I'd entered Top Circle. His expression had been tight-lipped and fierce, but the action had been smooth and surreptitious.

My magic was so twisted, cuff number four probably wasn't even necessary to keep my unconscious impulses contained.

As Marsgrove entered the building, magic flipped up between the buildings surrounding Top Circle, creating a clearly defined pen of students. Like gladiators—or farm animals—awaiting slaughter.

Panicked voices rose from the crowd, students too, freshly traumatized by containment.

The combat mages were encompassed as well, arrayed around the path edges and on the steps of various buildings. If we all had to fight our way free, at least we had firepower.

A number of soothing, well-spoken voices rang over the crowd, speaking in deliberately steady tones, directing everyone to remain calm and safe, and to tune into frequency 8136, or 25192, or 69036—I quickly lost

Chapter One

count and interest in the numbers. But they continued the broadcast for any mage needing a distraction, discussion, or soothing tones.

"Steady everyone," Mike's voice echoed in my head, coming through the scarves around our throats—a communication system we set up days ago in order to be able to speak outside the frequency system.

It had been an excellent decision—concocted because frequencies were easily hackable, and because I didn't have one. It had allowed us to stay in contact when everything else had gone to hell.

The bodies immediately surrounding me—all allies—steadied, on edge. Their mental presence was a simple buzzing through the scarves, most of them far too used to rule breaking to risk saying anything incriminating, even in a private communication.

The student peacemakers stopped speaking aloud, finally, jobs accomplished.

The unnatural quiet of a crowd of thousands of traumatized and panicking students made my skin itch, but frequencies were going wild around the field. It was obvious by the way gazes were tracking: touching on me, touching on others, and returning. No lips were moving, but information was being exchanged at a rapid rate and the facial expressions were mixed—anger, fear, resignation, hardness.

Gazes I could see, kept switching from Bellacia Bailey back to us—some discussion occurring over magic that I had not yet harnessed in my head. But anything involving Bellacia Bailey was not good for me.

Mike swore harshly through the scarves, his mental series of curses startling both Will and me.

Son of a...community opinion is not our most pressing concern, Mike said in a rush, his thoughts barely coherent. His gaze was completely frozen on something to our right. *Everyone—*

"The girl from the dome," said a deceptively compelling voice, easily heard in the unnatural silence of the crowd. "I want her in front of me *now*."

The crowd around me tensed, and I followed their gazes to the long steps of the cafeteria. A man from the Department—so identified by the buckled throat collar he wore—emerged from the shadows of a pillar—*out of the shadow*. His jet-black hair, smirking features, and long, flaring coat perfectly fit an anime villain. Power coiled tightly around him. Five other Department stooges, also dressed chin-to-toe in military black, emerged from other shadows to stand at his side.

Directly from the shadows. As if they had *been* the shadows seconds before.

The stooges stood at military attention, narrowed gazes searching faces and auras, while the man at their head stood casually, far better dressed and

* Aftermath *

supercilious than his counterparts. His gaze was cruel as it slowly and methodically dissected the enormous crowd, moving from group to group, person to person.

The vine that had wrapped around my ankle shot up the leg of my jeans, flattening itself to my skin as it shot all the way up my body and into my sleeve. It swallowed *whole* the stamp Constantine had given me and the tube of paint my golem had left behind, then dove back down the same path to wrap around my ankle again, vibrating in agitation.

Stunned by that, more than the emergence of shadow dwellers, I stared down at my bloodstained and torn clothing, to where the vine was hugging my skin beneath. That was an action as close to panic as I'd ever witnessed from Alexander Dare.

I tore my gaze away to look in his direction and saw the combat mages from Dare's team step minutely closer to him.

Panicked murmurs flew around the field.

"That's Praetorian Kaine."

"He'll wipe us all!"

"Shadow Mage. Right hand of Stavros."

Someone near me whispered in a panicked voice, "Why is he out here? I *saw* him go in with the others! Someone get Marsgrove!"

I tried to catch Dare's gaze, but the crowd in front of me shifted, and Mike slid slowly, but very deliberately, in front of me. Familiar, taller bodies pressed around me on all sides, blocking me from view.

"You have no authority here, Praetorian," Dare said coldly, addressing him only by title. "And you are supposed to be with the other Department heads, sealed in with our officials while the Administration uses the Truth Stone."

"I think you'll find that I soon will have far more authority than you can imagine, Mr. Dare," he responded with a cold relish that bespoke an ongoing acrimonious relationship. "As for *this* moment, they need me not, so I swapped seals. This sealed area works just as well under the terms I agreed to." He shrugged, lips wickedly lifting. "And while the Administration Magic is still coming online, I have every right to conduct a preliminary investigation."

Magic glittered above the crowd, and a number of students around me panicked. I could only see the edges of the magic, though—and I could see Praetorian Kaine through small gaps as he walked almost restlessly, weaving casually between bodies and groups along the cafeteria stairs, turning in small circles as he gazed harder at some mages than others.

"Of course, my acceptance of this seal is *slightly* different from yours, which was forced upon *you* by Administration Magic. Unless you have...*special* talents, Mr. Dare, then all of you have been commanded to

Chapter One

remain in place—a five-foot length, was it not?—a command that can only be broken if you are in danger of dying. It would be bittersweet were it to come to that."

My ragged magic reacted painfully to the threat I couldn't see, trying to compensate for my lack of visual stimulus. Marsgrove's cuff activated in order to control my subconscious impulse, but barely any magic was even stuttering upward for it to control.

Something hard shoved me in the side. I looked down to see a small handhold device with a viewer in the palm of Will's hand. The view was connected to Will's sight, and the praetorian's hawkish features were displayed prominently on the screen, along with those of the mages standing around him. Will's gaze was focused forward, but he held the viewer steady—hand only shaking a little—allowing me to see through his eyes what was happening without revealing myself.

It also displayed a number of facts around the edges of the image—most importantly that the praetorians answered only to the head of the Department. And were basically black ops with nearly limitless reach in the Second Layer—untouchable in the courts.

But they were *not allowed in educational institutions for underage mages.*

And yet, here one was. Scary enough, without seeing everyone's reaction to the man, shrinking as far from his presence as they could get, with their heads down to avoid notice.

In the viewer, Dare's arms were crossed, lips pressed tightly together, as he looked at the magic dissipating in the air in front of him. It looked as if a scroll had been momentarily displayed there.

"We have but little time before the Truth Stone seal lifts and the more traitorous of you contact your mommies and daddies. I will be watching and listening to see who does that, of course." His smile went wide. "Perhaps pay a few visits afterward."

Panic grew.

"You are taking too long." Kaine addressed an underling at his left, with a voice edged in steel.

The underling was looking at a device in his hand and swallowed heavily. "She's here, sir. On this field. Something was interfering, but it's narrowing in now."

Panic spiked. They were tracking me, and I was penned in like a farm animal.

Kaine coldly surveyed us, a crowd of nearly fifteen thousand students. "It will go better for everyone if you show yourself, girl." His modulated voice wasn't overly loud, but it was easily heard in the stifling silence.

There was a distinct pause when no one moved, as I watched familiar faces whirl through the display as Will scanned the crowd.

* Aftermath *

"The usual rules do not apply today, as you've seen." Kaine's lips parted in a shark-like smile. "Someone should point her out *quickly*."

Shockingly, even with the implied threat, and the terrified gasps in the crowd, no one in Will's view did. And there were quite a few who had one reason or another to do so.

Bryant—who had originally been part of our group, but had fled when he'd realized we were going to fight the terrorists—said nothing. But his sullen silence wasn't a surprise. Self-preservation was his primary concern, and both sides would punish him for speaking out.

On the other hand, I expected Peters, who was also in view, to say something. He gripped his Canary-yellow Justice Tablet, but his gaze stayed purposely fixed on a point opposite us.

Will's gaze, and the image on the viewer, switched to the front of the crowd.

Bellacia's neutral gaze was on Kaine, but she wasn't standing as casually as usual. She, like the rest of the crowd, was unnerved by this man.

Camille Straught, who had to have been updated by Bellacia immediately upon frequencies being reinstated, was staring in our general direction—probably right at me—but her lips didn't move.

Was the campus population protecting me?

"She's over there, sir."

A single thin finger pointed in my direction.

Keiren Oakley, a boy who had made life quite unpleasant for me in Layer Politics class and by very obviously recording my actions around campus, was pointing our way. I had breathed a sigh of relief when he had left with the privileged others to attend the combat competition live. At some point during the battle, he had obviously returned to campus.

Mike's back seemed to grow in size, blocking me even more completely from view of the men on the steps.

"And where've you been, you little slimeball?" Mike asked. "Suspicious, you getting off campus exactly when everyone was going to burn, then suddenly being back here now. Who told you about the attack?"

Oakley's pale skin turned completely white. "I attended the All-Layer Com—"

"Silence," Kaine said coldly.

But Mike wasn't done. "And spoke with quite a number of the Peacekeepers' Troop—who are all currently being questioned with the Truth Stone—before you did," Mike said, aggressively, ignoring Kaine's steely command. Mike's condemning gaze focused solely on Oakley.

"*Silence*." There was a definite threat in that single word this time, and Mike clutched at his suddenly shadowed throat.

I grabbed the back of Mike's shirt in one hand, and pressed shaking

Chapter One

fingers to the back of his neck, absorbing the pain Kaine was sending into him. My magic channels twisted and receded further inside of me, like the flame of a match lighting strands of hair.

It was a warning choke more than anything, and I had experienced worse while trying to resurrect my brother. But the feeling of absolute terror emanating from the students surrounding us seeped in as well. Neph grabbed one of my forearms and Will grabbed the other. Some of it leeched through, as they bore part of the pain.

Mike had protected 'feral' me for a long time, and even after learning about my Origin status today, he was still doing it. He hadn't run in terror yet.

Kaine released the punishing magic, and my fingers dropped from Mike's neck.

I fisted the back of his shirt harder in my other hand though, as we both heaved in breaths. The tie between us strengthened, shifting to a connection thread at his neck. Not yet on a level with Will, Neph, Dare, Constantine, my parents, or Raphael, but a far stronger connection than to any others. Breathing heavily, I sent through all the vestiges of healing magic that I could draw from the tangled, twisted mass of half-burnt channels inside of me.

I was *never* going to find Olivia with my magic so damaged. I couldn't even manage a proper spell.

The crowd began moving in tense jousts of bodies, and the vine tightened around my ankle, in a strange gesture of comfort.

Mike tilted his chin down, swallowing roughly. His lips didn't move, but his voice was clear, coming mentally through his scarf—still tied around his neck—to the rest of ours.

Hold steady, he said as the men around Kaine parted the crowd and headed in our direction. I stared at Will's device, gripping Mike's shirt as we watched the men quickly approach our position.

I could *feel* them getting closer, an unseen force unzipping the crowd in a four-foot vee as they strode forward.

Will abruptly pulled the viewing device back, jamming it into his pocket. His empty fingers clenched at his side.

Kaine's voice echoed, a mere fifteen feet or so away. "The six from the images we were sent. Tap each of them."

No official had confirmed that Olivia was missing. An unofficial death toll had started and I had heard the echo of it through the scarves as people repeated frequency broadcasts. But there were so many students receiving treatment in Medical and being revived, that the lists were constantly updating.

Olivia's mother's audible demands concerning the whereabouts of her

* Aftermath *

daughter had gone unanswered, and Marsgrove, who actually knew Olivia was gone, had disappeared inside the Administration Building with the other officials.

But five of us—Neph, Will, Mike, Delia, and I—were still standing after our attack on the battle field dome, and were available for whatever "tapping" was.

Will withdrew something thin from his pocket as he was magically pulled forward, Mike was physically pushed to the side, tearing him from my grip, and Asafa and Patrick, who had been part of the group flanking us, were thrown against the surrounding bodies of the crowd, in the small five-foot allotment of movement that Marsgrove's spell had invoked. Patrick's eyes glinted with malice as he eyed the Department mages who were tightly interweaving themselves among our group of five.

I took a deep breath, then another, nearly panting with panic.

A trickle of magic seeped through a leaf of the vine, unnaturally attempting to regulate my state back to calm.

But I wouldn't be able to reclaim Olivia, if they put me in a cell. All chance would be lost. And the others... The others would be lost as well.

No, no, no, no. Conscious thought to do magic whipped up in me, but was *immediately* yanked back and pinched hard by the vine around my ankle. I reflexively pushed against the restriction as the menacing officials in black prowled closer. The vine tightened further, battling for control of my magic.

I could feel the point at which I could break free of it. Right there... Just where the vine seemed to thin...

Dare's magic pulsed along the threads connecting us. *Trust. Let go. Trust...*

I abruptly let go of the magic, and the vine loosened. On impulse, I shoved Olivia's scarf into my back pocket.

Then I was staring at Kaine as he stepped directly out of a shadow formed from the crowd in front of me, and my gaze met his ruthless one directly, for the first time.

"Ah. Here you are." Satisfaction edged his cold gaze in icy, ornamental spikes. Silver eyes in hollowed sockets stared down at me. Surprisingly, he was much younger than I would have assumed. Maybe in his late twenties. Not that much older than the oldest students on campus, but the soullessness in his eyes seemed ancient.

One long fingertip drew a path from the outer edge of his right eyebrow, then curved beneath his eye. A haze of magic fell across the eye, turning the iris from silver to black, the entire pupil swallowed by darkness. Zips of polychromatic colors wove in and out.

I swallowed with difficulty, and eyed the other black-clad figures

Chapter One

surrounding us.

The vine around my ankle tightened, waiting to strike if I reached for magic.

Someone behind me fiercely whispered, "Where are the professors? Johnson and Marsgrove might be sealed, but the professors—well, get around the communication block!"

Kaine smiled—a slashing cut of his mouth and eyes. "Where are your professors indeed?" he asked aloud, addressing the whisper. "And where were they when all of you required their aid? No, I think it far better that you be under the Department's protection, and the Legion's, for the foreseeable future. And Tarei, do tap the student who was just speaking as well as these five."

There was a clap of sound, and the noise of the crowd dissipated around me.

"Now, to more interesting matters." With his magicked eye, Kaine took in the surrounding faces. His gaze rested on Neph, Patrick, then Delia, for the longest moments. Magic swirled up and over his blackened silver eye, like dark mist orbiting a sphere—giving data on everything that passed through his vision.

"What a riveting little group this is," he said. "Full of degenerates and sympathizers."

Patrick bared his teeth in a very savage smile, eyes glittering. Delia and Neph stood frozen.

Kaine smiled coldly, then turned his icy, spelled gaze directly on me. "Name?"

I shook my head.

He looked at the top of my head—which meant *he could see Raphael's spell*—and his cold smile grew colder. "There are so many reasons for me to take you to where you'll never again see the light of day, girl."

Raphael's insanity-laced words about the Department's basement slammed into my head.

It also made me very aware that whatever protection Raphael had placed upon me to avoid Department eyes was no longer in place. Whether it had gone with the chain I had unlinked between us over the past few weeks, or was due to something Raphael had done in retaliation during our fight, I didn't know.

And God, I was covered in evidence. Constantine's stamp and the tube of Awakening paint were in the vine wrapped around my ankle, my brother's bracelet was clasped on my wrist, Olivia's scarf—which was lightly, and very illegally leeching a small part of my ragged magic again, now that everyone was worried about frequencies once more—was in my back pocket directly connected to the one at my neck, and most damning,

* Aftermath *

the residue from Kinsky's papers had seeped into my skin.

"Should I question your friends first?" Kaine sounded disinterested and detached, but his gaze intensified and I registered a sickening pleasure increasing in his magic.

"Ren," I said immediately, my voice scratched and shaking. I cleared my throat, never looking away from him. "My name is Ren."

Never Florence. Not in this world, not a name that could connect me to my First Layer parents. I had changed my name in Excelsine's administrative system and it had been sealed as my "true" name when Provost Johnson had restarted my record after I'd accidentally destroyed the entire Shangwei Art Complex first term.

"Ah. Ren Crown, isn't it? We've come across your name in reports from a *variety* of sources. Quite a run you've had, so far, at this academic institution. Such a *short* run."

His gaze was hungry—and, so *very*, very merciless—as he looked at me.

He couldn't *take* me. I swallowed and mentally repeated the sentiment. He couldn't just take me. The crowd was too big. Too many people looked militant. I had just helped save campus. And even if people didn't know *how* it had happened, they knew who had done it. Everyone sitting in the battle field stands had seen us fight Godfrey and somehow secure the dome—had thought they were watching us die.

Kaine's magicked gaze tracked me, seeming to know exactly what I was thinking, as his smile grew.

"What happened to the Origin Dome that Vincent Godfrey raised? The one dismantled by Origin Magic—*new* Origin Magic. The one *you* dismantled."

There was a surge of magic in the crowd—whispers flitting over frequencies, judging by the nonverbal communication I could see.

Kaine's empty gaze surveyed the crowd as if he could hear them when I could not. His gaze landed back on me, reflecting a terrible pleasure. "Why do you look so frightened, Miss Crown? This is but a simple question. And one that *everyone* wants to see addressed."

The magic on the field stilled.

I could hear Olivia's clipped tones in my head, and what she would surely be saying: *He can't take you as a hero—he has to make people fear you first.*

I tried to send a mental request to Neph through my scarf, but silence was the only response. Kaine was sporting a terrible smile, and I looked past him to see one of his men pinching Delia's scarf between two of his fingers. Cutting off contact. Since the scarf was still around Delia's throat, it was an even more threatening gesture.

Mike was pulling at the hands holding him and yelling—lips ranting and throat working—but I couldn't hear a word of it. Kaine had managed to

Chapter One

eliminate the crowd from my reach—allowing me no audible way to judge what was happening around me.

"Such interesting stories still forming and being bandied about. Tell us, Miss Crown, how did you do it?"

Kaine hadn't seen what had happened firsthand. The terrorists' transmission from campus to the outside world—which had included all of the Council members, heads of state, parents, and citizens—had been cut the moment Godfrey had realized the dome over the battle field stands had been wrested from his control.

But I remembered the intense gaze, tracking Kinsky's papers. Not this man's cold gaze, but his boss's—Enton Stavros. I remembered the moment his absolute focus had switched from Godfrey to tracking the papers. He hadn't had time to see me.

But now?

The cruel smile on Kaine's face said everything. Piecing together the firsthand accounts, and narrowing down the variables, it wasn't hard to guess that it had been me. All Kaine needed was to get me to confess—to trap me in evidence, admissions, and lies.

I shook my head. The savagery in his smile grew as he surveyed the crowd again, his gaze calculating—as if he were actively listening to all of the secret and private conversations that everyone was having en masse in the moment. Eavesdropping on and parsing all communications on campus.

"The papers used on the dome over the battle field stands—where are they?" He pressed a cold fingertip against my forehead.

Kinsky's papers. A single piece of damning evidence that would out me for what I was.

"Papers?"

His finger sparked and pain shot through me, spiking in my forehead and spilling down my limbs like he had electrocuted me. I fell to my knees.

"Tricks do not work on me, girl. Nor on any in the Department. Better to learn that early. Now, let's try the same question again."

I opened my mouth to give the same answer, but the pain turned crippling. A hand pulled me back to my feet and harshly held me upright as my legs folded again. He was using a form of Justice Magic, but far more excruciating than the kind used on campus.

"Observe the lies she is trying to tell." Kaine's voice was dismissive, as he addressed the crowd I still couldn't hear. "Pitiful."

I hadn't signed any sort of contract with Kaine. He wasn't part of campus. How was he wielding Justice Magic over me?

"Now let's try again."

I concentrated on the pain, blanking my mind to anything else. If there

* Aftermath *

was one thing Raphael and my active delinquency on campus had taught me, it was how not to tell the truth yet still skirt the edges of fact.

Kinsky's sheets were somewhere in the Midlands—I had thrown them in that direction when I realized we were being forcibly marched back up the mountain. Because the tiles were constantly shifting within the Midlands, I had no *true* idea where they were inside those levels.

"I don't know." I couldn't give him coordinates or even a reasonable guess without further thought. I set my mind to the active task of reciting First Layer song lyrics.

Crippling pain made me drop again, lyrics splintering in my head.

"You do," he said with relish. "Where are the papers?"

"Somewhere in the Midlands," I gasped, the answer pulled from me.

The Midlands could hide anything. I had to believe that.

"Very good." He nearly cooed. "Now, what was on the sheets?"

"Vague human forms," I said. *Truth.* That was the last thing I had seen on the sheets—all of the trapped men inside. "I don't know who created them." I didn't know the parents of the men or any of their kin. "I can't be sure what they did." I had no idea of the men's pasts.

I repeated these notions to myself over and over, without letting my thoughts deviate from those truths.

"No? You are manipulating the truth of the magic. It's obvious by how you still struggle to stand. If you simply gave the truth, there'd be no pain. But you've given me plenty, Miss Crown."

His finger dropped from my forehead, but I could tell, by the sharp, malevolent look in his spelled eyes that he wasn't finished questioning me. Rather, it was as if he were suddenly on a ticking timeline.

"Such *reports* from the battle. Such unusual residue left lingering in the air." Kaine smelled the air, eyes closed. For a moment, it seemed like another face rippled across his features. "A scent not smelled in...much too long. The clear ozone smell of Origin Magic."

Sound returned to me in another clap of magic, and I heard the wave of murmurs break over the crowd.

"Not the reused, repurposed smell of the captured magic of the past." Kaine's lips turned down, as if he were dismayed, but everything else about him registered dark pleasure. "This is fresh. A new creator. And society can't have that type of danger running around unchecked. A danger like you."

He knew what I was. Clear as the sun sinking in the sky, and my heart to my toes, he knew. He couldn't just take me, though. Not on a suspicion. Not when I had just saved campus.

"Test her."

Hands grabbed my arm roughly and yanked me to my knees.

Chapter Two

TESTS THAT LEAD TO RUIN

THEY PUSHED THE crowd further to the sides, while keeping me in place. Sound had returned completely and I could hear people—Mike's forceful voice among them—protesting vehemently.

"Calm yourselves," Kaine said in disdain. "If she passes the test, we will reward her for her bravery and quick thinking, I'm sure." His smile was cold. He did not expect me to pass the test.

A small box was placed on the ground before me. Covered in iridescent swirls, it was a beautifully coated, but otherwise plain, square box.

Did he always carry this around with him?

Kaine smiled, as if he could read my thoughts. "We always carry it, little mage. Just in case."

He knelt down and caressed the edge.

The crowd nearest to us, who were able to see what was happening, pressed back as far as they were allowed, a few screaming in terror.

"Praetorian Kaine, don't you dare open—"

Kaine flipped open the box and the familiar, strident, panicked voice froze, drifting off into the ether as the world around me abruptly switched. Brilliant colors burst everywhere. Hues I had only dreamed of mixing appeared. The colors were alive, teaming with crystal and metallic bases. A wisp of Aurora Borealis Green, vibrant and coiling in the air, swirled suggestively around my head.

Draeger's box, in a practice room, so long ago, had been a little like this. Though less immersive. Visually engaging, but without the other sense attachments.

Kinsky's painting at the Library of Alexandria had been a little like this, but had possessed a far more personal touch in its otherworldliness. Kinsky's touch and personal thoughts had been dominant throughout the world inside the painting. This box was untouched—beckoning. No,

* Tests that Lead to Ruin *

demanding, that I stamp myself all over it.

Build. Shape. Change. Destroy.

A dot. A line. A circle bulging into a sphere. Three dimensional shapes began rotating in the air. As they rotated, they stretched and compressed, coming out of themselves, and diving back in—shifting perception to create four dimensions. Unable to resist, I reached for the first shape. There was a question within, asking what I could do with it. It was like being in a reading room and a practice room and the Library of Alexandria all shoved into one tempting complication of a shape that pulled me forth. Impossible. Inescapable.

Never able to resist the type of challenge that the puzzle represented, I manipulated it, breathing life into the shape and spreading it with my fingers, like peacock brushes on a canvas.

The tiniest, smallest part of me recognized that doing whatever this was would out me as an Origin Mage, but the magic was irresistible and I focused on that instead.

Unlike the domes, which had been out of control forces of nature, this magic whispered and teased, caressed and hinted, luring me with soft promises of what I could *do* with it. Telling me how it would reach to the raw, dulled edges of my internal pathways and reserves, and smooth everything. Promising it would fill the spaces.

Promising me that together, we could safely retrieve Olivia; we could wipe away the memories of everyone around us; we could save our loved ones. I just had to form the magic and give it to the box.

My magic *hurt,* though. It was twisted and tangled from all the mangled events of the past few hours that had taken, contorted, and incorrectly released my magic.

In here, the box whispered. Everything would be well and right. *Just give the magic to the box.*

I formed my mental pyramid, and the will of the box made it so that I didn't even have to use my own ragged bodily paths to engage the magic.

It would do everything for me, it whispered.

Love and enlightenment, Christian and Olivia, family and friends...if I just gave the magic to the box.

No more pain. No more heartache.

I eagerly lifted my hands, palms up and unfurled my fingers, then splayed them outward to pour the essence forth.

My love for Christian, always a part of me, forevermore. My bond to Olivia, who I would protect to the end. My bonds to my parents, Dare, Constantine, Will, Neph... The magic flowed faster.

External magic abruptly yanked it back, and I scrambled to keep my position, fingers outstretched to give, my twisted magic contorting further.

Chapter Two

The external magic yanked more forcefully, and my fingers curled inward, clenching, then fisting against my thighs. I felt the vine around my ankle suck the magic downward, swallowing it in long, greedy gulps, not allowing my body to process a drop. My heart beat a furious staccato. *No.* I wanted to give the magic to the *box*.

I pulled and pushed, but the vine continued to extract the magic from under my skin, taking everything that I was creating and devouring it like the carnivorous plant it was.

As it devoured, my view slowly grew distant, returning to the unexceptional shapes and absurdly dull colors of the normal world.

I tried to reach for the glory of the box again, but it was agonizing to do so. The raw paths of my magic were bleeding. Had *been* bleeding. The box had just temporarily taken away the pain and my knowledge of it.

My newly instated, unexceptional view of the world showed Kaine looking furious and venomous at my failure.

I let go completely—opening my hands to allow all threads to drop.

Kaine's minion hastily toed the lid of the box closed, then hurriedly backed up two steps.

There was silence, then a slow roll of murmurs.

"She passed," Mike said, shock in his voice that he couldn't contain.

The cloudy film of magic over Kaine's silver irises darkened, as if someone else were looking through his eyes. "No, I don't think so. Search her."

The vine, which had been slithering down the back of my ankle, released abruptly, and only my sense of it allowed me to register it diving into the ground under my jeans—ripping the smallest bit of energy from the dirt to aid its tunneling dive. Burrowed into the ground, gone, in a motion too quick for anyone not connected to it to sense.

Kaine's strange eyes were examining me slowly from head to bent knees, as if he could see through my pockets and to everything beneath. Another Department mage yanked me to my feet.

Mike stepped forward, lips thinned. His complexion was pasty and there was the slightest tremble in his limbs, but his chin was lifted, determined. "She passed the test," he repeated. "Time to reward her for her bravery today, as you said."

I could vaguely hear people yelling and feel the pushing against the crowd as I was jostled. There were officials spilling out of buildings in the distance and running around the sides of the student pen.

But I couldn't concentrate on anything but the way Kaine was staring at the ground at my feet, strange eyes examining the grass and dirt, as if the shadows held answers. The vine was gone, but there was the tiniest residual feeling, and I had no idea what type of locating or identifying devices these people had.

Kaine smiled suddenly, sharply, his calculating gaze going to the front of the crowd. Hungry eyes shifted back to me—as if Kaine had ordered chopped steak at a fine restaurant and found them serving a buffet of filet mignon instead.

"Indeed," he breathed, his smile chilling and all too alarming, as if he were speaking to someone else looking out from his eyes.

He tossed a silver coin to the praetorian nearest to me. "Bring her." Kaine scooped up the box and strode toward the steps. "We but need to retest Alexander Dare. A simple check."

The cloaked praetorian pressed the coin to my skin, and another man grabbed my other arm, yanking me forward. They marched me through Kaine's cleared path, bracketed by the solemn faces of the static crowd.

I craned my neck back and saw my friends frantically trying to move forward after us. But whatever the coin's properties, it allowed me to be moved, while no one else was able to break free of the five-foot cells Marsgrove had invoked.

Panic overtook me and I fought the hold on my arms. I heard the crowd nearest the steps—filled with combat mages—erupt in complaint and anger as we approached Dare.

"Your vendetta is getting tiresome, Praetorian Kaine, and edging into the ridiculous." Julian Dare was standing on the other side of the magical field, looking as if he were three seconds from bursting through. "Alexander was retested two days ago, the morning the competition started. It was the *fourth time* in as many months, and he tested negatively for Bridge powers, as *always*."

I struggled. Holy crap. *Monthly?* That meant Dare was exceptional at keeping his powers hidden—and the Second Layer officials were *very* persistent—if they were testing him over and over again simply because he was the extremely powerful son of a Bridge Mage.

As Dare had told me previously, *all* mages were dangerous, and to think otherwise was shortsighted. But there were controls in place for regular mages—like cuffs and intentions magic. Mages who could remotely take, without permission, magic from one person or object and transfer it to another, however, were specifically feared—as if they would suddenly decide one day to drain everyone surrounding them, and destroy the magic worlds.

Like Origin Mages, mages who could destroy the layers, were not to be trusted.

"Are you rejecting the test on his behalf, Julian?" Kaine said, his eyes cool, no surprise to be had as he stopped in front of them, his fellow praetorian dragging me to Kaine's side. This was a game that had obviously

Chapter Two

been played more than once. But the lift of Kaine's lips was a red flag, and Julian Dare's deep blue gaze shuttered, indicating he saw it clearly. The two men looked to be around the same age, somewhere in their late twenties or early thirties.

I looked at Dare, who was steadfastly watching Kaine. Dare's expression was neutral, but the feeling emanating from him...was not impassive in the least. He was coiled, ready. A fresh surge of panic surfaced in me.

"Maximilian's good will is starting to wane, Kaine," Julian said. "Prestige Stavros would do well to take care with his next actions and yours."

"A threat, Julian? Is Itlantes finally revealing its hand, overtly threatening the security of the Second Layer?"

Itlantes was the Dare's stronghold—an island they had successfully defended against the combined forces of the Second Layer before I'd been born.

"There is no threat," Julian Dare said.

"Alas, your brother does so enjoy starting bloodstained wars over women." Kaine smiled. His voice easily carried above the silent crowd, each word served to the bystanders, like a blow. "But what is this? You are *nervous* today. What could be the cause of this odd emotion for you?"

Their interplay was like watching a play where everyone had already rehearsed their lines. None of their questions or responses were anything more than movements replicated from an already laid out script.

"One of our premiere universities nearly wiped out? With two of my nephews in attendance? It's been a less than optimal day," Julian Dare said. "Cease your theatrics."

"*Theatrics?* The public always feels better when we test and retest. They like knowing that all is well. Keeping our layer safe means that we also have to protect it from within."

He lazily tapped at the collar around his own neck, and I saw the thin silver band that I hadn't seen on any of the others.

Without waiting for a response, Kaine stepped up on the third riser of the cafeteria's massive promenade and addressed the crowd. "As an upstanding member of our society, Mr. Dare will agree to be retested."

Everything in me went cold.

"Axer wasn't even *on* campus until the end of the battle," Fallon Lox said, his expression furious, focused completely on Kaine. "And *you* followed on his heels."

Ramirez and Greene, the two other male combat mages in Dare's personal group, were far less vocal, but their expressions were dark and focused on Kaine as well. Camille Straught, the sole female in their group of five, was staring at me, and she did not look pleased.

Still addressing the crowd, Kaine continued lazily, "Mr. Dare's

* Tests that Lead to Ruin *

dismantling of the Origin Dome around your Administration Building was laudable—I watched it myself—and we but need to make sure that he was untainted by the display."

Kaine pulled long fingers over a device at his belt. A pulse of familiar, tainted magic shivered over me in response. So this was where the magic of the Administration Building's dome had gone.

I had thought at the time of the dismantling, when I'd been far down the mountain on the Eighteenth Circle, that whoever had collected the magic from the Administration Building's dome had cared more for *it* than for helping campus. That opinion remained unchanged as I watched Kaine's coldly amused gaze move across the crowd, looking for dissenters.

No one said anything. Dare *had* taken down the Administration Building's dome.

Then died.

Hopefully, Kaine didn't know Dare had then taken down the dome under which Raphael and I had fought. Dare hadn't died after dismantling Raphael's dome, and I had a feeling that if it came to light that Dare was working up his tolerance to being able to touch and control Origin Magic, it would be an even worse strike against him.

"Excellent. Hold out your palm, Mr. Dare. Let's be prompt."

Alexander Dare wasn't going to pass this test. I could feel it. Something in me knew. He had blown whatever lid he normally kept on his magic in order to help me control mine. He was going to be exposed.

And Kaine knew it.

No. *No.*

Blind fury surged through me. I couldn't let this happen. Couldn't let another friend sacrifice for me. Another loved one. Christian, Olivia, Alexander...

Unable to access anything further up, magic lethargically oozed from my wrists into my fingertips, squeezing painfully as it twisted the magic channels completely excised by the strain of the days' events, and by being tested and drained.

But the box...the testing box had said that I didn't have to use *my* magic.

My hold on reason slipped as scenarios scrolled, one after another, dripping down my vision in a series of ones and zeroes, half-drawn lines and bursts of half-mixed colors. Consequences, actions. My likely death. Blowing up part of the mountain; creating a portal; disappearing in a blaze of glory—things that would make every Department agent mobilize to find me—that would give Dare time to recharge or cap whatever he needed to pass the test.

Dare's gaze whipped to me, and the line connecting us grew taut and painfully tight, interrupting the scrolling, and obliterating the feed. *Don't you*

Chapter Two

dare, everything about him said.

But the vine was gone, and he had no way to stop me. I fought to gather the streams of thought that, at a highly painful cost, I could still turn into magic. The Department mage holding my left arm swore and let go of me, as if he'd been shocked. The mage then grabbed me tighter.

The edges of Kaine's lips sliced upward as he watched. "Such an unexpected and intriguing discovery," he said as he looked between us, though, strangely, his voice no longer sounded like his own, and it did not carry to the crowd behind us. "The tests we will run in the lab..." He snapped his fingers and motioned to a man on his left. "Tarei, the device."

I could see Julian Dare doing something, finger moving at his side. Maybe he could break through the pen and stop all of this. But I couldn't trust him, and I couldn't let them test Alexander—the boy who had saved me, and who had let me have one last moment with my twin.

"Yes," Kaine murmured temptingly, his soulless gaze on me, reading whatever my facial expressions were exposing. "You should stop this from occurring."

I pulled at the streams and his smile grew. It didn't matter. It didn't matter that doing this would expose me. I would lead them on a merry chase away from Dare. I would find Olivia. Return her. Everyone would be saved and safe.

There was a sound registering somewhere in my brain that my thinking was *off*, but I was in a dreamlike state I couldn't shake.

"Ren," Dare hissed, completely out of character and off-script. I could see the absolute anger on his normally inscrutable face and feel his fury through the threads that connected us. But there was nothing he could do to stop me now. His powers didn't—

The jerk against my chest where the ultramarine thread connected me to Alexander almost made me drop the magic.

"Praetorian Kaine!"

I dropped the magic completely, shock vying with anxiety as Marsgrove neared our group, almost at a run. A sharp wave of his palm dropped the magic field holding all of us in.

The backlash of releasing the magic twisted my already burnt channels into an agonizing mass and I sobbed at the pain.

"Dean Marsgrove," Kaine said, turning toward him with nary a flinch. "You are just in time to stand witness."

"You will cease this spectacle," Marsgrove commanded, still striding forward. "*No one move.*"

Officials of all stripes spilled toward us in Marsgrove's wake.

Kaine's gaze was unperturbed. "Surely you are not suggesting that you disagree with the need to test rare mages?"

* Tests that Lead to Ruin *

"I do not see any reported, rare mages here." Marsgrove slowed to a controlled stride, making his way through the crowd on the promenade. "Only students who require physical and emotional care. Ones who, in the *five minutes* that we have been gone, you have sought to further terrorize. And through a loophole you exploited in the Justice Magic under which you have sworn to serve."

"Ah. I do miss our discussions on semantics. *Potential* rare mages, then," Kaine said, without missing a beat. "And determining threats is the thing most necessary to the long-term care of your student body."

"Instilling fear, you mean. Badgering and threatening."

"I weep for the generations to come," Kaine said, as if he were some sixty-year-old, jaded politician instead of a young, scary mage who moved in and between shadows. With a wave of Kaine's hand, his minion, Tarei, re-pocketed the device that had been about to test Dare. "How ill prepared they will be."

"They will manage," Marsgrove said through tight lips as he came to stand in an off-square formation against Kaine, the Dares, and whatever praetorians were holding me.

"Have you made an arrest, Praetorian Kaine?" said a bored voice two dozen feet behind Marsgrove.

My gaze followed the voice to see the cadaverous-looking man from the battle field projection standing behind a large number of Department mages. His gaze was as flat and soulless as his voice. In the blink of an eye, that vision disappeared and a plain-faced man—pale and profusely sweating—stood in his place.

Like an old moving picture where the frame flips, the face of the head of the Department switched onto a face twenty feet, fifteen feet, ten feet away, then swirled into place on the head of the Department stooge next to me.

A gaze full of dissecting malice looked down at me from its parasitic perch.

I stumbled away from him.

Only the pain pulsing through me as I tried to channel protection magic kept me from hyperventilating.

The anomaly cocked his borrowed head at me, his eyes taking in the scarf around my neck, his gaze narrowing on it. Everything in me said that if I had Olivia's scarf in hand, instead of stuffed in my back pocket, it would already have been taken from me.

His expression shifted to something falsely—so falsely—kind. "The lovely young mage who was standing in front of Vincent Godfrey and the Origin Dome. So pleased to meet you, dear." His voice was the one I had heard coming from Kaine—the one talking about the tests they would run.

Chapter Two

A shiver wracked me.

His head popped onto the Department figure to my left, then behind me, then to my right, flipping around me, cataloging all my points and angles, and where he could best place his dissection scalpel.

"Such a lovely surprise." His distant expression was at odds with the way his image flitted between hosts.

Whatever terror Kaine had induced in the crowd, this man tripled. It was tangible in the Community Magic throbbing at the edge of my numb state.

Marsgrove's lips were tight as he directed his remarks to the man's head as it settled back into a single position. "Praetorian Kaine has overstepped his bounds, Prestige Stavros. By edict of the Council, educational institutions are exempt from any oversight by the Department. He has no right and no authority to test or question *any* students."

"Prestige Stavros." Kaine gave a half bow—and there was no doubt in my mind that he was not one to follow such forms of conduct with anyone else. "Worry over the safety of the public and the underage mages here made me desirous of neutering any and all threats. Perhaps my concern over our safety *was* overly fervent."

My bracelet encyclopedia took that moment to unnecessarily inform me that "Prestige" was a title given to the head of large businesses or divisions.

I had a feeling the man in front of me would far prefer the Roman title of Emperor to go with his legion and praetorians.

"Praetorian Kaine questioned and tested students—waiting until they were penned in," Marsgrove replied. He seemed to be addressing this to the other officials rather than to Stavros. "I want charges filed."

"Praetorian Kaine, how aggressive of you," Stavros murmured.

"My apologies, Prestige Stavros," Kaine replied, not looking the least bit chastised, or concerned.

"Aggressive," Stavros said, in an indifferent tone of voice. "However, I think all concerned can see that you were only distressed for the well-being of our layer."

Whereas Kaine's face was decorated by smirking evil intentions, Stavros was an evil so polished that all emotion slipped right off him.

Marsgrove frowned. "I think that is to be decided—"

"This girl has valuable information on today's events, Prestige Stavros," Kaine smoothly interrupted. The expression on his face increased my worry. He still held an ace.

My heart thumped erratically.

"And she will be questioned under oath according to the rules of this campus," Marsgrove said furiously.

"If she were a *student*, perhaps. Alas, she has been expelled, and therefore falls under our jurisdiction," Kaine said, the side of his lips lifting. "This, I believe, also negates many of those pesky charges you were considering filing."

I clutched my bag, still slung around my frame with Justice Toad dead inside, fears becoming reality. I wasn't a student. *I was no longer a student.*

"Well that does change matters," Stavros said, waving a hand. "Take her. We will join you soon."

The man next to me yanked me forward.

I thrust my heels out. Voices were yelling behind me and people angrily surged forward. Julian Dare grabbed Alexander's wrist, fiercely whispering something as he stopped him from advancing.

"Calm yourselves," Stavros said to the surging crowd, one eyebrow cocked, as if surprised by the outrage. Every expression was a calculated act. "Expelled students are under the purview of layer authorities. Do remain calm. No harm will come to another student this day."

A neat way of not addressing *tomorrow*. Or non-students.

The man holding me thrust me toward Kaine, who grabbed me. I could feel darkness wrapping around the edges of my eyes.

"We will take care of Miss Crown's injuries and magical exhaustion, and return her to peak condition," Stavros said. "Worry not. We have a few simple questions for her, and of course, awards to give, I understand? At the Department, naturally. Where we can determine the best future for her. Praetorian Kaine?"

A band of iron clamped around my wrist.

My panic spiked exponentially, but no magic answered its call.

Chapter Three

THE STATUS OF THREATS

MY GAZE MET Marsgrove's and a series of frightening expressions washed across his face.

Justice Toad suddenly croaked and warbled, and the iron dropped from my wrist with a flick of Marsgrove's fingers.

A rush of warmth flooded my veins and expanded out in crystal clarity, brightening all of the buildings, flora, and students in my view. Community Magic swirled into me. I could feel campus fully again, in a way that I hadn't realized I'd been missing—mistaking the numbness I was already feeling for that disconnect.

I dove between Kaine and the man closest to him and put myself a foot behind Marsgrove.

"Prestige Stavros, Praetorian Kaine." Marsgrove's feet were shoulder-width apart and his hands were loose and ready at his sides. "You are mistaken."

"Is that so?" Stavros's smile was ice cold, while Kaine's was edged with a mania that was even more worrying. Stavros leaned forward so that just the five of us nearest could hear. "Such timing. And a truly illuminating action on your part to make sure I know exactly where your allegiance is in this war, Phillip. Perhaps it is long past time to make public your past alliances."

"And expose your own actions in this conflict from its very beginning? I think not." Marsgrove's voice was equally low and equally edged in steel.

One of them had erected a temporary privacy circle. It glowed around us in a dark, malevolent way.

"Ah, but looking over the mistakes of the nearly forgotten past merely provoke irritation. Current events are always more harshly judged. In light of what has happened, I think it will look *much* worse for you and for the precarious position in which your career has started to teeter. Besides,

* The Status of Threats *

everyone expects those that keep them safe to take...drastic measures at times." Stavros's lips curled coldly.

Marsgrove smiled tightly and with a wave of his hand the privacy field shattered. He raised his voice so that the crowd could hear. "Alexander Dare will be tested when he returns to the competition tomorrow, as is customary when a competitor leaves the field. That base test uncovers rare powers, so it will be more than fitting."

"Rare powers, but not *extraordinary* powers. The truly extraordinary often have ways to hide it," Stavros said dismissively, head resting on a new host in the circle of arguing adults.

"Your conspiracies are just that, Prestige Stavros," Marsgrove said, without concealing his words from the crowd.

The crowd tensed, and I got the feeling that Marsgrove was taking badass to new levels. That people didn't just say things like that to Stavros' face. And they hadn't even heard what he *had* been saying. I stepped minutely closer to Marsgrove.

"Phillip, you, of all people, should understand the need to restrain potential evildoers." Nerves spiked in me at Stavros's smile. He was staring straight at me, and I saw magic scroll over his borrowed eyes, like Kaine's. *What was he reading on me now? What was he communicating to the others?*

"You will not test any more students on this field," Marsgrove said, voice edged in steel. Seeing Marsgrove's enmity turned on someone other than me was a strange relief.

Stavros smiled, as if he had been given a perfect gift.

Provost Johnson chose that opportune moment to emerge from the crowd of officials. He strode onto the steps. A distinguished, white-haired man strode out after him.

"Prestige Stavros," Johnson said. "I assure you, any and all student involvement in the activities today will be dealt with. Internally. The Peacekeepers' Troop is available for continued debriefing and questioning at any time, as *they* are under your current purview."

Stavros's host stayed in place, but Stavros's head rotated like a terrifying owl. "Ah, Provost Johnson. So good of you to come to aid your dean. And Chancellor Barrie too. So prompt to his aid," he uttered as if he were complimenting dogs who had heeled alongside their master.

Nothing was said for a few tense moments as Stavros coldly surveyed the head of university life and the symbolic head of Excelsine, who was rarely seen on campus. I had never met Chancellor Barrie, who served as Excelsine's representative to the Second Layer Educational Council, but he looked and reacted like any privileged politician to a political threat—raised chin, narrowed eyes, clenched muscles.

Provost Johnson, to his credit, didn't cower under Stavros's pain-

Chapter Three

promising gaze either, though his words were careful.

"Be assured, Prestige Stavros, your concerns will be investigated fully within Excelsine's judicial system. We will deal with this entire matter in closed quarters, unless you wish to broadcast it across the layer."

"I would have you deal with your own mess, Provost Johnson; however, the Department is dedicated to the safety of the Second Layer. And it is obvious to all that oversight is required on this campus."

"Oversight is not wha—"

A praetorian flashed magic in the air and a seal appeared.

"And oversight was just granted." Stavros smiled. "By the same body that you are currently attempting to reach, Dean Marsgrove."

Marsgrove looked more pissed than I'd ever seen him. "Did they? How strange."

"There is no need to be sore at your inability to keep the populace under your care safe, Dean Marsgrove. We are, all of us, concerned with the safety of the underage mages in our layer. And will do what is needed to secure that safety." He snapped his borrowed fingers and magic appeared in his palm. The magic flickered into a heavy metal seal. "The Legion will provide campus security for the coming days. With the combat mages continuing their competition—showing a united front for the emotional well-being of all students in the Second Layer—surely this will be acceptable."

No one responded for long moments.

I desperately wished I knew what was happening.

"Surely the Legion is needed elsewhere where the security of the Second Layer has been repeatedly attacked," Marsgrove said, cold fury underlining every syllable.

"Nothing is as necessary as making sure our best and brightest are safe." Stavros smiled. "And if your security enhancements prove acceptable during this period, we will be more than happy to withdraw with minimal forces left behind."

There was something ominous about the way he said it. I sensed there was *no way* our security would prove acceptable.

"The *parents* of the students at this school, and the others, will also be having their say, Prestige Stavros," Stuart Leandred, one of the distinguished-looking mages in Johnson's wake, said, coming forward. "Few want a military body in charge of their children. Especially one that was willing to sacrifice our sons and daughters just mere hours ago. We are far from pleased with the actions undertaken before and during the attack."

I examined Constantine's father. He was a handsome man who seemed genuinely, paternally upset—but one who also knew how to channel that disquiet into effective political action.

Helen Price came to stand alongside him and smiled tightly at him. "As

* The Status of Threats *

one of those parents, we all know that some things must be sacrificed. I'm sure that we will come to wise agreement on the correct way to keep our layer safe."

I narrowed my eyes at her. In contrast to Constantine's father, Olivia's mother was *coldly* contained.

"Prestige Stavros," Chancellor Barrie said, "if you'd accompany us to my office, we can discuss these matters further." Barrie motioned toward the building.

"Of course," Stavros responded easily. "None of this should be a surprise, though, naturally. After the events of last term, we discussed what would happen if further events occurred. Our taking control of campus is simply a follow-through on those matters, one that has been elevated exponentially."

I saw Marsgrove's fists clench, and felt his anger. *This* conflict and interrogation is what he had been so furious about when he said that I'd had no idea what I'd started.

My sheer presence in this world gave the Department power. It drew attention to a threat that needed to be contained and controlled by them. *Me*.

Johnson ascended to the top step and addressed the student body.

"Due to the presence of the Legion and the need for a full campus sweep, lockdown will be initiated for the safety of everyone. I don't need to remind you that you are all still bound by Excelsine's judicial system and your contractual obligations. The judicial system will be undergoing a few modifications over the next few hours. Please pay attention to all updates."

A "lockdown" didn't seem a big deal. I'd been pretty much locked to campus since I'd stepped onto it. But everyone around me was repeating the word, voices tight with dismay.

Johnson held up a hand. "Two arches have been activated on campus. *Only* two. One from the edge of Top Circle"—he pointed in the direction of the arch—"that goes directly into the Magiaduct. And one from the Visiting Center that also goes directly into the Magiaduct. Once you take one of those arches, you will be unable to leave the Magiaduct. *No one* can be on campus while military personnel sweep for terrorists that are trapped or hurt on the grounds."

"I don't want to be sealed in again," a half-choked, hysterical voice said above the whispers. The sentiment was immediately echoed across the field. "I can't go back there and be sealed in."

I'd bet anything the speaker was a student who had been penned under the Magiaduct dome during the battle.

"You will not be alone, and the eyes of the entire Second Layer security forces will be upon you," Johnson said, with a forced smile. I could see

Chapter Three

magic scrolling around him and wondered just how many mental communications he was currently fielding. "Understand, you are all potential witnesses, and we are unable to release anyone until every person has been questioned and every nook and cranny checked. There will be no better security anywhere in the Second Layer. Five countries and the Department are contributing resources, and will be working together in groups that will contain a member from each country and one from the Department. Eighty heterogeneous squads will be manning both sides of the Magiaduct."

The "heterogeneous group" part seemed to settle a number of people. It appeared that no one trusted any one group on their own.

"At Gemini Rising, every student will be sealed into the Magiaduct under a lockdown witness enchantment. No exceptions. Assignments for where you will be in the hour leading up to it have been sent through frequency and feed and will be closely monitored. The penalty for any mage failing to abide by this edict will be expulsion from this campus, and detainment by the Department. Families are lined up in the Visiting Center, and each student will be able to speak to their family there. Select groups have been called for mandatory assembly."

Silence met the pronouncement.

"As long as the sweep goes well, classes will recommence on Monday. Indication will be given as to how that will occur."

Classes? I numbly stared at Johnson's back as he turned. *Who could think about classes?*

Marsgrove cast a loaded glance down at me. It was as much a threat as any he'd ever issued to me. *Don't even think about going anywhere except the Magiaduct* that look said, clearer than if he had spoken the words.

Johnson, Marsgrove, Stavros, and Kaine turned and strode into the Administration Building. Not that I fully trusted my eyes on such disappearances anymore. Other staff members were speaking to smaller sections of the crowd but I wasn't listening to what they were saying.

A crackle of magic echoed, and the hold on the field disappeared—the pen now extending out to include the Visiting Center and an arch to the Magiaduct.

Numbly, I registered the presence of my friends pushing in around me. The crowd lingered around us and I could feel gazes, like a thousand jellyfish stings, but I was too mind-benumbed to care. Then suddenly, everyone was moving.

Dare and the rest of the combat mages disappeared into the surging crowd that was pushing in multiple directions—some toward the Visiting Center, some toward the Magiaduct—while others stood as immobile objects in an otherwise flowing river.

* The Status of Threats *

I pulled Olivia's scarf from my back pocket and stared down at it. I pulled it against my chest.

"I need to check on Constantine." My voice sounded far away.

Will surrounded us with some sort of privacy field, and Neph slipped her hand under my elbow. I could feel her magic trying to comfort me, trying to navigate the tangled paths with a gentle hand instead of the machete that would likely be necessary.

"Are you okay?" Will asked.

Neph made a strangled noise as she traced the damage to my magic and body. "You need to go to Medical."

"Yes. I need to find Constantine."

Will shook his head, his gaze anxious, fingers gripping the device he had used to shut out the rest of Top Campus momentarily. "They won't let you see him. Not yet, not with the extent of his damage. I saw him." Will shuddered. "He's almost definitely in a healing coma right now."

I looked to Neph, who nodded.

"They won't let anyone into a room when a healing coma is in place," she said, her voice soothing. "Not even a muse for her charge, unless she has an advanced therapeutic degree. The regulation of the magic is too delicate. Slight changes can prevent things from healing correctly. The medical staff creates the healing environment, then vacates until the coma is broken. No one is allowed to enter except the mage who directly created the environment."

I needed to study up more on Healing Magic. Neph had been fielding that aspect for the group for the last term.

"I can—"

"They won't let you in now, Ren," Mike said. He was checking something by frequency; I could see the telltale signs. He looked at me and there was a tangled mixture of emotion in his gaze. Determination. Fondness. Pity. He put a hand on my shoulder and squeezed. "Wait for the coma to lift, then see if you can sneak in."

I nodded blankly, not even trying to prevaricate that I would be sneaking.

"Are we really not going to address the topic of Leandred and what we heard through the scarves?" Delia demanded, hands on hips, eyeliner thickly drawn and sharply pointed at the creases of her eyes.

Mike put an arm around her shoulders and steered Delia toward the Visiting Center. "We will see you all in an hour," he said over his shoulder. He exchanged speaking glances with Will and Neph, then shot me a supportive one. "Try to rest."

I could see Delia arguing with him as they strode toward where their families waited to see them. I thought I heard him say, "It will keep her

Chapter Three

here," but I couldn't be sure.

Will released the privacy field. It was always a risk to believe in privacy when there were so many mages around campus who either enjoyed breaking the rules or thought that they were advancing the judicial capabilities. The field was usually good for a minute or two of actual privacy, though. A good thing, when I usually cared.

"You can't leave while I'm gone," Will blurted out.

I blinked at him.

He fiddled with the skin behind his ear, clearly distressed. "My family is waiting and it will be really bad if I don't show. Stay in your room?"

I studied him for a long moment with sudden understanding. "You all think I'm going to leave."

"Yes."

I smiled tightly. "I can't." I could barely call up a spark of magic. Nothing was getting in or out. And with whatever the Administration Magic was now doing... I knew Marsgrove. There would be something specifically in there to keep me on campus. I needed far more juice in my veins before I'd even be able to try.

I tried not to be upset at the relief that splayed across Will's face. I *needed* to find Olivia.

Neph's grip tightened.

"I know. I get it." And I did. It would be stupid for me, even with full capabilities, to go haring off after Olivia with Raphael sitting in wait.

Raphael was waiting for me, right now. He at full strength, and me at a tenth. And he held my roommate's life in his hands.

I rubbed a hand over my face. "Go. I'll be here when you get back."

Will nodded, then grabbed me and pulled me against his chest. We collided awkwardly, but then it was all tightly gripping octopus arms and strained magic. I wanted to sob into the embrace. The lingering comfort of Christian still lived in Will. And even without his connection to my deceased brother, I loved Will for who he was—in his own right.

I gripped him tightly, and Neph's soothing hands wrapped around us.

Someone touched my shoulder and I looked up to see Asafa behind Will, with Patrick a few steps behind him. Both made eye contact with me. Saf squeezed my shoulder, not intruding on the moment, but making it obvious that he had something important to say.

"Activate the silencing spell on the plan and scarves as soon as possible, Crown," Saf murmured. "For the safety of everyone."

He gave my shoulder another squeeze then retreated to join Patrick. Patrick nodded at us, his eyes glittering with unhealthy emotion. Then they turned and headed toward the Visiting Center with the vast majority of the crowd.

* The Status of Threats *

Will pulled back from the embrace and his half-stricken gaze met mine. "Should have reminded you of that on the way up the mountain."

Neph made reassuring noises. "No one is thinking of everything. That is why we have each other."

Will shook his head at me, his gaze darting around. "Don't do it here. But as soon as you step foot through the arch, activate the spell." He looked around. "Soon. Now. Go now, actually." He looked devastated at pushing me away, but he gave me another nudge. "Every second counts."

I tripped back a step, nodding, not exactly sure how I was going to activate the spell.

Will gave me a tight nod, and I could see a flinch of something across his face. "They are calling us to the Visiting Center if we have someone there to see us. Administration Magic. I have to go. An hour."

I nodded—all I could do at the moment—and watched him go. He glanced back three times before he was swallowed by the crowd.

Neph put her forehead against mine.

I felt a tug in my own gut telling me to return to the Magiaduct. The Administration Magic was fully kicking in for me as well. No one waiting for me in the Visiting Center. My non-magical parents were blissfully unaware of what was occurring in the layer above theirs.

I looked at the Magiaduct. Lockdown took on a new meaning.

I looked at Neph, who seemed unaffected by the Administration Magic. As a muse, she was somewhat outside of its control, even as she was bound to it.

"Neph, I need you to do that thing to me. That thing where you get me out from under the control of the Administration Magic."

She frowned. "I cannot."

"I need to get to the Midlands."

She gave me a severe look. "Absolutely *not*. They are already combing the Midlands' levels. The terrorists did something to them." Neph looked down the mountain, a frown on her face. "I don't know what."

She turned back to me. "But they will definitely find you, and then nothing will save you."

"I could—"

"Ren." Her hands framed my cheeks, making me look her in the eye. "You do not fully appreciate the power of the Legion. They are *not* the Peacekeepers' Troop. They do not wave flashy magic and vow to protect. They are the force sent in for assassination attempts and brutal takeovers. They will have no one watching them while they test and break you." Her lips pulled into a grim line. "Then they will take you."

"I won't let them catch me."

Neph pushed the pads of her middle fingers into my skull. "If you go to

Chapter Three

the Midlands right now or find a way to leave campus before we return, I will make life unpleasant for you."

"But it's not safe for any of you. I'm not safe for any of you." I was panicking, I realized. Shock had flipped again from numbness to panic. "I got Olivia *taken*. They will come after me, and get all of *you*."

"Olivia made a *choice*. You do not get to make our choices for us."

The dam broke. "I want everyone to be safe. I can't take it again."

"Yes, you can," she said, her voice firm, but hands gentle.

I put my hands over my face. "I almost ended campus. Again."

"And yet, it still stands."

"I'm dangerous," I said, looking up at her.

"So am I." Neph's brown eyes glowed for a moment. "You've just never attempted to figure out *how* dangerous I am."

My shoulders drooped. I leaned my forehead on her shoulder. "It doesn't matter. I love you."

She sighed and wrapped her arms around me. "What part of you being *different* and the three of us knowing months ago and still being around you at every opportunity did you misinterpret?"

"The interpretation part?"

She jabbed me in the back at my weak attempt at humor.

"I'm being called to assemble in the muse's hall." She lifted my chin and forced me to meet her eyes. "Wait for us, unless I give you this signal." A wrench of feeling came from the area around my heart. "Then, you run, however you can, as fast as you can, and we will find you later."

It was such an about-face from what she'd just said, that I stared.

She shook her head. "The community is being called to account. The Department is trying to gain more control of us. I will handle it. But should you ever feel that tug over the next few weeks, you drop what you are doing and run, do you understand?"

"Yes."

"Good. I will see you in an hour or two."

My feet automatically started moving me toward the arch that would take me to the Fifth Circle of the mountain and into the Magiaduct. I dug my fingernails into the skin of my other hand to keep myself from crying.

Chapter Four

ROOMMATES FOREVER

TOP CIRCLE THINNED quickly, most students going to the Visiting Center. But a decent number of stragglers—people without family, or with family that weren't able to come—ambled zombie-style in the line that had queued up for the arch to take us to the Magiaduct.

I could see black-collared Department mages scanning students at the front of the line.

"Your attention," a magnified voice called out from the ether. "This broadcast is via Community frequency and streaming live on Top Campus. All students who are missing a roommate due to the events of today will report to their Dorm Reassignment Chaplain by Libra Rising to stand in front of a counseling ball in order to be matched with your next closest match on campus."

I barely got my translation spell to switch back to producing regular times again in my hearing—Libra Rising meant ten p.m.—before horror and denial were pumping through me at what was being suggested.

I would *not* get a new roommate, some replacement for Olivia. I would not let that happen.

The voice continued, more stridently, as if someone had already started arguing with it, "*Every* student who will not have a roommate available tonight *must* report to your Dorm Guide for an analysis. This is for the health and safety of our community."

"I'm not going."

It took a few moments for me to realize that *I* had been the one to say that aloud.

"No, I'm not either," someone near me muttered into the crowd's silence. "If I don't meet their *safety* standards, I'm not bunking with someone who has a one-eighth compatibility. My roommate is in Medical. I'll bunk down there."

Chapter Four

Other mutters joined ours. "I'm fine taking the hit to my reserves. What magic am I going to do anyway while Lou is down? And this will just add a tiny shred of magic to the community fabric anyway."

"A lot of threads equal a shirt," someone said in a too-reasonable tone.

"Yeah, well we don't need another shirt tonight," came the angry reply. "I'm skipping."

"Stop being a shivit," another said bitterly. "They won't let you skip. Just do it, and stop complaining, so the rest of us can get back to normal."

"Complaining?" The girl who had angrily spoken had a wild look in her eyes, the skin of her face sheet white. "Shinsara is *dead*. I'm not replacing her like a *sock*."

"It's not like that. The Community Magic needs all of us to—"

"Shove your magic!" The girl wildly detached herself from the line, her motions jerky and uncontrolled as she blindly hit out at the hands reaching out to help her. "I won't! Let me *go*. I won't—"

A bolt of soiled green magic hit her and she fell, only barely caught by the hands she had been fending off.

People were shouting about accommodations and being responsible for the health of their room if their energy dipped below thirty-percent capacity, and if *that* happened, only at *that* time would they accept automatic reassignment.

I gripped Olivia's scarf in my hand.

The line was still moving, even with the arguments. And as I neared the front of the line, the gazes of the Department mages who were scanning students landed on me, almost as one.

One said something to a campus official who was standing by. The official frowned, then nodded. He motioned toward one of the other campus mages. The mage padded over, listened, and nodded. He held a hand out to the arch.

The student at the front of the line—three people in front of me—went through, pushing into the crowd on the Top Track through the image. The others filed through.

I stepped forward and a Department mage put his hand out. "Wait."

I recognized his shock of white hair and purple-lensed eyes. Kaine's minion, Tarei.

The mage with his hand extended toward the arch, touched the arch and spun honey-colored magic at its edge. "Section capacity reached. Switching the port exit in 3, 2, 1, ready."

The image inside of the arch rotated—the vast expanse of the mountain and the vista tilted in view as the landscaped whirled. It finally stopped, and a different section of the Top Track of the Magiaduct was pictured on the other side. An empty section of Top Track. A little too empty.

"Proceed."

Tarei's purple-lensed eyes mocked me. Daring me not to go through. I stood woodenly and looked through the image of the arch.

Capacity on the previous section of Top Track reached or not, they had decided to change the exit point to the arch upon seeing me. If it took me elsewhere than the Magiaduct, or if someone was waiting on the other side...well, that is where I would make my last stand.

"Pardon me, miss," someone said behind me.

I glanced back to see a faintly familiar face. I didn't know him, but there was the faintest flicker of recognition pushing at the edges of my consciousness.

He strode past me and through the arch before anyone could say anything. A second person pushed past me and hurried after him. Tarei whipped out a hand in which he held a spiked device.

"Now see here—" the campus official said apprehensively, stepping forward with his hand extended to stop whatever Tarei was going to do with the device.

The two boys appeared on what *seemed* to be the Top Track of the Magiaduct. The first one nodded to me in confirmation. With the way the arches worked, he appeared less than ten feet from me, when in actuality, he was hundreds of physical yards away.

"There's a bit of an energy rush when you are one of the first ones through," the boy called back with a forced smile, his eyes focused on me while decidedly not looking in the direction of Kaine's minion. "Thanks for letting me go first."

He was sweating profusely and abruptly—anxious moisture gathering along his hairline as if he'd been bespelled with something that he was trying to combat internally.

I looked over at the officials. Tarei's white knuckles were wrapped around the spiked device, and he was gritting his teeth as he argued in low tones with the campus official. I jolted forward and nearly dove through the arch, not allowing Tarei any time to use further trickery.

The section of the Top Track on which I emerged was nearly empty, save for the two boys. The other mages whose heads suddenly appeared at the stairs leading up to our section disappeared before I could identify them.

Turning around I met gazes with Kaine's minion. His eyes glittered and he turned abruptly on his heel, striding away from the arch. I could see one of the other officials running after him.

Although I was trapped in the Magiaduct now, for a moment I felt stupid relief wash through me.

Special dispensation had to be obtained for anyone other than a student

Chapter Four

to enter the Magiaduct, and only those already associated with campus could currently obtain it. Using the thick soup of crisscrossing communications on Top Circle, I'd heard the officials arguing about it along with everyone else in line.

I followed closely behind the boys, trying to orient myself with the mountain landscape splayed below and around me to figure out where exactly I was on the dormitory building.

I could see magic glittering around the first boy, but the second one was clear of such magic. The first shuddered, then the magic broke like a crystalline cage of frost, falling to the ground.

I didn't know what had been in the magic that had encased him, but it had been intended for me.

I caught up to him and touched his arm. He turned toward me.

"Thank you," I said, somewhat fervently, wishing I could relieve whatever pain had been done to him.

"No, *thank you.*" He smiled at me, then limped ahead to join his friend.

I watched him for a long moment, before beginning the long walk to my dorm. The previous exit would have taken me far closer to Dorm Twenty-five.

Further down, campus officials were spread out on the edges of the Top Track, coordinating more port points for groups of students to come through en masse. It had been smart of them to port us up here. If they wanted us contained in the superstructure, they couldn't very well dump us on the grass outside, nor could they create bottlenecks in the common areas of the dorms.

Students started to drift toward the staircases and disappear inside the superstructure. Many of them looked emotionally spent.

As I neared a large group of mages, an older boy opened his arms slowly, magic pulling between his hands. He nodded at unseen individuals. At unseen frequency tidings. His expression was sober and determined. He started speaking aloud, voice magnified by whatever magic he held.

"Everyone, please. All emergency protocols have been activated. Samson, put out an emergency notification."

A boy near him nodded, and the first boy continued his speech,

"Steady, everyone. Mages are available, *at this moment,* for comfort, counseling, discussion, basic healing, and activity. Mages at the Visiting Center will be ported here in an hour. If you are still missing a friend, please check the sheets for health and welfare status."

I wondered cynically how many girls were checking on Constantine's status and exclaiming in dismay.

"Over the next few hours, the dorm common rooms will hold discussion sessions. Attending one is mandatory. After the mandatory session, a channel will be available for those who may want to sit in on discussions, but not leave their rooms. For those needing to talk or problem solve, many groups are scheduling meetings to discuss events or devise solutions for the future. The Young Politicos Club will be debating...everything to do with this. The Rational Engineers' Club indicated their intention to meet and discuss ways to dismantle or stop the construction of Origin Domes in the future and figure out what went wrong with the Administration Magic."

He nodded to the group, then nodded again at someone speaking in his head. "Yes. Yes. Alternately, there will be at least three group activities tonight in every dorm quadrant for those who cannot think or talk about the events any further. The rec center in Dorm Thirty is already setting up for sports activities."

He shook his head again at someone mentally. "No, Lorraine is leading, not Jaxon."

His lips tightened for a moment before he took a breath. "He lost his roommate and best friend. He's on the immediate attention list—we'll have someone to him in the next hour. The rec center in Dorm Thirty-three is setting up for parlor, board, and card games later tonight. Magical Meditation will be available on Top Track. An all-around meeting to discuss logistics and scheduling for the next few days will take place in the open space in Dorm Twelve in ten minutes. Ronnie is bringing the updated emergency procedures document. People, it's time to execute recovery plans. Campus is counting on it. See everyone in ten."

The students who had been whispering to each other in line and vibrating with anxious energy during announcements were the ones leading the charge on the Magiaduct. They had looked over their fellow students and simply thought, *How can I help?*

I noticed a bright blonde head weaving between students. My hands twitched, their deadened nerve endings trying to reach and form a connection to the magic blazing from her.

The girl I had healed.

Recognition hit twice, then realization. There was a familial relationship between the boy who had preceded me through the arch—the one who had deliberately taken the hit intended for me and the girl I had saved on the battlefield. Siblings or cousins.

She hurried onward, with a visible energy aura blazing around her like a beacon, toward Dorm Twelve. My hand covered my mouth shakily. At least my magic would help someone to somehow, piece the campus population back together. It didn't alleviate the crushing guilt and shame, but it made my determination stronger.

I started moving again, my steps a little shaky.

Chapter Four

Will, Mike, Delia, Trick, Saf, Dagfinn, and Lifen were somewhere in the Visiting Center with thousands of others. Their parents, like all parents in the Second Layer, had to be absolutely mad with terror.

I'd seen it on the adults' faces, in the projections that Godfrey had displayed on the battlefield.

I was so tired of seeing terror.

I made it back to my dorm room, drawing only a minimum amount of attention—people were too concerned with getting somewhere themselves. Once they weren't concerned with that, though...

Shutting the door behind me, I leaned heavily against it. The silence was overwhelming.

I stared blankly at the walls of our room.

Though extremely active in her legal communities, Olivia had usually been *here* when I arrived home. Elegantly hunched over a giant tome or drafting a statement to take down a worthy opponent.

I ran my fingers along her desk and swallowed. Her scarf felt heavy in my hand.

It had only been three *hours*. Three hours since I had first initiated the Red Alert. It felt like three days—every minute experienced in frame-by-frame high definition.

Meeting with our Dorm Guide—whoever that was—in order to assess my mental health and stability to last through the night, was the last thing I wanted to do.

I lifted the scarf to my mouth.

"Olivia?" I whispered into the threads. A cool fleeting touch whispered back against my skin. A desire more than an actual sense.

Magic twisted within me, the corrupted channels letting nothing out.

I closed my eyes, clenching them. I couldn't pull Olivia out of the threads. I could only lament.

Too close. Too close to Christian.

I had to get my magic back. I had to get off campus. I had to rescue Olivia.

The scarf suddenly wrapped around my hand and squeezed so tightly that I would have dropped it, if it hadn't been strangling in the intensity of its hold on me. A silken constrictor.

I stared at it, then jerked forward. The silencing spell. I gripped the scarves and rubbed a shaking hand against my chest. Did I have enough magic left to do it? What if I messed up something and the locator to Olivia that I had captured in the threads was altered or ruined?

A sudden *whoosh* of sound blasted from the vents. Tipping my head back, I could see the hazy white magic puffing out like unfurling steam.

I clutched Olivia's scarf tighter.

* Roommates Forever *

I shied away from the first touch of magic, and willed myself to relax at the second. Calm quickly overtook my limbs.

I remembered Will's quip about Mike keeping track of the level at which we were being doused with calming magic. That it said a lot about the Administration's emotional state.

This level had to signify that they were very concerned.

I let the pumping spell calm me, just a little, before I touched the wall at my side. Although magic wasn't pumping through me, I could still affect spells that were already in place. I didn't need to fit a key into a lock. I could just turn the dial. Left two turns, right two turns, left.

I smiled without humor and dialed back the calming spell. But unlike weeks ago, I couldn't turn it off completely.

I'd have to ask one of the others what I was doing wrong, but at least the motions had given me enough hope to try affecting the silencing spell in the scarves. Closing my eyes, I focused on the spells in place—pinching the one in my scarf that visually connected to my mouth, then rippling it through the control scarf.

It *should* stop anyone from talking about Plan Fifty-two with anyone outside of the plan, or communicating in any other way. The mouth visual was just what the spell showed me, tailored to how I saw the idea of it at present. I loved magic.

But I couldn't use it incorrectly again.

I shut my eyes.

Chapter Five

EXPLANATIONS AND CONFESSIONS

I STOOD UNDER the hot spray of the shower. I had chosen the First Layer kind of shower, complete with nearly scalding water. The bathroom was fully equipped with the magical kind of "showers" too—ones where you could just be whooshed clean, others where you would get doused or coated with anything you wanted—skin and sun protection, a layer of magical protection, a rehydrating charm, a light spray of a thousand different skin and hair colors, makeup charms.

None of those would allow me to see the blood swirling down the drain and feel the blistering heat against my scalp and shoulders. Maybe I was far too rooted in the First Layer, but there was something soothing and calming in watching the swirl of the drain carry away some of the day—the dirt, grime, sweat, and blood. The pain and heartache.

I stepped out and allowed the bathroom's instant drying charms to keep me warm and slightly on edge. Slinking around with wet, bedraggled hair seemed the opposite of what I needed.

Exiting the bathroom brought the reality of the situation back into view. Olivia wasn't normally very loud, but the steady turn of pages—of one piece of paper sliding against another—or the even hum of magic as she extracted information or performed a deft maneuver, were deafeningly absent.

I touched the open tome on her desk.

Knock, knock.

Startled, I threw out both arms and the tiniest bit of recovered magic followed painfully. The book I'd been touching smacked one wall with a heavy thud, while Olivia's crystal inkwell was propelled against the wall above her bed. It shattered into glistening, inky shards. Black ink ran down the wall and onto her bedspread like fresh, splattered blood.

It was far too reminiscent of my bedroom walls at home in the First

* Explanations and Confessions *

Layer after I'd tried repeatedly to resurrect my brother.

My hands shook, and I flexed my fingers like an arthritic with gnarled and twisted joints.

"Ren?"

At hearing the voice in the hall, relief and a new panic swallowed the alarm.

I quickly fumbled with the door, unlocking it, surprised that I had even thought to lock it. My first term need to break and enter the room repeatedly had left me with a habit of leaving it unlocked.

As I whipped the door open, I blurted, "I had a key, so I locked it."

Olivia had given me the key so that we could be true roommates.

Dare stared at me for a long moment, and if I didn't know better, I'd think there was a look of sharp relief on his face. He took a step forward.

I shoved him back a step. Relief at seeing him mixed with alarm. "No," I said. "You are in danger. You cannot be around me anymore."

Nearly a foot taller, and far broader, he could have easily stopped the action. He raised an eyebrow, looking down at me, as I tried to push him back another step.

I growled and pushed harder, completely forgetting in that moment to try magic.

"Ren." My name sounded like a sigh.

"*No.*" God, wasn't that just it too? The obviousness of my feral position. Not even remembering to try magic, even if it likely would have ended in agonizing pain and failure.

I could see people slowing down in the hall, decelerating to a snail's pace in order to observe the exchange.

"Why are you risking this?" I whispered, pleading.

His gaze was piercing, his position immovable. "Some things are worth risk."

My shoulders sagged and my hand fell from his chest as I leaned into the doorjamb. "I'm not okay."

He nodded slowly. "I know. May I come in?" He stayed where he stood, allowing me the choice.

"Yes," I said in defeat, stepping back and awkwardly shuffling to the side so that I could close the door behind him. And lock it. That seemed important. Olivia always liked the door to be locked.

Dare's gaze took in every facet of our room as he walked over to my side. I felt conflicting urges to cover up my disorderliness and to show him some of the items in the storage paper affixed under my bed.

He'd never been in our room.

"How did you find me?" I asked.

He'd been so cagey about meeting in *his* room—caginess that I hadn't

Chapter Five

realized was due to the fact that Constantine Leandred was his roommate—that I'd never invited him to mine.

"You aren't in the directory, but it's not hard to find you. Many people are aware."

People who were likely watching me even more fiercely now. Stavros and Kaine's people, maybe. Definitely Bellacia's. And Raphael's.

"My roommate—"

"Helen Price's daughter. I know."

"Olivia," I stressed quietly.

He tipped his head. "Olivia." He examined me. "When I looked into everything about you months ago, I'll admit to being surprised at your roommate choice."

"Choice" was an interesting word. More likely it was "fate."

I waved a hand around in a vaguely uncommunicative motion. "Mine makes more sense than yours."

"Neither Leandred nor I would have *chosen* the other. You, on the other hand, had a choice."

I blinked. "Not really. It was a rather happy accident. She would have tossed me out otherwise. We just happened to be highly sympathetic."

He stared at me for a long moment. "I forget how new you are sometimes."

He looked down at my desk. Notes that I had taken on his fighting style and tactics in the practice rooms were scattered on the top.

I hastily ran over and pushed everything into a pile. "Why aren't you at the Visiting Center?"

His gaze raked me. "I'm exactly where I need to be. Julian and Nick are taking care of family matters."

"Don't you have to get ready to go back to the competition?"

"Not if I'm not returning."

I fumbled the papers. "*What?*"

He lifted the sheets from my unresponsive hands. "I actually anticipated that you'd be gone already, and that I'd have to chase you down somewhere outside of campus tonight."

That would explain his relief at seeing me, then.

He looked down at the pages in his hand. "You think I could be tricked with a three-strike projection?" he said, reading the top page of the stack—all notes on *him*. "I'm offended."

I grabbed the papers out of his hands and stuffed them into a pile in the corner, then put a book on top. I crossed my arms and tried to stop the heat that was broiling my face from within. "What do you mean, chase me down? And what do you mean not returning? You can't miss your competition."

* Explanations and Confessions *

"Why not?"

I stared at him. "Because the tournament is...important?" It had been the most talked about thing for months. It was the event of the year, the one that earned all of the accolades. The one that had earned Dare the lofty reputation he had.

"It's a competition. A game. A sport."

I stared at him.

"You didn't think I was just going to let you break through the perimeter ward and wave good-bye, did you?" He looked unimpressed with me.

I processed his remark for a few long moments, then nodded slowly. "Okay."

He looked distinctly amused. "Okay?"

"Having you along will be quite helpful, when I flee," I said. I didn't have the first clue about what I would find when I located Olivia, other than that Raphael would be waiting for me.

Dare smiled, the edges of his eyes crinkling in genuine amusement. It was a smile I had gotten used to seeing, but it always made my heart rate increase.

I smiled tentatively back.

"Tell me about Emrys—or more accurately Raphael Verisetti."

And just like that, my stomach dropped to stone.

"How...? You know?" I asked woodenly. Raphael hadn't been wearing his own face in the golem. The golem had worn the face of the real Emrys Norr—though I had no idea where the real Emrys was—then when Constantine had broken through some of the spells, it had worn the face of my brother.

Dare gave me an unimpressed stare in answer.

"Did you know before today?" I asked, feeling drained again.

His eyes narrowed with an edge of cold anger. "I would never let Verisetti remain on campus."

I wiped a shaky hand across my face, unable to look at that expression; still I held firm in response. "Yeah? I have a bad habit of being the last to know around here. Aren't you going to ask me if *I* knew before today?"

"I know that you did not."

I looked back at him. None of the anger remained on his face. Instead, there was a sort of casually dissecting regard.

"You show your emotions freely," he said. "No one could have faked that level of distress. And, you don't have it in you to kick in with a terrorist. Not even with your bad taste in 'business partners'," he said, referencing the conversation we'd had the night I'd found out Alexander and Constantine were roommates.

Chapter Five

"Besides, I heard a small part of your conversation while I was trying to dismantle the dome he erected," Dare said.

Exasperation swept through me, which was a relief in the wake of all the other coiling emotions.

I collapsed on my bed, drawing my feet beneath me.

"You could have led with that statement, you know." From my bed I had a clear view of the emptiness on the other side of the room. Instead of dwelling on it, I focused on Dare.

"Raphael was present when I Awakened. He tricked me. Took advantage of my grief. Over..." I ran a hand over the photo near my pillow—the edges of the photo soft and distressed. "Over my brother." My twin who Dare had seen dead on a street in the First Layer.

"Raphael's been haunting me ever since," I finished.

Dare drew my desk chair forward, and sat with his arms on his thighs, leaning toward me.

"Verisetti was with you when you Awakened?" Dare's gaze was piercing. "What did he make you create?"

"How did you...? Marsgrove asked me the same thing."

"Awakening magic is stolen more often than most people think." He kept his gaze steady on mine. My brother had been murdered for exactly that reason.

It had been less than a week since I'd found out that Dare knew I was the girl he had saved in the First Layer the night my brother died. It felt like far longer. This past day felt like a year's worth of time alone.

"It explains the weirdness between the two of you. You and Emrys," Dare said, staring at the protection enchantments disguised as art that I had drawn directly on the wall—enchantments I had learned in the Library of Alexandria. "There was something strange between you two from the beginning."

"I...I made a golem." I flinched. "When I was trying to bring my brother back to life. I made lots of things. But the golem—I spent a lot of time on it. Made it out of professional-grade blob matter." Which I had gotten from Constantine—that part was going to remain secret.

"And I made it with my brother in mind. Raphael stole it from the Midlands during the—" I gripped my fingers together—"the whole bone monster incident. Then he came here—" I indicated my room "—and taunted a bit. Froze Olivia. Told me about the true potential of the picture I made during my Awakening. Other stuff," I finished lamely.

"What picture?" Dare leaned forward, intent.

"One that I could have resurrected my brother with." By sacrificing Will.

"Where is it?" His gaze drilled into me.

* Explanations and Confessions *

"In the First Layer. Marsgrove came to collect us when I nearly blew up my parents' house again." I winced. "And I left it there, hidden."

Dare narrowed his eyes. "Where is your house?"

I stared at him for a long moment. "I'm not telling you."

I trusted Dare with my life, but I thought on Constantine's words—that due to Raphael's magic, my house was protected against detection unless I specifically gave up the address. With my parents' lives at stake—I wanted as few magical people to know their location as possible.

He smiled. "Good."

Whether he was being truthful or not, I felt relief. I would do a lot for Alexander Dare.

Currently, only six mages knew the address. Of those, one of them, unfortunately, was Marsgrove, and another was a psychopath. But Olivia and I had spent most of winter break shoring up the base wards Raphael had put around my house to act *against* Raphael instead.

Olivia, Will, Neph, and Constantine completed the knowledge set.

"Your shield set. Verisetti did it, didn't he?"

"He saturated me in his magic," I said bitterly. "Before I Awakened. The shield set that Marsgrove gave me was created, at its base, by Raphael." Like everything else that I had in this world seemed to be.

Dare's gaze lifted to the top of my head. "It's untainted magic. Created long ago—maybe here at Excelsine. Marsgrove and Verisetti were best friends and roommates."

My heart stuttered over this new information. "I...noticed they seemed to know each other well."

"My uncle attended at the same time they did, though he was a few years behind. Verisetti had a brilliant group of friends, many of whom are still affiliated with Excelsine." He watched me carefully, waiting for me to figure out the connections.

Stevens. My professor, my mentor. It wasn't a shock—I had guessed she might know Raphael—but I still felt the confirmation like a blow.

Dare's gaze switched back to my hair. "One of Verisetti's gifts is in protection magic."

"Ironic," I said bitterly.

"Protection magic can be switched to destruction as easily as healing magic can be used for killing. The skill is the same—the intent and application are what matter."

"He's good at destruction."

"Verisetti skirted the edge of being labeled a rare when studying here. Combined with his artistic gifts, he was tested for Origin talent. He barely failed and it is very little wonder that he can wield your magic. Julian said Verisetti was getting called back in to be tested as a Protection Prodigy

Chapter Five

when he disappeared."

Unease slid through me. "The Department took him. Stavros. They experimented on him."

Dare's gaze sharpened. "Verisetti told you that?"

That wasn't a part of the conversation Dare had overheard then.

"I think Raphael wants me to kill Prestige Stavros," I said numbly.

Lightning fast, Dare leaned forward and grabbed my wrist. His gaze unfocused. Talking to someone via frequency. "Don't tell anyone that. Don't tell *anyone* that, do you understand?"

"Yes," I said quickly, panicked by his reaction.

His lips tightened at my immediate response. "You don't understand. But you need to believe me. Stavros never leaves the Department, and no one ever knows quite where he is within it. He continuously travels as a parasite. His hosts have been assassinated more times than the press can count—each time the assassins thought it might finally be him beneath the spells—and each time they were wrong."

I nodded, not really comprehending such notions.

"It is absolutely possible that Verisetti *has* triggered you as a sleeper agent somehow—that he did so during your Awakening. Such a plan makes brilliant sense. Stavros wants you. He will do *anything* to get you."

"Kaine—"

"Kaine is dangerous. And remorseless. And one day Stavros will need to watch his back. But not yet. Kaine will carry out his commands. Stavros holds more power than anyone in the Second Layer. Dressed up as protector and spouting concern for the people—no one can get to him. And anyone who does, doesn't end up *right* afterward."

I licked suddenly chapped lips.

"If he gets you, Ren, even if you are triggered to kill him, he has ways of...altering such things. You will not survive the Department. Do you understand? And even with Stevens on your side—maybe *especially* with Stevens on your side—you won't be able—" Dare touched his head sharply, nearly wincing. It was worrying to see him wince at *anything*.

His other hand was still wrapped around my wrist and it clenched then loosened, but didn't let go. "Later. What else did you make in your Awakening?"

"I...blacked out. Other than the picture, I only know of the box and the portal pad." I bit my lip. "The pad works in the First Layer. Marsgrove had a pretty terrible reaction to its existence." Will, on the other hand, had been over the moon.

"The box?" Dare's gaze was penetrating. "The one Verisetti has been carrying around for the past few months?"

"It's a conduit to my magic. In some way. A leech and a way to translate

* Explanations and Confessions *

the magic for Raphael, I think. I mean when Con leeched me, he had—"

"When Constantine *what?*"

"—had, er, already been studying my magic..." I trailed off on that very concerning note. I had forgotten momentarily that Dare wasn't in the "know" category on the leeches.

"Leandred *leeched* you?"

"I gave him permission." Sort of. A few of the times, at least.

"I'll end him." He started to rise. His fingers slipped free of my wrist and I immediately clamped my hand around his before he could leave.

Here we'd been talking about Raphael and the world-ending powers I had seemingly given him, and Stavros, who was like the ultimate villain, and he was going to go crush Constantine for leeching me?

"You will do nothing," I said.

"I've turned the other cheek a thousand times. But not on this."

I could feel his magic vibrating under his skin. The vibrations would be an implicit warning to any mage touching him that he was dangerous. He usually kept his magic reined in pretty tightly—only the aura of it enveloping him. It was always a bit heady being around him when he loosened the reins. There was so *much*.

I gripped his hand more tightly. "With the exception of Raphael, everyone *else* who has leeched me has done so with good intentions." I deliberately maintained eye contact with him.

Dare had called his mother a natural leech with her Bridge powers. And Dare had used and manipulated my magic to keep me from revealing myself to the Peacekeepers' Troop. He had used his hidden skill on Top Circle to keep Kaine from outing me—at great personal expense both times. It would be devastating for him to be caught displaying Bridge abilities.

But Dare was far too incensed for me to ask *why* he was putting himself out for me.

"*Everyone else?* What exactly have you been doing? I thought all those weird pulls on your magic were because you were making more illegal, living creations in the Midlands. *Leeches?*" He drew his free hand over his face. "Yes, that's exactly what those pulls were. But I never thought you'd do that."

It was like having a friend who knew all the bad things you did and disapproved of exactly half of them.

I let go of his hand in order to push the hair from my forehead. A telling, nervous gesture from me. "We were building leeches in order to unlock Raphael's. Raphael has—had—one on me. From my Awakening. That enabled him to take my magic remotely. The box. Constantine was only trying to help me."

Chapter Five

At least, he had been after the initial leech. I thought it better to keep mum on Constantine leeching me in the First Layer for his own ends.

I could see the pieces of the stuttered puzzle assembling in Dare's quick, strategy-driven mind and I sought to direct the conversation away from Constantine.

"The thing with you—that helped me piece it together," I said quickly. "It unlocked a single link of Raphael's chain. I think that's why Raphael in the guise of Emrys started getting so testy. His work was unraveling around him."

Dare gave a short laugh, his expression dark. "All of the attacks in the last few months. The lack during the last few weeks. Did Leandred know? Who the Emrys on campus was?"

"No. Not before today. It was a...very unpleasant surprise. I have a feeling that they'd spoken a few times on campus."

"I'll bet Verisetti loved that. Constantine has been stalking him for years."

It wasn't really much of a surprise that Dare would know that. He obviously knew Constantine very well in some ways. I wondered if he realized he had switched to calling him by his first name for a moment.

But yes, Raphael had undoubtedly been delighted to be right under Constantine's nose. Until the end. "He was very displeased with Constantine right before you showed up. The worst of Constantine's wounds were inflicted when Raphael revealed himself."

"Serves him right," Dare said bitterly. He cut a hand through my automatic denial. "No. I can read the signs on campus of what happened. And I can feel the magic. Leandred was clever about it. He's always clever about it. Nothing to tie him to the crime. Everything he did to set this up, he then overrode with spells that 'helped.'"

I swallowed.

"And you are covering for him."

"I..." I didn't know what to say. Additionally, the words about Constantine accompanying me to find Olivia, if he woke, were stuck somewhere between the guilt in my gut and the apprehension in my throat.

Dare froze. "You were *not* thinking of taking him with you?"

It should be more than mildly concerning that Dare had somehow made that jump based on a single trailing letter of the alphabet, but my apprehension and guilt combined into a super emotion of anxiety in my chest, and wiped away anything else for the moment.

"Yes," I said, voice going a little high.

"No."

"It—"

"Ren, you can't be serious."

* Explanations and Confessions *

"I know you don't trust Constantine," I said. Dare gave me a look of disbelief. "I know no one does. But he will keep his word once given. He always keeps his word."

He just didn't *give* his word very often.

Sort of nearly never, really.

Dare said nothing, and only the pulses from the threads that connected us let me know what he might be thinking. Acknowledgment—he actually believed that last statement to be true. Grim determination—probably not in Constantine's favor. Hatred.

Then he went blank. His expression, the connection threads, everything.

"Fine," he said, voice entirely calm.

I blinked, then narrowed my eyes. "Really?"

He smiled. "Really."

I could read nothing but calm honesty from him. "You are scary."

His smile dropped. "You should never forget what I am," he said, his expression remote, his gaze never leaving mine.

"The guy who saves my life all the time?"

He didn't respond. He just stared at me with that remote gaze. I didn't like it.

"I think I'm scarier?" I prompted.

He rolled his eyes, and the tension dropped from him like a heavy coat shed in a warm room. Easy, tranquil feelings were once more resonating between us. It was a heady relief.

"Do you warn everyone away from you?" I asked.

"I don't bother speaking to most people," he said dismissively, magic igniting in his hand.

"You are seriously awful." But slipping into regular banter like this was comforting. Like everything was okay, and Olivia was fine, just waiting to give me hell for mooning over Alexander Dare again.

He smiled.

"Seriously awful," I reiterated.

But truthful. He didn't bother speaking to most people. Even after saving me from the reading room at the beginning of my first term at Excelsine, he'd barely spared me a glance. And he'd only spared me the glance at all because my magic had fought him, and actually given him a fight. He'd barely responded with a dismissive hand wave to Peters, who had been uttering an obsequious Justice Squad litany of thanks to him.

Like Bautermann. The Second Layer superhero who saved everyone, but didn't allow himself to care about any of those he saved.

"Whatever you are thinking has your face all scrunched up." His fingers pulled the edges of my eyebrows upward out of their frown.

I blinked at him through the frame of his fingers, and he smirked back,

Chapter Five

releasing me slowly.

"I have—" he started to say. But then his gaze narrowed suddenly and his body tilted toward the door.

A forcible rapping made my head jerk in that direction as well. I ran the quick identification spell on the door and caught my breath.

Marsgrove, Helen Price, and an unidentified Department stooge stood on the other side.

Chapter Six

OF THOSE MOST HATED

"IF SHE DOESN'T ANSWER," the cold feminine voice said from the hallway. "Then we will be within our rights to enter forci—"

I yanked open the door. Marsgrove, Helen Price, and a Department stooge stared directly at me.

My heart stuttered for a second. Raphael's spell wasn't working on me anymore. Helen Price could see me.

My gaze met hers and sizzling hatred passed through me. *Good.*

Iced blonde and elegant, Helen Price smiled coldly and tilted her head, her arctic eyes taking me in and filing every piece of information. She had to be in her upper forties, but she had an ageless look. Likely a side effect of whatever deals she had already struck with the devil.

Her sharp gaze dropped to my clenched hands and her eyes narrowed in abrupt cognition. "Certain things become apparent."

The woman who had given birth to my extremely intelligent roommate had an equally agile brain.

"I do wonder what would happen should I test any spells that have been recently laid upon me," she mused. Her gaze met mine and I could see the promised retribution in the depths of her soulless eyes.

Dare, hidden from their view, didn't make a sound, but I *felt* him shift.

"Interesting, but irrelevant at this time," Marsgrove said coolly. "We have other things to discuss, Miss Crown."

I did *not* want this woman in our room, but I could clearly read Marsgrove's expression, and it said not to argue. I nodded stiffly and stepped away from the door.

Marsgrove and Helen entered, while the stooge planted himself in the hall, facing outward to guard the room. Marsgrove closed the door, sealing the four of us inside.

Helen Price's gaze immediately zeroed in on the fourth, unexpected

Chapter Six

occupant in the room.

"Mr. Dare." Helen Price's gaze was calculating at seeing Dare sprawled out in my chair. Marsgrove's expression, on the other hand, didn't change. I'd bet anything he had known Dare was here already—through Administrative Magic or from Julian Dare.

"Councilwoman Price," Dare said.

"We need to take Miss Crown's statement now, Mr. Dare. If you'd be so kind." She motioned toward the door with a small, empty smile.

"You need to take mine as well," Dare said casually, his ever-present ball of blue magic once more at hand as he slowly rolled it across my desk with his palm. "Now you don't have to go through the trouble of finding us both."

I swallowed, watching him. The timing of his presence in my room had been no mistake. Marsgrove's as well. There were layers here that I didn't yet comprehend. Each of the three facing me had obvious motivations and also ones that were insidiously hidden.

I glanced at the clock. Thirty minutes remained before the muses and Visiting Center inhabitants—which included nearly all of my friends—were released. The Department, sending Helen, had hoped to get to me before any help returned.

Dare had timed his visit to the same clock. He had purposely not gone to the Visiting Center.

Marsgrove nodded. "Both of you were on scene at the end of the conflict, and there are questions about that. Your presence here is satisfactory."

Helen smiled—all teeth. "Very well."

She took in everything on Olivia's desk, focused on the ink drying on the wall, then looked to my side of the room. "How interesting that I didn't see you or your things when last I was here. Curious, that everything was so bland on your side of the room, when now I see how colorful you keep it." She said *colorful* as if I had tacked loaves of moldy bread on the walls.

Raphael's spell had prevented anyone in the Department from noticing me. Unhooking that spell had obvious consequences, but I couldn't regret it. Raphael had used my magic to do unspeakable horrors. Better for me to be locked up in a government basement somewhere.

Letting them use me to do unspeakable horrors?

I shuddered. Okay. No. I needed an option three, where no one was using me to do terrible things.

I was just lucky that whatever magic Marsgrove had wrought to allow only Helen Price into my room, and not Stavros, Kaine, or any others, had been applied. Not that Marsgrove would have done that *for me,* considering how much he detested me.

* Of Those Most Hated *

Helen moved around the room, almost absently, but as she touched our stuff, little zings of magic darted from her fingertips. Like she was marking items. Marking items in *our* territory. Putting who knew what magic on Olivia's things, and on our room.

She walked over to my desk, disregarding Dare's large, dangerous, sprawled presence in the chair, and touched the edge of the desk before I finally stepped forward, forcing her to step back, not caring how aggressive she thought the action.

"*Mmmm,* it's as if you have something to hide, Miss Crown."

"I do not recall reading anything that said you have the right to touch anything of mine."

My *roommate,* included.

Her eyes narrowed. "Phillip, I feel quite uncomfortable. I think I would be far more pleased to conduct this interview in the safety of the Department."

"We will continue here until such time that Miss Crown oversteps herself." Marsgrove sounded dismissive, but there was a clear warning to me in his posture.

Helen smirked and pulled out a tablet. "You have been my daughter's roommate for how long now, Miss Crown?"

"Two terms."

"And yet, I see no record of you as her roommate last term." She tapped the tablet.

"My academic record has undergone a few mishaps."

"Yes, I see that it has." She was looking straight at me, so the tablet was likely a prop and her information was coming by means other than visual. It suddenly made me aware that the three of us were probably not the only ones in on this conversation.

My hands turned clammy, half expecting Stavros's head to pop up on her shoulder in some grotesque parody of paternal concern.

"You appear to be a constant drain on the university's vast resources, Miss Crown. Two thousand hours of community service." She shook her head. "I do think there are things that I need to discuss with Provost Johnson."

"Helen, Excelsine is not under your command," Marsgrove said in clipped tones, and my eyes widened at the clear warning in his voice—a warning not aimed at me for once.

"Yet." She smiled coldly, her gaze never leaving mine. "Not yet, Phillip."

"You are allowing your delusions to show again, Helen."

"You've had your play time, and your pursuits, and look where that has gotten you." She looked him over. "Older and more pathetic."

Chapter Six

"We warm-blooded types do what we must," Marsgrove said dismissively, though his gaze, always sharp, never lessened in intensity as he examined the room as well, studying his environment. He and Dare, both combat mages at heart, had that in common.

"Let's get to it then." Helen sealed the door, and with a flick of her wrist a spell circle enveloped all four occupants in the room. "Name?"

"Ren Crown." I had already given it to Kaine.

"Home address?"

Panic skyrocketed. "Pass."

The circle flashed yellow. I looked at it cautiously. I was far more knowledgeable about defensive and protection wards than offensive magic fields. I hadn't needed to study offensive magic yet, and had been planning on registering for Mbozi's *Volatile Engineering* course next term. The class would help patch that knowledge, but future course work wasn't helping my present situation.

"You cannot 'pass' a question, Miss Crown," Helen said, far too pleasantly.

I looked at Marsgrove, who stared back with a blank gaze. Dare was equally unhelpful, though he tipped his head in some form of support.

"I am between residences," I said.

The circle flashed white and a shock of electricity ran through me.

"My goodness, what lies you tell, Miss Crown," Helen said, with a sharp smile.

I shuddered and pulled my scattering wits and exploding panic back together. I *was* between residences—what with Olivia gone, me being assigned a new roommate, and not being under my parents' roof. "I am between residences," I said again, believing it.

The circle flashed green.

Helen's eyes narrowed. She tapped her finger. "You will find us unforgiving of verbal recreation at the Department, Miss Crown. It is by the edges of your teeth that you hang. If you fail to answer the question again, I will be required to take you to the Department for questioning." She looked as if she'd like nothing better. "Let's try again, shall we? Where do you *call* home?"

Dare and Marsgrove were both silent and unreadable. Why weren't they *helping*? My parents...

Marsgrove knew where I lived, but he couldn't tell anyone. It was part of the incredible protection set that Raphael had put into place, weaving blessed protections with far more diabolical ones. And not sending anyone after me was part of the oath that Olivia had trapped Marsgrove into agreeing to last term.

But having *me* reveal my home... Anyone listening in—*and I didn't know how many people were listening in*—would have the address. Helen could send troops immediately to the designated location.

Where do you call home?

I looked down at my heart and the red connection threads leading through worlds, all the way to the First Layer.

Where was home... No. I wouldn't tell her.

No. Never.

I mentally grabbed, pinched, then snapped the eighteen-year tie to my parents as home.

Shock flashed across Dare's face, as if he'd seen what I'd done and it had been something beyond his comprehension.

The recoil in the tie snapped back. Mental pain flooded me, then despair. Fingernails dug into my thighs, pressing so hard through my jeans that there would be crescent-shaped bruises decorated with blood left behind.

Physical pain was a frequent companion, though, and I focused the pain downward, capturing it to deal with later.

It had taken little magic to break the tie—only the tiny bit that the room was still trying to regenerate within me—but a great quantity of emotional strength. The kind that I desperately needed not to expend.

Empty devastation was the only thing I could now feel—as if I had walked up to my house and found only ashes.

"Where do you call home, Miss Crown?" Helen was leaning in, waiting to tick off the box on her mental form; to send the completed address field via frequency to a crew of black-clad operatives.

"Ex-cel-sine," I forced out.

The circle paused, then flashed green.

Victory and desolation mixed, then settled into something far more morose. I didn't let my parents images flash to mind. I allowed only the triumph of keeping them safe to focus me as I met Helen's gaze again.

Olivia's mother looked as if she'd bitten into a sandwich of nails, but her gaze was also sharper. I remembered Olivia saying something about how there was nothing her mother liked more than worthy opponents. How she liked to reward and punish those she found useful—that she liked nothing more than to keep riveting enemies close.

"Let's see how far you can dance, Miss Crown, before you collapse. Next question, shall we? What were you doing on the Eighteenth Circle?"

I gave a concise, Olivia-approved recitation of the events, keeping emotions and tangents absent. It was easy enough to do when I was still feeling the emptiness from the broken tie, and my destroyed magic. When questioned about why I had felt the need to guard campus, Dare stepped in and fielded the answer.

Chapter Six

"We were working together with the Troop, and I encouraged Ren's commitment to campus safety." He smiled at Helen—a charming smile that didn't reach his eyes.

"How did you break the Origin Dome?"

I could feel Neph and Will on the other side of the door. Could feel it when they were turned away by the Department guard stationed there. Could hear the whispered beep of my tablet indicating a message. If there was one time I wished I had a frequency, it would be now.

"Through joint effort and a lot of luck," Dare said.

Grilled for the better part of half an hour on what had occurred, it wasn't until we got to questions about Constantine and Olivia that I faltered.

"You are going on record as saying that Mr. Leandred was not working with the terrorists? There is some evidence that he helped at least one of them."

"He fought them. And he deliberately sabotaged their plans." All true.

I answered dozens of questions about Constantine, making sure to highlight his part in helping me and to think *nothing* of anything else.

I never looked at Dare. I didn't want to see what his expression was.

"The Justice Magic here is pitiful," Helen said scathingly, "even with the field in place." She motioned to the circle. "You need to be questioned in the Department. Such statements cannot get past our truth devices."

"It was determined that all students would be questioned on campus unless flags were raised," Marsgrove said smoothly.

"I believe there are plenty of flags here, Phillip." She tapped her tablet, smiled, and started to rise. "In fact, I've just entered one into the system. Come, girl."

"The flag has been overturned."

Helen stopped in the middle of her rise, and folded slowly back into her seat, long legs crossing to the side. "Is that so?"

"Check your tablet."

Helen tapped her finger against her thigh, but didn't even glance in the direction of her device.

"Burning your political capital on her?" She gave a laugh. "Ridiculous. There is zero chance that she will last three months more without fully revealing what she is. *Publicly.* And you *know* it."

Marsgrove said nothing.

Helen observed him for a moment more, then glanced down at the device. "And yet you waste it." She tilted her head. "You always were an idiot."

Silence fell on the room as everyone reexamined the invisible chessboard—playing a game out of my reach.

* Of Those Most Hated *

Helen dissected me with her gaze. She didn't believe a word of my "truths," but because of whatever ace Marsgrove had spent, she was unable to do anything about it. "If we realize that Constantine Leandred was connected to the attacks and you deliberately withheld information—"

"You will imprison me. Yeah, I got tha—"

"Where is my daughter?"

I faltered, expecting another question on Constantine. The truth spell took hold. "The Third Layer."

Helen leaned forward. "How do you know?"

I sharply wrangled my thoughts together. "The terrorists took her. They belong to the Third Layer."

I didn't realize I had taken hold of and was squeezing Olivia's scarf until I saw Helen's smile of satisfaction.

"Hand me that article."

"No."

"It is evidence. And you have zero authority to withhold it."

"No."

Helen smiled coolly. "This is not a request, Miss Crown. You will give me that scarf."

"I will not."

"She is under no obligation to give you anything, Councilwoman Price," Dare said. "She is not being charged with anything."

"She will give me that scarf, or she will be charged *immediately*."

"No," I said.

"Send up Praetorian Kaine." Helen touched the skin under her ear. "Tell Stavros we have found evidence from the terrorists inside the Magiaduct. He is free to begin his investigation now."

I saw Marsgrove do something—body strung as taut as a violin bow that was already showing flayed horse hairs—and the truth field around me was wiped away.

The two adults faced each other suddenly and I could see the magic flying between them.

"You wouldn't dare, Phillip." Helen smiled.

"Give me the scarf, Miss Crown." Marsgrove held out his hand without looking away from her.

"Now," he barked, when I didn't immediately respond.

I gripped it more tightly. This was the only way to find Olivia again. I wouldn't do it.

Administration Magic ripped through me, forcing my hand forward toward Marsgrove. *No.* I put my other against the wall. I'd blast a hole through space and time. I'd—

Magic twisted violently within me—a backlash caused by the surging

Chapter Six

magic that my body couldn't currently handle or manipulate—I bent over, senses scrambled. A light began glowing at the edges of my tunneling vision. A light that said I could accomplish what I needed with one...more...blow.

A world-ending blow.

I shoved away from the light. A hand landed on my back and another pried Olivia's scarf from my grip. My own scarf was pulled from my throat and I shouted and clawed.

I physically reacted, but was easily subdued without normal magic to aid me. Not even the enormous protections Olivia and I had layered in our room would deny the Administrative Magic—wielded by a dean. We had signed over our school lives to obeying that magic.

There was no "second chance" magic here. No "extra bit" that I could channel. No "just a little more" that I'd dug for and found a hundred times when I'd been drained before.

I'd already used all of those extra bits and second chances on the battlefield. I'd twisted and broken already broken channels earlier. There was nothing left to try now. Nothing except the magic glinting around the dark hole. And everything in me said that was not the correct option.

"Give them here, Phillip," Helen ordered.

"They are property evidence under Section 4.84.5234.62 of—"

"I don't care if they are the property evidence of *God*. You will—"

"I have three measures right now that—"

"Are you really that stupid? You waste your precious capital on—"

"Ren?" The voice was close to my ear and the owner was leading me over to the bed.

I shoved Dare's hand away and sat without his help. Shaking, I looked up through my lashes to see the scarves firmly in Marsgrove's hand, and tried to calculate what chance I had.

Hemmed in by three people who were at full strength and ability—while I had none—and with two of them combat mages most mages feared, my chance was nil.

Coasting through high school in Christian's shadow, happy and oblivious and utterly without care for social power, it would have seemed absurd to me, then, that I would become excessively reliant on having an overabundance of power at my disposal—magic that would let me do most anything.

And to be so scorched of such means when I needed them most was a bitter pill.

"Ren," Dare said.

"Don't," I said bitterly. He had helped Marsgrove take Olivia's scarf. I didn't care about mine, but I couldn't look away from hers. In a more rational mood, I might have responded differently, but nothing unemotional was making its way through my head.

"You are a coddled magelet, Miss Crown," Helen said coldly, focusing on me again. "Your *protectors* cosset you."

I gave a short laugh. *Coddled?* Mages had beaten, shocked, imprisoned, leashed, threatened, used, and fed me to monsters. I had forgiven that last one, but I hadn't forgotten what falling into the Blarjack Swamp had felt like my first day on campus, when I'd had few magical skills to assist me.

It was little wonder that I had taken the enormous magic well I had access to and run with it.

I had died twice by magic's hand, one of those times in order to save Dare and campus. And I'd been left for dead, completely physically broken, in the non-magical world by mages trying to steal my brother's magic.

I had been living a pretty un-coddled life since discovering magic.

I stared at Olivia's scarf in Marsgrove's hand.

"Get out," I said.

"Enjoy your pampered life while it lasts," Helen said pleasantly, her eyes hard. "For I can guarantee you, Miss Crown, that it will not."

A tendril of magic slithered over my skin, then pinched hard.

Chapter Seven

CHOOSING A PATH

I SAT A LITTLE ways off from the rest of the students in the dorm's common room. I could feel them watching me, as I stared at the notebook in my lap, my fingers trying to grip the scarf that was no longer there.

Helen Price had made me miss the window of time with Neph, Will, and the others. Every dorm had enacted mandatory procedures, backed by Administration Magic, which called the members of each dorm to the dorm's community area upon the designated return hour.

All I wanted was to reunite with my friends. My emotions felt as knotted as my magic. But trapped in an Olivia-less dorm, I had instead taken up the position as freak and spectacle for the residents of Dorm Twenty-five.

I jolted as a member of Delta and one of Epsilon took seats on either side of me. They silently met the gazes of the other students. They weren't wearing their Plan scarves either—and I wondered if theirs too had been confiscated—instead they had small blue scarves tied around their necks, symbolic reminders.

They stared coolly around the room, and the intensity of the gazes on me lessened and became sporadic—people were forced to take quick inquiring glances in my direction instead of the blatant staring they'd been doing before. I didn't know the Delta and Epsilon members as well as I did some of the other delinquents, but they'd been involved in Plan Fifty-two, and they were providing steady support that I desperately needed.

The dorm heads assembled in the open space in the center and began enacting spells.

Magic shifted between and among residents of our dorm. Community Magic was using the paths that we all already possessed to recharge the group faster. It was the way Community Magic worked, building small, localized communities, then tying those to each other—most potently between two roommates, to four friends living near each other, to groups

* Choosing a Path *

of six and ten in hallways, then onto inhabitants of larger spaces like a single dorm, then the whole Magiaduct, then to places where the entire community met—the cafeteria, the libraries, the fields and halls—until powerful magic flowed freely around the mountain.

The Dorm Twenty-five heads gave a spiel, repeating much of what had already been shared via frequency, community, and campus communications. They reiterated that as soon as the last student was secured in the Magiaduct, we'd be locked down, and the whole Magiaduct would start to regenerate and focus Community Magic more swiftly.

The words "locked down" resulted in fifteen minutes of panic for many in the room.

The words "roommate reassignment" caused an additional fifteen.

I tried to block both episodes by closing my eyes and doing mental calming exercises Draeger had claimed would help my magic refocus. The traumatic magic swirling around made me nauseous.

Apparently, the crystal ball that we'd all had to pass our hands over as we'd entered the common room had coded and locked those of us without roommates into the system. Once everyone on campus was entered into the system, each of us without a roommate would be paired.

"Okay, everyone. Calm down. That's right," said the soothing voice of one of the dorm heads. "We are going to search and flag magic levels. We want to make sure everyone is physically well. Depletion, usage, mindset, and state of recovery all count in the color that is generated. Panic and trauma to a mage's magic levels will affect your final color as well."

I was going to have to look into Psychology Magic at some point, as I found that distantly fascinating.

As an introvert and artist, and studying with Christian for sports psych, I had always practiced a lot of mind and visualization techniques, so knowing that mindset affected a person's magic wasn't mind blowing, but it did make me think about how that reality could be *used*. My mental pyramid took on new dimensions.

If ever things on campus went back to normal, Mbozi was going to have to start running away from my questions.

It was hard to imagine normal, at the moment.

I yanked my eyes open when I felt the spell scan me. It then moved to the Epsilon member at my right. Everyone's level was visible to the rest of the room.

Green meant healthy in body and mind, and was represented across the spectrum in various verdant shades.

No one showed green.

The yellows were a mix of issues, physical, emotional, and mental. Every shade of yellow was represented across the broad spectrum of the four

Chapter Seven

hundred or so people in our dorm.

The Delta and Epsilon members next to me, who had been stuck in the Magiaduct during the attack, showed butterscotch limned in purple, but the dark outlines were easy to ignore due to the steadiness of their neutral central color.

The purple outlines were likely due to a backlash through the scarf system. It made me wonder *what* everyone else had experienced when I'd taken a turn toward the insane after Olivia had disappeared.

Purples necessitated heavy concern, both emotionally and magically, and they were horribly present in pockets of students scattered throughout the sea of yellows.

Black encompassed the emotional and physical turmoil of the purples, but also indicated something was *severely* wrong with the person's magic.

I was the only one in the entire room showing black.

I folded my arms tightly against my chest and refused to look up again. There was nothing helpful in seeing the looks of horror and fear...or of seeing the more calculating and sly glances.

"He-her-here," someone stuttered. Magic "supplements" were shoved into my hand by a scared-looking slip of a mage who had been tasked with delivering them where needed.

"Crown, back to your room," the dorm head said, frowning. "Medical will come for you."

I pushed out of my seat, happy to leave the staring behind.

Back in my room, I chucked the supplements into the trash and started scrubbing my desk. *They wanted me to feel better?* Destroying the taint that Helen Price had left behind would make me feel better.

I hoped she had accidentally ported to hell.

A discordant tone rang through the air like a mangled foghorn. From my tablet, I could hear voices on the main frequency channel stilling, then a voice that sounded like Patrick's said, "Here comes lockdown, hold onto your butts!"

I sat on my bed and leaned against my window, magic sponge in hand. Outside, the magic shimmered, then grids of air flipped like invisible louvers, one after another, molding together and locking—sealing us in.

Trapped.

From my tablet, I could hear the voices of the other students. It was a discordant background mix—a low hum of nervous, traumatized voices, blending with calm and steady ones. How officials were justifying this to the parents across the Second Layer, I had no idea. Although, until mages reached the age of twenty-two, society considered them unsteady—not yet ready to be out in the world making independent magical decisions. Even in the First Layer, where eighteen was considered adulthood, none of the

* Choosing a Path *

adults really seemed to trust anyone during that four-year spread.

It was some sort of weird limbo where we were expected to act like adults, but always with the air that we *weren't* really.

They'd trapped us in here. *For our own good.*

I looked around my room. Olivia's things sat immobile.

I looked out the window. At the Department stooges combing campus. At the panels of magic keeping us locked inside. Safe against the outside. Trapped within. With supplements, and calming spells, and empty reassurances.

While they chose our paths for us.

I would have traded myself for Olivia today. I would have bitten Raphael's obvious lure.

It would have been a stupid choice. I *knew* that—because with me under his control, Raphael could pinch Olivia's life force between two fingers—but the choice to go with him had been made from emotion, instinctive.

Emotion that had been telling me that only *I* could fix things.

I looked at the empty bed across the room.

But I wasn't the only one involved. I hadn't been for days now, weeks.

I dropped the sponge, and slowly picked up my tablet. Before we'd had the scarves in place, we had used a temp system.

Taking a deep breath, I clicked a button and said, "Hello?"

A flurry of voices answered, magically wrapping around me.

"Lady-in-waiting, we've been waiting for you to call," Patrick said, in a satisfied voice—though there was a large dose of relief to his tone as well.

Other members added their comments as well, *their* voices more subdued. They were waiting for me to speak. Justice Toad was vibrating with the tension of it.

I wondered how long they'd been waiting for me.

I swallowed and activated the charm that popped everyone's full-color holograms into view, then spread them out in a visual grid before me. It was similar to what Godfrey had done hours before—spreading nearly the entirety of the Second Layer in view.

Faces appeared, arrayed in front of me. I was so overcome with relief that I had to get hold of myself for a moment. These people had helped me save campus.

Patrick said, "Got to tell you, Crown. Was worried there for a bit."

I focused on his hologram.

"Worried you might go all—" He made a looping motion around his head. "And scupper without any of us the wiser."

I cleared my throat. "No. I, uh, worked through a few things."

Whatever that tunneling light had been when Marsgrove had taken the scarf from me... The light had felt world-ending. Whether I might have

Chapter Seven

blown a hole in campus, or the layer, or Earth, or *existence* with my mangled magic...yeah. Relying on my emotions made me extremely responsive and focused. But when I didn't temper that with practical planning, it made me actively dangerous.

It was something I'd have to put real effort into working on...the tug against my chest to go after Olivia was getting tighter with each hour that passed.

Everyone was watching me closely.

"Plan Fifty-two is complete," I said. "You have no further commitment to fulfill. And our...previous line of communication is unsafe."

Thank God, Saf and Trick had already had the presence of mind to have me silence the scarves, though. In the Administration's or Department's hands...

Mike, Delia, Will, and Neph said nothing, and I didn't look at the other members of Plan Fifty-two, concentrating instead on Olivia's terrible twosome.

Asafa stared silently, while Patrick's eyes were manic and deadly. "Do you think that is why we answered this call? To be released?"

"No," I said softly.

The edge disappeared from his gaze. "Good."

I swallowed around the emotion. I smiled—a smile that started out strained, but gradually worked into something more real. "I would really appreciate your help with..." My voice came out far more steady than what I felt, but I still had trouble finishing. "With making sure every last one of our members returns to full health and safety."

Every single one of them knew I was talking about Olivia.

If there was one thing I had learned this past term—wasting willing help was not an admittance of failure. Christian and I had always been a team. So much of one, that we'd really been more an extension of each other. When I'd lost him, then arrived at Excelsine, furiously trying to revive him, I had been a one-woman squad of destruction. This past term had taught me a lot about the value of teamwork: working with Dare, working with Olivia, Will, Constantine, and Neph, working with Patrick and Asafa, working on Plan Fifty-two...

No, I wasn't going to go off half-cocked this time. Not when I *understood* there were better ways to proceed.

"Excellent, that is exactly what we were hoping you were going to say." Asafa's voice was even and calming. "There's another mandatory assembly in our dorm in an hour to discuss habitation and roommates. They are checking everyone." I heard Will and Neph chime in with their assembly times too. "When do you want to meet?"

I felt a stirring along one of my strongest connection threads, and some

* Choosing a Path *

of the tension I'd been holding dissipated as I recognized that the magical coma that had been holding Constantine had started to lift, somewhere in the bowels of the Magiaduct.

They might not be letting anyone in to see patients yet, but I'd been mandated for a medical check, and I wasn't going to wait here to be called. Not when there were other places I could be.

I gathered my things together.

"An hour after the last mandatory assembly?" I asked, and was met with a flurry of positive responses. I looked at the empty desk across from mine. "And...maybe in your room, Saf? Trick?"

I didn't want a new roommate. I didn't want to leave our room. But I also couldn't stay in our room right now, surrounded by the moroseness that was swallowing me. It was unhelpful to action. I needed to get out. To plan.

"Absolutely. See you soon, Crown. Saf out."

The others called in their agreements, and I gripped my tablet fiercely and walked from our room toward the underworld below.

Chapter Eight

RELATIONSHIPS WITH THORNS

THE MEDICAL WARD under the Magiaduct was bustling with activity and magic. Carved slightly into the interior of the mountain, the "recovering" ward was more easily able to access the magic that circulated throughout the mountain, allowing the patients to get the benefit of the rejuvenating magic swirling around from so many powerful mages living above it.

Especially now, with none of us able to leave, the circulating magic was heady and thick.

The pass that the mage had shoved into my hand, along with the supplements, had gotten me inside the level without having to resort to more nefarious tactics.

The long, wide corridor stretched forever. Every dozen feet there were small arches in the wall that led to other areas, and other wards. Unlike campus proper, the arches were labeled clearly here. No freshman hazing for the medical students. Healing people was serious business in the magic world.

Patient rooms, labs, sitting areas, and offices lined the four-mile corridor loop on each side.

A number of the windows were darkened, but many were clear and allowed the viewer to see through to the "windows" on the other side of the rooms. Charmed windows displayed views of fantastic landscapes—deserts, oceans, mountains, and forests, all filled with beasts and magic—for the recovering patients to enjoy. Some displayed environmental cross sections, like a Midlands' puzzle, stitching together multiple landscapes.

As I walked the long corridor, a haphazard grid of crisscrossing color snapped into place, overlaying my view with their hues. It was like looking at ward lines, but these weren't wards—they were active magic trails.

In the different rooms, and through the corridor, tools and magic flew

* Relationships with Thorns *

through the air. Their long arcs of color trailed their path, and thinner rays of light showed where the magic was headed, with the intention of the caster connected to the destination of the magic.

I blinked, but the paths remained for a few moments, fading like tracers after their mission was complete. Being able to see the trajectory of magic was new for me. Something to examine later.

Rubbing the inside of my elbow, I stopped in front of the room to which my crippled magic had led me.

Constantine wasn't awake to have chosen a landscape, so someone had visually perched the room on a cliff overlooking an ocean. The slight tang of sea spray and soft sounds of gulls completed the full-sense illusion.

I wondered idly what view he would have chosen. A jagged pit surrounded by beautiful flowering meadows to entice the naïve?

I put my hand against Constantine's window.

"Ren Crown."

I turned sharply to see a Medical mage striding toward me. She was looking at a tablet in her hand, which had to be displaying my name, and probably my medical status.

"You shouldn't be in this wing. Your pass is for the scanning and regulation section with..."

Her gaze took in my hand against the window, then traveled to the ceiling. I looked up at the crisscrossing lines, but I didn't know what she was observing or why her expression looked suddenly conflicted.

"Wait here."

I hadn't been planning on going anywhere else, so I did as directed.

As soon as she disappeared into a doorway farther down the corridor, though, I withdrew my picks and picked the magical lock to Constantine's room. I could feel the wards testing my depleted magic, looking for my intentions.

I entered the room and the wards welcomed me in.

I immediately strode to Constantine's bedside and touched his forehead, painfully "asking" his magic if anything harmful had been done to him since I'd put the painted spell in place while he'd been laying broken on the battlefield.

I didn't have the medical knowledge that Doctor Greyskull contained in his pinkie finger, but he had given me a very positive demonstration when he'd fixed my broken toe. The medical practitioner helped tweak the magic of the patient into fixing itself. It felt like ages ago that I'd watched in awe as he worked to patch me back together.

The paint I had placed on Constantine had strengthened the link between us. I could feel him stirring toward consciousness, reaching toward my stroking fingers. He was unable to block the new connection, at least

Chapter Eight

while in such a deep state of recovery.

He would be...displeased about that.

But it allowed me to see that everything seemed to be positive about his healing.

I had very little magic available to me—unless I used a device to pull it out of the Earth or air and set the northern hemisphere on fire.

Or unless I had *paint*. Awakening paint.

I hesitated for a second, finger tracing his forehead where I'd placed the painted line, then gave into the urge and directed my limited energy to go to Constantine, working through the echo of his painted skin.

It was second nature for me to give whatever I had, and I directed the energy hovering beneath his skin to dive in and fix him. I pulled the zigzagging wards that were gently filtering through the air into view. One of the lines zagged toward me, tapping against my chest in polite question. I opened my twisted magic in permission and the healing field in the room hooked into me, then connected to Constantine's forehead.

The process would sap more energy from me, before it would eventually return in the continually circling feedback loop, but I'd deal with that. I always did. I put my head in my hands for a moment.

Looking back up and around the room, I noticed that Constantine's scarf—Bryant's scarf—was nowhere to be seen. Someone had taken it too. I grimly sat in the chair next to his bed. It was likely that they had them all.

People were filing past in the hall. More than one person slowed as they saw me inside the room. I located, then fumbled with, the spell connected to the outside window. The glass finally dimmed.

A few moments later, the door opened and I stiffened, but didn't rise. Settled in the chair next to the bed, I tried not to look up as the familiar presence approached.

"Miss Crown. You aren't supposed to be in here."

"Oh?" I looked up. "Good evening, Doctor Greyskull."

He looked between me and the door, his gaze unsurprised, but still calculating. "How did you get in?"

I shrugged. "I opened the door."

"The door was locked." He gave me a half smile. "And no one is allowed inside. The wards are very specific."

"I won't hurt him," I said, not answering his implicit question of how I'd gotten past the lock.

Greyskull looked at the ward lines around the room. "No, I don't think you will. The wards are showing that your presence is helpful. Very unusual."

He pulled up a chair next to me. "But you are used to the unusual, are you not, Miss Crown?"

* Relationships with Thorns *

I'd probably pay for the proof that my presence was helping rather than hindering Constantine. All of those very long looks from the medical staff probably didn't precede anything good, but the Band-Aid had been ripped from my anonymity hours ago.

"It is a good thing you are here, in the medical ward," he said. "An Administration summons would have been issued otherwise."

"I'm fine," I said with a smile. "I've been worse."

"You were far less untruthful last time I saw you."

I let my smile slip. "It is hard to determine where truth should be placed these days."

He tipped his head. I could see his tattoos moving along his skin, peeking over the collar of his coat as if peering at me before retreating again. "I am in charge of this room's wards. I can do your examination here, though it would be better to do it in another space."

"I'm fine here, without an exam."

"Are you?"

I couldn't answer in the positive again.

"Come then," he said gently. "Let's take a look at what has been done to you."

A tattoo slithered down his arm and wrapped his pointer finger in dark coils that ended in a point at the tip. The tip touched my skin and the tattoo rotated forward, like a screw being drilled into my flesh. I could feel the magic, the familiar foreign energy searching and examining blocked pathways.

Scanning me.

"How does that work?" I asked, slightly breathless and trying to control natural panic.

Even if my magic weren't working as well as it normally did, I could still trace the path of his. It flowed down the twisted routes, mapping the blocked paths rather than trying to heal them, navigating the knotted coils, as if trying to flow through a garden hose that had been yanked into a series of knots that was stopping the water from going further down the tube.

It was pretty bad.

"Someone used a leech on you today, and poorly," he said, almost absently. "Multiple leeches."

I tensed and couldn't prevent my gaze from going to Constantine, who was still out cold and doing his best impression of Sleeping Beauty on the bed.

I tore my gaze away and met Greyskull's. "Godfrey. He had...something."

"*Mmmm.* You have remnants of other leeches too, but those have been able to naturally unwind themselves. You could file a report with the

Chapter Eight

Magisters, if you desired," he said casually. Too casually—I could tell he was angry on my behalf.

Still tense, I replied, "No, thanks." I hadn't thought that type of thing would be revealed by a scan. "Is that how my magic got so twisted?"

"It was a contributing factor, but not the only one. You drained yourself, replenished your magic...in some manner...then drained yourself again. This happened a few times. Think of it like stripping a ribbon, then badly stapling another ribbon to its tail. It will hold for a little while. But it will eventually break and leave the ribbon more frayed than before. Do this a couple of times? You can damage the original ribbon more than can be repaired."

"Can it...be repaired?"

"Yes." The tattoo slipped from underneath my skin and slithered back up his finger, disappearing beneath his sleeve. "I would recommend a healing coma. However, you would be out for a minimum of three days and the Department's healers would have a look."

"No."

He nodded, as if my response had been expected. "With this level of damage—internal damage, repeatedly battered—natural, slow healing is the best method. With therapy, you will be good as new."

"How long?"

"Two weeks."

"*Two weeks?*"

He tapped the knuckles of his left hand. "As long as you don't overtax anything, yes."

I stared at him. I couldn't wait two weeks for my magic to work itself back to normal.

That I could maybe now get into the Library of Alexandria without worry was an unwelcome and idiotic thought under the circumstances.

"Can I do anything to...speed that up?"

"There are always methods for speed. They are usually not in line with a healthy path."

I'd made sacrifices before. I could cut a few corners.

"If you make those choices, your magic may never work quite right again," he added idly.

I looked at him sharply. "Like overtaxing it now could make me not a specific type of mage anymore?"

"No, much of *that* is incumbent upon the way you view things and your mental processes. It might just never let you do something again with the ease with which you've become accustomed."

There was going to be a balance here, a tightrope that I would have to walk. I didn't have to be at full strength to go after Olivia. I didn't have to

* Relationships with Thorns *

use the full extent of my magic to do so either, if I focused on cleverness and cunning rather than brute strength and overwhelming magic.

"Things that are already drenched in my magic...could I, like, bathe in those?" *Could I dump an entire tube of paint over my body and let it work its magic?*

He looked amused. "You could. And while you are waiting for the paths of magic to reconnect between the "drenching" and your cores, you can enjoy excruciating pain while watching some very pretty world-ending fireworks."

"So...that one goes in the "break only in case of emergency" category?"

His smile slipped. "There are many things that go in that category." His gaze lifted slightly—to my crown, where everyone who knew Raphael's magic well always looked—then dropped to meet my eyes again.

I recoiled from him, immediately and sharply.

I'd had an "older man, awesome, safety crush" on Doctor Greyskull since he'd gotten my Ewok reference when I'd been recovering from Death #1. I'd never questioned my instinctive liking of the man and how my magic hummed alongside his when he was fixing me.

But now... Now that I was looking for it, and with the very large clue he'd just given me, I could see it. The same sorts of magical connections that Marsgrove and Raphael had, and that I was sure I'd find on Stevens, now that I knew where to look. Affectionate threads that were worn, frayed, and aged.

Another mage who had been friends with Raphael at school.

He sat back and held his hands down and away in a position meant to reassure me he wouldn't attack. His gaze was steady, honest, and infinitely accepting of my horrified reaction. "It is beyond time that you knew. Do you have questions?"

"You...you were friends?"

"Yes," he said, voice steady. "Very good friends, at one time."

Doctor Greyskull had been nothing but helpful to me, and the pained look he had given as he'd scanned my magic, told me he wanted to fix all that was broken within me. But...

"I can't trust you," I whispered.

He smiled. It was a little sad. "It is best you trust yourself. Know that I will *always* help you here in Medical and on campus."

"That is...awfully specific. And if we are off campus?"

"Something you don't need to worry about for a few years, no?"

"Sure," I said strangely, off-footed. The world had tilted and I had to gain my feet again.

"I could reassure you of my positive intentions off campus as well, but... Well, maybe it is best for you to place your trust in your own generation. I, too, want to help old acquaintances...get better." The skin between his

Chapter Eight

brows pinched. "Perhaps at the expense of newer acquaintances. Such is the tangled web woven between friends and family."

Of anything, him telling me not to trust him—and that he might help Raphael over helping me—made me relax more than any denial he could have given.

Trustworthy, no, but *honest*. Honest about his own loyalties.

He'd given me a wealth of information in very few statements. That his primary concern was his oath to the University—here, he'd put the students, any student, above Raphael. Off-campus...he might have a different order.

I nodded in acceptance. "Did you speak with him while he was here?"

Greyskull tilted his head and narrowed his eyes. I could see him rifling through internal data, trying to determine *when* Raphael had been on campus.

Greyskull hadn't been aware of Raphael posing as Emrys. Relief trickled through me.

Perhaps Raphael, too, knew that Doctor Greyskull would not help him hurt campus, or he'd thought that Greyskull might stop him completely.

I saw the grim realization show on Greyskull's face. "Ah. I believe I will need to speak with Phillip, yes?"

I nodded again, a short jerk of my head. Maybe if Marsgrove got raked over the coals by his friend, I could sneak in and nab Olivia's scarf.

Greyskull smiled tightly. "Not here, in his own skin, though?" He didn't wait for me to shake my head. "Not after fall term, he wouldn't be. He's always been quite adept at hiding. At protecting his location. Only once did he fail, and that was because he never saw the trap." He shook his head. "I've never met anyone better at stealth, and I've met a lot of exceptional mages in my line of work, Miss Crown. If he wants someone dead, that person has to be equally exceptional at something pertinent to their own survival."

"He didn't want to blow Excelsine," I said, with a sudden, strange need to reassure him. "That was Godfrey. Godfrey said that Ra—that *he* didn't want campus destroyed." It was better not to say Raphael's name aloud.

Godfrey's actual words had been, *Verisetti may want to coddle whatever pets he has here, but I've wanted to obliterate this mountain for the longest time.*

I fiercely examined Greyskull. I wondered if he qualified as a pet.

"No." Greyskull's smile was tight. "He is very certain in what he wants to destroy. Places where happy memories still exist are generally off limits for his psychopathy."

"He killed Godfrey."

"Of course he did. I can put two and two together, now that you've given me the decryption key to today's events, Miss Crown."

* Relationships with Thorns *

That it had been *Raphael* on campus at the end.

"It's been a very long day." He pushed his chair back. "One that I will discuss with Phillip and...others."

"Marsgrove hates him." And Marsgrove hated me. "He won't help you aid him."

I didn't want Dr. Greyskull to help Raphael.

"Phillip maintains a...less neutral position than I do. But there is a far different history between the two of them." He packed up his materials. "Our actions define our positions, not our discussions. There is a reason, Miss Crown, that Phillip is rarely on campus, and that I always am. He is far more assured of his goals. I find that sometimes a coward's way is a far more *comforting* path when friends and family are fighting to the death." He smiled self-deprecatingly.

"But back to your treatment, Miss Crown," he said. "Two weeks to return to *full* strength, but depending upon the connections you maintain and the care you take, you should be ready for normal classwork when classes restart."

He gave me additional supplements that—but for this conversation—I might have tossed into the trash with the others. But I believed him. I believed that he would help me on campus. That he held strictly to the lines he had drawn in the sand. That he would do everything to keep me healthy and alive while I walked the mountain's paths as a student.

Off campus... Off campus might be a different story.

He smiled wearily, gaze holding mine for an extra beat before lifting to the top of my head. He exited and said something to the medics who were gesticulating wildly on the other side of the glass. The window went dark.

I took a deep breath and sat back, thinking of my options. Two *weeks*.

I stared at my hands. Magic wasn't shooting out of my fingertips, but I wasn't without resources.

I rifled through my bag, to the small portfolio that I had brought with me. Lifting it, I looked through the contents.

I had badgered Professor Stevens endlessly about working on paint alone. But she'd never given in. She'd made me work on all sorts of things. Made me imbue my magic into different mediums.

Like paper.

I slowly lifted one of the papers. I had pieced together every fiber of it with my magic. Magic that was awaiting activation.

As my fingers filed through my portfolio, I counted ten sheets like it. Ten sheets made from magic that I had created while thinking positive thoughts—my work with Dare and protection of Olivia had been going exceptionally well at the time of their creation. These sheets would help someone who needed an emotional recharge, and campus was swimming

Chapter Eight

with people in need. The sheets only needed someone to activate the magic within.

I tapped them against my knee, then set them to the side.

Ten more of the sheets were swimming with thoughts of destruction—that had been a less-golden day. Ten more had resolute purpose sown into every fiber—anything one of them was used for would continue until it burned itself into a crisp. And there were dozens of other options in my stashes around campus—my room, Okai, the vault—all created under different constraints and emotions.

I had hundreds of things that I'd *already* created, and that were available to *use*. A mage didn't even have to be at half strength to be able to use powerful devices that were already filled with magic. Like the containers in the First Layer. They allowed mages who couldn't use their own magic to use the *containers'* magic.

Like I'd said to Olivia back in the Library of Alexandria—normal mages could create exceptional things with time and focus. Just because I was hobbled and couldn't whip out a game-ending spell didn't mean that I was without power or use.

I pulled a blank pad of paper out—no magic in it—curious to see what my charcoal pencils would do without my usual extra mojo flowing through them. After all, I had made the pencils too. I made everything I used. Raphael had initiated that path with my Awakening paint. And I'd become Stevens' student to continue the path. She had made damn sure I had.

I focused on my lines, drafting out a trap that I would recreate with a piece of paper filled with deception later, depending on the outcome of my test. Or I could set it with ultramarine paint when I found the paint tube the vine had eaten. That would compensate for the horsepower that I didn't have.

I'd get this done. I'd get Olivia back. I'd keep everyone safe. And help heal campus. I'd deal with *everything*.

"You look like shit."

Startled, I jagged the pencil line across my page and reached out a hand automatically. "You're awake."

"So it would seem." Constantine grimaced and touched his cheek, then his chest. The horrible, open gashes that had nearly split his body in half had healed fully half an hour ago while I'd been sitting with him, but Dr. Greyskull had said magical healing couldn't automatically take away the body's phantom memory and pain.

I touched his free wrist, letting the trickle of magic that I had recovered over the past hour flow into him, and put my pad on the edge of his bedside so that I could complete my drawing while still maintaining contact.

He cataloged his injuries, his healing wounds, and his vanishing scars.

* Relationships with Thorns *

"The doctor is competent, at least. Everything is in the right place."

"He will be thrilled to hear it." I shook my head and continued drawing.

Out of the corner of my eye I could see Constantine touch his forehead, his expression doing something typically complicated. "But this." He drew his thumb across the smooth, perfect skin beneath his hair—the paint I had laid there had long since disappeared, but obviously something remained for him to feel. "This is not the work of a doctor. What did you do to me, darling?"

I could feel a spike of anxiety beneath his amused tone. Dampening and prodding, like a system that was testing itself, troubleshooting lines of code or the angle of a charcoal sweep, one at a time.

I kept my eyes focused on my page.

"No answer? Even more interesting."

I had done it reflexively—wiped the ultramarine paint across his brow—when I'd been overwhelmed, traumatized, and barely coherent.

"I'm not in prison," he mused. In the background hum of the connection, I could feel him still testing and prodding at the magic of the paint. "And there are no brutish-looking guards at the door—the kind that make sure people stay where they are placed. I'm starting to question your judgment."

I smiled and kept drawing without responding.

He moved his arms, as if stretching sore muscles. "My magic feels...penned in."

I grimaced. "Campus is on lockdown. Magiaduct-only access for students. It's a good thing that the student medical facilities are underneath the dorms, or I wouldn't be lounging here."

"Waiting for me to wake like a good Prince Charming."

"Except that *you* are the witch." I sketched another line.

"A far more clever creature." He stretched again, sheet slipping to his waist as he pushed himself up. "Where is your knight in shining armor? Surely he doesn't know you sit here," he said, tone as unpleasant as it always was when he spoke of Dare.

I chewed my pencil top and looked up. I was pissed at Dare, but... "He carried you here."

A tight smile pulled Constantine's lips. "Can't lose his investment. As painful as it has been."

I watched the emotions play over his face, lightning quick, and said nothing. We descended into silence and I knew he was accessing whatever mental communications he had, updating himself on what had happened while he was out.

"Why are you still on campus?" he asked in a far too casual manner.

After Olivia was taken, Constantine had saved campus from destruction

Chapter Eight

by my hand. When I had thought Olivia was dead, I had completely lost my wits. It wasn't hard to guess I would be going after her.

"My magic is twisted like pumpkins placed too closely together in a patch, then left to rot," I said. "And the item that has her location...is no longer in my possession."

Constantine didn't say anything for a moment. He was, perhaps, the only person who didn't require an explanation. He had protected me from enemy fire while I placed the magic into the scarf.

"So, you will be leaving as soon as you recover the item and have enough magic to slip through the protections and patrols?"

"Yes."

"I am going with you."

"I know," I said simply. He hadn't betrayed the entire Second Layer only to give up on his vengeance. "But there are conditions."

"Saving your roommate comes before my revenge?"

"Yes."

"*Mmmm.* I suppose you'll need that confirmation in blood?"

"No, just your word."

He closed his eyes and leaned back. "Darling, it's like that lovely brain of yours learns nothing sometimes."

"You'll keep your word," I said, leaning back, propping my feet up on his bed, and returning to my work. "Feel free to be dramatic about it, though."

The edge of his lip curled upward even as his eyes stayed closed. "Now I am *your* entertainment?"

A piece of my anxiety unfurled a measure. This was normal. I *needed* normal. "I figure fair is fair."

"I've never been a proponent of fairness." But his face stayed relaxed. "What happened to you while I was dozing like the wrong fairytale creature?"

By the time I was finished with the retelling—leaving out the bit about Dare's vine—Constantine's mouth held a smile that was concerning. "Praetorian Kaine, *hmmm.*"

"Constantine..."

"I'm not even going to ask how you got past that test, darling, as I know you are leaving out those details, but as to the other—"

"I'll deal with the Department."

"No one *deals* with the Department. Even Stuart Leandred steps softly around them."

I tilted my head. "Your father seemed quite concerned about you."

"Yes, as always," he said dispassionately. But there was something weird about the way he said it.

* Relationships with Thorns *

And as if our words had somehow conjured the man, there was a knock at the door, and the windowpane cleared to show the person on the other side. The knob brightened with magic and turned.

Stuart Leandred, a handsome, distinguished man, looked wrecked as he entered.

"Constantine." He walked into the room, but his movements were hesitant, as if he were uncertain of his reception. "I was alerted that you had wakened."

"Stuart." Constantine smiled thinly. "How good of you to come."

Stuart Leandred didn't precisely wince, but there was a distinct hesitation under his political expression of cheer. I could see his magic trying to reach out to the healing wards in the room, stopping just short of connecting. Everything about the motion was desperate and uncertain.

I wasn't sure how he was able to be in the Magiaduct during lockdown. Special dispensation because of Constantine's condition, or because of Stuart's connections?

"Ren, darling. I'll see you later." Constantine gently pushed my foot from his bed. "Don't get into too much trouble," he said with a falsely casual tone.

I looked between them and quickly gathered my stuff.

Stuart Leandred smiled down at me. Whatever his true expression would have been, it was completely masked by a political one full of courteous interest. "Ren Crown, isn't it? Charmed to meet you. Your name has been on everyone's lips today, and your face on everyone's frequency."

"Nice to meet you, sir," I said politely.

Constantine gave me a more forceful nudge. "Go on then. Go help your starving orphans and downtrodden creatures," he said.

I stared at him, sharply reminded of Olivia and how she'd told me to get out when her mother had been on her way to our room. There was something equally electrified in Constantine's gaze.

"Go." His tone turned more forceful.

I had left Olivia's side, and Olivia's mother had tortured her.

I moved my hand to set my things back on the edge of his bed. "You know, I think I'll—"

Constantine grabbed my elbow, and slightly grimacing, opened the old path between us. Turquoise and copper blazed into view, completely unhidden for the first time since he'd become aware of the connection's existence between us.

There was no fear in the absolute tumultuous ball of emotion that was vibrating the connection threads. The ringing emotions that *were* present were *exceedingly* concerning, but Constantine had no fear of his father torturing him. Hatred was, by far, the strongest emotion. Bitterness,

Chapter Eight

abandonment, fury, coldness, righteous betrayal.

The only thing pointed toward me in the connection—Constantine was *so* good at only showing what he wanted to show—was the fierce desire that I have nothing to do with his father.

Shaken by the emotional feedback, I nodded and pulled my belongings back against my chest, then sidestepped his father and headed toward the door.

My last view of the room was of Stuart's hands thrust forward in entreaty, and Constantine's dark gaze pinning him in place, full of nearly the amount of hatred he had shown for Raphael.

Chapter Nine

COUNSELING IN A SEA OF GRIEF

WALKING THROUGH MEDICAL and back to my dorm, I wondered at the relationship between Constantine and his father. I didn't understand what could have—

My steps stuttered as I passed a room that contained a semi-familiar face. The girl who had lost her roommate. The girl who had been yelling for "Shinsara" on Top Campus before she'd been magically sedated. She twitched in her unnatural sleep, her features pinched.

I touched her window. Unlike with Constantine, though, I had no connection to this girl that I could use to bypass my twisted magic channels.

I tapped the side of my bag, my thoughts racing. I looked at the wards and magic zipping through the halls. I didn't have the ability currently to throw my magic directly to her. I had to allocate resources *differently*.

I waited for the hall to clear a fraction before palming my picks and making short work of the girl's door. She didn't have half of the wards on her room that Constantine had. Hers was an emotional pain, and there was less physical reason to keep others out of her healing area. On the contrary, calming and Community Magic was absolutely being *pumped* into her room.

I set my bag down and carefully withdrew a sheet of paper that I had created while I was thinking about Christian—healing thoughts of him, brimming with memory and forgiveness, acceptance and love.

I slowly folded the paper into an origami rose, concentrating my thoughts on my goal. I had no active magic at my disposal; however, I hadn't lost my hard-won ability to distinguish wards and intent.

It was easy to watch the streams of magic zipping around the edges of the room—the same ones that zipped through the entire ward. It was easy enough to see which ones were rootless and not seeking anyone specific. Easy enough to see which one was available when a healer needed a boost.

Chapter Nine

I held the rose up and caught one of the streams, moving the paper in a spiral as if I were filling an ice cream cone, letting the magic coil and settle inside the folds.

The magic immediately started to push at the magic in the paper. I swallowed, as an echo of my love for Christian seeped slowly from the paper onto my hand.

I set the rose carefully in the girl's hands, crossed on her chest. She shuddered, then stilled, and some of the pain in her expression eased.

"I'm sorry," I murmured.

I let myself out and hurried down the hall, not wanting to look in any more rooms.

A blonde head bounced in the distance. Familiar magic encased her. *My* magic. My breath caught.

I could see her stopping and tweaking something. Helping. Sending comforting magic to one room, then another. My magic still heavily laced hers—revealing remnants of the enormous amount of power I had blindly channeled into her, in order to resurrect her on the battlefield. And with the power, the blonde was giving her all—to help everyone she could.

I fumbled with my bag and a few minutes later I was shoving an armful of paper roses into the arms of a wide-eyed orderly who wasn't much older than I was. "Give these to the blonde." I motioned. "Her. Please."

He looked horrified, as if I had just handed him bombs, but a moment later, his expression morphed into one of wonder and he looked down at the papers.

"Please. Don't tell anyone," I said. "Just." I motioned again.

He looked at me as if I were crazy, but I just walked quickly away. He ran toward the blonde and I ducked into the stairwell as he reached her.

I made the long trek to the dorm, nearly shaking by the end of it. I turned the corner to our hall and put a hand to my mouth as I saw who was waiting in front of my door. I sprinted the last few yards and flung myself forward.

~*~

Curled on my bed, I tried to let the rejuvenation magic in our room do its thing.

I was more tired after visiting Constantine, and because of the emotional turmoil experienced afterward, but something had worked free during the visit to Constantine—and a single knot released from a twisted mass of muscle. Only forty, or four hundred, more knots to go...

Neph hummed and the magic worked around us. We'd been holed up in "comfort position" ever since we'd hugged ourselves inside the room.

Justice Toad beeped, informing me that Dorm Twenty-five was holding

* Counseling in a Sea of Grief *

its mandatory roommate-less assembly in five minutes. The idea of getting a new roommate and listening to *why* I needed one filled me with bile. But I couldn't skirt the assembly. My magic was in no shape to do anything rebellious at the moment, and Administrative Magic would make me attend, the same as every other roommate-less student in my dorm.

Just like the girl in Medical would be expected to attend in her dorm.

Neph had tried to obtain an exemption to move in with me—as my muse, she was allowed certain privileges outside of the usual ones. But she had been denied. Neph's roommate was a high-profile daughter of a politician, and without permission, roommates couldn't swap rooms in a lockdown situation. Roommates *had* to stay twelve hours out of every twenty-four in the same space, for the safety of all involved.

I was a little tired of hearing that last statement.

For the safety of all involved. My entire life was stretching before me in a series of cells with a giant red banner and those exact words scrolling the top.

Neph paused, then tilted her head as if listening to something.

"What?" I asked, pushing upward on my hands.

"Beta was just taken offline."

Neph's scarf had been taken at the mandatory muse assembly. She'd been tight-lipped about what had occurred at the meeting.

But she still maintained a connection to the scarf network. It was a muse thing where the connections that she formed no longer required the physical objects. We'd made tentative plans to channel Olivia's scarf through her when we found someone else who had retained their scarf. I was reluctant to try it, though, due to the way Neph had hesitated before agreeing. There was something she wasn't telling me. And Neph would sacrifice herself as easily as I would. I had to make sure I was the buffer.

No one else was going to sacrifice themselves for me.

"Do you know who took Beta offline?" I asked.

"Lifen. Or at least someone using her threads. She took Epsilon and Delta offline earlier."

Lifen and Delia, as the physical creators of the scarves, had the ability to unravel them.

Panic spiked in me. "Tell her not to unhook Alpha. No matter what."

Neph nodded and gently pushed me to the edge of the bed as a ding sounded—an alarm from the walls—indicating that I was past due for being assigned a new roommate.

For going to the roommate recycling session.

"Tell Lifen that she can't unhook Alpha, Neph," I stressed, refusing to move further.

"I did." She nudged me again. "She says she can't, Ren. We'll discuss it

Chapter Nine

in an hour. It's time."

I felt emotion bubbling up within me like the girl in Medical on Top Campus—a little hysterical and willing to fight for my right not to *recycle*.

"I don't—"

She placed her hand on the back of my neck. "I know."

Nothing more was said as I dragged together my things then locked the door behind us.

Because the Magiaduct was the only place students could be now, there were students everywhere. Students who would normally be meeting up in any of the thousands of public campus spaces—the libraries, the battle rooms, the focus-specific buildings like the Legal Hall or the Art Annex, Top Circle or the fields—were here instead, crowding into rooms and splaying all over the large track on the top of the aqueduct-like stone structure. Even on the stone stairwells that allowed students to head into the different dormitory segments, knots of students were arrayed on the sides of the stairs.

"Olivia would hate this," I said to Neph as we navigated the groups, keeping our sides tightly pressed together.

"She would not enjoy sidestepping bodies, that is certain," Neph concurred.

Fifteen thousand student bodies on campus, as of a week ago. Less now.

Up ahead, I could see a group trying to console a girl.

"I can't do it!" she said to the person on her left, an older girl who looked to be trying to counsel her. "They can't keep us here like trapped rats! Like the terrorists—they can expunge us at any time!"

"No, *shhh*. Lockdown isn't like that. They can't kill us with it or cut off any magic or air. All they can do is stop those possessing magic from entering from the outside, or from leaving from within."

"Trapped, without food! They could starve us. Siege us!" The girl laughed hysterically. "And there's nothing to siege! I don't want to be here!"

"You can apply for a pass," the older girl said calmly. "They are taking fifty students an hour to other locations—"

"To interrogate them."

"To help them. I believe some questioning will be—"

"*Wake up*," the girl hissed.

"We have to be here for another week. Mandatory surve—"

I was never so happy to turn a corner and leave a conversation behind, even if it caused me to draw closer to my goal—a location I did not want to reach.

But there were similar groups all over Dorm Twenty-five and spread across the Top Track of the Magiaduct. Inescapable.

Second Layer folks were a bit hardier than most First Layer folks, in that

* Counseling in a Sea of Grief *

they were far more accustomed to daily surprises and death. But like anyone who had had their home attacked, they were shocked and unnerved. And even though ninety-five percent of Excelsine students experienced at least one death while enrolled, almost all of those deaths were reversible. But today, twenty-six students hadn't made the ten-minute timeframe for resurrection—or had otherwise been unrecoverable.

Neph touched my elbow, accompanying me on this thankless task, while navigating the sea of grief.

Dorm Twenty-five's session was being held in the ground floor lounge—a roomy area that was usually rather inviting. Today, it might as well have housed Iron Maidens on the walls.

A small line of students stretched behind a sitting area, and five people joined behind us. But other than that, this seemed to be it for Dorm Twenty-five. So lucky, all those others living here who didn't need to be in this line.

I reached the front, and Neph smoothly withdrew to the side to wait.

An older boy, one I had seen many times inside the dorm, but never spoken to, motioned me to the chair on the other side of a small table that held a crystal ball. The boy was straight out of an alternate reality mashup where people dressed "punk" Princeton style.

I'd always thought he would be an interesting person to talk to. This hadn't been what I'd had in mind.

I sat slowly. I had learned to be wary in this world—chairs could tie you down, magic could spring at you like the face huggers from *Alien*... It paid to be paranoid.

The boy looked at me, then surprisingly, at Neph. Even more surprisingly, I could see that he could see her. Usually, I had to introduce someone to Neph in specific ways for them to be able to speak to or see her. Muse magic and mages' stupid reasons for distancing themselves from muses at large—wanting to sample *all* muses instead of binding themselves to one—usually made it impossible otherwise.

Of course, there was that whole thing with muses being able to control mages they were bound to, but I had shrugged that off long ago.

Princeton Punk looked back at me, eyes narrowing and mouth thinning around his lip ring, which I could see was an ouroboros, a snake swirling around the ring, constantly swallowing itself.

"The Crown girl, right?"

I swallowed. I really hoped he'd gotten that information mentally because he was the Dorm Manager, and not because I was now infamous. "Right."

His lip ring stopped swallowing itself, and the eyes on it blinked at me. The boy tapped his magical pen against his thigh. Something complicated

Chapter Nine

was happening in his expression, but I wasn't sure *what*.

Finally, he shrugged. "Have to go through the list, no matter who is on it. Chin up."

I blinked at him, but he touched his starched Oxford-like collar—which like many things in the Second Layer, was *close* to its equivalent in the First Layer, but with subtle differences. Magic reached up from the chair and wrapped around me, giving me a moment to think *I knew it*, before the magic retreated, leaving me unpinned and unharmed.

He tilted his head in the way that people here did when they were getting information mentally. "Ren Crown. Dorm Twenty-five. Room Twenty-five. Roommate Olivia Price, listed as missing."

I nodded jerkily.

"Your magic reserves are listed in the black, though you've recently edged into purple." He grimaced. "You could enroll down in Medical. Get a fortnight recovery stay."

I shook my head. They would keep me for the entire two weeks, probably in the healing coma Greyskull had recommended. Way too long to save Olivia. And they might start letting anyone poke at me while I was unconscious. It was best to remain in the general population, even if that meant other horrors were in store.

I couldn't trust anyone in the Administration, which was slowly being eaten by the Department, and that included Medical.

"Is your preference to stay in your room and have someone added, or to move to a different room where someone already lives?" the boy asked.

"Neither," I whispered.

His expression wasn't without sympathy. "This is not a punishment. I know it doesn't seem that way, but this is for the health and safety of the students and campus. We can't play with the magic dynamics too much without risk, do you understand?"

I nodded, understanding mentally, while at the same time not understanding *emotionally* at all.

"Which do you prefer?"

Being in my own space was preferable. But did I want some stranger invading our space, sleeping in Olivia's bed, using her things? I put my hand against my lips, swallowing down the bile.

"I'd like to stay in my room alone," I said, fingers pulling over my chin. "But if I have to have someone with me, I'd rather go somewhere else."

He looked relieved. Relieved to have me out of his dorm, probably.

"Put your hand on this."

I carefully reached forward to touch the crystal ball in front of him. It looked so benign, just as it had when I'd touched it earlier. The milky white haze swirled and pictures rapidly blinked through the space, like a deck of

* Counseling in a Sea of Grief *

cards being professionally shuffled. I thought I caught sight of a few familiar faces, but it was hard to tell in the rapid flip.

Princeton looked into the depths and the skin around his eyes pulled tight, moving the shape-changing ring in his brow, like the ring in his lip.

With a wave of his hand, the crystal reset, stagnant once more. He tapped something out on his wrist, and I saw magic scroll through the swirling tattoos on his skin.

"Dorm One. Room Sixty-two."

Dorm One? That was where Dare and Constantine lived. That was their floor. That was...

"No," I whispered.

The world tilted. Literally. Warm, soft hands pushed beneath my armpits, pushing me back upright, and soft words murmured in my ear.

"She has enough base power to support you." Princeton's words sounded far away. "And she filled out a very specific form and opened herself to a new magic source that is highly compatible to yours, which makes her the best singly available mage on campus."

Princeton looked at Neph critically, but didn't tell her to move away from me as he continued speaking. "Without stuffing you in with a twosome, Bellacia Bailey is the best qualified applicant right now."

"I'm not doing it."

There was a bit of pity in his expression. "You have to, kid. It's already logged."

"No."

"You should have seen the *other* option that came up in the ball." He shook his head. "Come on, kid, it won't be so bad."

It could not be *worse*.

"What were the other options?" I asked desperately.

He shook his head. "Doesn't matter. Bailey is now logged, and it will be a good match—she procured exactly the right source of magic to help you. With your magic as it is, the recommendation is for fourteen hours spent in her room. Report immediately," he said, looking at my magic. "For your own health and safety."

He must have seen something pretty devastating on my face, because his expression softened slightly and he swirled a hand over the crystal, gazing inside. He moved nimble fingers over the cloudy swirls. "I can give you...approval for twelve hours. Okay? Room Twenty-five here has a bonus layer of magic from whenever Price was without a roommate. It allows it to tap into campus. Not great, but not debilitating either. I can hook it into your mix in the Dorm One room to give that tiny bit of flexibility."

I swallowed, insanely feeling like I was going to cry. "Couldn't I just stay in twenty-five, then?"

Chapter Nine

"No. Twelve hours spent in a room with an assigned compatible mage gives the *base* benefit in an emergency situation."

Twelve hours with Bellacia? Even split into parts, that was horrifying.

"Listen, kid. It's best for you to have stabilizing influences around you at all times. And that muse of yours is going to be on thin ice for the foreseeable future." He looked at Neph.

What? I opened my mouth to ask what he was talking about, but he waved a hand to forestall me.

"Crown. Stop. Even the dorm had trouble not assigning you to Medical." He waved at the walls around us. "Probably why it offered that strange other choice," he muttered.

He shook his head. "You need this. Your magic is twisted and tangled, like barbed wire on a magical fence. You shouldn't even be upright." He examined me clinically, like a scientist who had found a strange, new animal. "I've never seen someone with magic twisted like that who wasn't screaming."

I stared back.

His gaze slid away first. "Listen, kid. This is temporary. Just get better and worry about other things later. But if Price doesn't show in a week, your temporary assignment will be permanent."

"No."

He heaved a sigh. "Don't kill us all, okay?" His ouroboros ring started moving again.

"Yes?"

He closed his eyes and adjusted the crystal ball. "Don't make it a question, Crown."

"Right. Yes."

I pushed away from the table. I *would* get Olivia back before the week was up. Until then...Bellacia Bailey was going to get her feral roommate.

Chapter Ten

BELLACIA BAILEY

I KNOCKED SOFTLY on the door, sounding the death knell of my dorm life. A door opened further down the hall and I turned to see Dare looking out at me, eyes narrowed on the duffel bag around my shoulder.

The door in front of me opened and I hastily turned.

Bellacia smirked at me, hand lightly on the frame. But it was an odd smirk. Tension and unease were layered beneath it.

She pushed away from the frame and allowed me to walk inside.

"Daddy thinks I'm crazy to room with one of *you*, even for a sennight," she said as she closed the door with a click of finality. "But I told him that it would be worth the fear. And Daddy knows risk is worth it when it is as fantastic an *opportunity* as this one is."

"I passed the test," I said woodenly, not wanting to think of my own parents.

"Of *course* you did."

I took a quick glance around. It was like Alexander and Constantine's suite. There was a main living space, a bedroom, and two workrooms. I had never been in their bedroom, so I walked in that direction. A bathroom was off to the side.

The bedroom was far smaller than Olivia's and mine—just two beds, nightstands, and closets—which made sense considering the added space in the rest of the suite.

Seeing the empty bed against the window wall, I walked over and plunked my things on it. The view out the window was all wrong, looking up the mountain instead of down, and on the sixth floor instead of the second.

"And if you think I want to room with one of *you*," I said, looking at the firesnake grove in the distance, a level up. "You can tell *Daddy* that you *are* crazy."

Chapter Ten

I turned in time to see her eyes flash. Her Sirenic abilities were just as freaky to me as my Origin ones were to everyone else.

Her expression smoothed out just as quickly as it always did and she laughed. "This will be so much *fun*."

"Yup," I said woodenly. "A real joy."

She smiled and sat cross legged on her bed, entirely too close. "Get cozy. We're *roommates* now."

"*Temporary* roommates."

She waved her hand. "Let's get better acquainted. Why don't we start by having you tell me exactly what happened on campus today."

"You were there."

"Should I go first then?"

I plopped hard on the bed and whacked the back of my head against the window. I started a six-hour timer ticking in my head and concentrated on setting out the few things that I always kept near my bed.

"You will explain everything to me by the end of the night," she said, voice lilting.

"I actually will not."

"Tell me, Ren. What did you do today?"

I could feel her voice wrap around me. And as it did, my pocket warmed.

I removed the warm, sand-colored scarab stone, and held it up. The waves of sound produced by the enchantment of her voice moved around the scarab as I moved it in the air. The scarab was blocking the waves from attaching to me.

I looked over to see her poleaxed expression. "Try again, Bella."

Fury overtook her expression. Had she really thought that this was going to be that easy?

"Where did you get that? They never... From your little *muse*? How is that working out for you?"

"Very well, thanks." Oddly, I was calming in the face of her rage. Muses weren't allowed in Bellacia's room—and I *would* be doing something about that once I knew how to keep Neph safe from her—but Neph had tucked this into my hand on the way over and told me never to remove it.

"You *owe* me," Bellacia said, voice harsh. "You owe campus."

"I owe one person, and she's not you," I said pointedly, tucking the stone beetle back in my pocket.

"Your *last* roommate? Price? They've listed her as missing, not dead. Where do you think she is? Such an interesting tidbit for our readers," she said bitingly.

"Go to hell." I shifted and laid the back of my head against the foreign pillow and closed my eyes.

∗ Bellacia Bailey ∗

"I don't think so," she said melodically, poisonously. "You *owe me*."

"Thanks for the save today," I said, eyes still closed. "Surprised the hell out of me. There. All done."

She laughed, a tinkling thing. "I don't think so."

"No? Then you can *kiss my ass* and thank me for saving you from suffocating to death, along with all of your Magicist friends."

"Such language. Are all those born to the First Layer so linguistically challenged?"

"Most. Normal people are good that way." I kept my eyes closed.

We sat in silence for a good minute. It probably wasn't wise to let someone like Bellacia regroup, but I was exhausted.

She hopped off her bed, landing on cat feet, but in the silence it was like planting a steel post in the ground.

I cracked an eye, on alert. Olivia had shown that roommates could do ill things to each other, if opportunity presented. Of course, I wasn't going to hook myself into the wards here like I had done for Olivia. I wasn't going to leave myself vulnerable to Bellacia.

She stood above me, eyes narrowed on something near my head.

I hadn't been able to leave Christian behind.

She cocked her head, examining the picture. "He looks familiar."

I frowned, then the blood drained from my face. Under Raphael's hand, my golem, looking exactly like my brother, had *very likely been seen* fighting Marsgrove. By some anonymous student. By someone who would sell such memories to the press.

I shoved it under my pillow, closed my eyes again, and tried to keep my breathing even. "Probably. The terrorists used some sort of familiarity enchantment to make themselves look like loved ones."

A tinkling sound of laughter, far too close. "How interesting. What new tech is that?"

"How should I know? Look it up." I turned toward the wall. Twelve hours in here. Maybe I could figure out how to get the workroom to hook directly into the rejuvenation wards and sleep there. But if *Dare* couldn't... He had a thousand things set up to ignore Constantine, but he still had to sleep in the same room.

I focused on breathing.

"Why would I look it up?" I could hear her sitting back on her own bed. "There are plenty of people who can look through captured memories and find the edges of the magic—to see what was actually at play today."

"Where's *your* roommate?" I asked, going on the offensive. With someone else, I'd never dare risk bringing someone pain. At the moment, with Bellacia, well, I didn't quite care.

"She switched temporarily to her sister's room," she said lightly. "Her

Chapter Ten

sister's roommate is in Medical, and they set up a triangulation. She'll be back on her feet in a week."

She laughed. "It's perfect really. You'll be here for *just* the right amount of time, then everything will be back to the way it used to be."

I understood clearly. The way it was before I came to campus. Because after a week, she was expecting that I'd be *gone*. Locked away for the good of all.

"Because of what you are, of course," she said in a musing tone.

"Female?" Everyone *knew* what I was at this point. They just couldn't yet *prove* it.

"What I don't know is how you got onto campus and where you came from," she said, ignoring my response.

I said nothing.

"Maybe I need to find the boy in the picture. Women would do a lot for a guy that looked like that. He's gorgeous."

I laughed, the sound short. "Sure. You do that. You find him."

"Hmmm... I think I will."

I wanted to see that. I'd pay for a lifetime subscription to her stupid newspaper.

"I need the full story after all."

"There is no story."

"No? Not in how you are able to wield and collapse Origin Magic?"

"I found a device on the ground," I said flatly.

"No. You pulled a device out from under your bracelet. Constantine Leandred wields a similar one, and he seems...enamored of you. Perhaps he made you one? Illegal, I'm sure," she mused. "Where is it?"

"You are the one who saw something," I said to the wall. "You tell me."

"So very interesting. But the evidence of it is unimportant. You were recorded by nearly a thousand memories."

I closed my eyes and tried to do deep breathing exercises.

"And those papers? The ones Praetorian Kaine was so very interested in. You used them, but no one else touched them. And while Delia and that boy—Michael Givens, isn't it?—looked shocked, two of your other little friends seemed unsurprised by your display."

Bellacia had gathered a *lot* of information. And she was stitching things together at an incredible rate.

It was obvious what she was implying with her name dropping. The underlying threat to my friends.

She should be thanking her *lucky stars* that I couldn't eke out any magic at present, and that my control cuff was completely intact. Subconsciously, I would have already tried to destroy her for such threats.

"What do you want?" I asked.

* Bellacia Bailey *

We wouldn't be talking if she were planning on simply outing me and making Constantine, Neph, and Will into my accomplices, with a side of Mike and Delia. I recognized this opening gambit from debate practice with Olivia. This was the beginning of a negotiation. Or blackmail, to be less euphemistic.

"Why, dear, I want you to rest and recuperate." She clucked her tongue, her voice still melodic around it. "You saved campus. Such actions deserve a grace period."

A grace period. *Right*.

"The information that you willingly share will extend such a period, of course," she added.

"Why not simply tell your little story—what you *think* you saw happen?"

"You don't understand the news at all," she said patronizingly. "Why have one delicious story, when I can have *three*?"

"There is more information out there right now than can be quantified."

The events of the day were all over the feeds. They were all over the Baileys' papers.

At the end of the battle, the student magical community had been freed to use frequencies again, and had "live updated" the crud out of everything. Conflicting information abounded, but much of it was damaging. Students had seen crazy stuff without being able to record it, but they could still describe their experiences.

"But that information is not *real*," she said.

Images of people dying flashed in my mind. Phantom sense memories of explosions rocking the world around me. "Seemed pretty real."

I rubbed my arms and wished Neph had been able to accompany me—but, no, I needed to keep her safe from Bellacia. Overcoming the muse block on the room seemed less desirable now.

"The reports. The accuracy. The truth. It needs to be told."

"I thought you were a Second Layer Magicist, first and foremost."

"I am. And accurate information will benefit the cause. However, I'm also a capitalist. With subscribers and quotas to fill. And you, you are a story that I will have on my front page whenever I need to put you there."

"I don't think so."

"Oh, you will." I could *hear* the smile in her voice. "Be happy with your grace time, Miss Crown. It is all downhill from here."

Knock, knock.

I was so startled that my eyes shot open to look at Bellacia. I figured she wouldn't allow anything as pedestrian as someone knocking on her door. Hooked into all of her social and political media, it seemed like she'd find physical statement distasteful.

But that was my bias showing itself. An early lesson in the magical world

Chapter Ten

had taught me that competent mages tended to practice many things without magic, so that if they drained themselves, they weren't completely helpless. It was like using my right hand sometimes to do tasks that were better suited to my left.

Still, when not being attacked, Excelsine tended to be a limitless zone, magically, and many mages took advantage of that fact.

There had been a dearth of "knocking" in our household growing up, but it was all the more important here in a world where information could be gleaned so quickly, and where a probe of magic could be taken as an offensive maneuver.

Bellacia's expression pinched, then grew wide and gleeful. She knew who was on the other side.

She leaped from the bed and gracefully disappeared from view.

"Axer," she said, voice charming, as I heard her open the door.

I scrambled upright and flew to the bedroom's doorway.

"Bellacia." Dare was looking past her, his gaze on me.

"What can we do for you?" she said sweetly.

"I am borrowing Ren." He looked at Bellacia as he said it, and didn't look away again, waiting for her answer. There was a challenge here that I wasn't privy to.

"Of course," she said finally. "Are you returning to the competition tonight or first thing in the morning?"

"Ren?" he looked at me, pointedly ignoring the question.

Even though I was still angry with him, a stupid thrill of vindictive glee ran through me at him ignoring her. "Yup. Coming."

I grabbed my bag from the bed, grabbed Christian's picture, and ran out after him.

Chapter Eleven

WORDS WE DARE

THEIR DOOR WAS only five down, and on the other side of the hall, from Bellacia's suite.

"Convenient, at least," I muttered, as he did something complicated over me, stripping magics from me. Whatever they were—probably listening or tracking enchantments courtesy of Bellacia—I didn't care at the moment.

I trooped in after him and he shut the door behind me. It was nearing eight, and the adrenaline highs from the day and my overextended magic use were taking their toll at an increasing rate.

"They assigned you Bellacia Bailey?" Darkness underlay his tone.

"Yup." I let the 'p' pop. "Great, isn't it?"

"Ren—"

"Constantine back yet?" I dumped my bag onto the round table that had suddenly appeared in their living room. I more carefully placed Christian's picture on top. I had a feeling that I was going to be carrying a lot of things around with me until I got Olivia back.

Dare eyed me, leaning back against the door, perfectly proportioned features taking me in. "He will be released in the morning. Something happened to the healing dynamics of his room that sped up his recovery."

"Hmmm. Imagine that." I collapsed into an armchair. "What do you want?"

He sighed and padded toward me.

"*No.*" I leaned forward in the chair. "You do not get to sigh like I'm the unreasonable one."

Exhaustion was starting to affect me, obviously, because I could feel tears threaten.

He squatted in front of me, balanced on the balls of his feet, forearms

Chapter Eleven

on his thighs, fingers crossed, and held my gaze. "What, exactly, did you think Helen Price was going to do when you refused to hand over that scarf?"

I pressed my lips together. Nothing intelligent was going to emerge from my mouth.

"Kaine was on his way, Ren. It was all Phillip could do to keep the barrier in place that keeps Kaine out of the Magiaduct. Marsgrove did the only thing he could. And so did I."

"That scarf was the only way to track Olivia," I said, voice hitching.

His hands unclenched as if he was going to reach toward me, but he crossed his arms over his knees.

"And Phillip still has it on campus, Ren." He kept his gaze locked on mine. "Marsgrove burned a lot of favors to do that. And, even so, the Department *will* have all the scarves in their possession within the next twenty-four hours."

That was even worse news. But— "Marsgrove won't return the scarf to me."

"No, he won't. He knows what you'd try to do with it."

I closed my eyes again and leaned my head back. "You are full of good news." I could take a small nap. Right here. With their wards humming around me. Surely something would look better afterward?

One of my knees bumped against his, and too tired to be twitchy, I left it there. I searched the connection to Olivia that sprang from my chest. She was still alive. I could feel that. I just didn't know *where*.

"You have to go to the Midlands."

I parted an eye. "What?" Dare was all laser-focus like usual, but there was an unusual edge of unease. It seemed to jump straight from his eyes into my belly, where it curled, waiting for the other shoe to drop.

I *very* much wanted to go to the Midlands. To check on Guard Rock and Friend. To hide some of the more illegal things we had in our room. However...

I tentatively touched the Administration Magic that was layered all over me, making sure that it was as intact as I thought it was. I did the same to him.

"I can't get out of the Magiaduct," I said slowly. "No less sneak four circles down campus and into the Midlands."

"Not easily, no."

I poked at the magic again, and analyzed the way my own was stuttering its way through me, then stared blankly at him from the cocoon of my chair.

"People keep telling me I have unrealistic expectations. And then my magic gets drained so that I *truly* have unrealistic expectations, and now you're feeding into my mad delusions?"

"We can do it."

"Okay. Great. Let's do it." I threw a fist into the air. I was so tired. "Should we go now? Is now good for you? With your superpowers tricking out everything, we'll be back in time for tea."

"Ren."

I blinked blearily at him, head unable to move from its position against the back of the club chair. "Listen, I'm all for this brand of insanity. But I don't think you are getting it, which is really strange." I looked at my hands, clenching and unclenching my fingers as if it would take away my magical arthritis. "I can't portal you a hole from this Tower of Babel to Eden tonight, then tunnel us to Hades."

And I was stuck with Bellacia for twelve of the next twenty-four hours, and I didn't think she'd just let me out of the room with an, "illegal things to do, magic to skirt!" reply.

"I can get you access to your roommate's scarf in the Midlands. For two minutes."

My eyes shot fully open and I leaned forward, face no more than a foot from his as I examined his expression for truth. Everything on his face said it was not a lie.

"Marsgrove is probably keeping the scarf at his house," I said slowly. Which was down on the lower levels of the mountain, far past the enforced school barrier. "And I know he has proximity alerts for me now."

Dare's eyes narrowed.

I didn't wait for him to ask a question. "He held me there, hostage, before I broke out and moved into the Magiaduct. Tricked me into enrolling here so he could keep me in a vegetative state locked away in his house. I'm *only* a real student here because of Olivia."

His expression darkened, then smoothed. "It doesn't matter where the scarf is right now. Only that I can get you access to it for two minutes in the Midlands."

I leaned back.

Two minutes? I tapped my fingers on the arm of my chair. With time to plan, I could figure out how to transfer Olivia's location from the scarf's threads without needing active magic. Disregarding the lunacy that the scarf would be in the Midlands—because, what?—Dare believed that he could get me those two minutes. And it was in my nature to always believe Alexander Dare.

"Okay." I put both hands against his chest and pushed. I couldn't concentrate fully with him so close. He rose and dropped into a chair that magically appeared across from me. He sprawled out in a mirrored pose to mine, one brow rising in challenge

Chapter Eleven

"But how do I leave the Magiaduct? My magic sucks right now."

"Someone else creates the hole in the spells, and duplicates our presence here."

I cocked my head, mind working even if the rest of me was waving a white flag. "You want me to use the others," I said finally. "Plan Fifty-two."

"During the memorial at midnight, the entire Excelsine community will be on the Top Track lighting memory fireworks and holding a vigil for those still in Medical."

I drummed my fingers while going over probable repercussions and deterrents. I already had consensus with at least some of the club members, but there was a difference between searching for Olivia using magical means and ingenuity, and actively baiting the Department on our front lawn.

"I don't want to put anyone else in danger," I said finally. "I can't. Not tonight." I swallowed heavily.

"Just you and me." He spread his hands. "We only need their trickery, and the guarantee that it won't be either of our magic focused upon in the diversion. Nothing will happen to them, my team will make sure of it."

"*You* also count. I'm not putting *you* in danger either. I will go to the Midlands on my own," I decided. I lifted a finger. "Stop looking at me like that. You are the one who just said—"

"There is no option that has you going there without me. And you have to go, unfortunately. Your building won't open for me." Implied in his statement was a strangely distinct *yet*.

I tapped my leg. "Then it won't open for the Department." When had *I* become the rational one? Maybe it was the exhaustion.

"The main directive Stavros gave his people was to find those papers. They gathered a magical trace on the battle field stands that will lead his men to them eventually. His men have been combing the grounds since lockdown—they are out there right now. Julian is doing all he can to be the nuisance only he can be, and he said that they haven't seen the building I described to him, yet—your building—but the praetorians are better than good. And they *will* find it. They will not stop until those papers are found, or until the trace of them disappears. And you *know* where the papers are."

I had shied away from thinking about it all day, in case I was questioned. But I knew they were in Okai, or on its front step.

"If Kaine gets the papers, along with whatever else you have in that building, they will have the proof they need and they *will* take you. No edict will stop them, only war."

"The scarf—"

"Isn't what I'm worried about at the moment," he said angrily.

I crossed my arms. "It's only a matter of time before they grab me. Even

* Words We Dare *

I know that. Maybe I make it to graduation. Maybe not. What I can do in the interim is what matters. And if I can secure the futures of everyone I love, then I will, first and foremost."

"And you should rely on those people to do the same." His expression was heavily charged, and for a long moment, I couldn't look away.

My tablet buzzed, reminding me of the time. I leaned forward and fished it out of my duffel bag, glad to have something to do other than feel the way my insides had knotted up. "I'll talk to the others, then come back here after. I'm leaving my things here." I grabbed my portfolio bag from the interior of the duffel bag and stuffed Justice Toad inside, then slung it crosswise over my body.

"Leave your things, but stay away from Dorm One. I won't be here." He looked resolute about something. "Contact me the usual way. I have things I need to get elsewhere."

He rose, as if the plan was already decided. "I'll come for you during the memorial."

I looked at him critically. "Yeah, that sounds like a terrible plan."

"You should be pretty used to that, no?"

I made a rude gesture over my shoulder as I left to the sound of his amusement.

Chapter Twelve

A DELINQUENCY OF PLANS

NAVIGATING THE TOP track of the Magiaduct was more horrifying now with twilight casting its shadows. It seemed like more than half of the school's population were arrayed along the four mile track, many igniting balls of swirling light in the darkening eventide.

With reassignments settled and the dorm meetings completed, people were setting up for the memorial service, or joining the lamentations in progress.

The edges of the walking track were crowded with bodies, spilling over into the track lanes that were only supposed to be used for forward momentum in either direction. The spell that allowed people to "flash" around campus on the well-worn tracks was still available, but I had never learned to use it, since Olivia was certain that I would run right through the fabric of reality instead and end up in the Bermuda Triangle, Mount Olympus, or hell.

Groups huddled, and magic lifted into the sky, only to swirl around in the magical magnetic field that surrounded the Magiaduct—siphoning from the students and re-energizing the inhabitants inside the dormitories and the grounds outside the Magiaduct.

Other mages milled about, lost and absent, unwilling to be enclosed in their rooms below.

But even though bodies were spilling onto the track, causing walkers to skirt them, it appeared as if the crowds sucked in their body parts as I passed—a rolling mass of flesh that never touched me.

They grew silent, and stared, as I passed, lights in hand. Creating a solitary, lit runway for me to traverse.

Patrick and Asafa's dorm was over a mile from Dorm One—and Top Track was the fastest way to get from one dormitory section to another without the use of arches. It gave me plenty of time to experience the

* A Delinquency of Plans *

horror of my new found fame.

I tried to focus on the magic that was lifting and pulling back into the stones of the Magiaduct, and not on the solemn faces I passed, lit by their memory lanterns/illuminations.

The students were still powering the mountain, as the university had been designed. Though, even from here, in the darkening night, I could see something was wrong with the Midlands, which took all of the backlashes and corrupted magic and recycled it back into useable energy. The constant fog was darker, almost crackling with black lightning, like something wasn't working quite right inside.

Raphael's doing most likely.

Someone brushed against me, making me blink. I was being given wide berth for the most part, as if there was an invisible, cautionary force field around me, so someone reaching out to touch me was new and weird.

Another hand, then another.

The path undulated as many pulled back as I passed, while others reached out.

Justice Toad beeped against my chest, where I had it gripped tightly like a shield. I looked at the screen to see a note from Patrick scrolling across.

God and leper, that's what you are now, Crown.

Patrick—who had to be watching my approach via someone's feed in the crowd—sounded entirely too amused. I gripped Justice Toad against my chest again and increased my speed.

Gazes followed me. Broadcasting my path to others—who knew how many others—as I strode past.

My breath grew shorter and quicker.

A moment later, I felt Neph's magic approaching, sweeping into me. My shoulders sagged automatically with relief. And I set my pace to her stride as she came alongside me, joining my gauntlet.

Neph touched my elbow, and warmth seeped in. I bumped against her, sending the equivalent back. Cycling and recycling.

The vigils that had already begun—the vigils for students still in magically-induced healing states or for the departed souls of those less fortunate... I tried not to stare as I walked, though I let some of my precious, recaptured magic seep out to join and strengthen theirs in solidarity.

I could feel two of my roses in the crowd, recharged with new magic.

Conversations ebbed and flowed as we walked. One particular argument caught my ear. A number of students were discussing the Fourth Layer. Whatever I had done during the battle with the dome's magic had directly affected something there. Blown something up.

"...ability to shift. The entire system's down! *One person.* And the *beast.*

Chapter Twelve

Chaos and anarchy..."

Fewer people were brushing against me now that Neph was alongside, the majority of people drawing back with the contracting crowds as we moved forth.

More than a few followed us on our path. I couldn't stop myself from looking over my shoulder. Seeing those blank and focused gazes staring at me as they followed.

Creepy.

Getting to Patrick and Asafa's dorm was more of a relief than I was willing to express.

Without knocking, I entered Patrick and Asafa's room, as they always encouraged when meetings were prearranged.

Everyone inside turned at our entrance and there was an immediate feeling of relief in the room—like a concurrently exhaled breath. It felt simultaneously like someone had squeezed my heart and given me more room to breathe.

"Sorry we are late," I said in a rush of too quick breath. "I got caught with—"

"Wait."

Patrick pulled on a green glove, snapping it against his wrist as he let go. He reached out, as if he was about to put me under the knife, then turned me, causing the room to spin in view.

He plucked something from the back of my shirt. As I turned on my heel, he held up a small yellow spell. "Let's get rid of this first, shall we?"

He blindly outstretched his covered hand to where Asafa was holding a clear bag, Patrick's gaze already searching over the rest of me. Patrick dropped the spell inside without pausing to look Asafa's way.

"Fifteen markers, twelve trackers and four listeners." He plucked each in turn and deposited them in the bag.

Asafa walked over to their wall of instruments and devices and dropped the bag inside of one. There were other bags inside as well. Asafa sealed the device and nodded to Patrick.

"Need to be double checking yourself at all times, Crown. Markers, especially, are inoffensive as far as shields or Justice Magic is concerned. Anyone can stick one on you, and experience no ill side effect."

Like the people brushing against me on Top Track.

He waved away my attempt at a question.

"Markers just flag you. People don't have to know your face—markers light you up like a Partridge Tree on Partridge Day. We'll get you all set up with a strip device."

"Great." I'd basically been a walking flare for the past fifteen minutes.

"But you only passed like twenty percent of the school's population," he said cheerfully. "So, there are plenty who won't know to run screaming yet until they match you up from the live feed and all of the million frequency exchanges that have already shared your face, your dorm number, and your class schedule."

I pulled a shaky hand through my hair, tucking the loose front strands behind my ears. "Great."

"Buck up. Normal is boring."

"I am a live bomb everyone steps softly around. A little boring would be good."

"Welcome to rare magehood." Patrick clapped me on the back, not bothering to lower his voice. "The club where only the best are welcome."

I stared at him.

"Not me. I'm merely a troublemaker, my lady." He winked, and handed me a piece of spelled paper. "But we are all-inclusive in our troublemaking sets."

Neph touched my elbow and Patrick's gaze followed the motion for a moment before snapping back into action.

"Read that. Agree. Chop, chop. Things to do, people to fleece, rules to bend."

I wasn't sure that I believed Patrick's words on not being rare.

I looked at the paper. It was a standard meeting secrecy oath. Olivia had made me read standard secrecy clauses in harsh, exacting detail, so it was easy enough to scan the paper for traps. There was a scanning frequency for such things, but Olivia was a stickler for knowledge over laziness and ease. I pinched the paper between my fingers, murmuring my assent, and it disappeared in a puff of gray smoke.

A puff of smoke bloomed from Neph's fingers as well, and Patrick herded us inward.

I looked at the rest of the room, at the team members from Plan Fifty-two, and my heart clenched again, fierce relief washed through me at seeing them alive, if bruised, slashed, and battle-weary.

Delia and Lifen were seated on the couch knitting something that looked like liquid silk. In front of the couch, Mike and Will were sitting at a long table with Dagfinn and Kita. Papers were spread out around them. Members of Delta and Epsilon, including the two from my dorm, solemnly gazed back.

We all took a moment. Gazes connecting. Plan Fifty-two had succeeded. We had made it. We'd survived. Against the odds, we'd survived.

And we'd get Olivia *back*.

Neph touched my wrist. I nodded and moved forward.

A round table formed from the long one—pushing and pulling its surface and slowly widening outward, giving everyone a chance to rearrange

Chapter Twelve

as it did. Delia and Lifen's couch grew upward and rounded, merging into the arrangement of chairs, all around the edges of the round table. Another small, half-rounded sofa appeared between Will's chair and the other rounded sofa, and Neph and I sat together in it. Like a lot of shared spaces in the magical world, our loveseat enabled a small feedback loop of magic to recirculate between Neph and me.

When everyone was settled in, Mike asked, "Where is Yapsley?" Yapsley had been part of Epsilon.

"He's not coming." An odd series of expressions crossed Lifen's face before she continued. "Said he wouldn't work with an Origin Mage."

Heat stole over me. I nodded mechanically to show my understanding.

I had a feeling that Yapsley's words hadn't *quite* gone like that. Yapsley wasn't one to use polite phrasing or tone. There had probably been a lot more general unpleasantness in that statement.

"It's okay," I said.

"It's not." Mike's mouth tightened. "It's not okay. And you passed that test."

"Mike—"

"No—"

"We don't want or need people involved in this who aren't willing to work with all of us," Asafa said, shutting the argument down. "We all took an oath upon entering this room, and we will all abide by it. *This* is our group."

He waited for everyone to nod before continuing, "Good. First, updates. Tilsia is in stable condition and recovering in medical. Loudon and Derkins got to her at nine minutes and thirty seconds."

My heart squeezed. God. Thirty more seconds...

Tilsia had been taken out by Raphael. My mind could connect the points in reverse, Monday morning quarterbacking the events. Raphael, under the guise of Emrys, had been doing something inside the Midlands—and Tilsia had been just outside of them before her last transmission.

I touched my bag and the unused papers I had inside. I'd visit Tilsia in Medical later.

"Tasky, Givens, Peoples, Derkins, Dagfinn, Lifen, Yapsley, Adrabi—" Patrick's voice continued listing people until it seemed as if he had mentioned everyone in the group. "Every one of those mentioned added another life or eight to their totals. Bau managed to revive *one hundred and seventy-three* people on the battlefield, many of them connected to one of us in one way or another. You're getting an honorary club statue, Bau."

Neph's gaze dropped to her lap, but her cheeks turned rosy.

"Second. As the media is already verifying, Price was...taken...from campus. We will be discussing the matter in more depth. All of the people

* A Delinquency of Plans *

sitting here have expressed interest in taking part in that discussion, and have signed oaths in that regard."

Glances were exchanged around the room.

"I know many of us lost friends today." Patrick looked around the table. "And we will grieve, and we will court vengeance for them. The latter, is contingent on our abilities to remain free."

He met the gaze of everyone in the room—a maneuver that took several tense seconds. "Not everyone desires vengeance. But for those of us who do, our goals align with those who do not in our need to make sure the Department does not imprison half of this campus after their review. We know who will be targeted first."

The Delinquents' Club, by pure definition, was comprised of delinquents, but in order to attend Excelsine, you had to be a top tier mage, and the top tier of delinquents, at the top tier university were *brilliant* mages. Mages who would be a feast for a government organization that could chain and use them.

"They grabbed Iosef's scarf," someone said grimly. "And mine."

A flurry of "mine too's" echoed around the table.

"They got everyone's then," Trick said, looking at Dagfinn, who was nervously chewing the skin of his thumb. Dagfinn, whose entire existence was dedicated to staying one step ahead of the authorities, looked as if he was one step from buying a one-way ticket to the psych ward.

"We took Epsilon offline immediately after Iosef's scarf was taken," Lifen said, her usually mischievous and mysterious smile completely absent from her delicate features today. She looked weary and drawn, like everyone else. "We quickly unhooked the others as well—all but Alpha, which has a failsafe. But even with the others dead, the threads are there. They can reverse engineer them. We need to torch the entire network. We just need Crown's magic to give permission."

I gripped my fingers together, as if my scarf was still within my grip. "I can't."

Lifen's worn gaze met mine. Her straight dark hair was pulled into a ponytail, and her almond skin was lacking its usual luster. "You don't have to do anything magically, just authorize—the magic is permission based, tied to you and Price. Delia and I can unweave the threads. We can kill the lead scarf, or at the *very* least make it a complete mess."

"No." I shook my head. "That's not it. The lead scarf—it contains the link to Olivia. I won't let it be unmade."

They all stared at me.

"I put the remnants of the magical...essence"—I circled my hand in the air for lack of a better descriptor—"around her disappearance into the scarf's threads."

Chapter Twelve

Lifen and Delia exchanged looks, kohl darkening both of their eyelids as their magic reacted synchronously.

My shoulders sagged. That was the type of exchange that usually didn't end in my favor. "What did I do? You aren't supposed to be able to do that?"

"No," Lifen said quickly. "We put location magic into threads all the time. It isn't a terribly difficult piece of sorcery, and it is a quite common request—finding one's objects, keeping track of possessions, they are all frequently desired enchantments. But...it's the other part of it," she said, somewhat delicately.

"What part?"

Lifen pressed her lips together, and Delia turned to me.

"Ren," Delia said slowly. "What layer is Price in?"

"The Third," I answered immediately.

"How do you know that?"

Helen had asked me that too. But with her, I hadn't wanted to answer, and therefore, had avoided thinking more deeply about it while under the truth spell.

I thought about how I knew. I'd become very used to the comfort of knowing where my parents were in the First Layer. The same feeling of separation was there with my connection to Olivia, but in an opposing direction. As if I had to pinch together space to breach it.

And I'd had a somewhat odd seven second adventure in the Fourth Layer over the holidays, due to a...mishap...I'd made in the Second Layer Depot while traveling to and from the Library of Alexandria with Olivia. The fleeting impression that had remained when I returned to the Second Layer had felt *farther* than the First. The impression from the scarf earlier had felt *as* far as the First, just different.

And, intuition told me she was in the Third, no question about it. I didn't need fully functioning magic to know it.

"I...just do?"

No one seemed surprised by this, but Lifen and Delia exchanged another quick look, and the others seemed to cotton on as well to their silent communication, tensing.

"Spells and enchantments that go *through* layers...are *not* common, Ren," Delia said. *Origin Mage* uncommon went unsaid. "Port mages get tagged early by just such feelings."

I knew a little about Port Mages from Will. Regular mages who were skilled in travel, like Will, could make arches, ports, and pinches, and other forms of Travel Magic like portal pads. And even those unskilled could do some of that as well, especially once the magic was created—like when Mike had been tasked with switching the runs in the skiing arches.

* A Delinquency of Plans *

The real skill of the Port Mage came in their ability to create ports *between* layers.

There weren't very many of them—five or six, I think I recalled someone saying—and they were feared just a little bit less than Origin Mages. They couldn't destroy or remake the whole Layer System, like an Origin Mage could, but due to their abilities to rift the layers they could do damage.

That's how the Department justified keeping them under their control. An extremely powerful thing—controlling those who could open and close magical doors to magical worlds.

"I'm not a Port Mage."

Delia shook her head slowly. "No, but you could be."

Door number two...being the lesser monster. It still got me a one way ticket to the Department's basement.

Trick clapped his hands together. "Everyone, stop looking so grim," he said, but there was a manic, worrying light in his eyes. "We've all taken our oaths, which will give protection to *all* of us. And Crown invoked the silencing spells on the scarves, which will at least give us a modicum of superficial protection there. So, back to what to do about the scarves and our communication angle. Unmake all but the lead scarf?" He looked around, sharp eyes reading each person's expression.

"It's risky not to do them all," Loudon said, shaking his blond head.

"It's our link to Price. We aren't destroying it," Patrick said, venom leaking into his voice.

Loudon put his palms on the table spread apart from each other, a gesture of compliance. "I'm here, aren't I?" he said very deliberately. "But it's risky. For all of us. And every moment increases that risk."

"Were there any scarves that weren't taken?" Will piped in. "Perhaps we could draw the captured magic through another one. What about Bryant's?"

"They have his too," I said. "It wasn't in Constantine's room in Medical. I checked while I was there."

Looks were exchanged that I couldn't interpret.

"Where *is* Olivia's scarf?" Saf asked me.

"Dean Marsgrove took it. It was either that or letting Helen Price take it." More than one expression grew darker at that statement. "I've been told the scarf is still on campus, but that it will be requisitioned by the Department within twenty-four hours."

"The dean must have burned a bridge for that one." Loudon tapped a finger against the table. "You think he will let you have it back now that Priggy Price is gone?"

"Not a chance," I said grimly.

"If it gets taken by the Department, you have to burn it, Crown,"

Chapter Twelve

Loudon said, examining me. "It won't do anyone any good, least of all you."

They'd all either seen the leash aspect in effect on me—or been told later about it. Leashing my magic to the scarf's network was what had kept the network active when the Administration Magic had gone down.

"I'll get it back," I said. I *would*. "Or transfer the locating spell to something else."

"Okay." Patrick clapped his hands again, but his skin looked even paler. "Unravel all scarves except for the lead." Patrick motioned to Lifen, who held her hand out to me.

I gave the mental permission, making sure to keep at the very *forefront* of my thoughts, that I needed the lead scarf whole.

Lifen's free hand went to her mouth as her other hand gripped mine. "Your magic." But then she got it together and delicately weaved a pattern in the air. She sent it splintering in all directions. Tendrils whooshed outward, then down through the vents, under the door, through the cracks in the window, and joining with the ward lines filtering everywhere in the air, seeking out all pathways.

Lifen quickly let go of my hand, as if she couldn't bear touching my broken magic any further.

"We are all subject to dorm meetings, club meetings, emergency meetings, and general Administration Magic shivit for the next few days," Patrick said. "And you know that the Department is going to grab some of us as soon as they can. We could be interrupted at any minute here, so we can't tarry on the subject. We need an alternative communication immediately."

"Not frequencies. Not even the dark channels. It's open season right now," Dagfinn said, dragging a hand over his freckled skin.

"Mate, you need to reeeelax. No one's going to hack your pits," Loudon said. "And if they do, they're going to take you and strap you to a command center somewhere and feed you continuous olives. The rest of us are the ones who are getting deep troughed."

Loudon was a thin, blond-haired mage with wild curls and an angelic appearance who specialized in Demolition Magic—dismantling magic, and *sometimes* getting it to a recycling device. He loved his explosives a little too much. And like Patrick, he was fey and unpredictable.

Not characteristics that were desired in good government assets. They were more likely to be treated in whatever way rabid dogs were treated in this world.

"Command center," Dagfinn muttered somewhat hysterically. "I'll take them *all down*."

"Wearables?" Lifen said, getting the conversation back on track while

* A Delinquency of Plans *

simultaneously pulling Dagfinn's hand away from his ear.

We were all just trying to back away from true panic.

Loudon angled his thumb down. "When you say wearables, I hear shiny and pink and hangs from my ears. Tattoos?"

"When you say tattoos, I hear, skulls, glow snakes, and vibrating pixels," she shot back.

"You could make them pink," Loudon said with an angelic smile.

Lifen made a scathing hand gesture.

Dagfinn nervously drummed his fingers against the table. "Something easy to remove, without magic."

"Another garment?" Saf asked, leaning back in his chair.

"We stood out with the scarves," Lifen said in her deceptively soft voice. "It was great for earlier today, during that initial confusion of the attack. It gave a central, trusted group for people to rally around. Identification made things *much* easier when there was no set plan in place for campus. But now, now that we want to blend in, now that the population is enacting its *own* contingencies for the next few days and weeks, we don't *want* to stand out."

I looked down at the leather band Will had made for me. To replace Christian's band. Christian and all of his friends had gotten their bands during the previous summer, and the rest of our year had followed suit upon school restarting.

I slowly twisted the band around my wrist thinking about what it represented.

"The memorial ceremony," I offered. I wasn't sure exactly what would happen during the ceremony, but mages were *people*. And people sought community. "What about a memorial tag? A token offered to everyone on campus on Top Track. Something without too many spells—something nice. But in *our* pieces, we hook spells into place. Hiding in plain sight."

Lifen nodded decisively. "Yes. That." She started flipping the air with her fingers, looking at something I couldn't see.

She pushed her palm against the clear magic and colorful designs twirled into view in the center of the table, rotating slowly. "We can start that trend in the Craft Circuits. My roommate's friends are littered throughout the Goodwill Clubs. With the memorials and vigils, people will wear them for weeks. Delia, can you give your next hour to this?"

The two of them had grown closer in the last week, with all the Plan Fifty-two theatrics and crafting the scarves. Many of the members had—a bit of fun mischief inherent in Plan Fifty-two bringing them together. I looked around the room, at the links between the mages at the table now. Today had turned burgeoning affiliations into something far stronger.

Delia nodded, eyes narrowed on the designs. "Let the Goodwillies pick

Chapter Twelve

the design, or make them think they are picking it. The knit bracelet, choker, or armband would really be ideal. Maybe with a memorial plaque that the band runs through—we can use enclosure spells on the metal. Get the prototype activated, then we can do our own thing with it later."

Lifen flipped her fingers to add a plaque to the designs, then nodded. "Frequency sent." She let her fingers drop and tilted her head to the side. "Fannie just spread it through a thousand students—twelve hundred now—fifteen hundred. Should hit max load in five minutes."

Gaping, I quickly shut my mouth before I uttered something like, "hive mind!"

In the First Layer, communication was nearly instantaneous now. It shouldn't be a surprise that with the ability to send *thoughts,* that it would be even quicker here.

No wonder everyone was already staring at me around campus—tracked magic or not. Frequencies really were that fast.

"With the Legion heading up security and the current sweep ongoing, we are going to have to do some massive trail wiping around campus, and fast." Saf looked around the table. "Everyone is at risk."

The regular members of the delinquents' club all looked steely in their assent.

"They are going to be looking over all the magic trails on campus. All of the little traps we set? And anything that looks 'evil' or 'unusual' will get reviewed," Patrick said. "They'll especially target anyone who has gotten Justice Magic hits. The more hits procured, the more the mage will be scrutinized."

I didn't know how Constantine would survive that procedure.

"The Department being here is *very bad*. And if they can show that the administration has been too lax, which, it *has*, then they will have grounds to take control. And with them taking control..." Saf shook his head.

"They've always wanted an in to campus," Will said to me. "Stavros wants to track rare mages. Too many mages that attend here slip by. If you make it to Excelsine, you've gone to schools that already test, and you've made it through those tests. Rare mages that have gotten to this level aren't rabbits awaiting slaughter like you might find in secondary school with mages who've just Awakened. If he can show that we have more than a few..."

Great. No way was I letting that happen.

"I can do it," I said.

Everyone looked at me.

"Crown, you, uh—" Lifen delicately cleared her throat. "Your magic—"

"I know." Two weeks to get back together magically? Far, *far* too long. "But if I can get out of the Magiaduct during the ceremony tonight, I

* A Delinquency of Plans *

can...convince the mage accompanying me to wipe at least some of the trails."

There was no way that Dare—ridiculously overpowered Alexander Dare—wouldn't be able to do that. And I was probably going to need to accept the fact that he was going. That I wasn't going to be able to stop him, even if I wanted to.

Looks were exchanged around the table.

"Who?" Saf asked.

I opened my mouth, but Dagfinn shrugged sharply. "Frankly, I don't care who it is. The shadier the better. I'll do whatever you need if you can get the comm trail clean. And you don't need someone else, if you have this." He fished a device out of his pocket and started fiddling with it. He held it up, face out. "*This* will get you ten years in Department hell, if you are caught with it, Crown. You activate this in a chaos spot and it will take care of every spell listed inside, including its own destruction."

I took the device, examining its silver edges. "So the Midlands will work?"

Dagfinn's lower lip sagged, then he snapped it shut. "Yes. Yes it will." He looked far happier, straightening in his chair. "Whatever you need, Crown." He spread his fingers, and kept his gaze locked with mine. "You do this, and *whatever* you need."

After a quick, traded glance with Saf, Trick turned to me. "You going to get the Queen's scarf back tonight?"

It wasn't a hard guess. Why else would I be courting such trouble?

"Hopefully." I was going to get it, or die trying. I pressed my hands together in my lap, palms clammy. "I won't be able to do magic or get out of the Magiaduct on my own, though. And my companion...can't afford the spotlight tonight."

There was no way Dare would have me seeking help if he could do it on his own.

I looked around the room and was unsurprised to see a flurry of discernment crest over most gazes at whom that might be.

Loudon swore softly, shirt sleeve pulled over his right fingers and pinching the sides of his mouth together. "Yeah?" He swore again, looking at Trick. There were many similarly small exchanges between the others. "Yeah, okay. This is happening. Why not."

"We are going to need an exit and a slew of distractions," I said, heart threatening to beat right out of my chest.

"Oh, Crown." Patrick's smile was edged. "You leave that to us."

Chapter Thirteen

RECONNECTION

NEPH, DELIA, AND I went to Mike and Will's room after the meeting. It was the first time just the five of us had been together since we'd been on Top Circle.

Delia hit Mike in the shoulder, hard. "What were you thinking earlier, Givens? Kaine could have *killed* you."

Mike stepped out of range and put his hands down in a gesture of surrender. "I was thinking that controlling the word of the community before the media does was the best thing we could do. And now anything that Oakley and his lot say will be looked at through a heavy lens."

Delia's lips pressed together. "You are on Kaine's list now."

"We already were, D." Mike's words were gentle—the type you said to the cat long cornered. "From the moment Godfrey showed us to the world, any sort of privacy was stripped from us."

"I'm sorry." I swallowed harshly, pulling at the trial memorial band newly strapped to my arm. "I'm so s—"

Mike looked at me. "What? You think you are the reason? Did you drag us to the Eighteenth Circle?" he asked, voice hard.

"No."

"Did you put us on the worldwide feed?"

"No."

"Did you try to kill the student body?"

"I came close when Olivia was taken," I said, letting go of the band and mashing my hands together.

His expression softened, and he touched the pin he had chosen as his temporary memorial object. We were all currently wearing different forms of wearables—pins, bracelets, drop necklaces, armbands, chokers, forehead bands, belts—allowing Delia and Lifen to tweak spells and ideas while they worked on the form we would all adopt.

* Reconnection *

"Ren. You saved campus. You created the other dome that saved the students in the battle field stands. You cleared the ports. You and Olivia and Plan Fifty-two made us all available to help. You were the nexus of everything *right* that happened today. And *we* willingly volunteered to save the students at the battle field knowing the outcomes. I knew death was likely before we stepped into the Blarjack Swamp."

My heart rate sped up again and I ran an agitated hand over my lips, staring at my lap. "I want to keep everyone safe."

"Yes. So do we," he said, voice turning gentle. "And that includes keeping *you* safe too."

"I nearly didn't pass that test," I said, lifting my gaze reluctantly to his.

"I know," he said bluntly, holding my gaze. "And I don't know how you passed it, but you *did*." He held up a hand to forestall argument. "And even if you don't pass it in the future, your status means nothing to me. I will do whatever is needed to keep you safe."

Mike was a clean-cut, sport-loving, weather-roping, well-adjusted boy. He'd probably been one of the most popular boys at his magical secondary school. Happy with his place in the world, and intent on seeing everyone else achieve that state. Hazily, I knew his parents were somewhat involved in community works and personal liberties in the wider world.

What Mike wasn't, was a delinquent. He was plenty popular at Excelsine, and could be out sporting it up right now, happy, and with blinders firmly on.

But he was highly loyal, and Will was his best friend and magically-sympathetic roommate. His brother-from-another-mother type of thing. When Will had taken me under his wing, Mike had done the same. And when Mike did something, he *did* something.

I had always loved Mike—he was so similar in personality and interests to Christian that being friends with him was as natural as breathing.

Mike, like Delia, still did things outside of the circle of Will, Neph, Olivia, and me—but he always sat with us at mealtimes, marking us as his "school family" unit.

And for that family unit, he was descending into delinquency.

"It doesn't mean *nothing*, Michael, and you know it." Delia had already started working on the second draft set of memorial wearables she and Lifen had worked up between them, and she was loosely working a bit of knitting into an armband, weaving a spell into a fiber as she wound it through another, fingers shaking just a little.

"D—"

"Just because you want it to be like that and just because something is *right* means nothing next to fear." She made a loop in a thread. "Not even seventy years can change society's mind on some things."

Chapter Thirteen

A struggle appeared on Mike's face, as he watched Delia specifically avoid looking at anyone. It had been hinted at multiple times that Delia's family background was far too close to the Third Layer for many Second Layer citizens to be comfortable with.

That Delia didn't have a problem with me seemed...odd. She had seen me on the battlefield. She knew, just like Mike, that I shouldn't have passed the Origin Magic test.

Delia crossed her first spell with a second, tangling the two together, and setting them into the fibers.

"Delia, are you...is it okay that—"

She pierced me with her gaze, fingers halting their motion. "That an Origin Mage ruined my past? My family's legacy?"

I couldn't form words.

"I told you, that day in the cafeteria," she said, spearing a thread. "We were going to be friends. Knowing you can break the world, and that someday you probably will—Origin Mages almost *always* detonate somehow—doesn't change the characteristics that you showed then, and that you continue to display."

Her fingers started another series of knots. "Flavel Valeris' actions seventy years ago may have started the ball rolling, but the people in the Second Layer chose, and continue to choose, to treat my family as they do, even though my parents were *born* here. They chose to treat us *thirdies* this way all on their own. The Second Layer chose to keep the magic that Valeris ejected from the Third Layer—magic that could have been righted with Kinsky's return. They started this war that they are now fighting. You did not."

A ding sounded in the room. Everyone looked up.

"Good timing. I'm starving," Mike said, breaking the tension.

I touched the connection thread to Delia and some of the tightness in her shoulders loosened. Mike squeezed one of her shoulders as he walked toward the food area of their room. He hadn't been kidding then. It wasn't too surprising that we might grab a second dinner, as mages ate more than First Layer folks did. All that energy use tended to burn far more calories.

"Magi Mart?" I asked. It wasn't ideal, but I'd had breakfast burritos and magic wraps on worse. I'd had one earlier with Neph after returning from Medical.

"Nah, the bell was a reminder. In lockdown situations, they send menus around, then send the food to us. Trying to simulate the cafeteria environment. Get everyone eating simultaneously and refreshing campus with our magical calories," he said jokingly. "Since everyone is going to be attending the memorial far past midnight, now is the perfect time."

Mike opened the delivery box and removed a sheet of paper. He

* Reconnection *

scanned it with his eyes, then pressed his finger down. A tiny bit of magic was enveloped.

"Second dinner. Order up," Mike said, while passing around what I could now see was a menu.

I took it and looked through the options. Caniopidas was listed—the delightful food item that was created by the ten-eyed people who worked a small section of the cafeteria. I pressed my finger next to the item. A small suction of energy took an imprint of my magic. The Decaclops people read the magic from a person and created a combination that was tailored exactly to the consumer. It was usually done in person in the cafeteria.

It was my favorite choice, and I didn't understand why other people shied away from it. I said so aloud.

"Because it is invasive, Ren," Will answered.

"This world is all about invasiveness," I said, looking over Mike's bed and out the window. The Legion warriors in their spiky black garb were striding between the vetted troops from five surrounding countries that had assembled to help "sweep" campus for any remaining threats. The mixed scouting groups were designed to stop anything from being covered up or hidden. No one trusted anyone, it seemed.

"And giving up rights," I added. "Why anyone would be against the perfect meal from a scan far less invasive than what I get every time I enter Top Circle, I'll never know."

The others exchanged looks.

I sighed. "What?"

"Part of it has to do with the Decaclops people, the Fourth Layer beings that make it," Neph said softly.

"Great. Racism?"

"Most mages like to call it *caution against things they don't completely understand*."

I sighed. "Fine. You can call a potato whatever you want."

"Magical creatures and beings live in the Fourth Layer for a reason. There, they control all. There, *we* are the potatoes."

I rubbed my neck. "So what did you all get to eat?"

"Caniopidas." Will winked at me.

I smiled slowly. It was a good reminder that the world could be burning, but that didn't mean that everyone inside was fanning the flames.

I looked out the window, smile slipping. "Campus still looks scorched. After the bone beast, the green mages had everything cleaned up in hours."

"Campus will be fine," Neph reassured.

"The green mages are probably *itching*," Will said. "They will have it all cleaned up in no time as soon as we are released. They are probably hatching more firesnakes in someone's room right now," he said ruefully.

Chapter Thirteen

Which reminded me of my new view and my new dorm. Delia looked at me sharply.

"We should discuss what is going to happen with Ren's roommate situation," Delia said, spearing me with a glance, reading my mind. It wasn't a surprise she knew—I'd bet my remaining magic that everyone in the Magiaduct knew at this point.

"I'll deal with her," I said tiredly.

"You will not be alone," Neph said.

Delia squinted at Neph suspiciously. "There's no way you can be in there."

"I must spend six hours of sleep time in my assigned room," Neph said smoothly. "It has been ordered. Other than that, though, I can do a work around in Ren's room."

Will stared at Neph, eyes going wide, whereas Delia's were narrowing. "But—"

"It will be fine."

"But—"

Neph put a hand on Will's arm and he abruptly went a little glassy-eyed.

I looked between them suspiciously. "What?"

"Will is unnecessarily worried. Everything will be fine," she said soothingly.

Will nodded, his expression a bit too blissful.

I looked at him even more suspiciously. "Did you just whammy Will?" I asked Neph.

"Yes," she said unapologetically. Mike looked resigned. Delia's lips were pinched even more tightly.

"Why?" I asked.

"He is worried that I will force my way into your new room."

Mike looked at Neph, brows pinching. "Why would you use force?"

"It is off-limits to muses."

"*What?*" Mike said, his face growing stormy.

Neph shrugged, as if they weren't discussing the same issue. "It matters not."

"It matters a *lot*," I said, letting the anger come back—pushing aside for the moment the knowledge that it was better for Neph to stay away from Bellacia anyway. "The dorm guy *said* that you were my muse. It's *known*. How—?"

She put her hand on me and some of my anger ebbed, slipping away.

"Did you just whammy me?"

"Yes."

I sighed and rubbed my forehead. "It is best for your safety to stay away, even though the reason completely sucks. Bellacia doesn't want you in the

* Reconnection *

room, but she wants access to you."

"She will get no access to me as long as you do not introduce us."

"How did the dorm head—"

"He has access to a muse. Bellacia Bailey would never stoop so low." Neph smiled thinly.

"But all of the people I introduce you to don't have access to you."

Her smile strained. "Oh." She dropped her gaze. "You *didn't* know."

"Hey, it's okay," I said, reaching out. "Do I need to?"

"Every time you widen our circle—*my* circle—you share my specific abilities with the others. Abilities that they don't get from a passing muse or the community. They can draw on me, diluting it from you."

"Wait." My voice rose in pitch. "You are subservient to all of us? We can basically *leech* you?"

"No." She looked at me carefully. "Not with how you defined our relationship. I get to choose. The muse has the choice in what to give and to whom."

Relief made me sag. "Oh. That sounds okay, then. Right?"

"No. It means that you get none of the benefit, should I decide to place my affections elsewhere." She reached out and gripped my arm fiercely. "Which I would *never* do."

"Um. You...could?"

I was completely out of my depth on this. I really should have read all of those muse books that Delia—who was now looking at me darkly, stabbing one thread blindly through another—was always surreptitiously suggesting. But I hadn't wanted to read any of that magicist crap.

Neph smiled. "Will does rather well these days, all things considered. And you...you connect better with the people you accept into your circle more than anyone I know. You share your magic, and create circuits that rejuvenate all who you take into your group. That is powerful Community Magic."

And something that I'd had no idea I was doing. Or at least not understanding that it was anything out of the ordinary.

"Community Magic is something that many mages accept—it's in all aspects of this campus—but that many have trouble trusting in their own circles. Mages are...not to be trusted, in a lot of cases. When power can be transferred so easily between people, it makes it easy to....abuse."

Delia cleared her throat. "Back to *Bellacia Bailey* being Ren's new roommate?"

"I have twelve hours with her a day," I said, trying to keep my voice upbeat. "If I spend eight of those at night, that should be no problem, right?"

"She can do a lot in twelve hours," Will pointed out, free of his

Chapter Thirteen

whammy again.

"Which is why Neph gave me something awesome."

Neph smiled, though she cast a nervous glance at the others.

"Like Leandred's *awesome* gift?" Delia asked darkly. She had seen the clicker in action the day I'd used it.

"No. We aren't allowed to harm mages without explicit orders," Neph said quickly. "It's a protection only."

"Explicit orders?" Delia's lips were pressed together, and she jabbed a thread through a hole.

"The scarab doesn't do anything to anyone," I interrupted quickly, seeing the way the conversation was headed. "It just prevents Bellacia from manipulating me."

"A scarab?" Will said, voice nearly a whisper.

Neph straightened the hem of her decorative blouse. "I...requested it from the elders during the meeting earlier."

"And it works great. Thanks, Neph," I said, wanting to ease whatever was making her nervous. I touched my pocket, smiling.

But Will was looking at Neph through narrowed eyes. "A scarab? What did you have to—?"

"Nothing that I was not willing to—"

"But *what*—"

Whammy number two was deployed, leaving Will incongruously grinning in a silly fashion.

I withdrew the scarab and examined it more closely. It was pretty, and I couldn't see anything leechy about it, but that didn't mean that I would *use* it again if it was. "Neph?"

She sighed. Having moved to get Will again, she was too far away to whammy me too, and Mike was crossing his arms now. "Godfrey almost...you can't be vulnerable like that, Ren. It required some sacrifices to be made in my community standing, but it is *done*, and if you don't *use* it Ren, we will all suffer and that sacrifice will have been in vain. Do you understand?"

Sacrifices? I clutched it in my hand. "That you play hardball? Yes."

Her expression softened and something pained appeared there. "You must allow us to shoulder some of your burdens."

A cleared throat made me look to the side.

Delia's gaze was narrowed and skittish. Anything having to do with Bellacia Bailey or muses had always made her uncomfortable—combining both in one conversation was probably more than she could stand.

"I can't do anything for you tonight," Delia said reluctantly. "But give me until tomorrow. I might have some things for you to use with Bailey...in conversational combat, if needed."

* Reconnection *

"Delia," I said gently. "You don't need to—"

"I won't hex you like Bau to make you shut up, but you aren't going to change my mind about helping."

"You're already helping," I said, touching her connection point on my wrist.

Delia's fingers were shaking as she started threading again. "When's the food coming?"

"Soon," Mike said, squeezing her shoulder.

"So, um, what's the plan tonight?" Will asked, looking for a redirect. "With Axer Dare."

Everyone looked at me, wanting to know the answer.

I shared the little he and I had discussed, and what we'd been sending back and forth through cryptic messages. We'd hooked up a few members of our two groups—and that seemed to be going as well as it could with Loudon freaking out over "going respectable" and "working with shiving *combat* mages."

The food finally arrived and we went over some plans for the scarf while eating. Delia was integral in the plans—having made the scarves with Lifen.

Throughout, Neph sent comforting vibes through all access points. But toward the end of dinner, Will was frowning. He and Mike exchanged a glance, and Mike nodded.

"Listen, Ren," Mike said, turning to me. "We know you work well together and trust him, but it is our duty since Olivia is...not here...to be suspicious of his motivations. Why is Axer Dare leaving the Magiaduct tonight?"

"To help?"

"He's skipping *essential* rest for the All-Layer Combat Competition—the premiere event for every university in the magical world, the only thing that gives him any challenge, and the event that he is, or *was*, likely going to win—in order to court incarceration and ruin by exiting the Magiaduct tonight? Running afoul of the men who want nothing more than to have him under their thumbs?"

"Er, when you put it that way it sounds sketchier."

"Yes," Will said baldly, taking over. "If the person taken was one of the combat mages, then it would be a non-issue." He splayed his fingers. "They wouldn't rest until their comrade was found. That's what they do. But he doesn't know Olivia personally at all."

"Maybe I'm one of his people?"

Will looked skeptical. "They've been fighting together—life and death—for years."

"Well, I'm going after Olivia, and I've only known her for two terms," I said aggressively.

Chapter Thirteen

"Yes," Will said anxiously, expression edging to panic. "And we are going to do the same. You don't have to be fighting together for years to make bonds. You are right."

My shoulders slumped. They were posing questions for all the right reasons. And playing Olivia's role as Devil's Advocate, a role to which Will wasn't suited. "No, you are right to put forth an argument. I'm sorry I snapped. I just don't know. I can't do this on my own—a truth I've painfully accepted. And he is coming whether I want him to or not. Is there harm in having him along?"

"Well, your odds of survival greatly increase," Will said frankly, anxiety erased with my reassurance, like so many things were in Will's accepting nature. "Like tripled or quadrupled. But...if you get caught *together*..."

"Why is together worse?"

Delia broke in, obviously irritated. "Do you know what a Bridge Mage could do on a battlefield? A *warrior* Bridge Mage? A combat mage already as gifted as Axer Dare?"

I imagined it. Dare standing in the middle of a melee. Magic flying in arced beams directly into and out of his control. Freezing his opponents in place—with them unable to do anything. Magic seeping into him from all directions, refreshing him and draining his opponents. A battlefield full of puppets. Or batteries. Unlimited control.

"Huh. Yeah. Okay."

Delia leaned forward. "Now imagine a mage capable of manipulating the fabric of the reality that we exist inside—the worlds that were created for us to populate and live within—and imagine that mage under the *direct* control of the mage who could control *everyone* around him if he releases his powers—what could a mage like that do with the world and all its inhabitants under his direct control?"

I swallowed. "I guess it's a good thing he's not a Bridge Mage," I said lightly.

Delia's brows drew tight. "Whether he is or isn't—they've been trying to pin him for years. And, I saw Kaine's expression, heard his words. *They* believe. And they saw a link between you. Any government would want the power of you both under their control. You, you are *specifically* what the Department was created for. They exist above, separated from all governments, in order to secure layer safety. They cannot *allow* such powerful mages to be free of their control."

My heart was beating double time.

"Pretty sure Dare's actively seeking to make sure neither of us get caught." Top Circle had made that pretty clear. Not that I could tell any of them about the vine. I rubbed the side of my curled finger over my mouth.

"You can't get caught, Ren," Mike said, expression dead serious. "If you

* Reconnection *

do, that little incident on Top Circle will look like a toddler's warm-up in comparison to what will happen."

"You'll drop your student status, Kaine will grab you, and you'll disappear." Magic appeared in Will's hand, then he fisted it closed. When he opened his fingers, there was only air.

Disappear like Raphael...maybe only escaping when I was just as insane...

"Understood," I said.

Will leaned forward. "You have to be quick about getting out, then getting back. I mean, not even *five seconds* can pass after you reach the time limit, Ren."

"Understood."

"They are professional kidnappers."

"I got it, Will."

"They will have nets."

"And pickling jars, yes."

"Ren—"

"Will!" I grabbed his shoulder. "I'm trying *not* to freak out."

"Okay, okay." He grabbed my hands and took a deep breath. "Me too."

"Where's dessert?" Delia said. Her fingers were shaking too hard to make the knot she was trying to form.

Mike jumped on the subject change. "Got some."

After eating some hastily obtained chocolate, more planning, helping Delia work her magic, talking to the other delinquents via our new communication stream, and some silent bonding, I reluctantly re-packed my things. I touched my new memorial armband. Between Lifen and Delia, we all had them now—it had been the most popular memorial piece decided upon across campus. The little metal mountain plaques securing them glinted in the room's lights.

Currently, ours only had an extra auditory feed. We would hook more spells in tomorrow.

No one said anything about these not having the leeching capability of the scarves—a feature only Olivia and I had been aware of until the assault on campus had begun.

Neph touched mine. "It will be fine. Everything will be fine."

The problem was, I could see no one really believed that.

Chapter Fourteen

IN MEMORY OF THE FALLEN

TENDRILS OF MAGIC arced up and away from the Magiaduct then pulled sharply back to curve into the stones at the top of the structure, swiftly traveling through the stone arches that decorated all nine levels of the Magiaduct before shooting down into the base of the superstructure.

On the side of Top Track that faced the upper slope of the mountain, the same light show was playing, encompassing the entire giant stone doughnut of rock and light, impaling it with the combined Community Magic of fifteen thousand students.

Everywhere I looked, students had memorial bands wrapped around their arms, wrists, or necks. The silver plaque on top had an imprint of the outline of the mountain, and magic zipped around it. The magic could be set in different ways—most bands had a scrolling feed of magic on the outer edge with the names of each victim in that mage's signature color. Each name completed a circuit, then morphed into a new name.

Eight-hundred-and-thirty-two students had died. Twenty-six hadn't been revived in time.

Those twenty-six names were as etched in my memory now as they were etching the edges of the plaques.

Some mages had chosen to display only the flashing colors around the edges. And still others eschewed the individual remembrances and just had a single silver font that wrapped the plaque. *Excelsine United.*

The intricately wound knitted threads of the bands were as individual as the mages wearing them, but the aesthetics were secondary to the main design, which was unified across every one.

Like the Lightning Festival—a New Year's Eve remembrance for all things—the tone of the vigil was serious. Unlike the Festival's more cathartic expressions, though, most here were pinched and drawn—the pain too raw.

* In Memory of the Fallen *

Down a ways, a number of people were standing on the outside edges of the stone barriers that bordered both sides of the track. My breath caught as I looked at their feet. Familiar paper roses were dotted between them. Three were mine, while the others were channeling magic that felt intensely similar—a copy of the feeling that I'd imbued in their threads.

What did that mean?

The mages were arcing magic to each other, then back again, spreading a canopy of aqua light over the section of track between the two small groups. I didn't know what the magic was doing, but from the expressions on the people who passed underneath, it was something lovely and peaceful. A number of people turned for a second pass.

"What stops anyone from jumping?" I murmured to Neph, watching the display and how close to the edge the mages on each side stood, emotion clogging my throat.

Especially on a night like tonight...

"There's an enchantment that keeps people from jumping. And the lockdown grid will further prevent anyone trying to get around that enchantment."

It was easy to forget the grid was even there. The lockdown grid had become transparent as soon as all the squares had connected.

Stepping to the edge of the Top Track, I placed my hands on the cold, gray stone, then reached out and touched the air at the edge. The air shimmered in iridescent waves, then turned clear again.

Keeping us in. Protecting us. Encapsulating us.

I looked down. The Legion, dressed in black, with a red pin to the left center of their throat, stood in formation along the length of the Fifth Circle as far as the eye could see. Interspersed between them were troops from other locales and countries—personnel who had volunteered to help sweep the mountain, and were now participating in the vigil and memorial.

Protecting us from any threat still left on campus. Or making sure none of us escaped.

Down in the distance, I could see the Midlands—the tenth through twelfth circles of the mountain—swirling with white gloom. Troops were heavy there—dots of black disappearing into and out of the perimeter.

Dare and I would be breaching that border shortly.

"Madness," I whispered.

"It's what you specialize in."

I'd felt him approach—a slight tug on the connection that bound us. He wasn't trying to hide.

I glanced up at Dare, standing alongside me. His expression was battle ready as his gaze tracked quickly over the landscape. A memorial armband was strapped around his bicep, the metal plaque glinting.

Chapter Fourteen

A shifting in the shadows below caught my eye. Looking down, I could see the shadows moving, bulging in place, then thinning back to normal size. I concentrated on the path of expanding and contracting darkness. Thirty feet, twenty feet, then Kaine stepped out of the convexly forming shadow underneath the tree nearest to our position.

I pulled back automatically, fright response engaged. Stopping my jerk, I inhaled deeply, then leaned forward again.

He was nine stories below us, but I could make him out as easily as if he were in front of me. He was staring up, smirking. Wanting me to see him. Wanting *us* to see him.

Dare was looking down as well, his fingers gripping the stone. A small anti-listening spell was pinned beneath his first finger.

Neph ran a fingertip down the bridge of her nose, then touched the back of my hand, giving me a temporary protection against eavesdroppers. It would disrupt any spells already on me for a few minutes, giving the listener bursts of static mixed with other conversations pulled from the general vicinity. She then slid into the crowd behind us.

"You don't...you shouldn't come," I said to Dare, as I stared at the Legion members below, keeping my gaze away from Kaine. I had seen the awaiting horrors in Kaine's dead eyes as he'd looked at Dare. This plan was more than madness.

I was used to working at a fast pace. I was used to working when traumatized. However, my trauma with Christian had been enveloped within my determination to bring him back, and in all the tasks involved therein. Today, still in the midst of a new trauma, with everything so fresh, I felt like I had stepped onto a tilt-a-whirl ride at the county fair—and I couldn't step off.

Dare gave me a look that fully communicated what he thought of staying behind.

I gripped the stone harder. "This is my mess—"

"This is our mess."

"I—" I shook my head, unable to finish the thought that maybe we should wait. Maybe Kaine would grow bored and leave after a few days.

Olivia's rescue couldn't wait for Kaine's boredom, though.

I needed to rescue Olivia, but I didn't want to sacrifice *Dare* to do it. I swept a hand over my torso, and the bulk of my connection threads. I needed all of them safe.

I needed me safe too, so that they all wouldn't be stupidly heroic and sacrifice themselves for *me*.

"The papers. The vine. Kaine will find them."

The papers had Dare's magic in them too—they'd sucked some of it in when they'd touched him the afternoon he'd given the papers to me. And

* In Memory of the Fallen *

the vine—who knew what it held.

Okai. The items would go where my magic was strongest. Guard Rock and Guard Friend, and all our projects... Will would be toast. The rocks would be locked away, or destroyed. We'd, all of us, be thrown into cells, or shackled by a collar around our necks.

I nodded. It was a shakier action than I wished it to be.

"Princess? You've got five." Trick's spelled voice came from the plaque's enchantment, zipping through my skin and into my ear—along a slim, opened pathway of magic that Neph and I had spent an agonizing hour untangling.

I nodded at Dare, this time more firmly.

"Let's go."

Chapter Fifteen

SHADOWS IN THE NIGHT

WE WALKED TOWARD the stairwell where Dare's crew was standing. Camille's gaze was frosty as she looked at me, but she said nothing. None of them did. Camille, Lox, and Greene maintained their positions, but Ramirez folded out of his and followed us into the stairwell.

Patrick, Asafa, Neph, Mike, and Will were inside. The usual expressions were on their faces—Patrick looked manic, Neph was exuding calm, Will looked panicked, and Mike was trying really hard to exude support.

Ramirez said nothing, just looked at each person in the stairwell, gaze taking in each.

Trick put a finger to his lips, then motioned for me to twirl. Used to this now, I slowly followed his direction. He scanned me with his device and pulled off the spells one by one, then dropped them in a soundproof bag. He pulled the enchanted drawstring tight and thrust the bag at Asafa.

"Loudon, Adrabi, and Peoples have secured the entrance below, and the combat mages are above. We have one minute."

"You are certain of their ability to hold the entrance?" Ramirez asked in a low voice. It was rare to hear him speak at all.

"You don't know the half of it," Trick said, shaking his head, a small grin pulling up one side of his mouth. "They'll hold it."

I remembered Trick's words during the attack. About never again messing with Loudon.

Ramirez stared around the group for a long moment, then he circled a finger in the air, as if encompassing the group. An invisible grip tightened against my forehead—enough to make me gasp—then Ramirez snapped his fingers and a duplicate of Dare bloomed beside him.

No one said anything, but there was an undercurrent that I could only partially read. Ramirez had done something to us. I tried to verbalize it in my mind, but *couldn't*. He had mind whammied us so we couldn't talk about

* Shadows in the Night *

what he had done after.

His ability to duplicate Dare meant something big then—either about Ramirez's magic or about his past.

Saf and Trick exchanged a glance, and Mike swallowed, gaze not leaving Ramirez's for a few seconds. Saf broke the stalemate and motioned to Neph. She nodded, then visual enchantments bloomed all over her and I wasn't just looking at her, I was looking at *us*. She had become both of us, standing side by side.

Neph and Ramirez had both created doubles, but they had done it using completely different magic.

"Hiding in plain sight, Ren." Trick gave a rakish grin to cover up whatever nerves had gripped everyone. "Muses. You are so very, *very* scary," he said fondly to Neph.

I looked at Ramirez. He was not a muse. Then what...?

Trick was pinning something on my shirt and talking to me, making me tune back in. "—will be looking for the markers they placed on you and won't look further," he said. "Give them what they are expecting to see, and they become complacent in their tracking. These are neutralizers. Should dampen down your magical signature."

"But we won't be able to use these same tactics twice," Trick said, expression going serious. "Not on the same board of play. So use your thirty minutes well. It's all we can give you, and not a second more."

Saf held up a finger to regain silence, then carefully put the spells from the bag into place around Neph's double image. He left one in the bag and tied the strings tightly. "I'll throw that one into the crowd. Crown, you have to stop letting them put listeners on you."

"Yeah," I said, sighing. I motioned to the other me and to the other Dare. Both doubles looked at me. "That's a little freaky."

"But effective."

We had gone over the plan earlier and I'd been told that creating a double was not something that was easy to do. That it required a specific type of bond or mage.

"Okay. In order for the fireworks to get through," Trick said, a hologram blooming between his fingers. "There are localized blasts allowed through the grid panel closest to the charge. With all of the personnel below, these won't be monitored quite as closely—who's going to do anything with the Legion staring up at you?"

Dare nodded and his battle cloak whirled into view. He withdrew two things from his pocket, then the battle cloak whirled out of existence again.

"We have created a very special firework." Saf ran a hand over his elevated hair. I'd never seen him make that gesture, one full of nerves. "It will attract their attention. No one will look away from it for ten seconds,

Chapter Fifteen

guaranteed. You have ten seconds to get through this open grid panel"—he pointed to a spot in the hologram—"and into the tree line. Givens?"

Mike held out his hand; two small white boxes were on his palm. "Wind streamers. You can ride them into the trees." He placed the boxes in my hand. "Set them on the stones, activate them, then hold onto the box. *Don't let go. Don't lose concentration. Don't lose the boxes.* You must detach them before the grid flips back into place, or the alarms will sound." He speared Dare with a glance. "Are you sure you can get back in?"

"Yes."

Mike didn't look happy, but he nodded, then gripped my shoulder once for good luck. Will followed suit.

"The stairwell will be held for thirty more seconds. Don't get caught." Trick tipped a salute to me, as did Saf. "Ta, Crown."

Neph touched my hand, and I felt her magic flowing into my palm—a little reservoir for when I needed it.

Ramirez looked between us, expression blank, then turned and looked at Dare, the real one. Dare tipped his head. Ramirez and the other Dare turned and slipped back through the door to Top Track.

Will and Mike nodded, then they too walked out, Neph behind them. I watched my double disappear.

As soon as we were alone, Dare pulled a heavy black garment out of one of the objects in his hands and threw it to me. "Put that on."

I did so, quickly sticking my hands into the armholes, then crisscrossing the fabric to buckle along the edge of my body. I fumbled the red Legion pin—realizing what exactly I was putting on. The metal was cold beneath my fingers. They shook as I tried to latch it into place.

Dare reached over and drew the long hood over my head. "They aren't wearing these on campus. They are against the rules set forth by the officials earlier today. But we need them. They'll hide our magic and identity to any spells cast our way. And they will camouflage us to a certain extent so that we can travel by darkness. But we *cannot be seen.* And we cannot step too close to the edges of any shadows."

I nodded quickly, not really understanding the danger associated with the edge of a shadow.

"All they need is a memory tag of our faces in these and we are done," Dare said, hands pulling the hood tighter as he emphasized the words. He was shaded, rippling in my view from whatever property the cloak was providing. But his gaze was piercing as he forced mine to meet his through the water-like effect. "Worse than just slipping out of the Magiaduct during a lockdown, wearing these cloaks is an automatic detention. There will be no trial. They will take us both. The laws guarding us here will not exempt us if we are seen in these cloaks."

* Shadows in the Night *

"I get it. Seriously. I *get it*."

He held my gaze for another loaded second, then nodded. "Let's go."

We exited the stairway on the eighth floor, and walked past Loudon, Adrabi, and Delia. I could feel the shadows reaching down from the edges of the ceiling as we skimmed along the wall. I squeezed Delia's shoulder as I passed. She stiffened, then turned to the other two. "Okay, boys. Time to join the vigil."

They turned left toward a stairwell further south, while we headed north.

The countdown timer indicated we had two minutes to get into position. Exiting back onto Top Track two hundred yards away from the others, I looked at every face we passed.

Their gazes slid right by us.

So far, so good.

Loudon had made it very clear that we had to use a grid panel that opened on its own. That we couldn't force one to stay open without leaving damning evidence behind. Fortunately, a Fibonacci pattern was programmed for the sequence. A spiral of magic lifting slowly into the air one firework at a time. The others had slotted in their distraction somehow—through some Community Magic trick that they were confident in.

Confidence was a large component in the game we were about to begin.

Our panel—the one Saf had indicated—was set to open in thirty seconds. In the generated sequence, it would open the moment after the panel some five hundred and twelve to our left lifted and let loose the boys' distraction.

Dare gripped my elbow. "There is darkness, and there are shadows. Avoid the shadows."

I looked at him from the darkness of my hood and gave a firm smile. The kinship in the cloaks allowed us to see each other's faces.

Three, two, one...

A brilliant light burst five hundred yards to our left as the club's firework exploded in the air, and the crowd gasped in shock.

Our grid opened, and the waiting firework rushed into its spot, as we jammed the devices onto the ledge.

The murmur of the crowd grew louder.

The wind streamers shot like clear rainbows from the stones, in an arc buried in the treetops far beyond. The firework in our grid shot through the stone between our devices, and thrust up into the air.

"Go," Dare said.

Someone yelled. But if everyone was watching our escape attempt instead of whatever distraction had been planned, it was far too late now.

I squeezed the device, and shot through the air along the beam, legs outstretched behind me as Mike had advised earlier—letting the force pull

Chapter Fifteen

me like a diver, streamlined in an arcing plunge. Dare, gaining air beside me, looked like a dark wraith, wrapped in the cloak with the hood covering his features.

I could see the operatives below us, dots on the battle-torn green space of the Magiaduct's front lawn.

All gazes were fixed on a point far above the Magiaduct, and far to our left. Some of the Legion members even took a step in the direction of the light show.

As my body flew along the air current, I could see Kaine below. He was transfixed by the show and he looked...elated? I turned my head awkwardly to look at the firework. At the moving image.

At the visual reel of me fighting Christian under Raphael's dome.

Oh dear God. My concentration slipped, exactly as Mike had warned against, but I couldn't even process the feeling inside of me, as everything about me was in freefall. A gust of wind hit me, and I didn't even fight it.

They had chosen to show footage that hadn't made it into public view—of my golem, controlled by Raphael, but with my brother's face, fighting against me. Me, with my hands in the ground and paint splattered on my face. God. Everything—

I hit a tree, then hit the ground. Hands were beneath my arms and hauling me forward an instant later. Away from the Magiaduct and into the tree line. I could feel blood on my face. I was so tired of being bloody.

"How c—"

Dare's hand pressed firmly over my mouth and kept me moving.

How could they have shown that? Everyone would *know*. The paint. *Everything*.

The forest swam in my view, and the shadows shifted furiously. No.

I thought of Olivia and the expression on her face as she burst into a thousand lights, and pulled it together. The shadows were shifting *deliberately*.

I nodded against Dare's hand to show that I was fine, and he withdrew it, not needing extra incentive to increase our speed as we dodged through the trees.

What had been shown in the firework was over now. I couldn't control that anymore. I could control my part in not getting us caught.

I could see both wind streamers in Dare's hand as he shoved the boxes in his cloak. I mentally castigated myself—he'd saved me from plummeting to the ground, he'd deactivated both of our devices, then gotten us the hell out of Dodge.

Yeah, doing this without Dare would have been a bad idea.

I'd had a panic attack during the attack on campus, watching everyone around me being killed, and I'd just experienced a smaller one now. Two in

* Shadows in the Night *

one very traumatic day. Clearly, I was going to need to deal with that.

And that wasn't taking into account how I'd gone off the rails and nearly ended everyone when I thought Olivia had died.

This day was truly shaping into one to *remember*.

Heightened fight response and adrenaline kicked in at a response to my need and my senses narrowed in on a shadow shifting in the distance.

Pain spiked. Using even that amount of magic hurt.

I swallowed it down and grabbed Dare's arm in warning, pressing against his side as we continued to run. He immediately went with the motion, hooking an arm around me, and whirling us behind the next tree.

The edges of the darkness, bleeding into the illumination of the fireworks, grew longer fingers.

I looked up into the lower canopy of branches, and forced my breath not to breach my lips.

The air shifted on the other side of our tree and the shadowy fingers grew sharper. A human predator was hunting us.

Someone hadn't taken the bait. And I'd bet everything on who it was.

I just hoped the cloak I was wearing hid the frantic beat of my heart.

Dare carefully pulled something out of the pocket of his cloak, then held it up. The small paper phoenix that I had made for him sat on his palm. But it was looking less papery and far more feathery. It blinked and its body turned Midnight blue. It streaked upward into the boughs of the trees, circled a branch, then swept to the left.

A feeling skated over my skin—a sudden vacuum of space—then the knife-sharpened shadows released and shot after the phoenix, tendrils of shadows reaching upward and outward from the branches, trying to catch the little being in their grip.

My breath was coming in short pants, and I tried to deepen the inhales.

I had created the phoenix to keep Dare safe in the Midlands—or at least the location and status of his body safe. I had designed it as a learning creation, though, drawing on the free magic from campus and the chaos magic in the Midlands for its intelligence and memory. The phoenix had either learned some new tricks on its own, or Dare had taught it some.

I had seen it eat magic in order to save Dare during the battle. So for all I knew, it might start breathing fire any moment.

I rubbed my forearm. Maybe...I was a little scary.

Dare didn't need to nudge me this time, we both took off at a dead run toward the ninth circle. None of the arches were currently active on the mountain. They were dormant in order to keep any lingering bad guys from staying hidden by jumping around campus. But Delia had given us the locations of two natural root paths that, on our current trajectory, would get us to the Midlands fastest.

Chapter Fifteen

The first one was easy to negotiate, but the second required us to run a hundred yards across more open space.

Fifty yards in, I spotted Kaine cutting through the shadows.

"Come out, come out, little rabbits."

He knew we were here. And I could see that *this* was Kaine, doing what he did best. Terror and concealment. A nightmare wrapped up in a law enforcement robe. Appearing like death's hand to deliver a forever sleep.

Fireworks lit up the air above the trees, obliterating some shadows and shifting others.

But no one knew campus better than Dare.

He pushed me off course, and we ducked under a tree that housed feral raccoonkeys, then across a stone path that came alive if you stepped on the correct sequence.

Kaine swore behind us and said, "Both sides, three point two formation, *now*."

Adrenaline pumped, painfully pushing past a few of the looser blocks in my magic. Kaine was not alone. It had been very explicitly stated what would happen to us if we were caught. Not good, not good.

Dare whipped out a hand and a device appeared in his hand. A shadow on our right fell. Another zigzagged in front and Dare bowed briefly, a blade sweeping across the space of his stomach.

"Lovely, *lovely*," Kaine said, in a voice as insane as Raphael's, but, to me, far more terrifying.

Raphael was the monster I *knew*.

Dare whipped his hand left and a root burst from the earth and more than one shadow shrieked.

But it wasn't Kaine's shadow. Kaine's magic felt effortless, toying.

A pit of shadow, smoke, and fire rose in front of us.

Millimeters of air thinned under Kaine's thin, sweeping fingers, as they brushed the edge of my hood. Dare grabbed me around the waist, twisting us as we launched forward, then disappeared into the concealed opening between two roots.

Inky blackness, moss, splinters, then root-laden ground.

I fell heavily on top of Dare. But adrenaline was still pumping and I scrambled forward, knees digging into his stomach and thighs, in order to launch myself toward the large wooden knot on the heaviest root, three feet away. I slapped it with my palm as Delia had instructed.

The edges of the wood cavern, at the base of the tree we'd just been spewed from, spiraled and sealed shut. Flames *should*, at this moment, be lighting the pants off every one of the shadows trying to follow our path.

I pressed my hand against my mouth to stop the insane urge to laugh. If it issued forth, it would be high-pitched and hysterical, and the last free sound I would make.

Dare appeared in my view, and I could feel his hands on both of my cheeks. He didn't say anything, but his grip grounded me, gaze boring into mine. His image firmed, and the hysteria subsided, leaving behind an empty feeling in the pit of my stomach. I nodded.

The edge of the Midlands was...thicker. As if the chaos was being penned into place.

Not good.

The Midlands served as the area where all of the magical backlashes that occurred on campus—and in the civilian areas at the base of the mountain—got sorted out and the magic "cleaned" so it could be repurposed without unfortunate elements gunking up the works.

We sprinted into the gloom.

Chapter Sixteen

THE MIDLANDS

HUNTING THE MIDLANDS with Dare was familiar, but whereas, in the past, there had been an almost unreality to the danger, now it was fraught with peril of a far different kind.

The Okai tile appeared immediately, recognizing me even with my magic dampened, and we wasted no time stepping onto it. Dare knew it appeared for me instantaneously, and had, obviously, counted on exactly that occurring during our time-ticking trip here.

The tile whirled away in a fairground twirl that left my innards lurching. As soon as it connected up to the next tile, though, I withdrew Dagfinn's device from my pocket and started digging in the dirt of the connecting tile to the right.

Dare's brows rose.

"Yes, I've been told it's highly illegal, yada, yada." I continued to dig furiously with my blunt nails.

Dare sighed, and a moment later a perfect hole was bored in the ground.

"Awesome. Thanks." I stuck the silver device inside, activated it, and quickly scooped dirt on top, patting it down. I leaned back and the tile slipped away.

"I, uh, told the others that we would clean up some of the magic trails around campus." I ran a dirty hand down the back of my hood. "That seems a little silly, in retrospect."

"We'll figure something out," he said. "Come on."

I brushed off my clothes as we headed toward Okai. The Gothic and Classical mix of architecture seemed even more of an anomaly than usual, both freaky and inviting.

On the front steps, the vine undulated like a cobra. Its vibrant green skin gleamed as it swayed, leafy arms fluttering in a mesmerizing wave.

Gloves appeared on Dare's hands as he walked toward it with sure steps. The vine weaved back and forth. And, though it allowed Dare to lift it by its throat, it did so almost reluctantly as if reminding him he was not its master.

There was something very off-putting about the magic and intentions I could feel from the carnivorous plant.

But taking care of it was one of the tasks that had to be completed, so I said nothing as Dare followed me up the short stairs.

I unmuted my armband and exclamations immediately greeted me, piling on top of each other as everyone wanted to know what was happening.

Steps one and two complete, I sent. There was a small mental cheer and Dagfinn gave a whoop. *Going dark again.* A number of fervent good lucks echoed as I muted the armband again to all voices except Dare.

Placing my hand upon the door to Okai, the knob glowed and I turned it. Dare slipped inside behind me, and placed the vine on the floor as I closed the door.

I drew back my hood, and Guard Rock and Guard Friend converged on me immediately.

Guard Rock made a number of sharp motions with his pencil. I crouched in front of him and he waved his pencil, pointing and clicking it against the ground as he moved his hands and feet then thumped a wall with a solid thud.

"He tried to get in? You didn't let him?"

Guard Rock thrust out his rock, puffing his chest. Guard Friend hovered near him.

I touched both of their rocks. "Thank you."

I turned to look up at Dare, who was staring down with a completely unreadable expression.

"Raphael tried to enter again—he entered successfully, once before, when he stole my dolls and golem—but this time they repelled him with help from the building." I looked around. "Either because he was in Emrys's form and didn't have access to his full magic through the golem—or because the magic here listened when I was upset last time, and prevented him from entering this time even with him carrying my Awakening paint."

The building was spooky like that.

"Probably the building. It was constructed by an Origin Mage," he added, at my questioning look.

I looked around the room with new eyes. It didn't *feel* like Kinsky's painting.

Dare tilted his head. "You didn't know." His deep brown hair shifted on his forehead as he shook his head. "Of course you didn't."

Chapter Sixteen

I rubbed my temples. That knowledge was something I'd have to mull later. "The extent of things that you expect me to know sometimes is a little unreasonable."

"Not if you want to survive."

I looked up to retort, but my response died on my lips. Dare was kneeling down and inspecting the rocks.

Guard Rock puffed up like a sentry under a superior's inspection. But his spear was also twitching with uncertainty toward both the vine and Dare.

"He has good instincts," Dare said.

"Because he isn't sure about trusting you?"

Unlike his response to Will, who due to Raphael's sorcery—and unwillingly, mine—was seen as a threat by any creation of mine made with my Awakening paint. The rocks always wanted to push him into my Awakening sketch to be turned into Christian's vessel sacrifice.

But it wasn't like Guard Rock's response to Neph, either, who the rocks adored, or to Olivia, who they mostly ignored. The response to Dare was the response to a predator and a general.

Dare reached out a finger and touched the top of Guard Rock's pencil spear. It went rigid and Guard Rock stood the straightest I'd ever seen him.

"Don't ensorcel my friends," I said.

He smiled and rose, but then his gaze fell on the papers scattered on the ground and his smile slipped. He stalked the edges of the papers, then crouched down and scanned them with a piercing gaze. The gloves returned to his hands.

I nervously walked over to join him. Kinsky's papers had slipped into the building and were scattered across the floor. On the pages were figures of men, bent and broken.

I wiped a shaking hand down my face. I didn't want to know if they were alive or dead. Outside of the heat of battle, I didn't want to see what I had wrought.

"How many?" I asked.

"Twenty-two, maybe a few more if there are bodies completely hidden beneath others."

I gagged.

But Dare was completely unperturbed by the papers and their contents. If anything, his eyes were gleaming.

Then again, he was the one who had given the papers to me—right before he'd let us be attacked by a monster. I wasn't the only one who was a little scary on this campus.

"There's a preservation charm." He pointed to the way all of the figures were stock still on the pages. "Which is good news for them. Their ten minutes won't start until they are released."

"Can we release them like the trolls and Hydra?"

"Can you?" He looked at me through the hair that had fallen into his eyes.

I tested my magic. Okai hummed around me. "Better here, I think. But, it's still pretty stoppered."

He gave his head a shake and I was treated to an unobscured view again. "Not here. The fewer links to this building, the better. And better to let someone else heal and...debrief them. I have a way to do it—a way anyone other than you would discourage."

He frowned at my workbench. He rose, and I raised my hands in an 'I haven't done anything yet' gesture.

He stepped forward and visually scanned the projects on the workbenches, quickly cataloging everything. His gaze drifted over the glass shards in the scrap and cleaning box. I nervously brushed aside a few of the more concerning projects—the leashes, leeches, and part of Will's latest portal design.

I could see Dare looking for something specifically, but I didn't know what.

"Leandred doesn't work here," he said. There was a lot of Constantine's magic here, because a number of the projects we worked on together ended up here for safe keeping, but there was no remnant of him here personally.

"No." I shrugged. "Will calls this our secret lab. We go to Consta—to your room," I amended. "When we work with him, then bring things back here."

He speared me with a look. "Some of—"

"Yeah, I know, I know. Let's just get Olivia back, then you can all castigate me together."

A shuffling sound along the floor had me turning my head.

The vine was slithering toward me, weaving back-and-forth in the air as it drew closer, mesmerizing.

It launched itself forward and sunk barbed fangs into my skin. Swearing, I tried to shake it off, but the vine clung on. Then, just as abruptly as it had taken hold of me, it let go, barfed up everything it had swallowed on Top Circle—plus additional things that were unidentifiable in the midst of the green goo coating it all—dove under a table, then shot up the stairs.

"What...?" I didn't even know what question to ask, as I clutched my bloody arm against my stomach.

Dare was staring up the staircase, expression flat. "It's going to figure out how to get back to the Fourth Layer on its own—even though creatures can't escape the Midlands."

He lifted my bitten arm and pulled a finger over the wounds. They

Chapter Sixteen

closed up.

I shook out my arm, clenching and releasing my fingers. "You got it from the Fourth Layer?"

"Yes."

"Why?"

"Just in case." He prowled around the mess, then carefully formed a ball of magic and dropped it over the whole thing, encasing it all in a blue field. He made a motion and the entire mass lifted. The mess settled on top of a workbench area free of clutter.

Inside the mess, bones and other objects stuck up at odd angles.

"The good news is that it coughed up all the magic used earlier," he said.

"What? Like owl pellets of magic?"

"Something like that."

"It eats magic?"

"Sort of."

The blue field dissipated. I gingerly sifted through the remains and lifted the tube of paint and Constantine's stamp. Green magic goo dripped from them.

"Great." I propped them against the wall at the back of the table and hoped the goo wasn't going to form into a living Blob or something. Things like that happened here.

Then again, maybe I'd get blob matter out of it. Bright side.

Dare reached forward and lifted the stamp, then flung it outward like a Frisbee without the release. It unfurled into the air, a banner absolutely gleaming with the spent magic of Godfrey and his minions. All the magic thrown at me, I'd balled up in Constantine's stamp, then thrown at Godfrey's dome.

It snapped at the end of its course, flinging the last bits of green goo at the wall. The wall shimmered, then returned to regular stone.

"What's he playing at," Dare muttered. He looked at me, expression unreadable.

"Birthday present?" I attempted.

He frowned, and returned the stamp to the workbench—next to the tube of paint, where his gaze immediately fell next. The tube had a thin strip of ultramarine around the edge of the cap—the paint I'd mixed during my Awakening while remembering the hue of his eyes.

Embarrassing.

But Dare was already sifting through the rest of the regurgitated items. He lifted two silver rocks and one of the bones and put them in his pocket.

"Yours?" I asked.

He tilted his head, not answering, and continued cataloging each object. Many of them ended up in his pocket.

* The Midlands *

He didn't touch the tube of paint.

"So, the vine...eats magic?"

"Yes. And reforms it. But active magic usually, not devices." He indicated the intact paint tube and stamp. "At least not right away. Given a few weeks, it would have been the most dangerous greenery in this layer," he said dryly, looking at the tube of paint. "But it does similar things to the Midlands' processing plant. Recycling magic back to a 'clean' state."

As many times as I had been in the Midlands, I had never been in the building that housed the processing plant. "Is...is it a plant?"

Dare stared at me.

"The processing plant... I thought, you know, manufacturing?"

He laughed, then continued, putting his hand down on my workbench to support himself.

"Fine," I said, cheeks burning. "But back to the vine, it eats magic and, what, regenerates it into clean magic again?"

"Its primary use in the Fourth Layer is to create the right magic for creature transformations. It primarily processes the extra magic that was blown from the Third Layer seventy years ago," he said, far too mildly. "A magic that was then used specifically. But without the Fourth Layer system in place, yes, it will 'eat' and 'process' any magic."

I didn't have time to think over the implications of the other statements, I just quickly nodded. "So we can set it on the trails around campus."

Dare's gaze narrowed. "Yes." He moved with purpose to the staircase. "If you can coax it to, it will start eating all the trails you set it upon."

Eating our magic trails, then barfing up clean energy? Win, win.

"Even better," he said, as he took the steps two at a time. "Such a task will keep it busy."

I followed quickly. There were a number of rooms upstairs. I rarely ventured there, though. There were some pretty creepy things about Okai. Even though it was a secret hideaway, there was an element of villain *lair* to it, especially in the upper level.

"What about Kaine?"

"The vine can handle itself."

The hallway stretched—longer than it would be if First Layer physics were in play.

The vine was in the hall, weaving in front of one particular door. It was the door that I always kept closed.

Dare looked at me in question.

"There's a, um, creepy mirror in there?" There were little shadows slithering under the doorframe. The vine tried to poke underneath.

"A portal?"

I shook my head. "I don't know. I stay away from it."

Chapter Sixteen

His right glove reappeared and he grabbed the vine. "Wait here." He opened the door.

"Um, *no*, this is my secret lai—"

Dare shut the door just as quickly as he had opened it, gripping the vine a little too hard as it flailed in his fist, trying to lunge back in the direction of the shut door.

"—r, what's wrong?"

"Do not touch that mirror." His gaze zeroed in on me. His skin was pale. "*Ever*, Ren."

"What is it?"

"Danger." He put his hand on the handle, and it glowed briefly.

I wondered if it was the same kind of danger as a Kinsky painting. I'd never told Dare about our adventure in the Library of Alexandria.

"What kind of danger? And why did you magic the lock up? I can still get in there, you know."

"Don't." He thrust the vine at me.

I took it gingerly in my left hand, then grabbed it tighter in my right—holding it like a poisonous snake—not letting the head have its way.

"We are wasting time now," he said, brushing off my questions. "We must go."

Hesitance gripped me, oddly.

In Okai, we were safe. I was safe here. I could create freely, away from the Administration Magic in the Magiaduct. I could maybe use whatever the mirror did to portal me to an evil Timbuktu full of hobgoblins and misery, then find some way to a Third Layer port from there. No one would be staring at me as I went past, or crossing their fingers over their hearts, or anything else.

But everyone was waiting back at the Magiaduct. They had put their freedom and magic on the line. I couldn't let them be questioned when I was discovered missing.

And we only had fifteen minutes remaining to set the vine loose, to set the men loose, to retrieve Olivia's scarf, and to figure out a way back inside the Magiaduct. There was no lingering. No safety allowed.

"Okay."

Dare, with his glove in place, was already scooping up Kinsky's papers —and wasn't that a shock. He was building up a tolerance of some sort to Origin Magic, but he would still either be stripped of his shields or knocked flat on his back after touching one. He had *died* today from the first dome he had taken down. Someone—probably Ramirez—had revived him almost immediately, though.

But the glove... *He had something that resisted Origin Magic.*

He peeled the glove from his wrist and over the top of the papers. The glove flexed and expanded, then shimmered into a portfolio similar to the one that had initially held the papers.

I was already thinking how Constantine, Will, and I could make one, as Dare stuck the portfolio into his cloak. I still had that portfolio, and *clearly* had not thought enough about its possibilities.

The vine snapped its thorny jaws at me, with a rictus green smile.

Keeping its head an arms' length away, I sank down to my knees and gave last minute instructions and rubs to the rocks.

"Hold down the fort. But if someone gains access, hide. I don't want you to engage. There are...unnerving people on campus. They might come for you, if they find me missing."

The rocks puffed out their rocks and waved their weapons.

"No. I don't want you fighting. Protection only. Hide what you can and don't let them find you."

I put my left hand on the floor and echoed the instruction to Okai. I didn't have my usual magic, but my intentions were still readable, and my slowly regenerating magic recognizable. It made my desires into suggestions rather than commands. But I thought the building would protect the rocks without a command. To the end.

I rose. Dare tugged my hood back over my head, then slipped his on as well.

He exited before me, scanned the forest line, then motioned for me to follow.

"Lock it up tightly," he said, as I touched the ornate handle of the door. "Your friend Will isn't going to be coming here before you, and you do not want the Legion to get in any quicker than they already will be." He looked at me. "They will find a way. There's no way that Kaine hasn't already marked this building for search as soon as the other forces are gone. He can smell the Origin Magic on it."

"Should I move everything?" Distressed, I looked at Guard Rock and Guard Friend through the little floor window Okai sometimes made for them. They were staring solemnly out at us.

"To where?" Dare said bluntly, not trying to soften the words. "Bellacia Bailey's room? Yours? This is the safest place on campus for you. It just won't be safe forever, especially if the Department gets the go ahead to take over campus security after the temporary edict. As long as they are temporary custodians, they can only use the tools that they bring by person."

He tapped the stone under his hand with a fingertip. "They will need a large-scale anti-Origin device to crack this building. They have them, but there is no way to sneak something like that on campus. They need the permission still. The officials are watching them in the same way that they

Chapter Sixteen

are watching us."

He pulled my hood farther forward. "It's why we can't be discovered. In any of this. It will give them what they need. And they *will* take over campus."

I looked at him, suddenly mystified. Dare was the campus protector. Why was he putting himself out for this? For me? Allowing campus to be put into the betting pile?

"I could use paint?" I eyed the door. "I could probably make the door eat anyone who approached."

The Library of Alexandria would be proud.

"As hilarious as that would be, it would give them justification to use means to open it." He looked out at the grounds that surrounded the structure. "Better to reinforce the slippery nature of the land. Don't let them onto your 'tile' as you call it."

Nodding, I pulled out the tube and twisted off the cap with the same hand, since I was still holding the vine in the other one. Trapping the cap between the tube and my palm, I swiped my forefinger over the lip. Ultramarine blue glistened on the tip.

For a moment, all sound was blocked—and all sense of taste and smell. I could only see the blue images and possibilities. If I bathed myself in paint —rubbed it into my skin... I could pull some of the power from my Awakening. Recoat myself in the protective image of blue. Let it fix all of my broken pathways...

I could become my Awakening. I could find Olivia. I could be *more* than Ren.

No. I swallowed. Just Ren was good.

I touched the door handle, then moved down the steps. Kneeling down, I made an arched line with a strangely steady finger in the dirt. *Protection.* Protect this tile from being stepped upon. The blue shimmered, then spread.

The building already had that command in place—it had taken me forever to get on the tile—and this was strengthening that command in the dirt at its base. Rapidly. The blue spread outward, circling the building, until the line rejoined itself. The magic flared, then disappeared from view.

I looked at the vine flailing in my hand, then acting on instinct. I swiped my finger along the top of the tube and wiped it on the vine's green head. It went still in my hand, like a puppet waiting for its direction.

Shuddering, I screwed the cap back on and sent the tube back to Okai. I wanted to keep the paint. I wanted the reassurance of having an ace in the hole. But it would be disastrous if it was found on me. It wouldn't even be the nail in the coffin. It would be the fully dug grave, complete with chiseled headstone.

* The Midlands *

I hated this. This hiding.

We stepped off the tile and Okai immediately spun out of view. It was replaced with another landscape, a quarter piece of a river—where the river flowed for fifteen feet before disappearing into the ground—like a fountain that was reusing its own water. Except that the river magically continued on in a tile somewhere thousands of tiles away. And it started its flow on another somewhere else.

I set the vine on the ground and pressed my finger to its painted head. I channeled my desire through the paint, and let the parts of my mind that collected information relay the sensory information on all the magic of the others—the others who each had some connection to me.

Find all of the trails.

In fact, any magic that looked tasty and mischievous? *Feast on, my green friend.*

The vine weaved in the air, then dove into the ground.

The whole thing took but a few moments, but when I looked up, Dare was standing rigidly a foot away, whole body tense.

He was looking at something in the distance, his fingers clenching on the air, as if he wanted nothing more than to draw a staff out of his unlimited bucket of tricks. But that would be a dead giveaway to him. No one used a staff like Alexander Dare.

"Five seconds," he said in a low, harsh voice.

I jolted, hands scrambling in the dirt to get myself upright as my feet were already moving in the direction he was pointing. We had fought together too many times in the Midlands for me not to obey unquestioningly.

He stood stock still, the deep hood obscuring his features, then he was all motion, hands lifting into the air and spinning. The greenery in front of him rose in a too-tight way, then spun with the motion of his hands in the air, and launched outward, toothed mouths open.

I lurched from my scramble into a full-out sprint.

Out of the corner of my eye, I saw the shadows shifting. Curses were heard as a few were caught.

Trolls appeared in front of us—why always trolls?—conjured by someone behind us and only a football maneuver kept me from being splattered all over the forest floor.

Shadows reached down and grabbed for my hood. Dare spun both of us and the ruined city tile we were running through shifted and broke, pillars and marbles rose then were thrust backward at our pursuers. The shadows screamed and two disappeared into mist.

A castle tile opened up. Then another. I angled left, heading straight for them. The other castle tiles would be more likely to attract, giving us better

Chapter Sixteen

odds at shaking the tiles that the praetorians were moving on.

It was as if everything Dare had been training me for was coming down to this single minute.

A moor tile shifted into place in front of us, and there was nothing for it but to sprint across. The open, smoky moors were the worst places to be caught, if one was relying on subterfuge.

The fog lifted into shapes—forming into toothed clouds of smoke and lightning that were preparing to lunge at Dare.

No.

Dare's paper dragon came out of the sky, reflected lightning glinting on its wings, and breathed fire in a long arc around us, blowing the shrieking fog into vapor. I pushed my very real shock down—I couldn't allow emotion to distract me as I sprinted and kept track of my surroundings as we burst through the flames and onto a forest tile, then the open desert. Root, branch, quicksand, scorpions.

Dare, hard at my heels, did something, pulling the forest branches together behind us. They formed a thickening thicket of enchanted thorns. A quick look over my shoulder saw a number of shadows slipping through the forming holes, but the vast majority ran headlong into the poisonous barbs.

Insane cursing and laughter echoed behind us.

Okay. If Dare hadn't already been slated for an imperial dungeon, he was definitely on that list now.

And then Kaine appeared.

Kaine swiped left, black shadow glinting silver as it sliced across Dare. An arc of blood shot from Dare's midsection.

His blood, we couldn't leave his—

The vine burst from the ground and swallowed the red trail from the air before a single drop hit the ground, then dove back into the ground in one clean arc. The dragon dove down again and swallowed the shadow that had split Dare's skin—making Kaine swear foully—then the paper burst into flame.

I stumbled, but regained my stride.

It was excruciating when one of my creations died, but I had to push it *down*.

The phoenix swooped in suddenly and sucked in all of the flames of the dragon, twirled around one of the shadows trying to grab it, then swooped into the trees. The pain immediately numbed, as if the dragon was no longer dead, but in some strange state of limbo.

"Don't call them again." Dare's mental voice was breathing heavily.

I didn't... I hadn't called them, had I?

Dare's voice came through my mind, projected via the bands encircling our arms. *"They will get caught on a next pass. There is no way Kaine hasn't calculated the trajectories now. Only surprise let that work."*

I nodded, sharply and mentally, ducking a shadowy form.

The cloaks were doing some of the work at keeping us from being caught—and the garments were exquisite at it. They made it harder for us to be grabbed, as shadows tried to hitch onto shadows. I was pretty decent at duck, dodge, and evade, but hunting is what the mages following us had been trained for. On a level playing field...well, I would have been dead meat without Dare and the cloak.

The forming castle tiles had slipped away in a mass slide, but there was another tile—one that connected to part of the moat, and we sprinted for it together without exchanging a word.

Diving on at the last second, space tilted, then the ground jolted as our tile fastened onto two other moat tiles.

Dare was already on his feet, lifting me back to standing, then we were running into the outer bailey. He ran specifically toward a small guard outpost on the upper level of the inner wall.

He twirled me inside, slamming the door.

The air was eerily silent. The praetorians' shadows made a whistling noise that was noticeably, hauntingly absent.

Dare immediately pulled a black cloth from his cloak and pressed it against the wound in his midsection. I swallowed. I didn't know how he had kept running. It looked like he had almost been sliced in half.

"Can I do anything?"

"No." He closed his eyes, then the black cloth melted into his wound, closing it in a black line. Another pass of his fingers knit the cloak back into shape. "Faults in the cloth lessen the illusion of the cloaks, but it should hold well enough for the next five minutes."

I checked the time. Five minutes was all we had to get back to the Magiaduct. I tuned back into the armband chatter that I had muted before leaving the Magiaduct, then muted again in Okai. Distractions meant death in the Midlands, even on a normal day.

"Where are you, Princess?" Patrick's voice was tight and overly controlled.

Holed up, with no way to make it back. I kept tight rein on the thought, not allowing it to slip through the armband.

I closed my eyes and started to scroll through backup plans for how to keep everyone waiting for us safe and out of interrogation.

"The good news is that our magic trails are being eaten as we speak," I sent. "On me making it back...that's...not looking as good."

A flurry of voices responded, talking over each other. There was an enchantment that sorted voices out on multi-frequency or comm links, but I just let their voices wash over me in a wave.

Chapter Sixteen

"Activate Plan B," I said.

Plan B meant that Neph would accompany the double to Medical and leave. Leaving me to be discovered as "missing" later—likely reported by Bellacia. It also meant that they would wipe all traces of memory of the plan from their brains. Leaving me on my own if we *did* make it back.

"No." Neph's voice.

"Yes. It's the only way I can do this. Promise me."

"No."

They started arguing—at me—so I sent a *back in four* then shut them out. I closed my eyes, overwhelmingly exhausted with this whole day.

"You said I called the creations and vine," I said tiredly, looking at Dare, who was fiercely and unflaggingly scanning the perimeter through the arrow slits in the castle wall, one hand pressed against his gut splitting injury. "I still do some magic effortlessly, while normal magic twists inside of me."

Dare narrowed his eyes on a particular spot outside, then continued his sentry watch. "It's what people joke about as the retirement magic of a mage. Mages put a lot of things into place so they don't have to rely on dwindling magic or aptitude. A mage just needs to rely on the magic he already created."

He looked at me. "And you... You create very powerful things."

I leaned my head back against the stone. "I can connect to things I already have connections with. I did earlier with some of my paper. They didn't require active magic. Just the key of me."

"Yes. You might irreparably damage yourself if you keep trying to channel new enchantments. But you can rely on what you already have. You will *need* to rely on what you already have. While you are like this, you need to craft what you already possess into new strategies, not magic."

I nodded tiredly and looked at the hand pressed to his cloak, thinking about what else was beneath besides his nearly mortal injury.

"Kinsky's papers. We could use them. Suck up the entire lot following us. Praetorian sketches." I mimicked whooshing my fingers into a sucking vortex. They were papers made by Kinsky, but they had accepted my touch and modification. I was pretty sure they would still answer to me.

"While there is some evidence that the suspended state inside the magic wipes a block of memory on either side of the entrance and exit to an Origin paper, you don't want Kaine inside something that contains a piece of your magic." Dare's mouth pinched. "He lives in shadow. He thrives in otherworlds."

I wasn't quite sure what that meant.

"The one thing I never anticipated was his presence on campus. We need to get rid of the papers," he said shortly. "Hide them, especially from Kaine."

* The Midlands *

I stared at Dare. He hadn't shared the 'how' of that plan. "Um—" I waved my hands to our surroundings. The castle had started shifting around us.

"We need something, in order to do that." His expression was grim.

I grabbed onto one of the arrow slits as another third of the castle shifted away. I had never been in here, so I didn't know how the tile would slide. This was a trapped position I would never have entered into without Alexander Dare at my side.

"Hold on," he yelled as the tile crumbled. He closed his eyes and threw down a ball of magic. It splattered on the stone floor as we were ripped into space.

When we reformed, we were staring into the smirking face of Kaine.

Chapter Seventeen

NEGOTIATIONS WITH A BAD HAND

I LET GO of the arrow slit and scrambled backward. Kaine reached forward and gripped me by the neck, pushing me back against the reforming wall.

I could feel magic rising off of him. Horrible magic that was all focused on me. He smiled. "By the power invoked—"

Magic hit him. His voice cut off abruptly in a choke, but his fingers tightened. I scrabbled at the strangling grip of his fingers. Kaine shed a shadow, like a layer of skin, and the choking spell on *him* fell with it.

Dare, fully hooded and standing a few paces behind Kaine, gripped the air and pulled backward with his fingers. Kaine's expression went tight and I could see another shadow start to detach from him.

"Dear baby Dare," he spit. "Do you really thi—"

A silver sheen unfurled over Kaine's face and was sucked backward with the shedding shadow, pulled into Dare's closing right palm. A blade protruded outward from Kaine's chest at the same time, an inch from impaling me with him. Kaine's grip on me loosened as he stared down at it. I shoved him backward. The ground shook beneath us, and Dare grabbed Kaine by his neck and thrust him out of the open window and into the next tile slide.

"Oh my God." It was a litany from my lips as Dare kept his right hand in a tight grip, his other arm still pressed against his midsection. It looked like it had opened again.

Not only were we past our time limit—our five minutes completely gone, with no way to return to the Magiaduct—but we had been halfway caught by Kaine, Dare was mortally wounded again, and Dare had used *magic* on Kaine. Had skewered him on a blade.

"Come." Dare lurched forward.

* Negotiations with a Bad Hand *

"He. You." I clutched my throat, trying to ease the pain there, as I choked out words.

Dare reached out for me and I could see the healing magic on his fingers. I instinctively grabbed his hand and swept it back to press against his midsection, my other hand wrapped around the portion of his chest where the ultramarine tie was linked between us, fisting it and sending everything I could through the link.

Dare shut his eyes and I could see them pinch in pain as he grabbed the magic. He disentangled me gently with one hand and knelt down.

My throat felt epically better—like I was now just suffering a massive cold.

"He'll survive," Dare said grimly, eyes pinching again as he grabbed something from the forest floor and pressed it against his stomach. "He's already hunting us again, but now with actual wrath involved."

"He knew who—"

"No, he was fishing." He flashed his free hand at me and the last pains in my throat lessened.

"But your magic—"

"*Later*. Give me your hand."

I held it out. He opened his closed fist just far enough to envelop my palm within it. The magic he had taken from Kaine swiveled between our palms, making me shudder.

With his other hand, he withdrew a small piece of metal from his pocket. He worked it between our palms. Then his magic was pulling on me.

His eyes were intensely blue. "Think about how you would release the men from the papers. Concentrate and visualize, but do it quickly," he said, words crisp and brooking no questions.

I wanted us to get the hell out of here *now*, but I closed my eyes and did as he said. Because...

My thoughts reordered, scattered puzzle pieces locking together. Because he had *let* Kaine catch us. Whatever magic Dare had done during the tile slide, had pulled Kaine to us, or us to Kaine.

And we were already well past the time we could return to the dorms without consequence.

I shoved those worries aside and concentrated.

Dare's magic pulled the vision from me—similar to what Constantine had done when he'd leeched my magic in the First Layer. But this felt far more natural. This magic was a part of Dare already—he was a Bridge Mage—and was using the connection between us, and my trust, to absorb and direct my mental image stream.

He'd manipulated my magic and actions during extreme circumstances

Chapter Seventeen

twice already. This third time was slightly different—with him having to swallow my thought process too—but I could feel him adjusting to it already, settling it into a procedure he could repeat in the future.

He'd probably be able to puppet me on a string from afar soon, without any aid. And wasn't that a comforting thought.

A moment later he pulled away. The blue light was gone, as was the feeling of Kaine's magic. A silver dragon glinted normally on Dare's palm.

From his cloak, Dare withdrew the portfolio containing Kinsky's papers and placed the silver dragon on top. Small strings wrapped around the two items, binding them temporarily together.

It had morphed from Origin-proof gloves into a portfolio, and was now becoming...something else.

"Where did you get that?" I asked, a little breathless from the image transfer and being enveloped in Dare's magic. Hopefully, no embarrassing thoughts had transferred with it.

"It's on loan."

"From wh..." I trailed off as Julian Dare stepped out and into our space.

Unlike the two of us, Julian Dare's cloak didn't hide his face.

His gaze was entirely focused on me, even as he took the portfolio from his nephew.

I tugged my hood forward, making sure it was still fully in place. I trusted Dare with my life. But I wasn't sure I trusted my freedom to anyone he knew.

I remembered Will saying that the Dare family—and we'd been looking at Julian specifically at the time—would have collected Will while in my Awakening sketch. Left him in there, and put him in the Dare family library of treasures.

"The key?" Julian asked.

Dare pointed at the silver dragon. Julian lifted the wrapped bundle and examined the dragon in the shifting light. "Exquisite."

So the papers would be taken by Julian Dare to who knew where. Back to their island where they would release the men for questioning? Back to the Department?

A significant amount communication passed between them that I was not privy to. But even frequency users had facial expressions, and Julian Dare was very pleased about something.

There was a strong physical resemblance between the two. The positive kind, as they were both very good looking. And the two of them were obviously close. Julian Dare was the youngest of the older generation, nearly fifteen years younger than Alexander's father, Maximilian, and only ten or twelve years older than Alexander himself.

Dare's uncle wasn't part of the Legion, but he *was* part of the

* Negotiations with a Bad Hand *

Department, and therefore he answered to Stavros. He was a Hunter—part of a special operations task force designed to find and stop disturbances, and to apprehend magical criminals in the First Layer—which, for mages used to being surrounded by magic, was a magicless place fraught with peril.

The first and second times I had encountered Julian Dare had been in the First Layer. The second time he had been casing my neighborhood, trying to find me after my Awakening.

Hunters tended...not to be well loved. They were like the marshals of the Old West. Marshals who did their own thing and weren't well policed.

I would never feel bad about the hunter I had trapped in my gopher sketch the night after my Awakening.

Julian Dare stared at me. His gaze seemed to penetrate my hood. "If we had only taken you that day in the First Layer..." His gaze was dissecting, even though he shouldn't be able to fully see me beneath the enchanted cloak.

Taken me from the street, where I had laid, dying on the ground, with my brother dead beside me.

Alexander Dare had saved my life that day. And he had given me one last moment with my brother, using the limited container magic the Dares had been carrying.

Julian Dare had been in favor of leaving me to die.

I said nothing.

"You should let me take her now," Julian said, gaze never leaving me.

Tensing, I looked at Alexander. *Take me where?* He didn't respond, his unchanging gaze focused on his uncle.

"When she goes down, she will take everyone with her," Julian said, gaze narrowing on me as I turned sharply back in his direction.

"What does he—"

"Ignore him," Alexander responded mentally.

But it was hard to ignore someone who was staring at me like he wanted to put a slice of me on a dissection slide. Again, Will's words about the Dares reminded me of my potential danger.

"You should let me do it now," Julian said. "We could stage it to look like Kaine did it and cease waiting for a better opportunity."

"Do what now?" My mental voice was sounding increasingly uneasy.

"Enough," Alexander said, looking directly at Julian.

Julian smiled. There was something very wicked in his expression. "Don't you want to—"

"Julian." There was a warning in Alexander's voice.

Julian opened his mouth to reply, but both Dares suddenly tipped their heads to the side, and Julian smoothly tucked the bundle of Origin and Shadow Magic into his own cloak, then straightened his sleeves.

Chapter Seventeen

Marsgrove emerged from the trees a moment later, expression pinched and irritated. "Is this where we all convene before being blessed with eternal damnation?" he asked in a clipped voice.

He looked at the three of us, hoods still covering two of us from view. His gaze rested on me longer, expression deeply unpleasant.

"What are you doing, Axer?" he said finally, turning Dare's way. "There is no way you didn't raise that alert on purpose."

Dare bounced a ball of magic in his palm, the sleeve of the cloak revealing only a sliver of his wrist. He didn't respond audibly. He was standing as if he was in perfect health, but our connection was as open as it had ever been, and I could feel the agony of his half-healed wound.

Marsgrove looked between us and made a distinct noise of displeasure.

He pulled out a device and activated it. Immediately, a crocgoose and five birdsnakes that had been creeping closer to our area zoomed off in the opposing directions, as if a force field was pushing them away.

"We have five minutes for this *meeting*," Marsgrove said. He didn't want to be here. It was in every line of his body and face. "The Administration Magic will override the Chaos Magic for only that long, then the praetorians will be upon us."

Marsgrove did many things that he didn't want to do. It seemed to be his lot in life as the school administrator trying to field the chaos of the world from all sides.

"Now what—"

Marsgrove broke off abruptly, horror replacing distaste as he looked to the right of me. Tensing, I jerked around and followed his line of sight, certain that I would see Kaine sauntering toward us.

But the object of horror was not human.

The other animals might have scuppered, but our cursed vine had appeared out of nowhere and was launching itself upward into the air, then diving back into the ground. Performing lazy dolphin dives on an early Wednesday morn, devouring spells that were zipping around and heading toward the processing plant. Nothing to see here...

Nothing except a clearly dangerous creature that I had sent off on a quest to remove all our spell trails.

It had been, like, ten minutes. Tops. And the vine looked considerably thicker.

That...was maybe not good.

It opened its green mouth and smiled toothily at me, thorn fangs dripping with magic, as if it was showing me what it had done, expecting a kind word in return. I smiled painfully—lip splitting—and gave it a thumbs up before motioning it onward with a jerking hand. Its smile grew and it obediently dove into the ground, leaving behind only a displaced stone.

* Negotiations with a Bad Hand *

Marsgrove was looking at the stone as if some nightmare was coming true. "Where...? *No.*"

Realization formed on his face, and his gaze whipped to Dare. To *Dare* not to me. "*You.* Do you have any idea...?" Marsgrove looked on the verge of absolutely *losing* it. With *Dare.* Not *me.* The absolute unreality of this made me nearly lose track of the conversation.

Dare tipped his covered head in acknowledgment.

"We *will* be having a *long* talk," Marsgrove bit out. "You do *not* understand the path you are walking. As *stupid* as your—" He swiped a hand through the air, cutting himself off. Which was good, because whatever he'd been about to say had made Julian go deadly still. "I will back the measures against you myself, Axer, do you understand?"

Dare's gaze was calculating beneath his hood. I wondered, for a moment, if I was still the only one who could see it. "We all must do as we must."

Marsgrove looked ready to explode. "Is that what this is?"

"Of course not. You said you wanted a bit of aid, Philly," Julian said lightly, almost rakishly, stillness gone. "And here it is presented." He waved a hand in my direction.

I tensed, anticipation thrumming now. Dare had said... And Marsgrove was here... That could only mean...

Marsgrove grimaced, and my stopped magic beat heavily against its occlusions.

"This subject isn't finished, Julian. Your entire family and I will be having words." Marsgrove withdrew Olivia's scarf.

I took a step toward it automatically.

"Stay right there, Crown," he said in a warning tone.

It was hard to stop. I wanted nothing more than to have it in my palm.

My head jerked toward Dare, who inclined his own at me. This is why he said we'd find the scarf in the Midlands. He had called Marsgrove to him.

Anticipation thrummed hard now, making me shift on my feet.

Marsgrove's mouth was set in hard lines. It was apparent that he did not want to do this, whatever *this* was about to be, but he was holding the scarf palm up in his hand.

I could see the cracked magic at the edges of the threads. Marsgrove had been trying to get through to the magic. Trying and failing. I darted my gaze around the group.

Julian looked extremely amused.

Dare radiated boredom, like only he could—bouncing his magic between his hands and lazily watching us. Anyone fooled by that was an idiot, though. He could flick that magic at any of us before we could react.

Chapter Seventeen

It was a reminder—like a loaded revolver carelessly twirled on a tabletop.

He'd known. He'd known or had anticipated that Marsgrove had been trying to unlock the magic in the scarf. He'd been counting on this gambit the whole time, maybe ever since Marsgrove had taken the scarf from me.

It was a reminder—a constant reminder—of the dangerous mind he possessed.

And—with my gaze once more locked on the scarf as Marsgrove gripped it—I might owe Dare an extra apology. When everything returned to normal, I was making Dare an *army*.

"Crown, look at me," Marsgrove said, voice a bit harsh.

I did.

"Do *exactly* as I tell you and nothing more."

I nodded, eager to do anything that would put the scarf in my hand.

He pulled out a ball that seemed alive with electrical currents flowing around it. "Touch this. It displays magic for those maintaining contact with it. And it will help you get by your..." He grimaced. "*Blockage*."

I touched the electric ball and all of the magic in me stood on point, as if it had been electrified and was awaiting command. As if I could diagnose and debug everything that was wrong with me.

All I needed was the key.

Information on my internal systems filed by faster than I could comprehend it. I shook my head to clear it. That wasn't the important thing here.

I touched my other hand to Olivia's scarf. And I could *feel* her. Instantaneously.

A sob ripped from me. Like a dry creek bed that had been drained of its last drop, and here, at its last moment to survive, it was being deluged with rain.

It had been a helpless spiraling of thought in the back of my mind since I'd lost her. Trying to reconnect to her through broken magic, threats, and trying to control myself. Reaching out for what I had lost.

And here she was again. Alive. The living thread of her thrumming through the fabric.

Marsgrove's expression was hard to read as he watched me, but the overwhelming sense of disapproval that he usually radiated was dimmed. There was almost a measure of compassion leaking into his gaze.

I looked down at the scarf and took a deep, shaking breath. I sent a trickle of the ball's magic through the threads.

Information and magic burst back, forming in a cloud before my eyes. Since I wasn't using my own magic, everything was somewhat muted. The electric ball made it so that the experience of using it felt removed, like watching a scene through a clear glass shield. I could still see it, but I was

* Negotiations with a Bad Hand *

almost isolated from being a true participant.

Interconnecting threads pulled, trying to grab my attention away from my main task. All of the spells that had been put into place were laid out for me to view.

I had watched Delia and Lifen create the scarves. I had watched them create the new comm pieces. They were masters at this craft, where I was a bystander, at best. But I *had* captured the link to Olivia into the scarf during the battle today. Even if it was a pure intuitive burst in the midst of an adrenaline-fueled madness, I had captured the magic myself, and that gave me the ability I needed to do this.

Unweaving the pieces that I needed, and exposing the links of the others, I laid everything out like an engineer with a circuit board.

"You leashed yourself to it." Marsgrove's expression was tight, but there was also something else there, another expression I had never seen directed at me—concern?

I lowered my gaze back to my task, carefully parting the magic. Marsgrove's electric ball made things much easier in many ways. The separation from any emotion let me bypass things that would have ordinarily made me stop to examine. That might have made me luxuriate in the interconnectivity that once more was—

"There will be an *end* to these types of activities." That sounded far more like the Marsgrove I knew. "When we are finished with—"

"Phillip." I had never heard Dare call Marsgrove by his first name.

Marsgrove didn't look away from me, but his words were directed to the side. "You will watch your tone, Axer."

Dare continued to bounce magic on his palm.

"Yes, watch your tone, Ax." Julian seemed to find all of this highly entertaining.

Marsgrove's penetrative gaze remained firmly on me. We still weren't friends. But I had saved his life twice earlier. And he'd destroyed the golem after defeating Raphael, saving me from certain imprisonment.

I wasn't sure what game he was playing with me now. He could have wiped his hands of me earlier today without breaking the oath Olivia had tied him to.

"Can you decode the location?" He asked tightly.

The connections spread out before me in a complicated series of pathways.

"Yes."

Marsgrove withdrew another device, and a spherical astrolabe bloomed above his palm. Some of the rings gently whirled, while others more intensely circulated the ball in the center. The layers of the world.

Extracting Olivia's location required me to use some of my own magic.

Chapter Seventeen

It couldn't be helped considering how the spell was hooked into me, and it was a study in crippling pain and concentration. In the Midlands, the external chaos was feeding on the internal deep chaos inside of me. Some of it was helping, some wasn't. Thankfully, Marsgrove's electric ball was doing most of the work, requiring me to use only a limited amount of the magic that *could* bypass my blockages.

I swallowed and urged one of the spells closer, then another. They zoomed forward until the feeling that I had placed within the threads of the scarf while on the battle field bloomed before me, waiting for me to parse it into another language.

The magic swirled around me allowing me to feel its intentions and to test mine. A feeling of calm settled as the magic clicked and an intuitive path formed.

I pulled my hand away from the electric ball and blue light hovered over my hand—long tracers of light. I extended my fingers to Marsgrove and he gingerly placed his device on top of my palm.

I coaxed the threads to part slowly, like long beads hanging from a doorway, and put the astrolabe in the middle of the mass.

Four of the rings on the astrolabe immediately stilled.

I lifted a particularly vibrant Kelly green spell thread and wrapped it around my finger, then extended my finger to the astrolabe.

Passing through the outer orbits, I touched the third ring, centered between the others. It whirled beneath my finger. There. A fiery point of magic marked a spot. Removing my finger, the other rings started rotating again. On the spherical plane of the Third Layer's ring, a dot remained, like a tiny fingerprint of grease on metal.

That was where Olivia had been taken. That was where she was being held. .

I held it up to Marsgrove. He carefully took it from me.

"I know where that is," Marsgrove said, gently collapsing the astrolabe and slipping it into his pocket.

"It will be a trap," Dare said, almost casually.

"Undoubtedly."

"I'm coming," I said automatically

"Not a chance." Marsgrove sounded anything *but* casual.

"You need—"

He grabbed me by the upper arm. "Do you know what will happen to this school if you are found leaving it?"

"Phillip," Dare said.

Marsgrove's gaze didn't leave mine.

Relief in seeing that Olivia was still alive vied with impotence at being unable to go to her. The remnants of her location swirled around the

* Negotiations with a Bad Hand *

whorls on my palm.

"You will doom campus, should you step foot from it. Being found here, tonight, would be dire. Being found off campus? Everyone would suffer."

Olivia...

"Do you want your friends here to suffer, Ren?"

His use of my first name shocked me almost as much as the query regarding my friends' well-being. Marsgrove never called me by my name.

"No." And there was something in his expression that I *could* read. "But you already know that."

"Yes." He tipped his head. "That was born out today. And you *will* help them. By letting me find her."

I looked at him. Olivia was his cousin, and unlike Helen, Marsgrove *did* care for her. I could read it on him. And although we might not like each other, Marsgrove was...beyond competent in battle. When Raphael had been toying with me earlier, he hadn't been toying with Marsgrove. And Marsgrove had won.

And...maybe this was another instance of using teamwork. Letting others help, so I would not be making the disastrous mistake of haring off on my own.

Like...haring off to the Midlands with Dare.

I pushed back my hood just enough so that the spell wouldn't impede Marsgrove seeing me.

"Okay."

Relief spread across his face, nearly too fast to catch. He nodded. "You didn't lose everything today, Crown. Keep your head on straight for the next few days and avoid any attention you can."

Didn't lose everything? No, things could have been worse, absolutely. The body count could have been far, *far* higher. But I couldn't be happy about losing Olivia.

However...I looked at Marsgrove's expression through a different lens—as an ally instead of an antagonist. He was still clearly uncomfortable with a number of things about me, but he also looked...sympathetic. And like I was an actual student here who was under his protection.

I stared at him, lips parting.

I had always been an interloper to him before—scheming my way into student life. But today... I had protected campus. Protected it, at my own expense. And that seemed to have made a difference to Phillip Marsgrove.

Dare still looked outwardly bored, but there was a crease at the corner of each eye that said he was amused at my realization.

Julian, though... Julian's expression was concerning. There was amusement, yes, but also a glittering regard in his eyes as he examined me.

Chapter Seventeen
Like someone who had found a useful tool.

I had seen that expression on way too many faces today—on all the ones that contained neither affection nor terror. I pressed my lips together and pulled my hood back into place.

Julian's smile grew, which didn't reassure me at all, as he couldn't possibly see me now under the hood of the cloak, yet was reacting as if he could still read me just fine.

Julian cocked his head, listening to something in the distance. "I'm off. Phillip." He nodded to Marsgrove. Then he looked at me and the corners of his eyes creased in some morbid amusement. "Origin Mage."

My breath caught. Julian stepped away and disappeared in a tile slide.

And then there were three.

Marsgrove looked between us. Continuing his bizarre shift in attitude, he looked furious with Dare, not me.

"And what is your play now, Axer? This was a stupid choice for you, regardless of the outcome. You'll never make it back once the Chaos Magic reigns again. You have a *single* minute remaining. Kaine was playing with you on the way here. I can feel the echoes of both paths."

Dare didn't look concerned. Something was flashing between the two of them.

Marsgrove shook his head, mouth tight. "You court disaster."

Dare said nothing audibly. Marsgrove narrowed his eyes. "You get one. You will not get another. *Ever*, Axer. This is it."

Dare dipped his head and held out his hand. Marsgrove placed a black disk in his free palm.

Marsgrove stepped back and gave me a look filled with conflicting emotions, and issued a single statement, "I will find her," then disappeared into a slide.

The scarf—and Olivia's location—disappeared with him.

I swallowed, and the empty pit in my stomach expanded. It was the right choice. The adult choice. In my present condition I was magically unable to help Olivia like I needed to in the amount of time it would take. And an option that was motivated and capable had presented himself. It would be fine.

It would be a choice filled with regrets.

No. It would be fi—

"Oh, Ren," came Dare's deep voice. "Such a long face."

I turned to him, ready to say something equally unkind, but he was holding the same ball of ultramarine magic in his hand that he'd been tossing back and forth. But now, the center held a spark. The spark that had been in Olivia's scarf—the remnants of the magic she had used from my protection butterfly, and the magic I had channeled on the battle field to

* Negotiations with a Bad Hand *

secure a living tie to her.

My gaze jerked to his. "How—?"

"No one watches the person who isn't arguing. Especially when performing an extraction spell on a piece of magic they no longer need. It's not the same as—"

"I love you," I said fervently, staring at the orb while shifting on my feet, wanting nothing more than to launch myself in his direction. "You are all-knowing and awesome and I'll never doubt you again."

When I looked up, the expression on his face was one that I was unfamiliar with—the ultramarine of his eyes nearly swallowed in black. Just as quickly, he recovered, and threw the ball to me. It burst upon my palm, soaking into my skin and connecting with the remnants of the spell magic still there. A small origami balloon formed, sucking the magic inside before flattening. Unassuming. A spare bit of folded paper.

But it was nothing even close to *spare*.

I could feel the spark of *Olivia*. The magic that had been connected to the butterfly life cycle I had made her—the one that she had used to sacrifice herself in my place—was *in my palm*. Marsgrove hadn't needed that bit of magic to discern her location, and even though he'd probably notice it missing soon enough, he didn't *need* it. Dare had taken it and given it back to me.

I looked at him, heart clenching and unable to give voice to it.

"Come." He gently pushed me toward the tree line. "We have to get back to the Ninth Circle as quickly as possible. These don't work in the Midlands," Dare said, holding up the black disk in one hand, and softly moving me forward with the other. "The Administration has been trying to get them to work in here for years."

"What is it?"

"It's a—" Dare abruptly stopped speaking, and shoved me right. "*Go.*"

He raised his arms, the cloak giving him an eerie silhouette. The shadows parted, then formed in a wave in front of him.

I ran. Destruction rained behind me.

Chapter Eighteen

SHADOWS ON MY SOUL

BREATHING HEAVILY and hitting another branch with my shoulder, I dodged a root and the grip of a gnarled shadow.

Kaine was gaining ground. I could feel the shadows slipping from existence between us.

He laughed in soulless delight.

"I can feel your fear. Delicious." His voice was just beyond the shell of my ear. An audible shadow slipping into the hollow. "And I know the secrets of your terror."

Nightmares formed in shadowlike images in front of me. My friends dying, my family broken at my feet, Christian's lifeless body, my creations crushed and burned. The visions morphed and took shape as my reactions gave them life.

My motions were seizing, panic gripping me again, freezing my muscles as my legs stuttered over a beautifully manicured lawn that connected to a charming cottage somewhere leagues away. Small shadows from between the blades of grass stabbed upward, upending me even more. Panic, terror...my vision started to tunnel. My third panic attack for the day—though this one...*this one* I now had the experience to identify as it closed around me.

No.

I slashed my hand through a shadow in front of me. It whirled inward along my hand's path like sliced fog, then reformed its shape, wrapping around my palm, cutting off the blood flow and trying to seep under my skin.

Stumbling, but still running, I pinched at the shadow, trying to pull it off, like a bloodsucking leech that had a grip on my fears—raking over them with tiny, barbed teeth.

* Shadows on My Soul *

I slashed a mental hand through the fog closing in on my thoughts, and, though it felt far too similar to the same lack of result, it cut through enough that I could grab hold of something besides all-consuming panic.

Everything in me wanted to open up the Earth and have it swallow Kaine whole. To shoot him into another level of existence, or cast him right from it.

"Do it. Do it, Origin Mage," the shadow whispered in my ear. "Show yourself."

It was almost too much. Too many pressing needs crushing me at once—get rid of the fears, excise Kaine, protect Dare, myself, stay free to find Olivia, be free of the *fears*...

I looked at my palm. At the shadow trying to dig into the whorls where the connection magic to Olivia had swirled. Where Neph had laced a small pool of magic, in case of need. A last resort.

If I wanted to survive, I had no choice but to control my reaction to the shadows, the shapes, and the fear. Dare and I just had to reach the Ninth Circle.

The fog at the edges of the Midlands came into view and so did Dare, sprinting on my left, cloak flowing outward like shadowy wings. Something was reaching for him from above...

Now.

I blasted the magic in my palm outward in both directions, violently thrusting Kaine backward. Shadowed wings slowed him before he crashed. He laughed as we breached the fog.

"I will wait, little mage," he called. "It won't be long."

Then we were through the fog. The painful backlash of using the magic was spiraling tighter, inward, squeezing my core like a noose and making me stumble with weakening knees. Dare pressed his palm against my neck and pulled me against him. The black disk sparked against my skin, and everything went dark.

~*~

I blinked, then blinked again, as Medical formed into view. We were standing in an empty room and a small red light was flashing furiously in the corner.

"They'll be here in ten seconds." Dare put a hand under my arm and pulled me forward, not stopping for me to gain my footing, just carrying my weight right along until I did.

Striding quickly down the hall—with me hurrying alongside—he swirled off his cloak and reversed it, turning it into a collared white shirt that he slipped back on in one smooth motion. He didn't wait for me to do the same—without breaking stride, he unhooked my cloak pin and pulled my

Chapter Eighteen

cloak off. Pressing it between his hands, it shrunk into a chunky black bag. He handed it back to me, and I looped it over my head and across my frame, all without pausing.

"Do you have any shadows on you?" he asked, voice clipped.

I jerked my palm upward. It was clear. My breath came in pants. "No. No." The shadow must not have survived the trip.

Footsteps furiously echoed around the bend ahead.

Dare hooked a hand over my shoulder and opened a door, twirling us both inside. He carefully closed the door.

Seconds later, running footsteps banged past. I leaned my forehead against the cold metal of the door, panting.

"Emergency medical device," Dare murmured in explanation. "Brings whoever is touching it right to Medical. The cloaks should have hidden our presence enough in the room for it to appear to be a malfunction. Give me your palm."

I did, without pause. He examined it critically, pushing the sleeve of my shirt up. "Clean," he said, though his tone was skeptical. His gaze grew more intense. "Anywhere else?"

I shook my head, but uneasiness gripped me.

He looked grim. "There is no scan for them. You just get used to the feel of them, and deal each a dark death as it shows itself."

The idea of carrying around a sliver of Kaine's darkness made me nauseous.

He touched a ward at the side—a protection and anti-eavesdropping ward—and squeezed my hand. He grabbed an energy cookie from a medical basket on the counter and a bottle of salve, putting them both in my hands. I unwrapped the cookie and shoved it in my mouth and was trying to squeeze some of the salve into my shaking hand at the same time as I chewed. The salve immediately soothed some of the burn.

More footsteps pounded past the room.

Dare had a bottled curative potion in hand as he stepped backward and dropped into a chair next to a bed. I blinked, turning my head slightly. There was a person in the bed. My gaze traced up from the tented feet under the blanket to the person's face. I jolted, hit my head against a shelf, and swore.

Constantine's eyes glinted in brief amusement at my surprise, before he turned his unamused attention back to Dare, who was leisurely tipping the potion into his own mouth. "She can stay. You can leave."

"The wards have to be reset," Dare said, leaning back in his chair and tossing the empty bottle into the trash bin across the room. "Greyskull told me earlier. If you want to stay out of Medical, that is, when I leave." It was all said casually, but neither of their expressions reflected that ease.

* Shadows on My Soul *

Constantine continued the heated stare-off for a few tense moments, before turning to me. "Field trip?"

I looked between them. "Something like that."

A second chair whirred into existence. Dare hadn't moved, but completely free of his dampening cloak now, I could feel his magic in the furniture's addition.

"We have another fifteen minutes until we can leave. Take a seat, Ren."

I looked between them and reluctantly sat. No one said anything for a few stressed moments.

"This is all horribly familiar," I said. My fingertips skittered over the origami balloon clutched in my other palm.

Constantine reached out and turned over my hand. He didn't say anything, though his lips quirked the slightest bit as he looked at the paper. "You found your friend? And while holding Alexander's lead."

I frowned. "Con."

"Still think you are going after Verisetti?" Dare said. "I'm afraid disappointment must suit you once more."

Constantine's expression darkened dangerously. I shifted in my seat. If Dare were anyone else, I would be afraid for his health. Constantine turned to me, expression demanding.

I wrapped my arms tightly against my chest. "Dean Marsgrove has Olivia's location. He's going to find her."

He narrowed his eyes at me and leaned back. "Explain."

I nervously summed up the trip and meeting with Marsgrove, trying not to give away anything I shouldn't. I kept sending glances at Dare, but he seemed content to say nothing, and he didn't try to alter my story in any way.

Why he was letting me tell Constantine anything was unnerving. My nervousness increased, and I spewed more information as a result.

Constantine's narrowed gaze focused on me, completely pinning me underneath. His head tilted toward Dare the barest bit at the end. His lips turned down, as if he was biting back a remark, and his eyes unfocused.

Almost like they were talking via frequency. But there was no way.

Doctor Greyskull took that moment to enter the room.

Greyskull's gaze took in all three of us—our positions and the magic in the room. A series of complicated expressions switched rapidly on his face. I looked at the wards of the room to see why.

The healing lines were strengthening *fast*. Far quicker than they had earlier. Far quicker than I had ever seen them. I looked down at my skin. Huh. I probably should be in a lot more pain still. I had thought the energy biscuit had just had extra mojo in it.

Greyskull sighed. One of his tattoos slithered up to the opening of his

Chapter Eighteen

shirt and peered out, then ducked back down. It reminded me of the vine, a little.

The carnivorous vine that we had unleashed on campus. *Great.*

A pinch made me jolt. I rubbed my arm and shot a dark look at Constantine.

"What?" Constantine asked, voice deliberately guileless.

I sighed and let my hand drop. "Nothing. Just regretting some of my life's choices."

"You are too young for that yet, hmmm, Miss Crown?" Greyskull asked, going through the motions of checking all the stats and spells in the room. "I see you've been here for thirty minutes, or so, Mr. Dare?"

It was ludicrously obvious that Greyskull knew exactly what had been going on. And that we hadn't been here for even close to that amount of time.

"About that amount, yes," Dare said easily.

Constantine's cheek twitched in irritation.

Dare was playing with magic again. Not *quite* managing boredom, he wasn't hiding it as well as usual—he looked like a professional poker player who for once couldn't hide the fact that he knew he had a winning hand.

Adrenaline junkie.

"And you haven't yet been entirely healed of that earlier wound, I see." Greyskull looked pointedly at Dare's middle.

"It's fine."

Greyskull sighed and snapped his fingers. A lotus flower appeared on Dare's lap. Dare picked it up and lifted his shirt. The gash across his abs was ugly and sluggishly healing. He set the flower on top and it melted, white seeping into the deep slice. He pulled his shirt back down and raised a brow at me.

I cleared my throat and looked elsewhere—at Greyskull's face, which was amused. Then at Constantine, who was significantly less so.

Pounding on the door made us all look in that direction.

"Open up, Doctor Greyskull. By the power of Statute 9.143.35, I must immediately question *under oath* the minors in your company."

Doctor Greyskull didn't move to open the door, but a wave of his hand slid a small screen into the windowpane. "They have already been questioned. I was present for Mr. Leandred's interrogation."

I looked at Constantine, wondering how that had gone. Constantine's gaze remained fixed on the official, but his fingers nearest to me moved in a 'so-so' motion on the bed, answering my query.

"I don't care about Leandred. Any idiot can see he hasn't moved. The other two. Send them out."

"I'm afraid I can't do that, Administrator Tenk," Greyskull said, his voice apologetic. "These two students are directly helping Mr. Leandred, and are needed here for additional time."

"The Origin Mage? *Right.* Move aside, Greyskull."

Greyskull lifted a brow. "Origin Mage? I was under the impression that she hadn't shown the inclination on the test Praetorian Kaine illegally administered earlier."

"We all know what bunk that is. I saw the footage—something stopped her, but it wasn't her lack of abilities. Send them out. If we give up the girl, I'm sure our champion, Mr. Dare, will only receive a slight reprimand and be sent on his way back to the competition tomorrow."

I swallowed.

"Administrator Tenk," a smooth, new voice asked. "What seems to be the problem?"

Stuart Leandred appeared behind Tenk in the hallway. He was like a penny that rolled along the floor, switching direction, slipping into the cracks, and turning up when least—or most—expected.

"Senator Leandred, sir. You aren't needed in these matters. Anyone not a student or directly involved in student affairs was supposed to exit the Magiaduct at sundown."

Stuart made a conciliatory gesture. "I was given direct permission by Chancellor Barrie to remain the night since my son is inside that room."

"Your son has nothing to do with the current situation, Senator Leandred," the administrator said grimly. "Stay with him, of course. But both of you—" He pointed at Dare and at me. "Out here, now."

"Again, I'm afraid I can't let you do that, Administrator Tenk," Greyskull said, his voice calm, even as his tattoos slithered and morphed in a less pacifying fashion.

"Doctor Greyskull, it is interesting that you are standing up for the girl, in light of recent matters," Tenk said.

Greyskull tipped his head pleasantly. "Is it? I was questioned myself quite thoroughly earlier. I chose to do so by way of the Truth Stone even. I believe you were there."

Suddenly, there was something very *hard* about Greyskull under the kindly doctor smile. It reminded me of what Dare liked to say about healing magic and death magic. Healers could be more dangerous than people liked to believe.

I could picture Greyskull engaged on a battlefield, casually injecting death with simple touches—one tattoo shot at a time. Or at a fight club—all wiry, lean strength, tattoos, and vicious attitude.

My Doctor Greyskull crush? Still intact, it seemed.

"I was there." The official glanced distastefully at something on Greyskull's wrist. "Be glad you wear that."

Chapter Eighteen

"Every day, I'm overjoyed at its existence," he answered sincerely.

I looked at his wrist—at the thin black chain wrapped around it. It looked as benign as any other decoration in the Second Layer—assuredly magic of some kind, but unexceptional looking. But Delia's looked ordinary as well, and it tracked her magic—and neutered it, if necessary.

I wondered if Greyskull's chain had anything to do with whatever vows he had made to work at Excelsine. It wouldn't be a secret that he had been friends with Raphael to anyone with access to whatever the equivalent of a yearbook was at Excelsine.

At some point, I was going to need to look through one of those.

"As a medical professional, I cannot allow you to disrupt the healing in this room," his voice rang with truth, and he casually held up his arm. A glint of light glittered on the dark chain. "As I said, these two students are directly helping Mr. Leandred, and my patients are my primary concern."

"Those two helping each other?" The official's eyes narrowed on both boys. "I don't think so."

I sneaked a glance at them. Dare and Constantine both looked bored. Far more like the nineteen-year-olds they were, rather than the warrior and manipulator masks they usually wore.

Poker faces, both of them.

"Well, then what are they doing right now?" Greyskull pointed out. "One must be helping the other, no matter what you believe to be the truth."

"Cute. I want—"

"It doesn't matter what you want," Stuart smoothly interrupted in a calm voice. "Today was an exceptional day. And if old prejudices are put aside for the good of—"

"You are either blind or *complicit*."

"I am neither." Stuart smiled less pleasantly, steel in his voice. "All you need to do is look at the magic." He waved a hand at the stats in the room that could be seen from the hall. "The metrics are right there. Easy enough to read." He pointed at us, then at the room. "And the magic has shown an increase of fifteen percent since I was here an hour ago. Fifteen percent. If they had only been here for the five minutes you are claiming, the increase wouldn't be so dramatic."

I looked around, intrigued by this fact.

Neither Constantine nor Dare looked surprised by Stuart's statement, but interestingly, neither looked all that pleased either.

The official looked as if he had a lemon lodged in his gums. "Sorcery."

"That is certainly something that you can bring up in your review," Stuart said, clapping a hand on the man's shoulder and steering him away from the window. "Meanwhile, how about you track down the perpetrators of the crime you say has been committed."

"This isn't—" The window closed on the rest of his statement.

The argument continued in the hall for a full minute before the official stomped off.

Stuart gave a final wave to the man, then entered the room. The wards let him enter, though Greyskull narrowed his eyes at whatever the stats were telling him.

Stuart looked at each of us, in turn. I didn't know what sort of information he was gaining, but as with the case of Helen Price, intelligence hadn't skipped a generation.

Stuart and Dare said nothing as they looked at each other. Stuart's expression was remote, but friendly, like only a politician could master. Dare's boredom held a thin edge of distaste.

"Leave." Constantine's voice brooked less argument than it had with Dare. Of the two of them, Constantine very obviously disliked his father more. For a moment, there was a common enemy between the two boys. Then Constantine turned to Dare. "You too."

Dare leaned back in his chair and crossed his legs at the ankle. "Can't. Doctor's orders."

Constantine gripped the sheet covering his legs and something dark flashed between the two of them.

Stuart turned to me, forcing my attention away. "Miss Crown. So intriguing, seeing you here again."

I swallowed, but nodded. "Good evening."

"It's well past that. Shouldn't you be abed?"

"Probably?"

"Doctor Greyskull?"

"Another ten minutes will set these new wards. Your son should be free in the morning. It's a miracle," he said lightly.

"Yes," Stuart said, eyes going hazy, accessing some mental magic. "Might I speak with you elsewhere?"

"Of course." Greyskull looked at me. "Miss Crown. I trust you can find your way back?"

"Yes. Thank you."

Greyskull paused at the door. "There are...tidings on the wind. Perhaps it would be best if you left as soon as ten minutes have passed?"

I looked at Dare and Constantine, then nodded.

The door shut and the two older men disappeared from view.

"You court disaster," Constantine bit out.

I turned to awkwardly defend myself, but Constantine was speaking to Dare, his focus solely on his roommate.

"More than you?" Dare rolled his head around his neck, working the

Chapter Eighteen

kinks out. "I know what you are trying to do."

"Do you?" There was a thin, edged snarl on Constantine's lips. He turned to me. "Playing with the praetorians? I thought you had more sense."

"Whoa. We're fine. Everything's fine," I said, alarmed at this shift.

"Are you? You are entrusting your friends to your enemies. I had thought more of you."

Shocked and hurt, I shrunk back in my chair. "I..." It was true. Marsgrove had always been an enemy, and vice versa, regardless of the cautious change in classification that might be occurring on both sides.

Constantine opened his mouth to say more, but nothing emerged. He jerked his chin toward Dare, daggers in his eyes. But Constantine was in no position to enact any sort of revenge for the silencing spell. Not that either of them was incapable of slitting someone's throat with an empty Jell-O cup, but Dare was in mostly decent form and Constantine was still on death's door. It was not even close to a fight Constantine could win.

"It's either that, or we make the kind doctor sprint back here posthaste to try and salvage your mangled body," Dare said pleasantly. "I thought you might prefer this option after all the effort Ren has gone through to patch you back together at her own expense."

And...that was that. We spent an *excruciatingly* silent eight minutes in the room with me trying to look anywhere but at the two of them.

At the end, when the timer beeped, I practically leapt from my chair.

Constantine grabbed my hand. Complicated and twisted emotions ran through our connection, but underlining all of them was regret. My shoulders eased and I patted his hand. "It's okay."

He released my hand and leaned back against his pillows, then closed his eyes, dismissing us completely.

Even with the tense silence, the healing wards in the room had strengthened further with just that small amount of time.

"So," I asked Dare as we closed the door and started down the hall. "You didn't remove his vocal chords, right?" It was half joke, and half concern.

"If only I could get away with that here. The spell released as soon as we stepped from the room."

"He didn't mean it," I said quietly.

Dare looked at me in disbelief. "He meant every word."

"Well, yes, he was upset at whatever he was upset about, but it's not like I haven't been second guessing myself every moment of the last twenty minutes."

His fingers touched my side, a fleeting brush. "You did the right thing. You can barely create a spark of magic, and Marsgrove is skilled and has a vested interest in finding her."

"Yeah." I pulled a hand through my hair and focused on my surroundings.

Plan A of our scheme had included Neph meeting me in an empty room at Medical, where we would switch back and I would exit with Neph. Plan B should have had Neph coming to Medical to dump my double and to leave.

I now understood *how* Dare had planned we would get to Medical unnoticed. And what an excellent idea it had been. Neph had dumped my double here somewhere, using her student healer status to access the level. If people had been watching Neph—and I was sure that they had—we were at least on a timeline to indicate I had been in Medical since the fireworks ended.

Clever, brilliant Dare.

Of course, Plan B meant that none of my friends should now remember any of this, to save them if questioned, but I'd cross that bridge later.

"Be careful who you trust," Dare said, as we walked.

"Are you going to warn me off Constantine again? I know you don't trust him."

It occurred to me, though, that Constantine could have easily given us up. Or given up Dare. A few words to the official would have ended the game completely. Dare had to recognize that.

Dare examined me. Looking as if he were debating something. "I don't trust him, in general. But...he is ruled by his emotions. He can be trusted with something when he shows emotion for it."

I had never encountered anyone else who saw him that way. Most thought he was either completely soulless or just waiting to be "saved."

I nodded, though I wasn't sure to what Dare was specifically referring in this case. My expression must have clued him in.

Dare sighed. "He alerted me. When Godfrey was trying to take you on the battlefield."

I stared at him, shocked. But my memory supported the notion. Constantine had looked toward the Midlands—where Dare had been at the time—twice while trying to stall Godfrey. And he'd seemed especially certain when after his last glance toward the Midlands he had told Godfrey that Godfrey would die. Mages who'd had frequencies for years still tended to look in the direction of the person they were speaking with, their eyes feeling the tug of the shared magic.

"You *do* talk over frequency." It was like learning that two countries that had been fighting for a millennium had been secretly playing tag in the backyard all that time.

Dare sighed again. "*No.* Something else. Something you can't just get rid

Chapter Eighteen

of, once shared."

My brain stalled out on that for a moment.

Both boys were insanely private. Neither of them were the type to share any lasting connection freely. I wasn't even sure that Constantine *had* a frequency. I had never seen evidence of it. Even the magic that he used to link with his conquests were temporary spells that left no lasting ties.

That these two had some secret way to communicate...

Meant they had been *friends*. But then, I supposed that made some sort of sense—few people hated another so personally if they hadn't at one time been close.

I decided to roll with it and freak out later along with everything else.

"So...he called you? That...seems like a good idea? Wasn't everyone calling everyone else once frequencies went back online?"

"You don't understand, I know." He gave me a tight smile. "The last time he used that connection was when..." He shook his head. "To overcome his hatred and use it again? I know what he can be trusted with."

"He kind of hates everyone?"

Dare's eyes were hooded. "No, he hates a tiny fraction of the population, and doesn't *care* about the other 99.9 percent. And he cannot be trusted with people or things he doesn't care about. *Ever.* He'll wipe the entire board clean of those pieces as easily as drawing breath, while focusing his actual attention on the pieces that have provoked some emotion from him."

Based on every interaction I had observed with Constantine, Dare's remarks seemed pretty accurate. What he had done today on the battlefield stood as a good data point.

"I think he'd save Will," I ventured.

"Of course he would. Because Will's attached to you."

I blinked.

"Which is why I'm even entertaining the repellent plans that I'm going to have to implement if Marsgrove fails. Constantine will protect you. He will save your roommate. He will try to kill the man who murdered his mother, and he will try to have me captured. All in that order of importance."

He was looking straight ahead, but he must have seen my jaw sag because he smiled and added, "I can take care of myself—especially when I'm fourth on that list." He looked amused. "There won't be enough time for him to do anything to me if he wants to accomplish his other goals."

I shook my head. I'd think about all of that later.

"Dr. Greyskull knows...a lot."

"Yes, he does."

His tone said all I needed to know about whether Dare knew about

* Shadows on My Soul *

Greyskull's split loyalties, and the reasons he remained on campus.

We exited Medical, the wards slipping over us, and stepped into the stairwell.

"Outside—the thing with Kai—" My voice broke off into a strange gurgle as he wrapped his fingers around mine without breaking stride.

"They can listen here if a student leaves a device."

A remembrance of the devices in the walls of the Second Layer Depot skittered through my mind along with all of the other crazy thoughts cascading through my head; the feel of his fingers around mine, the heat of his palm, the absolutely gobsmacked look on the face of the medical attendant who was passing us on the stairs, the increasingly amused look on Dare's face.

"You heard all those thoughts, didn't you?" I asked mentally, somewhere between mortified and horrified.

"Maybe."

The look on his face said definitely. I locked down as many stray thoughts as I could manage. But lots of insidious ones kept slipping through.

"Why are you holding my hand?"

I kind of needed him to stop. Everything I was thinking was slipping through—I could feel the loss like valuable items fumbled down a sink drain.

"Skin contact completes the circuit of magic so it is only the two of us. We are still using the communication thread your friends set up in the armbands, but with no outside interference, no chance of being overheard. Your friend Dagfinn is certainly paranoid enough that the regular pathway is secure, but this makes it unassailable."

Okay. That made complete sense. Sure.

I tried not to panic. Or sweat.

"Kaine. The thing with the metal dragon," I said a little desperately, trying to get back on track.

I squeezed his hand, as if that would only allow the correct thoughts to go through.

"I wrapped everything into a shadow. Kaine is naturally resistant to all sorts of magic. It makes him very dangerous. But he is frequently blind to his own."

I mulled his answer for a moment—trying not to dwell on increasingly terrified thoughts of Kaine being *resistant* to magic.

"The shadow does...what?"

"It hides what is underneath. Julian would never make it off campus with the papers or key otherwise. With the shadow, the package will look unexceptional to the guards."

Chapter Eighteen

"Won't Kaine know—"

"Julian is already gone. He took the opportunity while Kaine chased us. Kaine will have discovered this by now, though he won't be able to prove anything."

"And Julian will release the men in the papers?"

"Yes. And deal with them."

We passed another person who stared strangely at our hands, so I stepped closer to Dare and stuffed them behind our bodies.

"You think that is going to work?" His mental voice sounded really amused.

"No. Yes? Shut up. This is going to be all over the dorms by the time we get up there and I'm sending all of the people who ask, to you."

"You can try."

A little growl escaped my mouth.

"So, Kaine—is he resistant to Origin Magic?"

"Untested. I'm sure he is dying to try it out."

"He scares me," I admitted.

"He should." Dare's mental voice was grim. *"There's a reason that the Department's activities have remained shrouded for so long. His magic doesn't just hide his own presence."*

I thought of Raphael, who would have been taken about a decade ago, right after he graduated Excelsine. Kaine would have been eighteen at the time, maybe? My age.

"Was he there when Raphael was?"

"No one knows where Kaine came from. Whispered opinion is that he was raised in the secret testing facilities that don't officially exist."

Horror filled me.

I had so many questions, but we had reached the top of the stairs. I disengaged my hand. No way was I walking out there holding Alexander Dare's hand. Though it would likely shift rumors away from other things. Still, I wasn't sure that I was up for the social repercussions. When he had sat with us at lunch for five minutes, I had fielded questions for *weeks*.

"Ready?" he asked out loud.

I nodded.

We stepped into chaos.

Chapter Nineteen

CONNECTIONS OF THE DESIRED AND UNDESIRED KIND

THE FIRST FLOOR of the Magiaduct was in an uproar in Dorm One, with students yelling and arguing over each other.

"They are demanding that we line up for review. That we wake up everyone who is asleep too. After everything else today—"

"There's no way the officials will let—"

"They can do *anyth*—"

"Would it be so bad to—"

"*Yes.*"

I certainly didn't want Kaine lining us up and looking for a wound on Dare that wasn't fully healed. I let myself be seduced by the steady reassurance of Dare striding next to me, looking unconcerned.

Dare's gaze was steady, but there was a little quirk at the side of his mouth. Something that I could only see now that I'd spent so much time with him. Before, he would have just looked bored or unreadable. Whatever he could hear through frequency or armband conversation from his combat group had reassured him.

Armband conversation...wait.

I touched the band, flipping it back on.

A flurry of voices immediately started yelling at me, their sweet, shouting voices a sure sign that they hadn't gone to Plan B. That they hadn't abandoned me when I'd told them to.

"Where are you, Crown?"

"What were you thi—"

"I'm going to murder y—"

"Tap once for okay, two for speaking under duress."

"I'm fine," I sent back, jerkily tapping once, just in case. *"Stop talking. Why*

Chapter Nineteen

aren't you all on Plan B? We're trying to get through the gauntlet—"

"*We almost* did *go to Plan B, Princess, regardless of our desire to stay the course. For the last twenty minutes, Legatus Shike, the head of The Legion, has been demanding that everyone in the Magiaduct be examined and questioned again. Provost Johnson has been working like mad to keep them out. And now Praetorian Kaine is backing the provost and telling Shike to back down."*

That...was worrying. I didn't want to be lined up again, but why would Kaine suddenly back away?

Whatever Dare was hearing was tightening the edges around his mouth too.

One of the students near us answered my forming question. "Mandatory curfew instead? Whatever. *Seriously.* I'll take it."

I looked to Dare, and listened to the chattering in my ear. As long as every student returned to their rooms for the night in the next five minutes —or was running in the direction of their room—we wouldn't be subjected to interrogation. Students were yelling at each other to get going. Administration Magic started pulling at my stationary feet, the Administration was obviously backing this effort not to have the Department line us up again.

Students started streaming around us, some running.

The voices in my armband reflected the anxiety.

The edges of Dare's eyes pinched, and defying the Administration Magic urging us to *move*, he grabbed my hand, holding me in place, and raised my hand inches from his gaze. Magic dropped over his eyes—not like Kaine's, but with enough similarity that I tried to yank backward.

"Steady," he murmured. He frowned as he examined every whorl. "It is the only thing that makes sense, but there is nothing there." He looked over the rest of me, inch by inch, as people ran by us on both sides—a tiny island in the midst of the swarm. I looked around and saw the blatant staring from the students as they passed. Great.

I gave a lame wave with my free hand—as in, "Hey, everything's fine, nothing to see here." It didn't quite go that way, though, as people interpreted my gesture as, "I'm going to mangle everyone and everything around you with zero regrets!"

They gasped and shrunk back—creating an even larger space between us and the crowd. *Crap.*

I balled up my fist and drew it so quickly against my chest that I hit myself, but a flurry of hands had already shot forth to defend themselves, and three bolts flew toward me.

With a flick of Dare's finger, the bolts fizzled in the air. He never turned around.

Someone screamed.

* Connections of the Desired and Undesired Kind *

"I'm out of here through the other door. No way. No how," a boy said.

A number of people sprinted after him, away from us.

Wow. Just, wow.

Only a few stragglers—those with the sharp, considering gazes—walked more slowly past, gazes switching between Dare and me.

"Clean." Dare let my hand drop and frowned at me.

I swallowed and looked around us. Administration Magic tugged me harder. "Are we really going back to our rooms?"

"Yes." Dare's mouth twisted. "Kaine is up to something, but there is nothing we can do while the Administration Magic is supporting curfew."

"Break it?"

"A one-way ticket to expulsion in this environment." He was already turning me and herding me toward the staircase. "And the Department will process and take you before you get a foot from the wards."

The voices coming through my armband and into my ear were echoing the same thing, some of them forming the same questions.

It didn't take long to reach our floor or rooms. The dorm hall was a wasteland.

Dare looked me over. "You need to sleep." Something passed over his expression—a fleeting emotion. "If you can't sleep..." He touched my cheek. A thin thread of magic remained when he removed his fingers. "That will tell me and I'll help."

I stared at him. Administration Magic was tugging *hard* now.

"I'll see you in the morning," Dare said, opening his door and handing me my bag, which I'd left just inside. His hand brushed mine. "*Don't do anything.* Just sleep."

I stiltedly walked down the hall.

"Ren—"

"I know," I said tiredly, without looking back. Sleep, I got it. I stared at Bellacia's door. It was mandatory curfew. I had to spend twelve hours with her anyway. Hesitation was dumb. And painful.

Magic yanked.

But...a night in the room would cement some sort of roommate bond. One that I didn't want.

No. I was looking at this stupidly. Emotionally. This was not giving in. This was a strategic move that would lead me back to Olivia. I needed the recharge. To untwist my horrific magic. I needed to do nothing more than relax for twelve hours and rejuvenate. Get back on track so that when Marsgrove came back with Olivia, we would be ready to go. To resume Olivia's plans for world takeover. To continue my experiments. To get back to having a great time at school.

I opened the door. I heard Dare finally stepping inside his room—

Chapter Nineteen

having watched me the entire time.

Magic zipped over me as I stepped inside—recognizing me and welcoming me back. There was a less organic feel here than in my room with Olivia, but still powerful. Likely to do with whatever Bellacia had done to secure me as her roommate.

"Had an interesting night?" her lilting voice came from the left.

Bellacia was in her work room. The door was open, so I stepped forward and looked inside, curiosity being one of my fatal flaws.

Her work room was half a movie den—with deep, leather chairs and a number of viewing devices—and half a communications studio. Devices and enchantments of all sorts were issuing news releases in multiple ways, information was streaming along the walls and through the air, and banners were swirling around her, waiting to be plucked forth and examined.

In the midst of the barrage, Bellacia was stretched out in a leather recliner in casual night clothes of green and gray, and she was holding a fully colored and textured hologram—rotating it in the air and carefully manipulating the edges, poking around the corners, trying to uncover secrets only she could see. It looked like a miniaturized room rotating above her palm.

"Welcome back. Have a nice midnight adventure?" Bellacia asked lightly, eyes focused on the image.

"Down to Medical? It was a blast."

She laughed. It was patronizing and sweet and I hated it. "Whatever you say, dear."

I had no idea what Camille Straught might have told Bellacia about tonight's activities. With Dare involved, I couldn't believe that it was too much. Camille Straught seemed pretty loyal to their group, but she was a magicist whose nouveau family was working its way up the ranks of the Old Guard.

Bellacia's hand flicked and the news streams surrounding her parted for a three foot span—skipping over the space she'd opened in the air, so that no visual magic lay between us.

She touched the image she held, nudging it casually—*just so*—so that it turned to the side to be easily viewed by both of us. Then she flicked her fingers and it bloomed fully on the opposite wall—a 3D full size vision. My eyes focused, and my breath stuttered.

General Telgent, the leader of the Peacekeepers' Troop was seated in a chair at the center of the image, cuffs binding his wrists to metal armrests. I clenched my fingers into fists. There had been evidence to suggest that he might have been involved—the interaction I had observed with "Emrys" had possessed me to tell Isaiah and the others to be wary of him.

Telgent's fingers twitched and flexed.

* Connections of the Desired and Undesired Kind *

I took a step closer automatically. It was not a static image. It was an animated feed.

"What is this?" I demanded.

"Telgent's third interrogation." The hooded, amused way Bellacia sent my way was telling. "Recorded after the events, while we were all settling in back here."

"Where is this place?" I couldn't help taking another step closer.

Bellacia shrugged lightly. "That is the secondary question, isn't it? I've already been through both of his interrogations that took place here on campus."

That admission was more than mildly concerning—that she had been able to access recordings or memories of what had surely been secured information.

Bellacia's gaze was serene. And it said—*I can get anything.*

I pressed my lips together and looked back at the image.

Telgent looked like he had been dragged through hell and hadn't made it back in one piece. I couldn't be too unhappy about that fact. I hoped Marsgrove had given him a good work over.

Telgent looked up as five mages appeared. His eyes skittered over Stavros and latched onto one of the women. "I have nothing further to say. I've said it all. I was blackmailed and I went along with it and allowed the terrorists access to Excelsine. I am guilty of that. I am not part of their organization, though, and you *know* it."

"Do you think that will matter to anyone? Twenty-six students and three staff are permanently dead. One of our most secure facilities breached. People want your blood. It is up to us how much we allow them to shed." She smiled. It was creepy. "Tell us what we want to know."

"They still have my family. You are crazy if you think I'm going to do anything to jeopardize that. My silence earns their survival."

She hummed a little as she tinkered with a small machine near him. "Of course."

"What are you doing?" he asked, obviously unnerved by her nonchalance and steady actions setting up the odd machine. "What is that?"

"Nothing to worry about, General Telgent. Nothing for you to worry about at all."

The feed went dark.

I stared at the wall. "What happened after?" I asked, unnerved.

Bellacia didn't answer. The twist of her mouth said she didn't know, though.

"Where did you get the recording?"

Bellacia shrugged. "Where does any good journalist get her sources and material from?" She smiled.

Chapter Nineteen

Telgent's family was being held hostage—that fact focused my rage elsewhere. "What was the machine?" They expected Telgent to answer the questions even though he had no intention to do so—that didn't indicate anything good.

"That's the primary question, isn't it?" Bellacia rubbed her lower lip, looking at the feed. "You've never seen it?"

"No. But that's hardly surprising."

It wasn't like I had to conceal the fact that I was feral anymore. Origin Mage, yes. Feral, no. That secret had flown the coop and was never returning.

"Mmmm. I suppose not. Still, you've seen far more things and far fewer things than many mages, have you not? You aren't exactly stable or normal."

I narrowed my eyes at her. "Ditto."

She gave a tinkling laugh, and leaned back. "Coming from you, that is wonderfully sweet. I know how you love collecting the *interesting* mages on campus."

"You mean the strays?" I said, stepping back, not willing to play this game.

She leaned forward. "The powerful." There was something greedy in her gaze for a moment, before it turned cajoling. "The *interesting*."

"You've been here for, what, two and a half years now?" I said, unimpressed. "You could have made friends with any of those people."

"But no one trusts *me*, kitten. They just see my father." A forlorn expression appeared.

I narrowed my eyes. "No, I think they see *you* just fine." I looked around us. "You love this. This *is* you."

She laughed, and the forlorn expression dropped, leaving real humor in her eyes. "It's true. I do love Daddy's business."

"Your setup is pretty great," I allowed, looking around the dynamic room. I could appreciate it. If it wasn't Bellacia, I'd be insanely curious about all of the gadgets and gizmo magic. As it was, I needed to become as lightly ensnared as possible in the traps she was surely setting for me.

"Thank you," she said graciously. "I've worked hard to be where I am." A harder glint entered her gaze. "And I am good at what I do."

It reminded me of Camille, who had said something similar about her own abilities once. Both extremely confident, and even though I wasn't much of a fan of Bellacia's views or tactics, I could respect her strength.

I looked at the other work room. Technically, it was mine now. But did I want a place where Bellacia could snoop to her heart's content when I wasn't around? Or where her previous roommate had been?

Who knew what sorts of traps Bellacia's roommate had left in there.

* Connections of the Desired and Undesired Kind *

Dare might be able to give me some pointers on securing the room—heaven knew he had his own locked down like Fort Knox. But tonight my magic wasn't up to it, even philosophically.

No, better to continue schlepping my bag. Or just put everything in Constantine's room. He already knew all of my secrets. He could poke all he wanted.

"I'm going to bed," I said.

I hauled my bag toward the bedroom and bathroom. I tried not to be unnerved by the lock clicking into place on the main door, locking us both in.

When I got back, Bellacia was stretched out on her bed in her black, white, and green tank top and shorts, looking over reports.

"There hasn't been a curfew in years. The Department is going to be going over all of the records and disturbances on campus," she said, as if we were continuing some conversation. "The decisions that the administration has made. Decisions concerning your enrollment and your little outburst at the Shangwei Art Complex."

I winced, as I placed things on the nightstand. She'd been following me for so long, she'd probably learned of it fall term after it happened. Those students who had followed me at the party ready to enact whatever social control punishment they'd intended, were probably there on her orders, searching for the mage who had destroyed the building.

"Such an interesting firework burst during the show. The man you were fighting looked just like that lovely one in your photograph. Did you two have a falling out?"

Her voice was lazy.

"I told you. There was a familiarity enchantment in place."

"Ah, yes. The mysterious enchantment. Who was underneath the enchantment then, Ren Crown?"

"Some terrorist." I lined everything up next to my pillow—Chapstick, my photo, magical ear plugs. The last, I desperately wanted to pop into my ears, but I was afraid of what would happen if one of my senses was dulled.

"It looked very personal, that fight between you. I fed all of the information about it and a recording of it to the mage on staff who tackled the article. It's up to fifty million views already. The recording stopped so abruptly, though, that all of us watching it felt cheated. There's a reward for anyone who supplies the rest of the footage."

Everything in the room seemed to be closing in. I pulled back the covers, keeping her visible in my periphery.

She twirled a lock of hair around her fingers. "You were just absolutely covered in paint, dear. What was that all about? And where did it all go? I saw no evidence of it on Top Circle."

Chapter Nineteen

They weren't questions. They were taunts.

"Maybe it was just hidden under the blood," I said tonelessly.

"I do so wish you would just let me scrape through that brain of yours. Make it easy for both of us."

I touched the scarab in the interior pocket I had quickly, magically, attached to my sleepwear. It had taken almost no magic to secure it, but it had felt agitated since I'd pulled it from my bag.

The scarab had possessed too much active magic to be hidden under the shadow cloak—and even Neph had reluctantly agreed it would be a red flag pointing right at her as two otherwise unidentifiable individuals illegally jetted across campus.

The small stone beetle was hot under my fingers. I wondered if Bellacia was trying to do something to me, even now.

"Good night, Ren." Bellacia's lilting voice was smug.

"Good night," I gritted out politely. I hopped in bed and turned toward the window. The view was all wrong.

And with Bellacia's light laugh in the background as she turned off the lights, all I had left was to think. We had all agreed that it was too dangerous to use any communication in Bellacia's room, even the armbands. After seeing her setup, I thought that wise.

But that left me very much alone.

Thoughts ran through my head like water overflowing an already full cup.

Olivia. Constantine. Raphael. Kaine. Dare. Julian. Marsgrove. Greyskull. Bellacia. Stavros.

Marsgrove had left campus already. While I was in the bathroom, Bellacia's audible feed had been playing the news of which officials had returned and which had left. She had been letting everything come through audibly. Taunting me with the knowledge she had access to.

A banner of news tickertaped the top of our room, like a soft blue nightlight. I couldn't take my eyes from the words, as they magically changed from reporting on the student status of Excelsine to reports on Raphael Verisetti, his plans and access to alternate magical technologies. Twins and death were next and I followed that rabbit hole for a moment until I shook myself and looked at another headline. Next were words on Stavros and Kaine, then on Dare. A stream of reports appeared about him and in the midst of "breaking news" I worried for a moment that he had left his room and gone back to the competition.

A report on how Dare had "escaped defeat" in one round of the competition heats made me narrow my eyes at the words.

Then horror took me and I shut my eyes.

Bellacia's laughter followed.

* Connections of the Desired and Undesired Kind *

The tickertape was magically changing to report on whatever topic I was *thinking about*. Automatically projecting the news I was interested in. I kept my eyes locked tight and breathed in deeply. An insight into my thoughts was *not* something I wanted Bellacia to have.

"Oh, Ren, you aren't being any fun. That is a highly advanced piece of tech you are ignoring."

"And the fact that I'm a highly unstable mage is what *you* are ignoring." My magic, recovering more now that we were both in here and resting, sparked.

She laughed again, but it was a much shorter sound. When I peeked up again, the tickertape was still going, but it was in some sort of code. Whatever Bellacia wanted to see, then.

My fingers clenched carefully around the deflated paper and tucked it half under my pillow. Close enough for comfort and for keeping it concealed from my new roommate.

I was too wired at first to fall, then stay, asleep. Waking nightmares plagued me with the standard fare of Dare dying and Olivia slipping away and all of my friends calling out for help with me being unable to do a thing as I slowly lurched toward them in nightmarish fashion. Too late, always too late. One dream followed another, jolting me awake.

But my thoughts soon turned sluggish, the exhaustion from a day of overwhelming emotion and physical activity taking its toll.

I breathed in the magic of the balloon as I fell asleep—the tendrils slipping into my mouth. Worlds turned in my mind. Then blackness descended.

Chapter Twenty

NIGHTMARES AND CONSEQUENCES

PERCHED HIGH ABOVE—as if I was a spider in a corner crack—I looked down inside a bright, vibrant room that was edged in the same blackness that had overtaken me. Two very familiar people were facing off below.

I opened my mouth to shout, but nothing escaped my throat. Locked in nightmare status—like with Marsgrove's ball, it was as if I was separated from what I was viewing by a clear shield of glass.

Below, Olivia coldly examined Raphael. "I think not," she said, continuing some argument.

He gave her a smooth, nearly mischievous smile. "You will." His expression abruptly changed to mirror the coldness of hers. "Or I will physically extract your magic through your fingernails. And such lovely ones, they are."

Olivia curled her fingers into her palm. "Your threats mean little."

"Of course they do," he said, voice taking on a cajoling quality. "You are the daughter of Helen Price. And action is everything."

Even in a dream, my heartbeat sped up.

"I knew her, once." Raphael's eyes glittered. "And once again. And I can see her magic, her marks all over you."

"Impossible." Olivia's voice was dismissive, but not entirely capable of hiding her unease.

"No? 'Helly' was such an adept student at figuring out how to take protection magic and turn it the other way. You forget that not only do I know exactly what to look for in her magic, but I devised most of the spells she uses."

He leaned into her space and pressed a finger into the hollow of one shoulder. Olivia stiffened, and her leg jerked uncontrollably, pain overriding her control.

* Nightmares and Consequences *

"She made sure to watch each spell I performed," he said casually, twisting his finger just a bit and making her other leg spasm as well. "And she made sure to test each back upon me. Do you know what it's like to have a nearly limitless pain threshold, but the sensitivity of those with the least allowable amount? You feel everything, but never pass out. The pain just keeps going and going and going."

Olivia lifted her chin, pain obvious in the motions as her legs continued to jerk.

"But you aren't the one who should suffer." He lifted his finger. "Are you?"

"Go to hell," Olivia said in her crisp voice.

He leaned forward and whispered in her ear. "I've never left."

His gaze lifted and met mine, and he smiled at me, then lifted his finger back into position.

Panic rocked me and I tried to launch myself forward. The dream immediately began to shatter. I felt a foreign excitement that was not my own. It made me pause long enough to stem my panic. I drew back and looked at the shattering cracks of the dream. Olivia and Raphael were still moving inside, the jagged lines making their movement jerk from one shard to the next. I took a deep breath and carefully patched the glass shards together, shaking hands working feverishly to put each back in place, then smooth my hand along the cracks.

The foreign excitement had dimmed, and I wondered at my strange, splitting brain.

Raphael was prowling around again inside the dream, but Olivia was now released from the chair. Whether this was the same dream, or a new one, I didn't know.

"Do you think while you have that, that you will be safe?" he said.

Olivia's fingers curled more tightly around the creation I had given her—it had bloomed into a butterfly when she'd used it to sacrifice herself for me. "I think that it gives you pause."

Raphael smiled. "Origin Mages are such interesting creatures. They suck in the powerful like magnets too forcefully attracted."

"You are trying to make light of our friendship."

"Yes." Raphael prowled around her. His gaze lifted to meet mine again and he smiled. He could *see me*. "I could kill it. That seed of trust you have in her. Crush it like a grain beneath a pestle."

If he could see and speak to me, then maybe—

I called out for Olivia, but one of the shards immediately started to crack again.

Olivia looked down at the butterfly for a long moment, then up at Raphael. Her smile grew slowly. It was tinged with darkness. Knowing.

Chapter Twenty

"No, you can't."

But she was speaking to *him,* she couldn't see me. I paced the edges of the vision, trying to figure out *how* to access it without breaking it.

Raphael laughed, suddenly and incongruously, like so many of his actions. "Delightful." He crouched in front of her. "I had that once, you know, that *knowing.* That someone would always be there. It was even truth, for a bit, but time savages all things."

"Or maybe you put your trust in the wrong person."

"Perhaps." He moved suddenly and touched a finger to her forehead. "But if I plucked out some of you, replaced it with something else. Would you still be you? Would you want to be someone else, Olivia Price?" His voice was low and hypnotic.

Her fingers curled around the butterfly and she swallowed with difficulty. "Before, yes." They were playing some dangerous game of bravery chicken and she wasn't moving as he lightly tapped her forehead. "Now, no."

"You wouldn't invoke that same debilitating loyalty from my Butterfly, if you were someone else. I could break that link."

"I don't think it would matter. Not to her." Fierce emotion underscored her words.

I was nodding wildly and my hand was pressing against the barrier. Another shard gave an ominous crack.

"No? What if I plucked out some of her? Made her into something *more.*"

Olivia's eyes narrowed and her breath started exhaling faster. "I would pluck it right back."

"Oh," he smiled and moved back. "So you want to keep her stagnant? Unchanging? But nothing stays the same. One can never go *back.*" His voice was mesmerizing and I could see Olivia fight against it.

"That is the beauty of loving chaos, then, isn't it?" she said. "It's always changing, always fluid and unpredictable. You never have to just *be,* do you, Verisetti?"

Raphael smiled, eyes dark. "Clever girl. Clever, clever girl. I'm going to enjoy pulling you apart."

He reached for her and I shouted. One of the shards flew forward and my voice echoed through. Olivia turned toward the sound and her gaze met mine. She opened her mouth, but the edges of the dream had cracked, a tunnel sucking it backward, sweeping the edges away into the vastness of space. I grabbed for the shards, arm shooting forward. A shard went tumbling from the center, the pressure pulling it all. My hand went through the opening.

Pressure pulled at my hand. *Pulled my hand.* I set my feet, prepared to follow my hand through.

"No, Ren!" Olivia's voice yelled. Her horrified gaze was looking at something to my left. Raphael's splintering gaze was narrowed on my ear.

It was enough to stop me for a single moment.

Something slithered faster than my eye could see down my extending arm and launched itself at them through the hole.

The shattering dream vortexed completely with the breech, blowing me backward.

Raphael reached up and snatched it out of the air, a shadow strangling in his hand. It started to curl around his fingers, then shadowy wings burst from its sides, extending faster than I could process.

Rage overtook Raphael's expression. "You *dare*—"

I was rocketed backward as the shards in the conical tip broke into parts small enough to be sand, then sent them splintering up like lightning toward me.

I gasped for breath, jackknifing in bed.

The clock enchantment on the wall read six a.m. Bellacia's tickertape scrolled madly with headlines of nightmares and visions and breaking space.

Emptiness pressed in to fill all the spaces alongside the panic as I looked at the foreign ceiling. I wasn't in my room. I wasn't in *our* room. I was in enemy territory, and Olivia was in an enemy world.

"Bad dreams?" a lilting voice said.

I shuddered and pressed my palms against my eyes, trying to slow my rabbiting heartbeat with shuddering breaths. I let my body fall back down.

Dreams. Just dreams.

"Origin Mages have them, you know."

I jerked my hands from my face and rolled over sharply to look at Bellacia, who was leaning against the other wall, lower body splayed out on her bed, body language amused at my night terror. She had an Ambrosia stick in one hand and a tablet under the other. The Ambrosia stick was weaving slowly in the air. I had seen a number of the more expensively dressed students at Excelsine nibble them while they walked.

"What are you doing up?" I asked harshly.

"Some of us have to wake up to work no matter the hour."

I closed my eyes again.

"Interesting whisperings across the layers woke me," she said lightly. "The praetorians have been busy in the past few hours, I see."

Unease slithered through me.

"Kaine and his shadows—how do they work?" The question was out before I thought better of it. Damn room in enemy territory during vulnerable times of the day...

Silence answered my question, and I opened my eyes to see Bellacia

Chapter Twenty

sitting stock still on her bed, eyes narrowed on me. I saw her dim her frequency feeds to concentrate on me fully.

"Why?" she asked. A beeping red light appeared on the corner of her tablet, but I had her full attention.

I laughed shortly. "He made it my business to ask."

She was watching me, trying to figure out the story.

"He's a rare mage, right?" I asked. "The scary kind. Yet he's walking around."

She looked as if she was deliberating whether to answer. "He's a Shadow Mage. If there wasn't a massive Department leash placed on him, people would have demanded he be put down years ago. Scary? No. He's the thing of nightmares."

"Yeah." I pushed shaking fingers along my brows.

"You are destined to meet more mages like him. No nice village life in the country for you. Monsters seek each other out," she said with a smirk, chewing on her stick again.

"Nice." I let Will's bracelet encyclopedia fill in the blanks on Shadow Mages. Ability to manipulate shadows, can morph into and travel through connected ones... I shivered looking around at the dozens of shadows in the room and reminded myself that they had to be *connected*. "His abilities are pretty terrifying."

"Kitten, you have no idea," she said, easily keeping up, used to knowledge being quickly and easily accessed. "However, it's not quite as world ending as a mage who can make the world collapse with a sneeze, no?"

"I don't know, personal monsters that focus on an individual are a lot scarier than some vague world-threatening possibility," I shot back.

"Only for children," she said sweetly.

"Pretty sure adults are just as susceptible to your Siren suggestions."

"Not the worthy, strong ones," she said. "And those are the only ones worthy of the power to make decisions. I weed out the others quickly enough in the media."

"You must be pretty popular," I muttered.

Her eyes glittered. She had a haughty smirk, but there was bitterness in her eyes. And I suddenly got it.

I had observed her enough to understand. While Bellacia held tremendous influence in circles around campus and was unequivocally beautiful—and therefore sought as a companion—people didn't *like* her. They respected her, they liked her on their arm, but, well, Bellacia was a *threat*. A social, media, and personal threat, and she didn't attempt to hide it. Ever.

She'd *made* those choices. I wasn't going to feel sorry for her.

* Nightmares and Consequences *

Much. A little thought of maybe if... *No.* God, she'd have me for breakfast.

I closed that line of thought down with a deep breath and closed my eyes. More information scrolled through on Kaine's rare abilities. Riding shadows. Attaching shadows. The more powerful Shadow Mages were able to see, hear, and feel what the shadows did.

I thought about my nightmare. About what it might be trying to tell me. My dreams often served up subconscious stew for review. My subconscious was obviously trying to work something out, what with the glass shards and the shadows and the butterfly.

In the dim light, I held up my hands and looked at them.

"What are you doing?" Bellacia's voice was far too interested.

"I think he put a shadow on me this afternoon." *Dammit.* I was too used to voicing thoughts in the middle of the night to Christian, then Olivia.

"Impossible," Bellacia said flatly. "Someone would have seen it—in that crowd, it is a certainty—and I've been over the footage. He didn't. He'd not be allowed to remain on campus. *No one* would let him remain. Even Stavros' largest cashed-in favor couldn't keep him here."

Not this afternoon, then. But tonight? Tonight, in the darkness, he could have slipped one onto me. Dare had sure thought he might have.

During the chase, Dare had been doing everything he could to keep the shadows from me. And Kaine's voice in my ear had...

My *ear*.

I swore, scrambling out of bed. Neph's scarab hadn't been with me outside of the Magiaduct, and Kaine's shadow had whispered in my ear.

That nightmare was trying to tell me...

Oh my God. *No.* I looked at the red alarm on Bellacia's device that she was still ignoring while she was cataloging every move I was making.

I grabbed the paper balloon and brought it to my lips, shakily breathing into the opening. It inflated, allowing the magic to swirl around inside the hollow, freeing it from the interior fibers. But only a fraction of the magic remained. My shaking hands lost their grip and the paper fell on my rumpled sheet.

Not a nightmare. What had I done?

I stumbled into my clothes, banging into multiple surfaces as I tried to yank everything on.

"Where are you going?" Bellacia demanded. Her expression was guarded, her body tense—as if she thought I might just issue that world-ending sneeze right this moment. I saw her switch her feeds back on, and a weird expression immediately pinched her features. She started punching buttons and swirling magic in her palm.

I grabbed the sweatshirt I had shed on the floor next to the bed.

Chapter Twenty

"Roommates," she said haltingly, obviously trying to do multiple things at once—listening to something in her feed. "Are—"

"I *know*," I said harshly, lifting the precious, used balloon. "I'll be back."

She sucked in a harsh breath, gaze slamming up at me, lips parted. "Did you—?"

Knock, knock.

Bellacia's eyes widened and her gaze jerked to the door. I tripped in my panicked scramble, but regained my footing quickly. Sprinting to the door, I yanked it open.

Dare stood in loose fitting sweats and a t-shirt, exactly as I had seen him the night before the competition. He was barefoot. "You aren't sleeping anymore," he said. "Why?"

Dare's eyes narrowed on something on the outside of the door. He slashed his hand downward. Sparks of magic flew from the wood.

"Was it a nightmare spell?" I asked, somewhat desperately.

But it hadn't been a nightmare. I knew this—more with every drawn breath.

I yanked the origami balloon to eye level. The magic was still there, thin, *so thin*, but swirling. Still alive. *Still alive*. My heart beat in an overzealous staccato of panic.

"No." Dare gave me a pointed look, then one in the direction of where Bellacia was. I stepped back, trying, and failing, to act calm.

He entered and shut the door.

"Poor girl had a nightmare," Bellacia said, chewing on her stick and leaning against the jamb to the bedroom. Her gaze was on the origami balloon, a calculating expression on her face. "And then you show up. How *interesting*. I don't think I've ever known you to visit a room in the middle of the night, Axer. What *have* you been getting up to these past few months without the grapevine knowing? I'm shocked."

He looked tired. It had only been four hours since I'd seen him last, and on top of everything that had happened on campus, he had put in nearly a full day competing against the best fighters in four layers.

"You always have been rather stupidly confident in your own knowledge, haven't you?" he said dismissively, tired irritation making the words clipped.

Her eyes narrowed. "What?"

He turned to look at her fully, expression dangerous. "You should pay more attention to what Cam tells you. Play your games with the others, take your revenge on Leandred, but turn in this direction, and I will destroy you."

I looked anxiously between them.

Bellacia laughed suddenly, but the look in her eyes didn't match the sound. "Oh, Ren, you become *more* interesting. You are just a tiny treasure trove of delight." Her gaze never left Dare's while she said this.

"Great. Can I speak to you...somewhere else?" I said to Dare, while looking at the workroom that I hadn't yet investigated.

"Don't leave on my account," Bellacia said, expression even more calculating. "The items filtering through the outer feeds right now are appalling and engrossing. Nothing has hit the main waves yet, and I'm going to be piecing together the exclusives for the next ten minutes to be first." Her smirk grew and her eyes narrowed. "And with such interesting insights too."

"Get your stuff," Dare said to me. He was looking around the room, expression tight.

"Now, Axer," Bellacia said. "Curfew might have lifted an hour ago, but you know what the room spells require."

"And you have hit the load, haven't you, Bella?" He seemed to be saying something else entirely.

He threw something toward her. She caught it midair, and pulled it against her chest. I couldn't see what it was, just that it was tangerine and asymmetrical.

"I have indeed." She smiled and tapped the wall, then took another bite of her stick, tightly gripping whatever it was he had given her. "Ta, for now, then. I'm going to be quite busy."

I returned to the bedroom and grabbed my bag—still packed. It even had my toiletry bag on top, and not in the bathroom, just in case Bellacia tried to stick some tracking magic in my toothpaste.

It would be like swallowing a shadow.

I shuddered, and followed Dare's swift exit from the room.

Chapter Twenty-one

KAINE'S REVENGE

"TELL ME," he said, as soon as we entered his room.

I dropped into one of the club chairs that was only here when Dare was present. My bag thumped down on the floor next to it. I carefully placed the balloon on the armrest, staring at the magic thinly, and fitfully swirling inside.

"Ren?"

I snapped my gaze up. "What did you give her? Bellacia?"

"A short term solution. Tell me what happened."

I raked a hand through my hair. "I had a dream. I thought it was a dream. Are...are you sure it wasn't a nightmare spell on the door?"

"I'm sure."

I rubbed a hand over my eyes. "Check my ears?"

He didn't even give me a weird glance at that, he came over and started running magic over them.

"There was a shadow inside?" It was less a question and more a blunt statement, reading the obvious answer in my actions.

I flinched. "Maybe. It...leaped through my dream."

His eyes unfocused. "The feeds are starting to report on a facility in the Third Layer that was destroyed. Julian said Marsgrove was in position and about to strike when Kaine jumped through. Fighting continues." Each sentence contained a weighted pause as he rifled through reports. "Bellacia is already scooping and reporting as much as she can from her contacts, and making quite a few good guesses."

The place under my breastbone went cold and hollow. I lifted the flattened origami balloon. I could still feel Olivia, connected to me, but here was a visual reminder that the spell that I had connected to the place where she was taken was no longer in play.

"Olivia is still alive."

* Kaine's Revenge *

"As is Verisetti. But they jumped location."

I closed my eyes. "And Kaine?"

"Still very much alive and in pursuit. He...is very difficult to kill."

I opened my eyes and stared at the balloon.

"Marsgrove still has a chance, Ren. He is tracking them right now."

"*Does* he have a chance?" I cupped the balloon. "I had their location. I gave it to Marsgrove. I gave it to *Kaine*."

"Yes."

I closed my eyes. "Marsgrove's not going to be able to find them again. He has been unsuccessfully chasing Raphael for years." I thought on Greyskull's words on Raphael's ability to hide.

"Marsgrove hasn't been chasing Verisetti with *Kaine*."

I looked sharply at Dare. "They are working together?"

"Never. But they can, and likely are stealing intel from each other. Tracking the other. Piggybacking the information they find, trying to be the first one to Verisetti."

I touched my control cuff and the steel gray connection there that I always ignored and denied. I sent a pulse of magic through it. God, how the worm turned. I was sending aid to Marsgrove.

"I should have gone," I said.

"You wouldn't have returned," his voice was matter-of-fact, but distant, still listening to reports I couldn't hear. "You would have gone and Verisetti would now have you, or worse, Kaine."

"I can handle Raphael," I said, knowing it was untrue. Raphael, of anyone, knew how to manipulate my magic and my emotions. In some ways, during that grief-stricken six weeks between Christian's death and my Awakening, he had *made* me into what I was.

"Ren."

I leaned my head back. "Yeah. I know. But sitting here, doing nothing? Not heroic."

"You can't fight every battle yourself. You have to rely on your team and your soldiers. And to do that, you have to *pick* the right team."

I swallowed. "The first seventeen years of my life were all about relying on Christian. One other person. I didn't need anyone else. And then he was gone. And..."

"And you repaired and moved forward. It's not a disloyalty. You would still do everything you could for him, were he here. But he's not. Death is preserved and unchanging, but life *moves*."

Never stagnant. Olivia's words uttered in another world through a dream. Always moving and changing.

"If Kaine catches them—"

"Verisetti has stayed free for a long time. He's been wreaking

Chapter Twenty-one

devastation for over half a decade. *He* is also very difficult to kill."

"Olivia is not," I said, voice strained as I opened my eyes to look at him.

He said nothing for a moment, fingers moving along the armrest, tracing patterns with ultramarine magic. "What did you see? In your dream?"

I told him all of it.

He tapped a finger against the leather. "Kaine's shadows watch and observe. Anything that happened between him placing it on you and it escaping is suspect."

My breath caught.

"The multiple fields maintained in Medical, and the ones Leandred and I separately use, should have been enough to disrupt him there. And Bellacia is full of tricks. But anything might have slipped through in either place, so consider any of that information compromised." He looked at my bag. "Nothing is fully safe."

I looked down at it and moved my foot away.

"He might have disengaged from you in order to go through your things —and Bellacia's—after you fell asleep, but it is more likely that he stayed with you in order to travel through your head and your dreams."

Nausea swept me. Without permission, my fingernails started clawing at my ears.

Dare reached out and stilled my wrists. "In order to make the jump, he would have had to go through completely. Nothing remains."

"He knew. When he let us go."

"Yes," Dare said simply.

I looked sharply at him.

"I never underestimate Kaine," he said. "And he always seeks revenge. There were variables that couldn't be controlled and sacrifices that were possible."

"Raphael looked so angry," I whispered, looking at the balloon. "What if...?"

The toying with Olivia, the verbal sparring...that indicated that Raphael found her amusing, and he kept amusing things *alive*.

But madness existed between Raphael and Stavros and Kaine, and I had accidentally sent Kaine there. And Raphael reacted poorly when things slipped from his control. Olivia would be—*was*—in the crossfire.

"If Marsgrove fails, then you spin the webs that Verisetti doesn't want you to spin."

"If you think he doesn't want me spinning webs, then—"

"The webs he *doesn't want* you to spin."

I tucked my chin against my chest, over the space where guilt was gnawing an aching hole.

* Kaine's Revenge *

He tipped my chin up, eyes serious. "You know what a shadow feels like now?"

I thought of the slide of it with its tiny cat-tongue-like barbs. Rough and slippery at the same time. Haunting. I nodded and swallowed, his fingers following the motions. "I think so."

"Then it won't happen again."

His fingers dropped, and that seemed to be the extent of his recrimination. Guilt settled in my stomach.

"I'm sorry." I closed my eyes. "Maybe you should have let Julian take me. Wherever he meant." I waved a hand in the air.

"Don't tempt me." His voice was intense. "Not yet."

I opened my eyes and tried to figure out what he meant. Unable to do so, I stared at the hollowed paper, at the thin magic swirling in the interior. "I had thought I had gotten past the feeling. Of being lost."

His expression softened and he reached forward as if reaching toward the tie dangling from my heart. "It's been a very long day. And you snapped your tie to your home."

Yes. And it still *hurt*. It hadn't stopped. I was a drifter now. No home tie to my parents, a muted, restricted one to Olivia, one that was insidiously trying to connect to *Bellacia Bailey* via Community Magic, and one that tentatively recognized this room.

"I couldn't let Helen Price get their location," I whispered, anguish rushing through me again.

"I know." His voice was soft. "You did the right thing."

I smiled with difficulty. "You should have seen your face. I'm not sure I've ever seen you shocked before."

"It takes a lot. And snapping a tie like that is..." He looked off into the distance. "But family...family is something you guard. Sometimes you are born to that family, and sometimes you create it, one connection at a time."

I looked at the balloon.

"And sometimes a part of them can be returned to you," he said, something unidentifiable in his voice.

I looked at him.

He flicked his wrist and carefully caught a shrouded, sphere-shaped object that came whizzing out of his workroom. He held it out to me.

"I tried to give this to you before leaving for the competition. Perhaps there has been no more opportune time than now, though."

I unwrapped the shroud. A glass orb sat inside. As soon as it was free of its covering, magic burst free from whatever concealment or protection spells were in the cloth. The magic immediately wrapped around me. I gasped for air, unable to breathe.

I could hear Dare cursing as he reached forward. I stumbled out of my

Chapter Twenty-one

chair and backward, tripping, clutching the orb to my chest as I fell, then scrambled along the floor. No one was taking it away. No one!

"Shh, it's okay." He stopped reaching for me, palms down. "I should have told you what it was first." He kept speaking, cursing Ramirez and his overly secretive influence.

But I was still trying to breathe. Loud, half gulps of air that couldn't make it past the constriction of my closed throat. The light in the orb was touching points of the glass like a plasma ball, and each time it touched me it ignited points all over my body with my brother's magic.

Christian. I gave a sob.

"How?" was all I got out.

Dare was kneeling in front of me.

"It was what was left of his magic. At the time...you didn't register as a mage. And in the First Layer...our senses don't work as well. But in hindsight, it is easy to see. You absorbed nearly all of his Awakening magic before we got there, didn't you? Then went dormant."

"The man...had my brother's bracelet. Put Christian's magic all in there. I grabbed it." Hazy and half-dead, I'd still felt the pull of my twin and I'd grabbed the magic.

Dare nodded. "Twins. You would probably have Awakened soon after your brother did. For a period of time, his magic nullified yours, for lack of a better word. Enhanced it, though, in the end."

He was looking at me, concern carefully, but not quite thoroughly, hidden.

"I know," I tried to reassure him, heartbeat still fluttering like a hummingbird's wings. Raphael had told me most of it. Raphael had kept me in the pressure cooker of dormancy as long as possible, trying to make my Awakening as explosive as he could.

Dare looked as relieved as he ever showed—relieved that he wasn't telling me new, painful truths. "We gathered the remnants in the air as evidence. I...retrieved them for you. Later."

I stared at him, still clutching the little glass ball to my chest. "When?"

"A month ago."

After we had been working for a while together around campus.

Four days ago, before he had left for the Combat Competition, he had told me he knew I was the girl in the First Layer. That he had known since the day in the library when I'd stupidly transferred the search spell directly to him. Touching someone directly with magic enabled a deeper connection and he'd known then.

He had anonymously sent a beautiful Firework sphere to me for the Lightning Festival. So that I could use it as a remembrance of my brother. The sphere had looked a lot like this one.

* Kaine's Revenge *

"Thank you," I whispered.

Dare pulled a hand through his hair, acting like Will for a moment, when Will didn't know what to say. It was an unusual gesture for Dare.

He waved a hand toward me. "Just in case."

"Of?"

He shrugged, looking around the room in some strange attempt at avoidance.

"Things? Stuff?" I deadpanned.

He smiled.

I rolled the ball around my cupped palms, staring down at it. "How do you hide it?" I didn't specify what "it" was, but I figured he'd understand without trouble. "Do you use it? At the competition?"

"No. The tests they give record and stamp a baseline. Anything that charts off of that is held for review. I've never used any abnormal abilities in competition."

Everything *about* Dare was abnormal. Abnormally competent at controlling himself, abnormally good at fighting, abnormally hot.

"Being a prodigy seems a little abnormal."

He spread his hands. "All abilities that are within measure, though."

"Have you ever used your powers in battle?"

"No. It's never wise to rely on skills that you want to keep hidden. I've never used them in practice at all outside of the island." He gave a twist to his lips. "Though, I would have, there against the Bone Beast, as you called it. I was readying to do just that when you ported to me."

The look of resignation he had shown. He had been resigned to using his restricted magic to save campus. I had thought, at the time, that he had been resigned to death.

Maybe they had been close to being one and the same, though, considering how people seemed to react to the idea of his powers.

I curled the ball more tightly against my chest, feeling the magic. Magic that Dare's powers had given me.

"What about the...?" I waved my other hand toward my ankle, where the vine had been wrapped. "How come it didn't register? Kaine seemed to know that something had been there."

"He sees much that I wish he didn't. But the vine has its own magic, and it swallows all magic around it. Thus, the absence of an alert."

"Can we get more of them?"

"I don't know. It depends on what happened in the Fourth Layer."

The reports were conflicted and sketchy. People kind of stopped talking when I came within range. If it weren't for my armband, Justice Toad, and Bellacia, I'd have started to live in a bubble of silence.

"The vine swallowed my magic on your command. Did it turn it into

Chapter Twenty-one

one of those odd rock bones you pocketed?"

He smiled, and there was something sharp about it for a moment, before smoothing away. "That is a question for another time. Get some sleep."

"I'm not tired."

"No, you are exhausted."

I huffed out a breath.

"You can't do anything right now," he said, rising. "And the best thing for your magic is rest. Sleep, Ren."

"You mean watch Bellacia cast up-to-the-minute feeds on the Third Layer situation all over the walls? No thanks."

But he was right, I couldn't do anything right now and the *best* thing I could do was to recharge so that I would be up to potential when I *could* do something.

I could go to Neph's. Curfew was over. It was early—dawn just peeking through—but Neph would open her door. I walked back to the chair, keeping a firm hold on the orb, and grabbed my bag, my toiletry items nearly slipping out.

Dare looked at me strangely. "What are you doing?"

"Going to Neph's."

"Do you know who her roommate is?" He must have seen the answer in my expression. "Ren—"

"I'm not going back to Bellacia's."

"Of course you aren't." He frowned. "That's why I gave Bellacia the recharger. You are staying here."

I fumbled my toothbrush holder. "What?"

"Here," he enunciated. "Your magic will fix itself faster here than anywhere outside of Bailey's room and Medical. You can even have your muse come when she wakes."

I pinned him with a look, trying to decipher what he meant by that. "I'm not getting rid of Neph."

"I think that's been made perfectly clear." He raised a brow.

"So...stay here? Sleep? Where?" I sank back into the chair keeping my gaze away from the bedroom. I knew what it looked like now since their suite had a duplicate layout to Bellacia's. There was no space for a third bed.

He looked amused and waved a hand. A flat couch appeared beneath me and my back—no longer supported by the club chair—fell with it. I flailed and caught myself on my hands.

"Very funny."

He headed toward his work room. "Today is going to be messy. Sleep." He left the door wide open, and I could hear him moving inside and could feel the hum of his magic.

* Kaine's Revenge *

With Christian's orb tucked against my chest, Olivia's balloon carefully tucked in my hand—far away from my pillow—and with the sounds of Dare close by, and the room's comforting magic swirling around me, I did.

Chapter Twenty-two

WAKING IN THE SAME WORLD

I WOKE UP with a blanket tucked beneath my chin and the raised brows of Constantine staring from a chair across from me. I smiled at him before realizing where I was.

I jack-knifed upward, blanket slipping down. I grabbed the orb and balloon before they could fall, and curled them back into my lap. "You're back."

Since there was a bag at his feet and he looked like death warmed over, then frozen, then warmed again, he must have just arrived.

"From the mostly dead," he responded. There was a scratchy edge to his usually smooth voice.

I pinged the connection threads, subtly checking him for spells. Dare liked Stuart Leandred about as well as Constantine did—which had not filled me with confidence.

Magic zipped clumsily into my fingers as I reached for him. I stopped and looked at them. I had *magic*. Taking a good internal look, I felt *so much* better. My magic was making it through paths that had partially opened and fixed at some point while I slept.

I grimaced. Whatever magic enhancement Bellacia had swapped her soul for *worked*.

Testing, I waved my hand in a circle and a butterfly made of fiery light appeared on my palm. I swirled my fingers around my palm and a silvered dragon appeared next to it, sparking rays of light. I tossed my palm up and they lifted into the air, flying in opposing arcs, then dove into Constantine's chest.

He lifted a brow at me, expression clenching, but said nothing while I investigated his state.

The paint that I had wiped across his brow gave me insight into his physical state, as well as allowing me...other things that I never planned to

* Waking in the Same World *

use. His state registered increased stability—large leaps from both times I had seen him.

Relief swept me, and I let the magic go, leaving it to swirl around him at his control.

I inflated Olivia's balloon. The thin magic still swirled inside. She was still alive.

Staggering relief.

Constantine pulled my magic from his chest and put it into a small pouch, then carefully pulled the strings closed. He tucked it into a pocket while looking at the paper balloon, then raised his gaze to me.

"You screwed up," he said bluntly.

I closed my eyes. "You have no idea."

"I have a pretty good one, actually." He held up a hand and headlines swirled around his fingers and drifted into the air.

I snatched a few of them, reading about the dozen attacks that had taken place all over the Third Layer. The reports had Raphael, Marsgrove, and Kaine stamped all over them.

"Yeah." I released them to the recycling grate and slumped back, rubbing my eyes as the bed reformed into an upright couch.

I filled Constantine in on the pertinent parts of what had happened with Kaine and Raphael.

He leaned back—looking like he was knocking on death's door again. "I don't know whether to strangle you or embrace you," he finally said, eyes closing. The strange thing was that I felt a humming satisfaction ringing through our connection. He was pleased about something.

He had been furious with me in Medical.

"Where is Dare?"

Constantine waved a blind hand toward Dare's workroom. It was devoid of the thousands of wards that were usually upon it. Dare had stopped blocking his presence from the room, or at least from me. I wondered what he was doing in there.

"Can he hear us?"

"He's *busy*. His precious mother opened a line to the room. Or else he would have been out here interrogating me already."

"How do you know what he's doing?"

He waved again without opening his eyes. "What is the plan?"

I didn't respond.

He cracked open an eye. "Oh, darling. Are you deluding yourself now?"

I shifted. "You don't think Marsgrove will succeed now?"

Constantine hummed. "Do you?"

I picked at the blanket, and gave a mirthless laugh. "I'm magically unstable. I'm being continually tracked. And I'm going to have a harder

Chapter Twenty-two

time getting out of my *room* than I will getting off campus."

He opened both eyes, examining me, looking for...I didn't know what. "Yes, I heard about your new roommate. I have been thinking of all sorts of lovely ways to remove you from that situation." He smiled.

"Without hurting her," I said hurriedly. I pictured him pitching Bellacia's body off the Magiaduct, safety spells in place or not.

Bellacia was one of the people in the very small fraction of the population Dare had referenced who Constantine cared about. And not in the good way.

"Of course, darling. You made me promise when you destroyed my lovely toy. I was thinking more of mental pain," he said with a smile.

"Without *hurting* her. Emotionally counts."

His smile grew. "Not a problem."

"She's not a cyborg."

He waved a hand. "She doesn't have enough emotion to be one."

"Con."

"I think your line is, 'It's lovely to have you back.'" His eyes glinted, amused, and there was something genuine in his devilish smile for a moment.

I reached out and touched his hand. "It is."

Dare chose that moment to exit his workroom. He looked between us, then at the wards, expression going grim. "Ren."

"Yes?"

"Your tablet is beeping," Dare said.

"Crap." I fished it out. The first thing I saw was that it was *noon*. The next was that I had thirty messages of increasing panic from my friends, and last, but definitely not least was that a mandatory Justice Squad meeting had been scheduled by Isaiah Gellis.

I stared at the blinking magic, then swiped a finger through it. A message from Isaiah popped up and swirled into my brain. Comfort and friendship and a clear directive of, "We are waiting. Get to this room, Crown, or the contract magic is going to penalize you."

An image of a room in Dorm Eight flashed.

I stared blankly at my tablet. "I have... I have to report to the Justice Squad. Everyone was put on the roster for duty today," I said out loud.

I still had Justice Magic responsibilities. Unbelievable.

Marsgrove was out there somewhere—rescuing Olivia or dead. Raphael and Kaine were waging war across the Third Layer. Stavros and Helen Price were somewhere, plotting my doom. And I was stuck here, in the Magiaduct, captive with everyone else, and responsible for campus *lawfulness*.

"Only you, Crown," Constantine said, his tone pretty uninterested again,

* Waking in the Same World *

and his eyes still closed. "Would be surprised by this."

"But—"

Dare dropped a sandwich and a piece of fruit into my free hand and pulled me upright. He magicked my day bag crosswise over my body and pushed me out the door.

In the hall, Justice Toad beeped for an entire minute while I stared in stupefaction at the tablet in one hand and the food in my other.

I gained myself an additional hour of service time in not answering the beep promptly enough.

Chapter Twenty-three

JUSTICE SQUAD

EVERY GAZE followed me as I swallowed the last bite of my sandwich and slipped into the only seat left—front and center, unfortunately—of the dormitory common room we were using as a temporary meeting spot.

On the way here, I had tried to eat, catch up on what had happened while I'd been out cold, answer the questions of the people who were brave enough to accost me in the hall, and reassure all of my panicking friends that I was alive. But I had too little time to process any of it, especially while apologizing profusely to the entire armband alliance for turning off my comm again. I was going to have to catch up on everything on the fly. Hopefully I didn't get caught wrong footed right from the get go.

Isaiah clapped his hands together, bringing audience attention back to him. "Okay, people. We had quite a day yesterday. A brutal one. The media is, unfortunately, labeling it Bloody Tuesday—I think we have one of our regular offenders to thank for that moniker, so make sure to give O'Leary an extra fun punishment next time you answer his call. But *Bloody* Tuesday, or not, we weathered the events and we *succeeded*."

A fierce surge of Community Magic pride swept through the room. It was not unlike what I'd experienced inside of Patrick and Asafa's room, and it was a powerful reminder that my community *was* larger than I sometimes realized.

"I'd like to single out a few outstanding efforts," Isaiah continued. "Prime support personnel took care of everything that came through the system during curfew hours last night with the help of Professor Wellingham, and with Provost Johnson granting exceptions."

Exceptions could be made to curfew magic? Interesting...

"And as most of you already know, last night and this morning we had *thousands* of calls," Isaiah said. "Thank you, to everyone on prime support who went above and beyond the call of justice duty."

I shuddered. I could only imagine the type of calls that had been fielded.

"Rewinding back to the events of yesterday," he said, "Travers, *excellent* work on the Justice Magic Negative Field. For all of you who are unaware, when the Administration Magic came back online yesterday, Travers managed to switch the flow of Justice Magic to attack anyone who was not a resident of campus proper. The praetorians were able to overcome the magic, but most of the rest, even members of the Legion, were put out of commission for a full minute, allowing us to identify those who didn't belong on campus. I heard some of the officials who journeyed in at the tail end of things got a right shock."

That startled an unwitting laugh out of a few people.

"Poor Travers suffered three thousand hours of community service for implementing the spell, but I've been assured those hours will be cleared before lockdown ends."

There was a large round of applause. I joined in, and visually identified Travers, a gangly brunette with large ears and pink cheeks who was ducking his head. I was very interested in what he had done to achieve that spell.

The list of mages who had performed outstanding actions in the service of the day was lengthy, but Isaiah wielded each recognition with aplomb.

Until the end.

"And lastly, Ren Crown."

Silence.

"Without whom," Isaiah said, without breaking stride. "We would have been blind to what was happening within the Troop."

More silence. All gazes on me.

"Furthermore, her actions allowed us to work together with all possible hands and resources to break free of the Magiaduct's dome and to protect campus."

I swallowed and looked at my hands, unwilling to meet all of the gazes staring at me. I was kind of hoping Isaiah would stop speaking. But no such luck.

"Actions that are directly prompting an immediate debate on how we can coordinate efforts further, and better, in response to large-scale attacks. All thanks to one of ours." He brandished a hand at me.

I cleared my throat in the face of the dead silence.

"There were a number of mages involved in keeping communications open," I said, shaking hands gripping Justice Toad tightly against my chest. "Mages who are, ironically, routinely punished for such actions. You might want to go easy on Patrick O'Leary for a few calls, even though, Bloody Tuesday? Yeah, I can't believe he named it that either. But if you want to thank anyone, Olivia Price was integral in every facet of yesterday, not least

Chapter Twenty-three

of which was making sure that we all remained connected to each other."

I took a breath and looked around. "Do not credit me. We were all, as a community, involved."

Silence.

Isaiah gave me an amused glance. "I know said community has many questions—" Hands and magic shot into the air. "Which will be answered during the strict fact based question and answer session at the end of this meeting."

The hands reluctantly lowered. Thank Magic, for Isaiah.

"First things first. We need to discuss, going forward, what we can do to aid the new forces on campus—" *More* new forces, was somewhat heavily implied, but not said. "And Justice Magic itself."

I settled in for a long meeting. Usually I had fourteen projects flying through my brain, and untangled magic slotting everything into neat mental piles to work on. Today I had one mission, and magic still too burnt to freely flow past all the knots.

That meant I was stuck...listening.

"We will need to account for mages acting out from stress and grief," Isaiah said. "Those on prime support have already been dealing with it, and there will be increased counts of vandalism, fighting, and provocation over the next few days. The mental health and well-being mages are working with the Administration to tailor the next two weeks of Justice Magic to include a trigger in the magic to identify magic tinged with a rota of emotional occurrences.

"If someone acts out of grief directly, they will receive particular sentencing. Sentences designed to help them, while at the same time not rewarding their initial outbursts. We are trying to help students get back in the pool and off the diving board."

I stared straight forward, unable to stop the thought spiral of how I had acted my first eight weeks on campus. Of how many charges I had racked up searching for a way to bring Christian back.

"We will coordinate grief counseling with large picture trauma. This is more than just our monster of the day, or out-of-control beast of the week."

"The combat mages will still be *gone* tonight when the top levels of campus reopen," someone in the audience said.

"But part of the Legion will remain here," Isaiah responded. "I think we can all concur that they can handle any surprises that occur."

Surprisingly, that seemed to bring no ease to the people in the room. They had been gung-ho at the Peacekeepers' Troop coming in to help. Either the idea of outside help had lost its shine or the Legion was outside their point of acceptance.

* Justice Squad *

When Isaiah finally reached the end of what we'd be doing during the next week, it was question and answer time.

Unsurprisingly, I got the first one.

"Miss Crown, what *happened*?"

It was a question I had been asked at least six times on my way to the meeting. I gave a rote recitation of the events. The same litany I had given every stranger so far. Stripped down and to the point.

But at least here, everyone knew what working with Alexander Dare entailed. No one questioned my statement that I'd felt like I needed to save campus when he left for the competition.

It was a nice change.

Unfortunately, there were more difficult questions to answer.

"Why didn't you use us? Why weren't we privy to this plan of yours?" an upper year girl asked, expression pinched.

"There was a good system already in place, which usually worked." I shrugged. "This was really more of a...panic response to being teamed with, er, Axer."

People kept giving me weird looks when I referred to him as Dare. Like only strangers did that. It was hard to change, though. He was Dare in my head.

Even though he'd made me a peanut butter sandwich an hour ago.

I was still processing that.

"But you could have set up that panic response with us," someone blurted out.

Deliberately and slowly, I looked around the room, meeting all of the gazes staring back at me. "Could I have?"

A few gazes turned away.

"Let's face it. I don't belong on this squad," I said frankly. "And many of you have felt that way about me from the beginning. It's not a secret."

"You've been a very productive member of the squad, Ren," Isaiah said, voice slightly chastising.

I gave him a strained smile.

"Listen up, everyone. I won't tolerate any breakdown in the squad or rotations," Isaiah said, expression grave. "If there is anything that yesterday has taught us, it's that we need to work together as a community."

No one said anything, but I could feel the enormous weight of their gazes on me.

"Schedules are on your feeds or tablets. Go forth and bring peace."

Chapter Twenty-four

DOG DAY AFTERNOON

LEAVING THE MEETING, I was able to take a better look at my surroundings, since I wasn't juggling five things. Gazes peered back everywhere I went—solemn and questioning. It was worse than it had been last night.

"Did you see that spell she shot through the roots?" one murmured. "What was it? Who was the boy?"

Everyone had seen the firework—the recording of me fighting "Christian" under the dome. I hadn't reviewed the footage. How much of the fight had been recorded? How much had Saf and Trick shown?

"Just the beginning." Trick's mental voice was reserved. *"And there was no sound. Sorry, Princess. It was the only thing that would grab everyone's attention."*

I swallowed. "It's okay," I murmured. It was going to have to be, at this point. "Are we still meeting?"

A meeting time had been thrown out in the flurry of communications I had been fielding on the way to the Justice Squad meeting.

"Yes. Come over any time."

Trick and Saf's room was unofficial headquarters at this point.

Most of the members were already inside. They caught me up on what I'd missed.

"The crowd went crazy after the firework, yeah, but Nephthys was brilliant with your double's physical responses and we herded around you. Even watched the rest of the memorial in full view of Bailey and her ilk. Eight thumbs up, on our end. Had a little trouble when we didn't think you'd make it back, but, luckily, we held off on Plan B."

They'd *waited*. They should have dumped my double and all the trackers and markers attached to it, erased their memories, and disavowed further involvement. But, now that we were back safely, I couldn't say that I wasn't relieved they hadn't.

* Dog Day Afternoon *

I couldn't tell them *exactly* what had happened on our midnight trip, or what had happened with my dream and Kaine, but I let them know that Marsgrove had Olivia's location and that he was chasing after her at this exact moment.

Trick turned on a feed.

"Violence continues in the Third Layer, as the Legion, praetorians, and terrorists engage in active warfare."

Most of the news outlets were reporting on the Third Layer violence that had been occurring all day. Many speculated that the attacks were direct retaliations to Bloody Tuesday.

"Some of the attacks have to be simple retaliation without deeper meaning," Dagfinn said. "Plenty of Second Layer folks are foaming at the mouth with the desire to dirty their hands in some vengeance. But if even some of those I've identified in the wires are Marsgrove and Verisetti and the praetorians—they are jumping all over the Third Layer in a mad version of a child's game."

"Marsgrove will rescue her," I said, a little desperately. "I'm so *sorry*."

Looks were exchanged.

"Princess, you made the right call. We were all in a bit of a tailspin last night after you went off grid with Axer Dare. It really brought it home. Hearing that Marsgrove is getting her back was a massive relief."

I closed my eyes. It would have been a solidly served plan, too, if Kaine hadn't used me to muck it all up.

"Dean Marsgrove is a right prick about a lot of things," Dagfinn said. "But he's a fighter and tracker. And he's always favored Price."

Olivia's familial relationship to Marsgrove wasn't a secret.

"Dean Marsgrove has a better chance than we do," Saf said bluntly. "You did the right thing giving him her location."

The others murmured their agreement. Their uniform accord that giving Olivia's location to Marsgrove had been the best option was unexpected.

I couldn't let them think that I was blameless for the current mess, though.

"Kaine used me to track them too," I blurted out.

More looks were exchanged.

"Ren." Mike sighed. "Kaine was going to track you to the ends of each layer of the Earth. What do you think was going to happen if you were the one to leave campus?"

They all exchanged looks again, and I felt very outside the loop.

"What happened?" I asked, dread coiling.

"They caught two students leaving last night, Crown," Saf said. "It was a good plan the two cooked up. We had it on our list."

I looked around the table, stomach dropping as I read their solemn

Chapter Twenty-four

expressions. "And?"

"No one's heard from them since the Legion nabbed them. Not a frequency exchange, not a peep. They took the two of them under the guise of worldwide security."

I looked down at my hands.

"They can't keep them for long. But with you? They'd find a reason," Mike said grimly. "Easily and quickly."

They'd test me. Properly this time. In the basement of the Department where they could manufacture any results they wanted.

Neph pressed her palm to my skin. Tension dissipated like a balloon freed from its knot.

The entire room seemed to take a deep, calming breath.

"Word has it that they are going to open the Magiaduct before dinner—get all of us rotating through the cafeteria," Lifen said. "Public spaces north of the seventh circle will be open."

"I don't know about you, but I'm not all that keen on getting out," Loudon said, rubbing a hand over his short curls. "The Legion is going to be scanning us at every turn. This isn't like the office stooges and scientists who were here before. The Legion is ruthless. And they have tagged every one of us from recorded feeds—identifying the scarf wearers, if nothing else."

Hyped up as we'd all been on the adrenaline from yesterday, today more rational heads were in play.

"That reminds me, we made this for you this morning." Will smiled and handed me a small, square jewel. "It doesn't stop people from knowing who you are, but this will absorb all the tracking and marking spells anyone tries to place on you. Like tracking spell flypaper. The jewel inactivates them, but keeps them inside."

He shrugged. "The capture allows you to go over them later, if you want, to see who tagged you—there's a brilliant spell decoder that Adrabi put in there. We're all planning to tailor and use them," he said frankly.

I examined the flat jewel, then tucked it into my armband—the interior lining had been made for just this type of addition. "It will absorb all the spells?"

"All the ones that can be scanned for."

Not shadows, then. But getting rid of all the spells that random—and not so random—students were placing on me was a boon.

"People will be scrambling to come up with better trackers before the day's out." Adrabi smiled, all flashing teeth and bronzed skin that looked far better today than the mottled look he'd sported due to a flaying spell cast on him the day before.

"Luckily, we know most of the makers on campus personally. We'll be

* Dog Day Afternoon *

having a challenging time staying a step ahead of the crowd." Adrabi looked like that suited him very well.

"Nothing we can do about Administration Magic, but I looked into the Department's permissions on campus. They can't hook into tracking individual students yet through Administration Magic. And their 'mission' here is to secure campus. So they are legally restricted to student help in tracking us."

As I knew well, they had plenty of those.

"They'll be trying to pin us. Hard. The Department not only wants to pin the blame on the Administration, but they want all of us under their thumbs, and *some* of us under their dissecting scopes."

I pressed my lips together. The Department wanted powerful tools, but anyone connected to me was most at risk. "I don't want any of you caught in the crossfire. There *will* be crossfire. And it will be my battle to fight."

Adrabi didn't break eye contact, and he didn't hesitate. "Nephthys *Bau* resurrected me four times yesterday," he said frankly. "Four times. And we all know she wanted to be at *your* side—she was leaking magic like a mother bear full of rage and purpose—yet she hunted each of us down, repeatedly, to make sure we survived the day. *All of us.* Other than Price, and that was an extenuating circumstance, every single one of us connected to the Plan made it to see sunset, and we were in the *thickest* parts of the battles in *separate* circles of the mountain. Bau waded into every one like a wraith and plucked us each from the eversleep."

Neph studiously didn't look up, busy as she was manipulating the emotions of the room. Keeping us all on even keel. I could feel the tight knot of emotion inside her, though, that she was trying to hide.

Guilt, shame, and fierce gratitude all wrapped together again inside of me. "I, uh, accidentally whammied her."

"Yeah," Adrabi said dryly. "We know. Obviously with instructions to save us all. Listen, Crown. You let us take care of things around campus for a bit, got it?"

Neph looked up and pierced me with her gaze. It wasn't hard to decipher what she was trying to convey.

I looked back at Adrabi and swallowed. "Yeah, okay."

"And don't worry about your muse. I've already got some things in the works for protecting her. We've got her back in the days to come."

Frowning, I started to ask, but the conversation mysteriously switched direction and I blinked for a second. What had I been about to say?

The thought slipped free of my mind as we started to discuss what could be done when we were released from lockdown. Loudon continued to fret.

"Think positively, lad," Patrick said. "Location protection charms and eavesdropping interference devices are a *hot* market right now. And the

Chapter Twenty-four

steady traffic wanting to ask us about Bloody Tuesday is only increasing those sales as they buy devices in an excuse to meet and ask questions. We are selling out across the board."

Patrick winked at me. "I'm keeping a log. Price will want to know all about it when she returns."

I nodded slowly at him. It was a foregone conclusion to them that Marsgrove would get her back. I wanted to believe it too.

"Chin up, Crown," Patrick said.

~*~

During my first round of calls, more than one person sputtered, stuttered, and dropped what they were doing, when I showed up. I was also nearly blasted four separate times in reaction. By the end of the hour, though, I was receiving far more considering looks and far less *accidental* blasts aimed my way. The news had spread that I might answer a Justice call.

I had my hands full with a slew of grief calls too. And those...those were both easier and harder to bear.

I made a side trip to Medical halfway through my first rotation and shakily whipped up a dozen more roses, this time using Christian's orb as the focus for my feelings and limited magic. I dosed each paper flower with a liberal swipe of the healing wards. It helped that when Greyskull passed me, instead of chastising me, he plucked a ward from the wall and draped it over my hand without breaking stride.

The ward, and the inherent permission within the action, had been similar to Marsgrove's device—and it made it easier for me to get past my blocks, allowing me to direct some of the Administration Magic instead of using my own.

I used all twelve of them within twenty minutes. Tucking them into the room when the Justice offender was looking elsewhere, or simply handing it to them, if their grief was especially fierce.

As each minute ticked by with no positive news about Olivia or Marsgrove, though, the feeling inside of me darkened as well.

I clicked out of service and opened the door to Bellacia's suite, determined to spend one of my mandatory hours logging reports and searching for any scrap of information on Olivia or on Marsgrove's location. Maybe I'd luck out and Bellacia would be out.

As luck had it, not only was she *in residence*, but five of her magicist cronies occupied chairs around a table in the main room.

Bellacia smiled sharply at me. "Ren, welcome back."

I nodded and walked quickly to bypass the table and get to the bedroom. There was no need to wonder about the tracking spell blocker

* Dog Day Afternoon *

Will, Adrabi and the others had made. I could see the panic in some of the faces around the table as they indiscreetly checked devices, wondering why they hadn't been alerted to my presence.

"Outrageous that she walks freely," someone said, jerking in the opposite direction as I passed.

"Her magic is up," Oakley said, making a note. "Too far up."

"Her magic can hear you," I said, without breaking stride.

"Don't antagonize the Origin Mage, Oakley," another chastised. "But I do agree it is suspicious. The lack of tracers could be due to a visit to her little friends. But, she should only be recovered twelve percent with the room's magic. Where is she getting the extra? What if she's pulling it from the earth or grounds? What if we are about to suffer an event?" He shook his head. "Record her levels and check them against the readings from this morning and yesterday. We'll need it in our report."

I slammed the bedroom door closed.

Clenching my fists and breathing heavily, I marched over to my bed. Was it worse or better for me to be here while their group was meeting? I shut my eyes. Whatever. Too late. One hour here now. One hour later.

I secured my things with a protection ward, and aggressively pulled Bellacia's streaming headlines into reach. Screw Oakley, Bailey, and their crew.

News reports soon scrolled every wall. Another Third Layer facility had been hit by the Legion. And a list of all the locations the praetorians had been spotted flashed for my attention.

I quickly absorbed those, and admitted temporary defeat—no news source, not even Bellacia's, had any mention of Marsgrove or Raphael being seen.

I touched one of the scrolls labeled "Campus: Live!" and a surveillance feed opened up. Someone had set a spell mimicking a drone on top of the Magiaduct, and it was circling the superstructure, giving a live, rotating view of the levels on either side. There were still members of the Legion, the praetorians, and troops from the surrounding countries visible all around the Magiaduct. But the latter were growing thinner in number, as the searches around campus were completed and the areas pronounced clear.

I touched another scroll labeled, "Campus: Report!" which indicated that the Magiaduct would be re-opened at Cancer Rising—six in the evening on the twenty-four hour clock.

The combat mages, it was reported, were leaving at the same time.

I closed my eyes, squeezing them tight.

I'd be able to get to the library and, maybe, the art vault. But I'd lose Dare.

I touched another scroll that said, "Latest on the Loss Report!"

Chapter Twenty-four

Olivia's picture flashed, making me jerk upright.

Listed beneath her image was the message, *Have you seen her?* Beneath that different methods of magical spotting were encouraged—gazing, printing, casting—along with numbers to call with information generated from each method.

The whispers about her being missing had started shortly after the battle, and had been confirmed with the student listings that chronicled critical, missing, or dead students. Most of the missing students had been magically transferred to one of the other lists as campus sweeps had taken place and bodies had been recovered.

Olivia was one of fifteen students who remained on the missing list the day after Bloody Tuesday.

There were a few groups dedicated to finding the missing students through gazing and other magical means. Eight had been identified hiding in their Second Layer homes, having somehow successfully escaped through the lower levels of campus during the chaos. Suspicions and rumors had been raised over *how* they had escaped, but nothing definitive had been discerned.

Three of the other missing students were hiding in their *Third Layer* homes. Students who had slipped by peer notice of being "Thirdies" and who had retreated in the wake of worrying that they would be harassed about their birth layer. Or who had been *allowed* to escape.

The final four students had proven to be beyond magical detection. One of those was Olivia.

I tightened my hand around the origami balloon.

Helen Price, meanwhile, had capitalized politically on her missing daughter—just as Olivia had known she would. She was maintaining a brave facade, denouncing the Third Layer, the terrorists, and the school's capability to protect itself.

"It wasn't someone on our watch, of course," Helen Price said to the interviewer. "It was someone who infiltrated the Troop who had already been cleared at Excelsine. In the direct aftermath of the attack, we found the body of Emrys Norr in a bunker under his home. Why the officials at the school didn't recognize that he was not the same person, I cannot speculate."

"Wasn't the Troop your pick for Excelsine's security?" the interviewer asked.

Helen lifted a brow. "Our pick? No. The officials at the school required *aide* after the unexplained events of the previous term. We offered Legion protection, but Excelsine chose the option of having the Troop. It's really been one blow after another for Excelsine's security. More and more, I'm coming to realize that it would be better for the educational system for the

* Dog Day Afternoon *

Department to oversee it in its entirety. We need a managing body. These are our *children*."

My fingers clenched so hard that my pencil snapped. Half-truths wrapped around past manipulations. She was making it sound as if the administration had made one poor decision after another, instead of being forced to pick between three bad options—two of which had the Department all over campus, and the other that had the Troop providing security for a week.

"Look at Excelsine, in particular, and their actions over the past few months. What is it that the school's officials have to hide? Why are they trying to prevent a security body from looking at administrative information? If everything is legal at Excelsine, why are they choosing to hinder routine investigations?

"If something isn't done, I'm not sure I can send my child back once she is returned."

My control cuff compressed around my wrist. I had enough magic back, that without it managing me, I would have blown up the entire hologram device.

"Speaking of your daughter—"

But I couldn't listen to any more. I punched off the feed with shaking fingers. I was far too furious.

Being Bellacia's roommate gave me firsthand access to every broadcast and piece of news—some before they went live. It was an unexpected benefit of living with the enemy.

And an unexpected downfall, as I sat shaking on my bed.

Bellacia slipped inside the room. I pulled all of the spells into my hand and pitched them toward the recycling grate in the floor.

"Oh, Ren, there's no need to hide anything." She twirled a number of news articles around her fingers, pinching them together, then splaying them out. The spell seemed to be looking for connections in my previous searches. "Archelon Kaine," "Raphael Verisetti," "Phillip Marsgrove," "Olivia Price," "Helen Price," and "Enton Stavros" all popped up. She twisted two fingers, and another report formed.

My breath seemed to be coming faster.

"Whatever is the matter, Ren? You seem to be concerned over something?"

I grabbed my bag.

"It's only been an hour," she called out.

"Yup."

I walked out the door, slamming it shut behind me.

The door five down from hers opened before I reached it.

Chapter Twenty-five

CIVILIZED COUCH WARFARE

CONSTANTINE GAVE ME a look. I sighed as I walked inside. He closed the door behind me.

Dare appeared in the doorway of his workroom.

"Hi." I wiped a hand over my face, looking between them. "I just...couldn't stay there longer than an hour."

"You are welcome here," Dare said, hands stretched to either side of the doorframe. His gaze narrowed on Constantine, then turned to me. "Stay as long as you want."

With the two of them prowling around each other?

"I've already witnessed enough bloodshed this week," I said ruefully. "I'll go to Neph's."

Though for some odd reason, I was already dropping into a chair, limp with relief, and my legs were lifting up on an ottoman that hadn't been there seconds before. I stared at my feet for a moment, then shook my head.

I let my head fall back on the club chair. Just a minute or two. I'd just stay here for a minute or two, then I'd go to Neph's.

Little bolts of magic were zipping along the edges of the room where the walls met the ceiling. I stared at them, watching the colors meet and meld or travel alongside each other. A week ago, two *days* ago, none of this magic had been freely flowing through the living room. Whatever else had happened in the interim, Constantine and Dare had put aside their hatred long enough to allow the wards free rein in the suite. The wards that shut the other off from their individual work rooms were still there, but even those wards were...laxer.

Perhaps it had to do with Medical, and the two of them being separated overnight. Or perhaps it was what had been set up for the competition, and finally turned on. I had asked, after all this roommate insanity had come to

* Civilized Couch Warfare *

light. All of the combat mages' rooms had been hooked into receiving extra Community Magic for the week, so their roommates wouldn't be adversely affected. The same way that Olivia had gone without a roommate for long stretches of time.

The emergency procedures in place now didn't allow for those dispensations, unfortunately. Though, Bellacia and I were benefiting from that extra magic in Room Twenty-five.

I nestled into the chair a little more. Constantine and Dare's magic was highly sympathetic to mine, but in a natural, organic way. As evidenced in Medical—we could probably overpower the grid given time.

There was a larger, active power boost in Bellacia's room, because whatever she had done to secure me as a roommate, worked. But it was an artificial feeling.

My eyes started to slip shut, as they'd been unable to do for the last hour in a place where I had to watch my back. I had only been awake for four hours, but I felt like, were circumstances different, I could sleep for a week.

"We will limit the bloodshed for the next few hours," Dare said dryly, though in a more serious tone than anticipated.

The "home" connection reached outward toward their wards. My eyes shot open and I aggressively reeled it back in.

"Why?" I said, trying to cover my actions.

Dare raised a brow, and I quickly added to my statement, "Not why on the bloodshed, why on the invitation to camp out on your couch? I *can* go to Neph's."

Even though my feet weren't currently moving me in that direction.

Neph's roommate didn't like me—probably was terrified of me now—but Neph would invite me in anyway.

Will and Mike's would be a fine alternative, as well, though our magic was neutrally sympathetic, and those news reports had increased my urge to heal *faster*.

"Have your muse come here," Dare said. "The room magic is helping you." He pointed to the zips of magic which had doubled since I last looked. "Helping you *slowly*, which is supposed to be the point of healing."

The expression on his face said he knew what I'd been thinking.

I shrugged.

"So, what did lovely Bellacia do?" Constantine asked. His lips indicated that he was amused, but his eyes were steely and...anticipatory.

I waved a weary hand. "Nothing. The normal. She keeps recording everything I do in there. She's exhausting. And she's probably right—I will be kicked out of here within a week. She'll have it all magicked up neatly too with pyrotechnics—*Bulletin at Nine, Wicked Girl Gone, Our Layer Saved!*"

I tipped my head back. "What happens if I *don't* stay there for my

Chapter Twenty-five

allotted twelve hours? I'll embrace a few hundred justice hits."

Neither of them responded vocally.

Dare's gaze strayed to the wards, then to Constantine. Constantine tipped his head and looked smug for a moment. Smugness turned to fury at whatever Dare mentally conveyed to him.

"You think it will always work out the way you want it to," Constantine said out loud, anger underlying every word. "Frequency flash—*Alexander Dare does not always get what he wants.*"

"You're being a child."

Whatever Constantine said in return was mental, but one finger jabbed in my direction. Both of their expressions turned pinched and unpleasant, the kind that happened in a heated argument. Sneering, in Constantine's case and lethal, in Dare's. But after a moment, their demeanors changed and they both gave short nods to each other.

"Do it," Dare said grimly.

Constantine's grin turned unholy.

They both turned to me.

I started humming the Twilight Zone theme music.

At their twin blank stares, I sighed and quit. "Never mind. What did you two just agree on? And, may I say how freaky it is that you two communicate somehow?"

Constantine turned on his heel, unholy grin still lifting his lips. "I think the word you are looking for is *unfortunate*. I'll be back, darling."

I blinked at him. "Where are you going?"

"Just down to Medical," he said lightly. "Have to check in, you know."

I didn't know. He *was* probably going to Medical—Constantine didn't lie usually, you just had to ferret the truth from his words. This likely meant he was going there, but not *only* for a check in.

"Okay, be sketchy."

"It is my best side."

As he walked toward the door, his clothes flipped into something far more tailored to a business event. Constantine was *expensive*. Everything about him reflected extraordinary wealth, even his dressed down clothes. But he usually wasn't dressed in the equivalent of a business suit.

Extra sketchy.

He left with a rude gesture to Dare and a blown kiss to me. Dare's face was shuttered as he looked at the closed door.

"Thanks for the sandwich," I blurted.

The edges of his lips lifted in amusement as he turned back to me. "That's what you are going to go with?"

"Yup. I would have starved without you."

He reached inside their magic fridge and threw a wrapped package to

* Civilized Couch Warfare *

me. I unrolled a crunchy veggie wrap. There were a few unidentifiable vegetables inside—the Second Layer had a lot more purples and pinks in their veggie options—but it tasted fine.

"Make sure to eat." He pressed a finger against my arm. A little diagnostic appeared above it— *magic level 33%.*

Considerably better than expected, but still a strong third away from feeling like I could keep things together without Dare on campus.

"You can boost that up another fifteen percent," he said, "If you eat three more meals before midnight."

I nodded sagely. "Feeding me after midnight makes monsters."

"You aren't a monster, Ren," he said, gaze intense.

"Thanks, Alexander." I sighed and took a bite. I wondered how much Second Layer pop culture *I* missed in conversation.

"You don't have to call me that."

"Thanks, dude."

That caused the edge of his mouth to quirk. Unlike pop culture phrases, words translated cleanly just fine.

It was clearly implied from his comment that I could address him in some diminutive form. I wondered what he would do if I started calling him Al.

He sat across from me as I ate and casually manipulated his fingers in the air. He was doing some absolutely compelling equations based on timetables, distances, and magic variables. I didn't even try to pretend I wasn't staring at them as they formed in the air.

A little alarm spell blinked the time and gave him a "time remaining" alert.

I swallowed the last of my food. "You're leaving at six?"

The same despair and tension that had overtaken me when he had left for the competition the first time, threatened once again.

He looked up, as if sensing my distress. "They are demanding our return to the competition. To make everything 'right again.'"

I balled up the wrapper in my hand, concentrating on the material as it compressed. "That's...there seems to be something wrong with that logic." Tension gripped me more completely, and I threw the wrapper into the trash, then crossed my arms tightly, trying to stave off panic.

Dare snapped his fingers and a hologram of Helen Price appeared in his hand.

"It is best for the emotional health of the Second Layer for the competition to continue," she said, in her cultured, hateful voice. *"Having the excellent combat mages from Excelsine do well will be a boon to everyone in the Second Layer. I think we will all be rooting for them."*

Dare extinguished her in his palm. It was a satisfying maneuver that I

Chapter Twenty-five

would have to try next time I was listening to one of her interviews.

"The other layers are also demanding that the competition continue," Dare said. "They say that what happened here is a tragedy, but that pausing the competition for a day and a half gives us more than enough time to grieve."

"Right," I said bitterly.

Christian's orb warmed in my pocket, as did the ultramarine thread connected to my chest. I released a breath. The feeling of kinship Dare was sending was not just warm, it was soothing.

"Thanks," I said.

He rose and motioned for me to follow him as he walked into his workroom.

My steps were tentative in his wake. Tension of a different kind gripped me.

His workroom was one of the mysteries of Excelsine that I had longed to solve. I'd been fascinated by the wards on the room from the first time I'd entered the suite—long before I'd known Dare lived here.

It had to be something *epic*.

Constantine's workroom was fantastic with all of its mechanical and material wonders, and Bellacia's news emporium was incredible. I expected Dare's to be some sort of labyrinthine maze of monstrous wonder.

What I didn't expect was for it to be pure white. Bare. Sterile. Without a shred of furniture or even a piece of lint inside.

Four white walls. A white floor. A white ceiling.

I stared around the room blankly—in a reflection of all that was blank around me. "Er..."

He raised a brow, and waved a hand. Color and light lit every surface. He pulled his hand toward his chest, and a full closet appeared.

I reached forward and my hand went through the hanging garments and touched the wall.

He smirked and lifted a shirt from the image. In his hand, the shirt appeared as real as any I'd ever held in mine. He flung it toward an image of a black bag and it disappeared inside.

Dare *shifted* the room, rotating it to show a different section of clothing. An endless walk-in-closet. I wondered if Delia had one of these. If she didn't, she'd be green with envy.

I was less interested in the clothes, though, and more in the abilities of the room, which I recognized intimately from the Battle Building. Dare switched the walls to display weaponry—showing some way overpowered James Bond Quartermaster level stock.

Chosen weapons went into the bag, too.

Medical supplies were next.

* Civilized Couch Warfare *

"You have a practice room, a department store, a hospital cache, and an armory," I said dumbly. "In your room."

"Not quite." He didn't elaborate.

"Can you battle people in here?"

He smiled. "Only mental simulations." He pointed to the floor. "We are limited here, where we aren't in Kratos."

In the practice rooms in the Kratos Battle Building, the entire realm of reality was turned on its head. The rooms weren't all that big, but the floors moved magically with the movements and intentions of the occupant. So running, diving, and even flying were all possible when the dynamics of the room were activated.

Mental simulations? Surrounded by his mind and imagination, I could just bet on what sort of mental chessboard or fighting strategy he could practice in here.

Maybe Olivia and I could move dorms next season.

"So, when you move in," I asked, "do you just decide what you want your workroom to be?"

Because I definitely wanted this. Something I could creatively decorate, drown in my art, then pull into smaller spaces that I could activate at will.

"The spells for the rooms are tailored by the mage."

Constantine had everything in his workroom *just so*. And everything was very real—real furniture, real stirring sticks. Sure, he could change things around—most things on campus were flexible. But he rarely did. He liked to pretend that he was quicksilver, but he was actually pretty dependent on things around him being reliable.

As I watched Dare flip through multiple scenarios to obtain everything he needed, a few things attacked at random. He easily dispatched them, but they were unpredictable—one stock room had no monsters, another had three, and another tried to suffocate us both. In Dare's self-made room...nothing was stable. Constant flux. Always able to change and adjust.

Dare's inherent stability—or my opinion of it—came from the feeling that he would be able to handle *anything*, no matter what happened. That's why it was effortless for him to wear the helm of campus protector. It didn't matter what happened, he would handle it, if he were on campus.

Though, not unlike Constantine, Dare, too, didn't like unknown variables. He actively sought them out. He'd done it with me. Made me known.

I shook my head and stepped over to the black bag he was filling and crouched down, watching as the items he tossed disappeared inside.

"So, this is how dressing spells work? You have a container with them in it—or with attachments to them?"

He nodded and continued.

Chapter Twenty-five

"You preload them." I crossed my legs and rested my chin on my hand, elbow on my knee. "Huh."

"But you have to have enough working magic to use them. Excelsine is overpowered, so many mages use the spells here. But, in other locales?" He shrugged. "It depends on the magic available. Many communities consider it a waste of resources."

I thought of my storage papers, and Kinsky's. The reason that they were dangerous and valuable was that they used a set amount of magic. Permanent magic. This spell, like most, used magic temporarily, allowing an ebb and flow to the usage, safely recycling it when not in use, and controlling what use there was.

Taken in a "good for the community way," it was a better use of magic.

But mine...wasn't dependent on the community. There was power in that, though even I could see that it was an easily misused power.

I looked down at my hands and clenched my fingers into a fist, then relaxed them. Magic inched its way through my palm. Better than last night, at least.

"So, I'm fed..." I began.

Dare—no, *Axer*—looked up.

"And...I noticed some interesting items when you flipped through your medical stash..." I continued.

He didn't seem to be taking the hint.

"Like at least five of those white bricks-of-resuscitation." I was hoping he'd take my leaning forward, brows-raised, hint.

Delia could be counted on for quick energy pick-me-ups, but Axer always had the best stuff. He'd given me the bricks before, and they were crazy power-ups.

He shook his head and continued packing. "They won't work on you right now. Your magic still isn't circulating through its proper channels."

"Can you..." I waved my hands around, then mimicked a cord being violently pulled from me to him.

He looked unimpressed with my charades. "No."

With his mother being a world renowned healer, in addition to being a Bridge Mage, I had made assumptions. Assumptions that he could fix what Doctor Greyskull might not be able to. Unfair assumptions, really. Just because a parent was exceptional at something, didn't mean that a child had learned or inherited those skills.

"I *can*," he said grudgingly, reading my expression perfectly, as usual. "But I won't."

"Why?"

He shook his head. "I can't have you running off."

There were a number of things loaded into that statement.

Civilized Couch Warfare

Conversations that we hadn't yet had, irritations that hadn't been smoothed over, trust issues that I hadn't prepared for.

Questions about judgment.

Anger curled. "Just when you say so?"

"Yes."

I had been angry at him before we'd gone to the Midlands. But this was something deeper, something edging on betrayal.

He watched me. He watched me in a way that said he understood exactly what my thought process was.

"Why?" I demanded, getting back to my feet.

"Because while you are brilliant and powerful, trustworthy and loyal, you still lack good decision making skills."

I couldn't argue with that, not really. But I tried. "And you can make better decisions for me?"

"Yes."

"Going to the Midlands was *your* idea."

"And we got exactly what we needed, all according to plan."

I opened my mouth, but nothing came out, I was so furious. I stared deliberately at his midsection, still healing after being torn through.

"You can be angry," he said.

"I am," I said with deliberate pauses between each word. "Very angry."

"Perhaps then you will do *very better*."

My chest was surging with breath, like I couldn't catch it after a long run.

He tipped up my chin, fingers like small fires set against my skin. "These next few days and weeks are important. Fate of the world important." His gaze switched between my eyes, then his expression shifted minutely, as if he'd read something there. "Fate of your *roommate* important."

I leaned further into his fingers, sending them brushing fire along my throat. "Which is why I need you to dive in and fix me. In *case*."

He stood there for a long moment, fingers spanning my pulse points, my life force beneath his hand, an easy twist for him to snap my neck.

He tapped one finger against my left pulse point, in rhythm with the beat beneath that was speeding along as it always did when we were this close.

His gaze switched from there to my lips, then back to my eyes. "Okay."

My lips parted, heartbeat skittering over a beat. "Really?"

"Yes."

"Why?" I wanted it—for him to fix me—but I was also extremely aware that he hadn't been planning on doing so, five minutes ago. Natural curiosity and paranoia made me question the change.

His fingers slipped slowly from my skin. "Do you want the true answer,

Chapter Twenty-five

the real answer, or the answer that will sound best?"

"Truth? Real?" The one that sounded best?

He smiled. "I *want* to manipulate the magic in you."

Unfortunately, because of how *I'd* answered, I wasn't sure *which* answer he was giving.

"Do you know what it takes to consciously untangle someone's magic, Ren?"

"Greyskull says it's about diving down, working with the person you are healing."

"How long did it take him to fix you?"

I considered. "The first time? Five minutes? Maybe three—for a broken toe. I only allowed him to scan me yesterday—no real fixes. We sorted through his old...friendships."

Axer didn't look surprised by any of those statements. "It will take me hours. Hours where I will be *swimming* in your magic. Blanketed by it."

I blinked.

"Where I can do anything at all with the pathways I find." He touched my left pulse point again. "Because you will let me, won't you?"

It wasn't a question. And he wasn't wrong.

"I will be able to do anything. Hook you in any way." His fingers slid down my throat. "Manipulate everything inside of you until you answer only to me."

And it was something that so many people wanted to do to me. To be able to use my magic without having to ask its *shell*, me, for permission. Or perhaps for me to just *be* a shell. Raphael, Godfrey, Stavros, Price, even Marsgrove. And I had seen some of the hungrier looks on campus yesterday and today. Some of my fellow students wouldn't hesitate. Some of the *club,* people I knew, would not.

"And that's why," he said, "if you want to prove your judgment to me, you will say, *no.*"

I swallowed. His fingers moved with the movement. "That sucks. You suck."

"And you need people around you who question you more."

He stepped back.

"Why?" Why go through with this type of charade, why not just do it and say nothing? *Why?*

"Perhaps I'm just trying to get you to trust me implicitly," he said.

It was a very Constantine-like thing to say. But, the thing was, Axer knew I already trusted him. Knew that I would pretty much do anything for him.

"No."

He was obviously amused by my response, but his gaze was piercing.

* Civilized Couch Warfare *

"Then perhaps I don't want a shell," he said.

"Are you reading my mind?" I demanded. I hadn't said the part about people wanting a shell of me aloud.

There was a slight curl of his lips. "Really, Ren? You know such things aren't possible."

I looked down at my armband, then narrowed my eyes on his fingers, which were now playing with a beautiful ball of ultramarine, zips of silver darting through and around the sphere.

Communication Magic was not my forte, not yet. There was a lot of auditory processing involved, which was not my strength. I'd be putting in some concerted effort on that, though, if I made it here another term.

"Why *are* you packing? Shouldn't you already be packed?"

"For the competition, yes."

I narrowed my eyes on him. "Then what are you packing for?"

"Inevitability."

Chapter Twenty-six

PROMISES OF BLOODSHED

CONSTANTINE STILL wasn't back as the clock ticked over to half past five.

Axer put a small silver figurine in my palm. A duplicate rested in his. "Keep this on you."

I tapped my finger against the silver dragon. It was exquisitely crafted. I stroked my finger down its head and the one in his hand yawned, mouth wide. I tucked it under my armband. I'd go to Delia's and sew a pocket for it later.

"Is this going to manipulate me while you're gone?"

"If it is, you shouldn't have put it in your armband."

I rolled my eyes. "Whatever. You had your chance, buddy."

He smiled—a far more self-satisfied smile than I was used to seeing. Axer tended to wear an "all business, save the villagers!" look as a default. "Did I?"

"Yup. So, what do they do?"

"They will allow us to communicate. Off tablet, off frequency. Only these two are connected to each other."

I fished it back out, more interested. "How did you do it?"

"It's an easy spell, and an old one. The hard part is usually synching up the two mages at either end. But in your case, it's simple."

"Yeah, yeah, you know all my magic and weaknesses. I've already been warned."

"Have you?" he said lightly. Too lightly.

"Don't worry. Good judgment hasn't kicked in yet." I held up a thumb. "You're all set."

His expression grew serious. "The dragons can work via dreams, if you need them to, though there is risk involved in that with you."

I stared at the dragon. "Yeah, I'm not eager to repeat that yet."

* Promises of Bloodshed *

"I know. But if it comes to it, hold it and think of me as you fall asleep."

My cheeks flushed. "Shall do." I was going to need to keep it *away from me* as I slept.

"If you leave campus, though, do not wait, tell me *immediately*, however you have to."

I examined him, suddenly tense. "You seemed pretty confident that Marsgrove was going to prevail. What are you saying?"

"I'm leaving in thirty minutes. You will be under Leandred's influence for days. I know him. And I know you. He's a viper *you* choose to pet like a stray cat."

"Why don't you just stick trackers on us. Everyone else has."

"I can already track him. And you too," he said, with a pointed look in my direction. "With both of you in one place, it's child's play."

"That's...weird."

"No weirder than those animated rocks in your workshop that carry pencils as weapons while they case the premises."

I opened my mouth, then shut it. "Fair enough."

The door opened.

Constantine strode into the room, expression still that combination of smug self-satisfaction that he had exited with.

"Sacrifices were made, and dear Daddy is over-the-moon at being able to grant a request. All systems go."

I frowned. "You went to see your father?" I checked the magic on him, probing the connections that were still vibrantly displayed. He looked fine.

"Here." Axer threw something to Constantine.

Constantine caught the band in the air, and turned it over in his fingers. "Astrophene. How modern."

"Too complicated for you, Leandred?"

"Only in the way that it doesn't allow me to choke you with it. Such a limiting material," Constantine mused.

Axer ignored him and walked into the bedroom. "This one's mine." He looked at me and pointed at the bed closest to the door.

"Er, okay. Looks great?"

"The charade will require multiple parts, if implemented." He looked as if he'd swallowed a lemon. He pulled a shirt from atop the comforter. "And you'll both heal faster with you jacked into them."

I stared at his bed, then back at him. "What?" What charade?

He looked impatient. "Tell me *immediately*, if you leave."

"Yes?"

"It's not a question, Ren."

"Yes."

He reached out and palmed the back of my neck, pulling me closer and

Chapter Twenty-six

making me miss a heartbeat. "If you let Leandred leech you in order to untangle your magic completely, I will destroy him."

Heart thumping, I examined his expression. He was entirely serious. Smart of him. To threaten Constantine's welfare instead of mine.

"That goes for anyone, do you understand?"

I nodded, reluctantly. It would have been a pretty good plan.

"Do not listen to him, darling. There is little he can do to—"

Axer's hand dropped from me, and Constantine abruptly stopped speaking. I turned to see him standing in place, throat working as if someone was slowly cutting off his air. His hand made an aborted motion toward his throat, then curled, as if he wouldn't give his opponent the satisfaction.

Dare's expression was entirely forbidding as he looked at his roommate.

"Make it easy," Dare said to him, voice coaxing.

"Axer?" I said, putting a hand on his arm.

Freed of the hold, Constantine took a large breath and smiled dangerously at Dare. "Scurry on, now. You have a *competition* to win."

I thought Constantine might die, in that moment.

I stepped quickly between them. "Wow, okay. That promise on limiting bloodshed, it's still in effect, right?"

Tall as they were, I didn't provide much interference for their lines of sight. But after a moment, Axer looked down at me. The death promised in his eyes lessened.

I patted him. "Yay. Okay." Then pulled him toward the side of the room.

With one hand on him—worried he'd obliterate Constantine, if I let go—I dug out the last paper rose. I'd kept a single one. Infused with fond memory.

I handed it to him, sending a burst of affection and continued health through our connection threads.

His mouth quirked and his lethal look fled completely. "I accept your token," he said, in a parody of what I'd said to him weeks ago when we'd been testing with the Troop.

"Thanks, again, for..." My hands automatically formed like they were holding a sphere, then nervously clasped together.

"You are welcome, Ren," he said, voice soft.

A bell dinged and he shouldered his bag and walked to the door. He gave us each very separate—and loaded—looks, then disappeared into the hall.

I let out a breath, and ran a shaky hand through my hair, refocusing on Constantine.

"You." I pointed at him.

* Promises of Bloodshed *

His expression was still dark, but he quirked a brow. "Is now when my promised beating occurs?"

"Ugh." I rubbed my temples, then threw out a hand. "What were you thinking?"

"Shall I be scared of Alexander Dare too, just like you? Darling, don't give him the power," he said derisively.

"I'm not *scared of him*. But you don't go poking wild animals," I hissed. "The two of you are more feral than *I am*. Metaphorically!"

He picked imaginary lint from his shirtsleeve. "You don't like it when wild dogs fight over you?"

I narrowed my eyes. "That isn't what this is. Why do you hate each other? When did you stop being best friends?"

The flinch told me all I needed to know.

"I'm *right*," I said, horrified.

He showed his teeth under a slashing smile. I knew what was going to happen next. He was going to unload *everything*, all cannons firing. And it wasn't going to be pretty.

Quickly, I reached out and put my hand on the bend in his arm. "No. I'm sorry." I closed my eyes and focused on the connection threads, pushing *friendship* and *regret* across them.

When I opened my eyes, his expression was completely different.

He looked worse, completely like someone who had been on the edge of death twenty-four hours ago—and less like someone magically reconstructed to nearly full strength. "I will break you, Ren," he said, voice heavy. "You need to understand that."

"It's okay," I said, soothingly, like how I used to coax Christian back into form after a game loss. "We'll be fine."

Constantine rubbed a lock of my hair between his thumb and forefinger. "You think people want to be *friends* with you, Ren."

"We are friends."

"Old magic users don't make *friends* with powerful game pieces, Ren. Families like the Dares have allies. They see your potential and what they can do with it. All without planning to make you an equal in the process."

I smiled, a tight smile. I could read between the lines of what he was saying. "We are friends. That is predicated on the assumption that you enjoy my company, like I enjoy yours. If your definition of friendship differs, that is fine. I can still use mine."

His fingertips pressed together tightly, the tips whitening. "I'll ruin you. If Alexander doesn't do it first."

"Of course. You are my friend," I said gently. "I've given you that power."

~*~

Chapter Twenty-six

I slumped against the closed door fifteen minutes later.

My magic was still tangled. I was no closer to reaching Olivia. Alexander Dare and Constantine Leandred were the bane of my existence. And Dare was right, with what he had said earlier.

I put my head in my hands and massaged my temples.

I trusted people, and then did whatever they wanted me to do. I *liked* doing things for my friends. It made me *happy*.

But it wasn't necessarily conducive to good long term decision making.

I'd really enjoyed having Olivia field everything last term. Having Axer do it.

I just needed to question things a little more. And do risk assessments.

I shuddered.

And Constantine...I didn't know how to help him. He was like my magic—twisted and burned and explosive.

I shared all those thoughts with Neph as I sat in a chair in the middle of her room. Her roommate was off with her boyfriend, leaving us blessedly alone.

She tilted her head. "You do trust rather easily. But you have good instincts." She danced in a circle around me, arms swaying, magic lighting the edges of her room and helping to shore up the wards around me that she had been placing for months. Each turn eased some of the broken bits in me. "I don't think you make those trust decisions without basis."

I hugged her pillow to my chest and watched her dance. She swooped around me, then swooped back into view. "Do you think I can trust my own decisions?"

She twirled again, and extended a leg upward. Magic shot from her pointed toes to the ceiling wards, bouncing down in a direct line toward me. "Yes. But I suppose this is what your Mr. Dare was referencing when he said you rely on others to make decisions for you sometimes. What do you think?"

I pulled my viewer into position and set it to tune in to the three most popular feeds, then to triangulate them. Living with Bellacia had taught me a few things about news spells.

As expected, the combat mages leaving the Magiaduct were on display. An arch had been set up on top of the Magiaduct, to cleanly and quickly escort the combat mages to Top Campus. The Magiaduct would be opening ten minutes after the combat mages were through, so most of the students had queued in the ground floor common areas, shifting on both feet, waiting to be released.

I watched the combat mages file through the arch. Cheers were blaring in the background of the feed, but something told me that it was an overlaid sound. The people in view were entirely too white-lipped—their

* Promises of Bloodshed *

eyes only on escape from the prison of our dorm.

"I think, I need to manage some of my stress," I said, finally, taking in all the faces shifting across the viewer. "And take back some control. What about you?"

Neph looked at me in question. "Me?"

"Will was worried. And I know you are keeping things from me," I said as lightly as I could. There was an insistent feeling in the back of my mind that I kept *forgetting* something, in regards to this, but I couldn't remember what. "I want to help."

"You already are." She gracefully sat on a padded stool. "I was sanctioned officially months ago. It's a light death sentence for many muses. We rely heavily on community. When I was...released...from Sakkara, it was due to family politics. A trickle down." She shrugged at my enraged expression. "We are influenced by our communities, and it is assumed that we are one with them."

"That's unfair."

"To someone used to doing her own thing, it would seem the most grievous of unfairness. Most muses are not used to being on their own." She looked out the window, into the distance. "I was sanctioned again yesterday."

"What? Why?"

"It matters little." A small smile worked over her lips. "They can do little to me now that would matter to me. It's a perk of being your muse."

"Because of the Origin Mage thing?"

"More because of *how* you are than what you are. You've given me freedom."

I sat up straighter and pushed the news feeds closed. "What happens, if I get caught or taken? What happens to you?"

"It depends. It is one of the reasons the elders give for not becoming attached to a specific mage. Certain authorities can use a connection as an in to the community. We already have heavy restrictions placed against us."

A knock on the door captured both of our attention, and answering it produced a harried looking mage who had two dozen long stemmed *black* roses in a hand vise—not a *vase*—held at arm's length away from his body.

It almost looked like he was afraid of them.

No, he was definitely afraid of them—it was how people in the movies held plutonium with tongs.

"I was told to deliver these here? To Ren?" He said nervously, his gaze traveling from Neph to me. His eyes widened. "Wow, it is you. I thought—I mean, I was paid a lot—but I thought, maybe, and—"

"Thank you," Neph said softly, taking the hand vise from him, and touching his skin as she did. The boy's gaze turned dreamy—like he was

Chapter Twenty-six

having the *best* dream—and he nodded, then turned and nearly skipped down the hall.

"You are handing out those whammies left, right, and center," I said, carefully taking the hand vise from her to complete the magic transaction. Both ends of the heavy metal rod held vises—one that was holding the flowers, and the other currently unused. I peered at the flowers. There was something weird about the stems.

"Those are Guillotine Roses." Neph sighed and walked to her desk. "Don't touch them. I have something that can either dispose of them or strip them."

I looked more closely at the stems. Each one was covered with wickedly barbed thorns, and as I drew them closer to me, they started to rotate around each stem in opposing spirals like small saw blades.

I could feel my lips lift. "No, it's okay. I think I know who they are from. Do the flowers do anything dangerous?" I clamped the unused end of the rod on the edge of her desk.

"The petal edges are blade sharp. But if you can navigate the thorns and petals, they are one of the sweetest smelling flowers."

They were raven black, but the petals glowed with an iridescent shine as they collected together in the center. Indigo and purpled black.

"Who sent them?" Neph asked.

I smiled and leaned down to carefully inhale the core of one rose, keeping my hands behind my back. The thorns rotated around the stems in spirals as I breathed them in. It was very Constantine, this apology.

"A friend."

Maybe...maybe we'd all be okay.

~*~

The campus clock ticked over to the Cancer sign at the western position of the twenty-four hour clock and a *ding* rang through the room.

Patrick whooped over our shared group communication.

Neph and I walked to the window. Outside, the magic shimmered once again, then the invisible louvers of air flipped, one after another, unlocking from their neighboring louvers—letting us out.

Immediately, mages streamed out from the building and up the hill. I had to assume that mages were doing the same on the other side of the Magiaduct, streaming down the hill as well. The top seven circles of the mountain were now habitable again.

Mages dressed in green streamed out of a dorm to the west, then broke off in multiple directions. The formation looked like a large snake slithering out into many heads. A hydra being born.

The green mages were going off to fix campus. To piece everything

* Promises of Bloodshed *

back together.

The combat mages were gone, but the rest of the student body was a tight, focused unit.

I put my fingers on the glass. I hoped it was enough.

Chapter Twenty-seven

CAFETERIA BLUNDERS

WE JOINED THE mass exodus from the Magiaduct at the tail end of the rush.

A shimmer of magic swept over me as we exited, like a layer of lotion washed away.

The mountain air was fresh and vibrant, and the weather spells were currently set at a pleasant seventy-five degrees outside the Magiaduct. The spells usually differed from level to level, depending on the geography of the area and what they contained. The firesnake grove, for instance, was always unbearably balmy, and the ski runs were cool enough to keep the snow fresh.

I expected far more Department mages clocking my every move. And while there *were* quite a few fulfilling that requirement, there was only one praetorian. Tarei.

When Kaine had gone after Raphael, the other praetorians had gone with him.

Tarei, however, stood like a figure in the mist. Watching—purple eyes glinting at us from the shadows.

I could still feel the echoes of the nullifying cuff he had placed around my wrist. Different than the one that Godfrey had clamped around my throat, but no less terrifying.

As if he could read my thoughts, something gold, round, heavy, and glittering appeared in his hand. He twirled the cuff around steady fingers, never breaking eye contact with me.

Neph's eyes narrowed on him. Tarei's gaze slid to her, and his smile turned more threatening. A second cuff appeared in his fingers, singing through the air along with the first. That response answered the question of whether he could see Neph.

I had a feeling that the Department made sure that each employee could

* Cafeteria Blunders *

see muses and any other group they sought to regulate.

"Cockroach," Mike muttered.

"Why is he still here?" I asked, keeping him in sight.

"He's Stavros' eyes on campus," Delia answered mentally through the armbands. *"Say nothing more."*

The arches that connected to other arches on the top seven circles had all been reactivated. We took the nearest one that would take us to Top Campus and the cafeteria, and away from Tarei and his threats.

Shadows shifted along our path across Top Campus, though, and adult gazes—the warriors and security mages from other countries along with Legion members—followed our trek. The cafeteria was only accessible by students, which made it a huge relief to enter.

But I had never seen so many people in the cafeteria all at once—campus tended to work in shifts due to classes and student life. Today, though, the lockdown had poured most of us here at once. People were packed around tables, barely a single seat to spare.

And, yet, our table stood completely empty in the midst of the mayhem. It stood out *very* obviously in the middle of a packed populace.

It was obviously deliberate. Whether people had tried to sit there and been dissuaded by something, or *someone*, whether the tables around were packed with mages specifically seeking to listen in on us, or whether people thought there might be something contagious where I'd previously sat, I wasn't immediately sure.

Caniopidas in hand, and trying not to make eye contact as the crowd shifted around me in the way I was becoming increasingly used to—some people wildly jumping to the side, and others deliberately trying to brush against me—I headed toward our table. I wasn't going to look a gift horse in the mouth. Sitting at a random table and making small talk with gaping, terrified, or angry people negatively affected the appetite.

The floor to ceiling windows showed the same magnificent view down the mountain and out over the river and valley that it always did. But the Department stooges staring into the windows at us and tapping code against their legs was new and unwanted.

And the calming spells *pumping* into the room were overwhelming.

I pushed my tray toward the center of our table, deposited my giant bag on top of Olivia's empty seat, whipped out a notebook, and started madly sketching before my butt landed in the chair.

"Ren, um, what are you doing?" Will asked carefully, taking his usual chair. The others arrayed themselves in theirs.

"Preparing."

I didn't have to see the exchanged glances to know they were making them over my head.

Chapter Twenty-seven

"Stop worrying," I said without looking up. "I'm not actively doing anything dangerous yet."

Axer was gone from campus again, which had naturally raised my fervor and stress back to Defcon levels, but I had a different focus this time. There wasn't an amorphous threat that *might* happen. We already had one. I needed to get my ducks in a row. I needed to be planning for what happened when we were ambushed from within.

I saw Will place his eavesdropping device on top of the table. It was one of the good ones that would make what I was writing and drawing unreadable as well.

Head still bowed, I cast a discreet look around. I could see a few people at the tables nearest to ours frowning and adjusting their own devices in escalating eavesdropping warfare.

A few moments later, however, a member of the Justice Squad swept over and sanctioned each of them for having restricted devices or using appropriate devices but with restricted settings.

It reminded me of Bellacia, who had been perfectly legal using her abilities on me up to a point. But when she'd gone past that point, she'd been hit with a Level Two, then a Level Three offense.

"Justice Magic, how does it work off campus?" I asked, watching one of the mages argue with the Justice Squad member.

Outside of campus, without the Justice Magic that bound us, I didn't want people like Bellacia whispering in my ear, scarab or no scarab.

"Towns and countries have different ordinances and statutes," Will explained. "When you move to a city, you enter into a social contract to live by the rules setup therein."

He pointed around us. "Like the contract you sign to attend Excelsine. The rules are different in different towns. Entering a town commits you to 'guest' standards."

I tapped my pencil against the page. "What about between towns?"

"Many town boundaries border another. Outlaw Territories *do* still exist, but the Department has made it so people are able to travel around them pretty easily. And layer shifts happen on a yearly schedule in the Second Layer—easily anticipated—so it lessens the danger."

"Outlaw Territories? Those what they sound like?" I asked, writing again, mouth directed toward the tabletop. The eavesdropping charm was supposed to protect against lip reading as well, but who knew what might happen in giant fishbowl warfare.

"No rules, no Justice Magic. Anything goes," Will acknowledged.

The Wild West then. I nodded.

"It's a reason Travel Magic and porting is so lucrative and popular," Will said, chewing on whatever the Caniopidas people had made him. "People

* Cafeteria Blunders *

want to move safely from one law-abiding settlement to another. The Department, for all their shadiness, has allowed Port Mages under their authority to work their magic frequently to help the towns under their jurisdiction. Which is pretty much the entirety of the Second Layer."

"Town rules are also why people are very careful with their social credit," Mike added, giving Will a pointed look. "You can't move into some towns if your social credit isn't up to snuff. Like if you have Justice marks against you."

Will shrugged, and winked at me. "That's why I'm going to one of the think tanks after I graduate. All of the project planning you want, and none of the justice hits." His expression went a little dreamy. "The hallways are safe zones—no magic—but in the labs, you are *free*. And they provide housing with the same rules. I can invent *all day* and not have to worry about what I'm doing."

That sounded...pretty good. But it wasn't important now. I needed to focus.

"Third Layer?" I asked.

Delia stayed silent, eating whatever green leafy thing was in her bowl and not making eye contact.

"Most of the Third Layer is Outlaw Territory," Will said. "Especially with the lack of stable or plentiful magic. Layer shifts are so common that you can barely use magic outside a settlement. And without the recycling components, magic attacks back." He made an exploding motion between his palms. "Been trying to get a permit to do some research there. The settlements have recycling centers, but many of them are not great. Ask Loudon about it."

I thought of the Midlands and the recycling plant, and what Raphael had been doing in there.

I narrowed my eyes and tapped my pencil again.

"That device you made to take a layer shift and power a generator, Will? Can it work in the Third Layer?"

"It'd still, um, strip you of your clothes and anything else containing a wrinkle." He rubbed a hand through his hair. "We've been working on other things," he said defensively.

I smiled. It was fleeting, but still there. Helen Price had been on the committee that had been stripped by Will's device.

"What is the range again?"

"Fifty feet."

I double tapped my pencil. "Can you throw it? Or trigger a delayed activation and run from it?"

"Maybe, what are you thinking?"

"Just mulling possibilities."

Chapter Twenty-seven

The Third Layer raised a myriad of challenges for me. Dead zones and lethal shifts of magic.

And that's where Olivia was. I gripped my pencil.

Neph's hand touched my arm. "Eat," she said softly.

I sighed and put my pencil and notebook away, then dragged my tray forward. I had an unidentifiable noodle, vegetable, and meat dish. The Caniopidas people seemed to think I required something sweet and saucy today. After the initial bite, I started eating quickly. They always made the *best* things.

Five bites in, a tray hit the table next to me. I looked up, half expecting to see Patrick or Asafa, and half expecting to see Bellacia.

I was not at all expecting it to be Constantine.

I rarely ever saw Constantine in the cafeteria. And when I did, he was always at one of the two person tables located on the tier closest to the windows, farthest away from where most people sat. He usually either sat alone or was joined by some girl in the endless rounds that always tried to keep him. Sometimes one of the more notorious and flashy club members would join him—they were always very obviously strictly business meals, though.

Constantine examined all of the faces at the table, his hooded gaze swinging from one to another and his smirking mouth not changing expression. He smoothly moved my bag from Olivia's chair to a conjured stool and slid into the seat, next to me. He swiped a finger across the edge of the table as he sat, then leaned back in his chair with insouciance.

He slid his plate, loaded with some sort of breaded concoction, toward him.

I blinked at his plate, my suspended fork dripping noodles into my bowl, then automatically looked at the faces around the table.

Delia snorted and went back to eating her salad, but her fork was stabbing harder than it had been. Mike looked nonplussed. Neph *felt* nonplussed, though she looked calm. Will looked surprised, but he gave Constantine a nod and a greeting of, "Leandred," as if this wasn't completely out of the ordinary.

It was just a good thing Olivia wasn't here. Murder wasn't a good look on anyone.

I sighed and set my fork back down. If I thought he was actually sitting with us because he *wanted* to, I'd not say a word. I'd be pleased, in fact.

However, the anticipation thrumming in him meant that wasn't a remote possibility.

"Do I want to know?" I asked.

"Do you want to know how many people are staring at us right now?" He said, lifting a bread wedge. "Probably not."

Cafeteria Blunders

He smiled, still practically *draped* across the back of the chair, body angled toward me, and ate the piece.

I ignored the urge to look around the room. "I was *going* to thank you for those awesome roses."

"I have no idea what you are talking about," he said, lifting another wedge. But I could feel his pleasure, and I could see his lips curve the slightest bit as he ate.

"You realize Axer did this a few weeks ago? Ruined mealtime for weeks."

"Please, darling, everyone was watching this table long before you sat down. And people aren't even bothering to hide their plebeian gawking now. It will take months to go back to anything resembling normal for you."

I met Delia's gaze and she gave a short nod, not without a little uncharacteristic sympathy.

"Lovely," I said. "And you sitting here? What prompted this little injection of future gossip?"

"What? I can't sit with my favorite?"

"Ren?" Mike asked, looking like he was willing to perform some sort of "eject" spell, if I asked. He had been the one most likely to get rid of unwanted "Axer Dare" questioners in the last few weeks. He looked far more concerned about Constantine than he did most mages, though.

Delia touched Mike's arm and minutely shook her head. Mike's gaze didn't move from us, and his frown didn't lift, but he said nothing more.

Will reached toward his eavesdropping device.

"Don't bother, Tasky." Constantine tapped a long finger against the tabletop, which shimmered for a moment when he did so. The table had never done that before, so this was obviously the result of something he had wiped on it with that initial finger motion. I was far too used to Constantine's materials and created concoctions to be surprised that whatever he had done had invisibly spread so quickly.

"Nothing beyond three feet gets through this," Constantine said. "And even then, the surrounding tables will only hear a truly entertaining conversation."

I sighed, used to his antics. "Are we all complimenting you?"

"You are doing a magnificent job at flirting, darling."

I put a hand to my forehead, rested my elbow on the table, and closed my eyes as I chewed another bite. "Just...just wake me up when this is over."

He gave a low chuckle and ate another wedge.

"So?" Delia asked, gaze sharp. "What *are* you doing here?"

"Planting some seeds."

Chapter Twenty-seven

"What? Why did you sit here, Leandred?" Delia demanded, gaze sharp, eyeliner drawing itself to thick kohl.

"To build some delightful tales, or at least the foundation for them."

Her eyes narrowed. "The foundation? With what happened on the Eighteenth...people are already talking."

There was something audacious about discussing anything in the press of people around us, even with layered eavesdropping spells.

"*You* don't even know what happened on the Eighteenth, Peoples," he said dispassionately, eating another wedge.

A slashing smile took her lips.

"Didn't realize that the Alpha scarves had a little more juice, did you, Leandred? You got Bryant's. He was a Beta. We didn't hear the conversation, no, but our scarves picked up a few things." Her lips pressed tightly together. "That there was a conversation with Vincent Godfrey at all, is peculiar. Interesting pieces of a jagged puzzle."

Constantine's eyes narrowed, and there was a glint there that made me concerned for everyone at the table for a moment, then the creases at the edges of his eyes smoothed. "The Alpha scarves just encompass those at this table." He gave the table top another tap with his finger. "A non-event. And no one else remembers the events anymore."

"Are you sure?" I frowned, interrupting their pressurized spat. "Maybe they're just holding onto it for a better time."

Someone had recorded footage of the fight under Raphael's dome—Asafa and Patrick had used a portion of it in the firework. And Bellacia had made it apparent that there were no secrets she couldn't find. I'd assumed that just meant everything would come out eventually, including my little world ending moment and Constantine's duplicity.

"Positive." His lips curled again.

"How?"

"How should I know why people forget things of import, darling?"

I sighed. I had an idea of how he might have changed people's memories. He had manipulated Origin Magic after I'd let him leech me to fix his wounds. He could have used it for a number of spells in that moment—like for spreading a memory enchantment to anyone close enough to see us.

He'd manipulated the minds of the men who had attacked us in the First Layer, and he was a lightning-fast learner. Once he had done something, repeating and adding to it was simple for him.

I was surrounded by quick and powerful mages—attracted to them, obviously.

"Remove it," Delia said suddenly and succinctly.

Constantine smiled and ate another wedge.

* Cafeteria Blunders *

"What?" I asked, looking around the table. "Remove what?"

"Mind trap." Will looked enthused. "Did you lace that in your eavesdropping potion? Those are tremendously difficult to coordinate. When Professor—"

"Will." Mike rubbed his eyes tiredly as if he was just done with *everything*. "It's an eavesdropping anti charm, Ren. That witchy piece of magic Leandred did when he sat down also contained something that would contain knowledge in anyone who touched the table. All those shiving finger taps he keeps doing likely activate different parts of the magic and the brain. I swear to Magic, if you make me incontinent, Leandred, I will make sure they never find your body."

Constantine spread his fingers on the table with an expression of innocence.

I frowned. "I didn't feel anything."

Constantine's finger was suddenly drawing beneath my chin. "I would never bespell you like that, darling," he said, gaze slowly roaming my face as his finger drew a path along my skin. "I'd save yours for something far more delicious."

"Son of a—" someone said, but I couldn't make out who was speaking. I could only stare at Constantine.

He sat back again and resumed eating.

"Price is going to love this," Mike muttered, and took a page from Delia's book and stabbed his food.

"Forget Price. Axer Dare is going to commit murder," Delia said, stabbing her fork at Constantine. "And I'm going to be an unhelpful bystander."

"What is going on?" I asked, dazed.

Constantine smiled. He looked *very* pleased. "It's rather simple. The populace will think you've succumbed to my charms. And that I picked you as my latest conquest based on your power, or wanting to one-up my beloved roommate. Simple and it will easily give us hours uninterrupted to do...whatever needs to be done."

My mouth opened, but nothing emerged. "You want...you want people to think we are going back to your room to...what?"

He raised a brow.

"To do...science?" I said halfheartedly.

"Yes." He looked suddenly quizzical. "What else would I mean?"

He reached out and curled his fingers around the back of my neck, tilting my head just enough to put us at a very interesting angle. "Lots and lots of science," he said, voice low, gaze hooded and hypnotic.

Nothing emerged from my mouth, which was trying, and *failing*, to form words.

Chapter Twenty-seven

His other hand touched my chin, urging it downward, gaze tracing the movements of my lips.

Delia cursed, leaned forward, and yanked his arm down and away from me. "Leandred, I swear—"

Interestingly, he didn't curse her for touching him. He just leaned back in his chair and smirked. "Don't be overhasty, Peoples. You might find yourself forgetting how to apply your makeup in the morning."

It was a definite threat.

Constantine finished his meal and pushed back his chair. He reached forward, turned over my fingers, and dropped something into my palm. I looked down at it. It was a key. Made of the astrophene Axer had given him.

"What is this?"

"Don't be thick, darling."

He lifted my bag and slung it around his shoulder, then strode up the steps of the cafeteria tier.

I stared after him, lips parted.

"Okay. I have a question," Will said, as we watched Constantine walk away.

"Just one?" Mike said, and stabbed his food repeatedly.

Chapter Twenty-eight

JUSTICE, THE GIFT THAT KEEPS GIVING

BY MY SECOND rotation of Justice Squad duty, I was mentally resolved to the inextricable realization that I would be committing murder by nightfall. The Department didn't need to send a Shadow Mage to torment me, a portion of the student body had it well in hand.

I had created and used two dozen more roses—once again with Greyskull strangely appearing again exactly as I began constructing the first one and handing me a ward, then continuing on his way through the Medical corridor.

The calls that used roses were fine. Or, not so much fine, but bearable. Helpful, in a way—with me being able to offer a moment to *share* the Justice Offender's grief, lessening their burden.

No, those weren't the calls that were going to end in murder. The imbeciles with far too much money in their trust fund accounts—that was the only explanation for how they had gotten into one of the most prestigious universities in the magic world—were the ones happy to torment me for free.

"Guys, she's here." The guy looked at me and leaned against the doorframe. It was such a similar action to the one Constantine had undertaken when I'd first met him, that I blinked. However, time and affection had softened my view of that memory. This guy and this situation didn't have that advantage.

Nor was he even close to being as hot or as smooth. I'd been ruined for normal assholes.

"Name," I asked in a bored tone.

"Anything you want it to be, precious."

Ugh.

"Bolton Haynes. Level One. Substance abuse," I said, reading from Justice Toad. It didn't increase the punishment if I had to look up the

Chapter Twenty-eight

offender's name, but Justice Toad gave a happy croak, sensing another productive visit to stretch out the kinks he still had from being nearly fried the day before.

Haynes leaned forward in the doorway. "I'd be happy to up that to a Level I Do You."

I pushed the button on Justice Toad and the guy turned into a toad.

The guy behind him narrowed his eyes at his friend, then at me. He took an aggressive step toward me. "No one likes it when uppity mages get—"

He turned into a salamander. A slender salamander. Easily misplaced.

"Anyone else?" I asked the others behind him.

The rest held their arms at fifteen degree angles and pointed their hands down to the ground, fingers spread, in the surrendering gesture mages used. Seeing as people frequently blasted magic from their palms, the First Layer "hands up" surrender was still a gesture I was trying to break. Hands up gestures earned magic bolts to the face.

Not that I was going to be bolting anyone with magic anytime today. Slipping in with greased palms, or not, Excelsine did have standards, and I was easy pickings at the moment, for even the lowest of the low here, if they possessed any degree of cleverness.

But I didn't need my own magic with a Justice Tablet in hand. I just needed justice on my side.

And maybe some sort of Justice Holster on my belt.

The crowd of guys stood, tense, in surrender.

I tapped my finger against Justice Toad and waited for the amphibious spells to wear off.

The toad morphed upward and an idiot human stood in place once more. He wiped at his mouth with both hands. The salamander followed suit a few seconds later.

"You—"

One of the guys in the back grabbed salamander guy and wrestled him into the room. Bolton stepped hastily into the hallway and the door slammed behind him.

"You didn't need to come out here," I said, flipping through punishments. I had far better places to be. Like at the new grief call that was blinking in Justice Toad's corner—it was becoming increasingly easy to identify the grief calls, and I'd bet anything they would be automated by the next day. "I could assign your punishment just as easily with you insi—"

"Would you go on a date with me?"

I squinted up at him. "What?"

He shrugged, and ran an uneasy hand through his hair. "I saw you with Leandred, and my father said that having an Ori—"

"Yeah. No. Clean the common area and let's call it a day." Justice Toad

* Justice, the Gift that Keeps Giving *

beeped in agreement.

"But—"

"I can find something else, sure." I shrugged. "Like cleaning the toi—"

"I'll clean the common area, by my magic, I so do vow."

The magic registered.

"Great." I tucked Justice Toad under my arm and turned.

"Wait, I—"

"Nope."

The next ten calls contained six that hit the "grief punishment" response, and four that had to have been on purpose, like Bolton Haynes's call—either doing something so that I'd show up and they could make some skeazy political alliance, or verbally—and once, *physically*—assault me for imagined crimes. The latter had gone very poorly for the girl doing the assaulting. Justice tablets *really* didn't like such things.

Justice Toad croaked happily, working out his own kinks.

Word had gotten out about my stint on the Justice Squad, and today it wasn't only the delinquents who were trying to get me to their door.

Anyone who truly wanted to talk—and there were a few social scientific types who had approached me in the halls in between calls to talk about current events or about the *fascinating* subject of Origin Magic or Origin Domes—didn't get sketchy groups together to stage an assault.

I felt no guilt turning the other kinds into amphibians of all varieties.

Like the ones who were plotting in a common area of Dorm Nineteen. Just my luck to be tucked around the corner filling out a report from a call on the eighth floor—a grief call.

I had sent out a note on the Justice Squad loop to see if anyone was interested in having the grief counselors accompany us on the calls that pinged with the parameters of a grief response.

More than a few members had sent back enthusiastic replies. It made me optimistic.

"Leandred teaches the *best* spells to his conquests, and I can't even imagine what her magic could power with one."

I blinked and peeked around the corner. A group of four boys were leisurely spread out in a circle of chairs.

"Power that can kill you," another said dubiously.

"Kill me in the *best* way. I'm totally approaching her after he drops her. I stole one of those roses she's been giving people from a kid down in Dorm Five. Trust me. It'll be worth it."

Lovely. I remembered the call to Dorm Five. I'd make a little side visit there after this.

I wondered what these four would do if I walked around the corner and flung my tablet at them. Justice Toad croaked optimistically, hoping.

Chapter Twenty-eight

"Leandred is...vicious. I wouldn't—"

"He cares nothing about his conquests," the first one said dismissively. "That's why you *wait*."

"They were fighting together Tuesday," the second boy said, more insistently.

"*Everyone* was fighting together Tuesday."

"But he was right there, in that dome."

"Yeah, on the *ground*. With a bunch of other bodies. Wrong place, wrong time."

"I don't think—"

"What are you guys talking about?" asked a new voice.

"The Crown girl. And approaching her after Leandred is done."

I wanted to say, *I can hear you, you shivits*, but immediately canceled the thought of any direct engagement. Not unless I was going to port them somewhere. Like the Second Layer version of the Arctic. Or Hell.

Olivia would have some ideas.

I gritted my teeth and kept filling out the report, jabbing my fingers on the tablet's screen magic.

"Are you insane? Two words for you—Alexander Dare. *No way*."

"There's no way she's Dare's. He doesn't date. And you *saw* Leandred in the cafeteria."

I really was going to kill him.

"There's something weird there, I'm telling you—"

"And I'm telling you that this is an opportunity. One that someone else will take, if we don't."

"She may not be dating Alexander Dare, but he is sure as hell protective of her. Have you seen the memories of them together?"

"That just means an alliance with the Dares, as a bonus," he said assuredly. "And I will be the utmost gentleman."

"No. That mother of his... You aren't thinking this through. *Maximilian Dare*. War with a *quarter* of the Second Layer. They only go for one, and they don't back away once they get their sights set."

"You are reading way too much into this. There are no 'sights set.' He's friends with Straught, yeah? Protective of her too, but they are just friends. This is the same."

"But—"

I pushed away from the wall not wanting to listen any further to the idiots who had far too much time on their hands to create rumors out of nothing. Sights set? Ha.

But, truly, there went any future notions of dating. Because mages like those sure as magic didn't want to date *me*. They were looking at *opportunity* not the person. I could mourn the loss of the "dating life I'd never had"

* Justice, the Gift that Keeps Giving *

once I got Olivia back.

I could still give Constantine *hell*, though.

I made my stop at Dorm Five. Poor sixteen-year-old kid had been sitting in the battle field stands and had seen too many horrors after the dome had collapsed.

As I gave him a new flower, his expression turned rapt with awe. More alarming than the sleazy calls were the ones from people who stared at me like this, saying nothing. I backed away with a quick, "Feel better!"

In some ways, the awed gazes were the worst. At least I knew what the harmful or opportunistic people *wanted*. The expectations forming in the gazes of the others unsettled me deeply. As if they expected that now that I was identified, I'd fix the world.

Dorm One held my last call—another frog. I signed out and tucked Justice Toad under my arm. It was a short trek back to my floor.

Constantine didn't answer the door. Probably a good thing for him, as I had *all sorts of things* to say to him about what his little performance in the cafeteria had gotten me.

I took the key he had given me out of my pocket. Staring at it, I figured, eh, worst thing that could happen was me ending up flattened in the hallway.

The key went cleanly into the lock and the door opened. A feeling of *home* hit me. Still a little weirded out by that, I called out, "Hello?"

Axer's room was locked up tight. The others were wide open. Constantine wasn't home.

My bag was sitting neatly next to the front door, as if Constantine had known I would drop by just like this. I deliberated for a second, then rifled through and removed all the things I needed for sleeping, but nothing more. I wrote a note on top that said, "Thanks! Still going to murder you, though," and tucked my duffel bag just inside his workroom door. If he brought someone home with him tonight, they wouldn't be going in there.

If Axer was to be believed, I was the only one who ever did. Sometimes Will tagged along, but never without me.

If Constantine wanted to *Sixteen Candles* my underwear, it was better than Bellacia doing it.

I couldn't wait for him, though. I had to get my time in at Bellacia's. I'd see him in the morning.

Four more hours would seal it up with Bellacia for the day. I'd be completely out of luck on the roommate penalty front, if Axer hadn't done what he'd done that morning.

With help from Will and Neph, I'd figured out what the tangerine device Axer had given Bellacia was. It tricked the room's magic for four hours by actively *giving* the room a reflection of my magic. It had to have the buy-in

Chapter Twenty-eight

of the other person involved, however. Axer had given Bellacia some of my magic, in exchange for her buy-in.

I was pretty sure I couldn't trick her into a permanent or semi-permanent solution. In fact, I was pretty sure that had been a singular event. And one that I might not have come out on top of. I shuddered at the thought of her freely investigating my magic. I had needed that rest, though.

But I needed another three hours for today and another twelve tomorrow at Bellacia's. I was going to catch up on all my missed sleep during those hours, or die trying.

I locked their room back up, and headed down the dreaded five doors with a much smaller tote.

In the wake of safely unlocking Constantine and Axer's room and becoming engrossed in my own thoughts, I made a mistake. I touched Bellacia's door without running a diagnostic.

A spell immediately shocked me, sending pain down my arm. I closed my eyes and refrained from thumping my forehead against the wood. I'd made *that* mistake once earlier, and received a very unpleasant daymare that some anonymous soul had thoughtfully left for me.

I yanked open the door, battling two other spells, and locked the door behind me.

I furiously located my "roommate."

Bellacia was watching a video in her workroom, though they didn't call them videos here—my translator simply made the word into the best description for me. There was far more magic involved in creating magical videos—and they allowed the viewer to examine the scene in greater detail than was possible with video in the First Layer, capturing everything in multiple dimensions at a set distance. But special recorders had to be used to ensure that the record was accurate, and not due to a magical memory, which was easy to fake.

"Back from another one of your little justice jaunts? How many hours do you have to serve again?" she asked idly, flipping to another view.

"Nope," I said, trying to shake off the last spell hooked onto my fingers. Looking at Bellacia and at the spells, I could see they weren't hers. She wouldn't be so obvious. It didn't lessen my ire.

I had signed out from Justice Toad too early. Next time, I was keeping him on until I reached the interior of the room. The Justice Magic would give the *thoughtful* mages who kept leaving spells a really nice return message.

Bellacia gave a husky laugh. "Oh, darling, these are the easy questions. The ones with already gathered answers. It will only be a matter of time before all of your secrets are mine. Best to give up early, yes?"

* Justice, the Gift that Keeps Giving *

"Nope." I successfully extinguished the spell with perhaps a bit *too* much fire. My base magic was looking up, finally, thirty some hours after Kaine had caused me to burn the ends completely.

"Are you sure?" Bellacia's voice warmed the scarab I had secured around my neck. I was keeping the small beetle there *forever*.

My gaze strayed to the video she was scrolling — pulled there as I'm sure she was *hoping* it would.

It was of Kaine. Leveling a town in the Third Layer. A little timestamp marked it as earlier today.

I swallowed bile as I watched the destruction.

Sure, I had seen Axer destroy dozens of opponents at the same time. Freespar was anything goes combat, and the Midlands were man versus supernatural nature. I had observed one of the best fighters of our age in action up close. But Axer killed cleanly and quickly. And he almost always resurrected and released the monster of the day into its proper habitat. He didn't...savor the kill. Didn't go in for maximum pain and damage. The shadows that swirled around Kaine were ever-hungry and vicious and motivated by pain. Lashing out, whipping skin, and tearing flesh. Making fear and death *last*.

Raphael also wasn't a clean killer. Though the madness in his killing was different.

I got the impression both from Raphael and from Greyskull, that Raphael had been different, once upon a time. I got the impression that Kaine had always been this way.

"Something wrong, Ren?"

"You really need to watch happier things," I told her, going for blithe as I tried to erase the images from memory. "Like *Dragon Talons—Rip or Tear?* or *Living in an Iron Maiden for Fun and Profit*. Quality, light entertainment."

Bellacia smiled. "You don't like the real thing?"

I dropped the act. "It's horrible. I don't know how you can stand it."

"Yes." She leaned forward. "It is terrible the things people will do. The people who are freed from their cages."

"Ah. That your angle? Kaine is too dangerous to be allowed out? Well, sister, you aren't going to get an argument from me. However, it's because he's *evil*, not because he has a little something extra in the backseat."

Her brows creased, then smoothed. "Ah. Such unusual expressions your First Layer tribe has."

"My tribe knoweth the best."

"But part of what makes Archelon Kaine what he is, is his own birthright. A Shadow Mage. He can't help his nature."

"What about Sirens? Lure anyone to their death lately, Bella?"

For a moment, I thought she would pull out all the stops, rip off my

Chapter Twenty-eight

scarab, and hammer me with auditory magic. But she just smiled.

It was a terrifying smile. It said that she thought she had all the time in the world.

I flipped her off and walked into the bedroom, tossing Justice Toad on my borrowed comforter.

My Picasso Guernica coverlet had been left behind in my real room. It had been easy to leave behind—it grew increasingly uncomfortable to sleep beneath with each ruined and devastated town attack that occurred.

I closed my eyes. Sleep. I could do this.

By the time I was done in the bathroom, Bellacia was getting comfortable in her own bed.

"You surprised us earlier, slipping your trackers. You are making us rely on the old ways. But the old ways have their uses too. Watching you specifically is fascinating. I've always loved visiting the Fourth Layer zoos the best. They keep magical beings in them sometimes. The ones who've been particularly...*bad*."

I didn't respond.

"I wonder what they would do for your exhibit," she mused. "It would probably be better there than with the Department. They'd probably give you an art studio so you could create works for visitors to see. A sort of museum prison. Cami has a sharp eye for talent and ability, and she told me she asked you once about painting her."

It wasn't a question, so I didn't respond to that statement either.

Bellacia continued, not needing a response. "I've seen many of Kinsky's portraits. Women make wonderful standard bearers. You should paint Cami. I'd love to see it."

"Nope."

She laughed again. I didn't know how she did it. I found her act *exhausting*.

I looked out the window. I could see the firesnake grove from here, one circle up. Distant, but still beautiful, their opalescent scales sparking vibrantly under the rays of the sun. The crimson leaves and vivid colors of the grove glowed.

It was a beautiful view. I hated it.

I leaned my head against the glass, watching the snakes blink in and out of their camouflage as they rebuilt their home, which had been affected in the attack, like most levels above the Magiaduct. Someone from our team had set up enticement traps around the grove, to lure anything not connected to Administration Magic there.

"Your little friends aren't helping you any, you know," Bellacia said offhandedly. "They protect you from the knowledge that you are a pariah. That you are dangerous."

* Justice, the Gift that Keeps Giving *

I pressed my lips together. "I got that picture fairly well on my own, actually. Pardon me for not wanting to *dwell* on the ostracism that I will never shed. Pardon me for not wanting to be a bitter, dangerous leper on society. Bitterness and brooding seem to lead to such positive life choices."

I thought she would persist with the interrogation, but she flipped off her screens and reclined on her bed.

"Goodnight, Ren. Don't kill us all in the morning."

"Goodnight, Bella. Don't die in your own delusions."

I closed my eyes, and took deep breaths, trying to calm my racing mind and heart. It was fine. Everything was going to be fine.

Olivia would be rescued. Bellacia would be a bad, buried memory. Campus would go back to rights. And I'd make good, long term, careful plans about what to do going forward. Solid threat assessments. We'd all be fine.

I should have known Raphael wouldn't wait for *fine*.

Chapter Twenty-nine

*DE*ADLINES

I STARED AT the cord attached to my chest as it pulled me forward, through time and space and dreamscape, and—like a rapid zoom in a horror movie—sharply yanked me into a crystal room.

Glittering crystal prisms reflected the light of a thousand dreams. I could see the blurred images of them—dancing about under the surfaces. Whether it was an assortment of my own nightmares, or a larger collection outside of me, I didn't know.

I looked around the room, details brightening as I pulled my surroundings into view.

Marsgrove was bound on the floor. Wide-eyed and staring at me, he yelled something at me behind his gag. I moved toward him, hand outstretched, but the cord at my chest was finite and yanked me back before I reached my goal. I followed the cord, seeking its origin. Shock stopped me mid-motion.

A crystal coffin stood in the corner of the room supported on heavy crystal legs. My cord stretched to the heart of it.

Olivia was laid out within. Like the fairytale Constantine and I had been joking about, but arrayed in the same bloodstained clothes she had worn on the battlefield. Her hands were clasped around a copper butterfly resting on her stomach.

Only the slight rise and fall of her chest kept my full panic contained as I tapped frantically on the glass.

She didn't wake.

I backed away from the crystal coffin. This was just a dream. Just a terrible, nightmare. My subconscious was picking up random items and forcing them together. I just needed to wake up.

A shadow slithered along the outside edge of the room, behind Olivia's crystal plinth. Long, sharp nails curled around the edges of the outside

* *Dead*lines *

glass, trying to find a way inside the room.

Just a dream. Kaine belonged in nightmares and shadow realms. Perfectly normal to find him in one.

This was just a dream.

"It's not a dream, Butterfly."

I jerked to see Raphael sauntering toward me. I stopped my sudden, backpedaling momentum and took a steadying breath, holding my ground and yanking rational thought into my grasp. He could have ambushed me from behind. That he hadn't, meant we were here for a conversation.

"I thought I ended your ability to visit me in dreams," I said, positioning myself for the best physical defense.

He smiled. "You did. Your connection with your friend—" He motioned to Olivia. "—brought you here the last time, so I simply...used it again." He twisted his fingers in the air, and I could see an outline of the cord on his palm.

Outside the dreamglass, the dark shadow issued a cacophony of grinding screams recorded from the pits of hell.

Neph's scarab burned on my chest. I moved a hand down to clutch it.

"Poor little shade, locked out from the event it wants to attend most." Raphael sent it a mocking wave. Long scratches of shadowed nails screeched against the glass of the dream as the shadow increased its siege.

"Such a shame he hasn't figured out a way to break the dreamglass. He truly learned nothing in all those years. A wraith without power."

In profile, I could see sharp, shadowed wounds on Raphael's skin, belying his taunting. He hadn't escaped the fight with Kaine unscathed. Whether the wounds were mental or physical, I couldn't discern in the dream state.

Raphael turned to me. "You've been a naughty mage, Butterfly."

I darted a glance at Olivia, who was as still as I'd ever seen her. I looked at my hands and the air in front of me. I was inside of the dreamglass, but the air was heavy, as if Raphael could lock me into my own crystal chamber at any time.

"I would never have willingly sent him," I said bitterly, looking at the shade.

"You let him attach to you," Raphael said. "Like letting that boy leech you."

I smiled at him without an ounce of warmth. "I'm not going to dignify that with an actual response. You called me here. What do you want?"

Mercurial as always, his expression changed to one of mischief. "Perhaps it is better to ask, what does your *roommate* want?"

I looked at the cord, which had solidified in his hand, and started pulsing in his palm. I looked at Marsgrove, trussed and trying to

Chapter Twenty-nine

communicate something through the power of his eyes. My last hope of Olivia being rescued with outside help slipped through my fingers like dream smoke.

I looked back at Raphael. "I'm certain we can come to an agreement."

He smiled. "You want your roommate back quite madly."

"I'm inclined to have her return in mint condition, yes."

"I've heard you had quite the nasty downgrade in the roommate area."

I licked parched lips. "Yes."

"I could do much with a Siren."

"Unfortunately, I'm pretty sure she's not rooting for your team."

"How about a trade?"

I looked at him carefully. "You want to trade Olivia for Bellacia?"

If I was home with Delia and Neph, I'd issue a sarcastic "win-win" comment. However, this was not a game.

Or at least, not a game I wanted to be playing.

"Would you take such an offer?" he asked, watching me through knowing eyes.

"No."

"You would protect your new roommate? Your vile, vindictive roommate?" He asked idly, making a loop and knotting the cord stretching between Olivia and me in his palm. He gave the strings on either side a little pull to tighten the knot. The end attached to me, stuttered.

I felt old, all of a sudden. "Pick a different game, Raphael. One, which I will play."

He smiled and loosened the knot.

"Oh, but I like this game. Who will you protect? It is an old game. The best kind. One that we have played before. You continually surprise me in your choices."

"You are unsurprised by this."

"Yes," he said suddenly, moving closer. "I am unsurprised by *you*, but baffled by why you continue to make said choices."

"You were a Protection Prodigy."

Something dark shifted through his eyes and his gaze went to the shade of Kaine, trying to break inside the dreamglass.

"Old identities, Butterfly. We forge new ones in the fires." He touched my forehead, pinning me like a fluttering insect on a pin board. "What will your new one be, when Stavros gets a hold of you?" The way he said Stavros' name was a mixture of hatred and something else.

"I don't need a new one."

"We all get new ones," he said with a vicious smile.

"What is yours then?"

"*Death.*"

* *Dead*lines *

A thousand rapid images flashed through the point at which he was touching me. Too fast to decipher, too many to remember. I shuddered under the onslaught of so much remembered pain.

"How do you handle it?" I whispered.

"Some would say I do not." He smiled, and it was a broken, jagged thing.

His finger dropped from my forehead, and it was as if it broke multiple spells. Olivia seemed to wake, suddenly. Her hands flew to the edges of the coffin surrounding her, her gaze shot to me.

She yelled something at me, but the sound was completely encased in her tomb. Or sound was encased in me. I touched the scarab.

"Set her free," I said, voice unintentionally breaking. "Save her, Raphael, even if you can't save yourself."

"Oh, but the saving is up to *you*." He held the cord aloft. "It is simple. You want your roommate, you need to come and get her. No more sending others to do the deed." He tsked, madness once more forgotten, and patronizing mentor back in place. "Bad form, Butterfly. I expected more."

"Did you expect me to be magically crippled?"

"We all must deal with setbacks." He looked at Kaine's shade, and his eyes narrowed. "You should have come with me, Butterfly, when you had the chance."

"I started to." It hadn't been a *good* move, but I *had* started the motion.

"I know, and it's the *reason* you will get your friend back. I will deliver her, but only into your hands. They are the only ones I trust," he said, mouth pulled into a viciously mischievous smile.

I looked from Olivia to Raphael. "So, I show up, and you set her free?"

"I prefer to appeal to *baser* incentives. You show up, or she dies."

My gaze flashed to Olivia, pain ripping through me. "No. Don't."

"Death dealing *pulls* at me, Butterfly. It's a one-time offer. And it expires at midnight in three days' time. Come get your roommate. She is languishing without you."

Olivia was screaming something inside her crystal coffin.

"You'll just kill her when I get there," I said, desperately, yanking my gaze away and trying not to look in her direction. It was too painful. "Or the moment after I arrive."

"No." He spread his hands, voice ringing with sincerity. "My offer stands as stated. Come and get her, and you both go free. Don't, and she dies."

He reached up and turned a dial on the dream. Glowing red magic gathered in his other palm.

"Wait." I scrambled to keep it together. "I don't know where you are. I don't know how to—"

Chapter Twenty-nine

"I'm not a monster. You have three days, Butterfly. You will figure it out, I'm certain." He smiled and tapped a single finger on the pane of the dream. It cracked in five directions.

"No! No, you can't, you have to at least—"

"Sweet dreams, Butterfly." He turned toward where the shade was coiled, ready, smoked eyes on its target, tracking Raphael's movements as the cracks in the dreamglass grew larger. The red glow in Raphael's palm increased in brightness, as did the edge of the savage smile that lifted the left side of his face.

The crystal coffin shattered and Olivia dropped and threw herself over Marsgrove.

Crack. Crack, crack, crack.

The dream shattered. Kaine leapt at Raphael, and I was thrust backward into space.

I shot upright, gripping my hair in both hands, and taking deep, gasping breaths.

"Another nightmare, dear?" Bellacia questioned sweetly. She was on top of her bedspread, painting her nails magically, one long strip of magicked black at a time.

I threw off the borrowed bedspread, ignoring her, and scrambled to ascertain my magic level.

50% blinked back at me. I held my hand to my mouth, forcing myself not to cry. It was hard.

"Poor dear. Are you *upset?*"

She smiled at me from beneath her lashes and blew magicked air across her nails. But I saw her discreetly checking her feeds. Wanting to see if this was a repeat from the night before.

When I didn't respond, she said, "Magic shared, is a burden aired." She smiled and started on her other hand.

She was *far* too close to me. These rooms were too small for living quarters with Bellacia Bailey.

I focused on her actions, instead of viciously telling her that I *should* have swapped her. Raphael might even have been delighted enough with my response to do it.

Still smiling, she made a long swipe with the brush. I took a deep inhale with each swipe she made and forced my focus. The magic of the polish allowed her to change her nails at will—lengthening them, coloring them, decorating them, edging the tips to barbs designed to cause pain, filling the ridges with magical ink...endless options for the fashionable and deadly mage.

The *free* mage. My focus broke.

Shaking, I checked the time. It was two in the morning. "Do you never sleep?" I asked, furious.

"With you in here, I sleep with one eye open."

"Why did you even set up this stupid rooming scenario?" I demanded.

She leaned toward me, brush aloft in the air, green eyes glinting. It was like she had suddenly taken off a mask long worn. "Because this will gain me everything I need. The last pieces of the puzzle. Assembling right before my eyes."

She visibly struggled for a moment, then she was once more the Bellacia Bailey that I knew. She shrugged lightly and laid down another perfect stripe. "Rooting out the unworthy. Making our layer safer. If all it takes is a little lost shuteye, I will make do."

I stared at her for a moment, contemplating a hidden depth and agenda that I hadn't previously considered, and didn't yet understand. Unnerving. "I'm surprised you haven't just killed me off. Done the world a service."

"The Justice Magic would never allow it. Besides, pet, you get a *dispensation*. For saving campus. Even Cami agrees, and she's not very happy with you right now. She's stupidly protective of her little clan of warriors, even though I've warned her a thousand times that being that way is not the way to move *up*. No." She smiled slowly, blowing across her nails. "I won't harm you. *Physically*, at least. That doesn't mean you don't owe some answers to all of us. And it doesn't mean you shouldn't be...monitored."

Controlled. There weren't really any lines to read between on that one.

I took a deep breath. Then another.

I'd been controlled since I'd Awakened. In one way or another, I hadn't been out from under a chain of some sort—Raphael, Marsgrove, Excelsine, my magic itself, my own choices.

But a leash placed on me by the Department would truly remove any semblance of my own agency. And leaving campus would put me directly on that path.

I pulled the covers back over me, and curled onto my side away from her, clutching everything against my chest—the orb, the balloon, the dragon, the scarab, the jewel, the rose—hoarding them like a winged serpent over a pile of gems.

Three days? I narrowed my eyes at the wall.

I'd show them all what I could do in three days.

Chapter Thirty

RALLY TO ASSIGN

MY MAGIC WAS at sixty percent upon waking. I had three days. And I knew exactly what to do.

I tucked away two hours of research in a library streaming room—furious, focused research on the Third Layer, Outlaw Territory, the protections needed to travel within it, and how to get there—with an acceptable five percent loss to my magic recovery.

Learning how to use the streaming rooms had been one of my best moves my first term here—the sheer load of material and connections that could be made between different texts was unparalleled. I also needed to get to Draeger once they opened the Eighth and Ninth Circles, or figure out a way to get through the restriction.

I started a list of threat assessments, protections, and queries that I would solve in the free moments I had the rest of the day.

Constantine wasn't in his room, but I had the key—which was still a little weird. I exchanged items between my day bag and increasingly burgeoning duffel, and locked up after myself.

I strode down the hall, Justice Tablet under my arm.

It wasn't that I suddenly had different priorities. I had the same priorities, and the same clear goal. I was just now possessed of a timeline and deadly motivation.

I fielded a call from Neph, one from Will, and one from Saf, saying I'd meet them after service duties. And I sent a quick, coded message to Dagfinn asking about comms in the Third Layer.

I was going after Olivia on my own—I couldn't afford to have anyone drown on my sinking ship—but I wasn't going to ignore the lesson learned from Bloody Tuesday and this past term, in general.

Mages working together could create incredible things.

And I wouldn't discount Marsgrove and his words about protecting

* Rally to Assign *

everyone here. I had to make sure that everyone I left behind was taken care of.

It presented complications both for my plans to leave campus and for what needed to be implemented to hide that disappearance.

I would have to deal with friends who would surely object to the plan, as well as keep information flowing uninhibited. It presented a challenge that I thought would be best approached from task setting first, permission asking later.

With all of those things in mind, I headed out on my first set of morning Justice calls with alternate goals.

Lifen opened the door, a bright orange pen in her hand, in contrast to her all black wardrobe. Her dark hair was even pulled back with a black band.

"Crown."

"Chen." I nodded, addressing her the same way.

"What alarmed me?" Her eyes narrowed on my tablet.

"Nothing. Sorry about that. I'm on my way from another call in your dorm and decided to stop by before the next one rings. Got a moment?"

She nodded and motioned me inside.

Her roommate, a blonde who had her frequency on so high that I could see the magic pulses around her head of the music she was listening to, was sitting cross-legged on a bed on the other side of the room. Upon seeing me, she stared for a moment longer than was comfortable and her frequency pulses increased in a cacophonous burst.

She touched something on her bed—was that one of my roses?—then touched the wall nearest her. Dragging her fingers across the space, a barrier erected itself and mounted into the wall on the other side, cordoning her off completely from us. The seeping waves from her frequency abruptly ceased.

I pointed to the barrier. "Sound proof in both directions?"

"By design," Lifen said.

I accepted the security of it without question. Lifen was not an average rule breaker. But discretion was always a good idea.

"What do you need?" she asked.

"Metalworking commission. Jewelry."

Lifen was far more of a blade girl. Sharp, pointy things. But she was a maker, and a crafter. And she had smithed the memorial plaques in the team's armbands herself.

I opened my notebook to the drawing of the ouroboros ring that the Dorm head had been wearing in his lip. After reading about what was needed in Outlaw Territory, and thinking about leaving everyone behind, a number of things had combined to make me think of this option. The

Chapter Thirty

swallowing vine, the lip ring, the firesnakes, the need for transmogrification...

Lifen cocked her head at me. "Protection charms?"

"Um, no, metal snakes that can slither, climb, swallow magic, and swallow themselves if discovered. A sort of...personal recycling system."

A slow smile worked over Lifen's lips. "You have enchantments in mind?"

I nodded to her, holding up a sheet of notes. "And I thought...Loudon?"

She tapped her chin. "Yeah, okay, I can see that. Never thought about working with him on anything before. He interested?"

I tapped him mentally, then gave a nod. "He said that if he could insert a spell to make something self-destruct, he was in."

She gave a light laugh. "Give me your notes and two hours to work up a skeletal prototype, Crown. I'll contact him."

~*~

I took three more calls, then dropped by Dagfinn's. Trick was there, like an imp keeping track of his mischief. I wasn't surprised to see him. He, Saf, and Dagfinn were close, and anything I told one likely was as good as shared with the other two.

Dagfinn had read between the lines of my note like the paranoid communication mage he was, and, with a flourish, handed me something as soon as I stepped in his door.

"And you can communicate between the layers with this?" I asked, examining the slim manufactured rock with its many streaked veins.

"Absolutely. And I've made a few modifications. They'll do whatever we want them to do."

"You aren't going to get in trouble with the SEC or FAA, or whatever it is here?"

His eyes unfocused for a moment, then he brightened. "Ah. FACE—Frequency and Communication Exchange—and no." His smile turned sly. "They've been after Mage X for years, and haven't caught him yet."

I stared at him.

Well, that solved my problem of thinking I was dragging everyone along with me into being enemies of the state. They all already were.

"I'm extremely thankful that you ended up on our team in this," I said finally.

Dagfinn winked. He looked more relaxed than I had seen him. He was usually paranoid and twitchy. "You cleaned up just about every loose end I had on campus Tuesday. *Before* the Department could get their claws in me. Excelsine policy doesn't allow students to be subjected to government scrutiny except in the case of extreme violation or expulsion. I was a lot looser on campus than I am in the outside world, and that was about to abruptly bite me in the canker. FACE and the Department would have connected all the dots."

He spread his hands. "Whatever you need, Crown, as I said before."

~*~

Delia was next, and I got right down to business.

"Have you ever made a battle cloak?"

"Yes."

I blinked. I had been expecting a negative response. "Oh, great."

She looked amused. "There's a class on cloaks in the stitching sciences department."

"Oh. I feel...slightly dumb for not anticipating that."

She laughed. "No one pays attention to our classes." Her eyes looked sly. "They should, though. They should pay far more attention to the stitches in what they wear."

Delia's frequency of small offenses was legendary.

"What about shadow cloaks?"

Her gaze sharpened and she drew an extra privacy rune in the floor with her foot. "The ones the praetorians wear?"

"Yes."

She sighed. "They are illegal to make or wear. They work like Kaine's Shadow Magic, but also separately from it. Listen." She held up a hand. "Seeking information about those is not something either of us need. But I can make you something else. Something that for you will work *better*."

She touched my neck, and a ghostly image of magic followed her fingers' path as she pulled her arm back.

She touched a roll of thread and I could see her magic reaching out and touching each string, sifting along and communing with each tiny thread. It was a little like how I approached paint and color. But there was a taste to the magic that spoke of texture over hue as Delia touched and stroked everything, whispering small enchantments as she worked.

Snipped threads littered the floor. I picked up one and touched it, feeling for the threads of magic.

This type of magic was the difference between a competent battle cloak and something truly extraordinary.

There was a change in the atmosphere of her workspace, and I looked up.

She lifted two fingers, pinched together, and held them out to me.

I stared blankly at her fingers. "You can make air?"

She laughed and shook her fingers. A ripple of material shifted in the air.

Chapter Thirty

I moved forward toward it. "Camouflage?"

"Works best outside." She leaned forward. "And works best with a mage who can *feel* the magic around her as well as the air. Or a mage who has access to someone who can imbue those qualities."

"Mike?"

"Weather mage, Origin Mage, fiber mage." She winked. "It's a quality combo, Crown."

A smile started slowly but moved quickly on my lips. "Fantastic."

My smile quickly slipped. "Wait. When did you start this?" There's no way she had just whipped this out today.

"Tuesday. Mike too."

Panic gripped me.

She chewed her lip. "We've known this was how things would go. I know that Price and I don't get along. But she sacrificed herself for you." Her head tilted, looking off to the west. "Never thought I'd see sacrifice in a Price."

"Delia, I don't want you involv—"

She looked back to me, heavily kohled eyelids half-lowered over brown eyes. "Too bad. Loyalty vibe. Told you, Crown. Count me in on whatever happens. Oh, and don't delude yourself that you are keeping this a secret from Will and Neph."

My shoulders slumped—I wanted to keep them all safe—but my internal joy couldn't dim at having them *know*, of not keeping secrets.

Thirty minutes later, with a sporty weather mage at our side, we were spinning threads between us.

Chapter Thirty-one

DEALS OF DISCUSSION

WHEN I FINALLY returned to the guys' room, Constantine was leaning against the full length window in their living room, staring out. He turned and his sharp eyes swept over every inch of me.

"You've been quite busy this morning," he said. He was holding himself very still, and I would have said he was amused if I couldn't feel the deep anger resonating across our connection.

"Long night."

"When are you leaving?"

I hesitated, then continued rifling through my things. After being confronted by Delia, it wasn't like I had thought I would sneak by *Constantine*, but I didn't relish this conversation.

Any thoughts on giving him crap about what the rumor mill had cooked up had faded far below my real concerns.

"He gave me three days."

"Ren."

My shoulders dropped, along with the shirt in my hands. I stared at it. "I'm seeking help. *Asking* for it. But I have to go alone."

On stealthy cat feet, he dropped down in front of me. He smiled when I looked up. It was less pleasant than the ones he usually favored me with.

"Do you think that's going to happen?" he asked, voice pleasant.

I gripped my shirt. "Raphael sucked me into a dream state last night. He said that he would release Olivia—let us both go—if I came for her. He doesn't lie. But I'm positive the no-kill agreement would not include you."

Before winter term, Raphael might have toyed with Constantine before delivering the blow, but after finding out that Constantine had leeched me, Constantine had been living under a prompt death sentence in Raphael's mind.

He'd dealt Constantine such a blow, even in the limited golem skin

Chapter Thirty-one

Raphael had worn. Constantine would have died on Tuesday if it hadn't been for the healing spells both Axer and I had placed on him. *Mine* had been super shady too. I still wasn't completely sure what the paint had done to him.

"He'll kill you," I said softly. "When it was a rescue mission, an infiltration, it was different." I rubbed my eyes. "Or maybe it wasn't different, and I just wasn't thinking clearly. Nothing about Tuesday was clear. There is no element of surprise now, though, and that's infinitely worse for you."

"You think he wasn't always expecting you?"

I stayed silent. Raphael had been expecting me from the moment that Olivia stepped in front of the spell meant for me.

Constantine lifted my chin. "I'm going to kill him. And you are going to get your friend back. That's all that matters in this."

I pressed my lips together. "Telling me you are going to commit murder is not the best way to go about things."

"It has been months since I've sold myself to you as anything other than what I am."

"Kaine is there. Somewhere. He attacked when Raphael cast me out."

"And we will deal with him too." He released my chin.

I stared at the shirt, rubbing it between my fingers.

"You weren't even going to tell Alexander, were you?" he mused.

I peered up at Constantine. He was smiling.

"Probably. Maybe. I have a few days. I need to plan. He'll try to talk me out of it. And...he's busy."

Constantine seemed to find something darkly amusing, but he didn't explain.

"Why do you think Verisetti wants you there in person?" he asked instead.

"Probably to strap a bomb to me or worse. Maybe just to get me arrested when I leave campus, so I'll be sucked into the Department. I don't know." I rubbed my eyes again. "But he vowed. He will let Olivia go, if I make it there."

"You look worse."

"It's been a rough few nights."

He looked me over. "Tonight will be better."

"Sure." I could be optimistic. "Where were you last night?"

"Medical."

"Do you have to stay there every night?" Maybe I could get Greyskull to admit me on a temporary order, and I could keep Constantine company and get away from Bellacia.

"No. Just last night. Tonight will be far better, as I said." He smiled

* Deals of Discussion *

slowly.

"If you say so. But, listen, since I have you now, I need to get into the vault."

Constantine raised a brow. "It isn't on the list of opened buildings."

"Right." I looked at him expectantly.

He looked back, amused, still crouched in front of me. "You think we will just break in?"

"Yes?"

"With all of your followers and trackers and shadows trailing you?"

"Yes?"

"That one sounded even less convincing, darling."

"Yes," I said firmly. "I need to make a number of things, and I need paint, Con. You know I do."

He pulled a lock of my hair between his fingers. "It would almost be easier getting into the Midlands, at this point."

"No." I shook my head in emphasis and he let the curl go. "I need to keep everything there safe. I will definitely be followed. Vault access doesn't put me off the campus grid. And I could even do a switcheroo with Neph for a bit."

"You realize she's a Bau, correct?"

"Con?"

He blew out a breath. "You exhaust me."

"No, I don't."

I caught his smile before he grew serious again.

"I'll see what I can do."

~*~

I left Constantine to figure things out and headed over to see Professor Mbozi. Mbozi sighed upon seeing me, then questioned me brutally about the domes and what I had done. It wasn't often that I was on the interrogation side of a Professor Mbozi/Ren Crown discussion.

Enthused, I told him everything I could—without disclosing secrets—and asked him for help filling in the blanks in my knowledge. Which he did.

He touched lightly on *other* subjects, mentioning that he had a class on rare magic fields that would be coming up in the fall, and also that he *might* have a few hours to spare on special projects in the spring.

Seeing as I had been hunting him down over the past two terms like a raggedy lion with a favorite gazelle, I was ecstatic.

I left his office with a smile and the magical blueprints for a portable chaos field. One that was "ideologically possible, but untested, Miss Crown."

I was pretty sure he was just as excited to hear about what I did with the

Chapter Thirty-one

field as I was, even though his facial expression had been long-suffering, world-weary, and like he was headed off for a stiff drink as soon as I disappeared from view. It was a lot like the way Professor Stevens looked at Constantine.

On a hunch, I tried to locate Professor Stevens too. I'd been itching to talk to her since it had become obvious that she was friends with Raphael. Her conversation with Helen Price a few weeks ago made complete sense, within that context. And, given that context, I could deduce that she wasn't a fan of Olivia's mother. That she might help me, was a possibility.

But she wasn't in her lab. Nor anywhere else that I looked.

It was possible she was trekking around campus with the majority of the teaching staff, who, unsurprisingly, were out and about on campus in large numbers, helping any student who crossed their path—and getting in the way of the Legion interrogating the populace, more often than not.

Rumor had it that in-person staff meetings were not being held for the time being, and that they were spreading resources all over the top levels of campus so that all of the staff could not be trapped in one place again.

Softer rumor had it that this was not just in case of terrorists attacking again, but also if the Legion decided to show their might.

It was becoming just as usual to see a professor briskly walking a tracked path through one of the levels, talking via frequency or hologram, than it was to see students doing the same.

But none of the faces who crossed my path were Lucille Stevens.

Tarei followed me on my failed quest, a shadow in the mist, and I tried to ignore him. Tried to ignore when he blinked at me with a gaze that was not his own.

I made sure to stick to the most well-traveled paths.

~*~

The dorms weren't much of a relief, but at least here, there was a sanctity Tarei couldn't yet breach.

The common rooms were packed with people watching the All-Layer Combat Competition. Even packed, though, there weren't as many students watching the competition in the common areas as there had been before the attack. Some people were too traumatized to watch more fighting, others were too traumatized to be in the same place that they were when the domes were erected.

But there were plenty who were still glued to their sets and feeds. Some looked desperate for some sort of victory—as if having our school win would give them some balm or security they couldn't otherwise find.

The transmission was tracking Lox at the moment, and he was doing a fine job in whacking his opponent. Well-enough that some of the people

* Deals of Discussion *

watching were switching their short attention spans elsewhere.

Strangely, even the perfectly respectable students at school—the ones who were *never* in trouble—were casting disturbed looks at the vents.

"Can't turn them off completely still," someone hissed. "System override."

It was a sobering reminder that while normally the Administration "let" us get away with some things, when they wanted to affect something specifically, we couldn't stop them.

And when they were being pushed by outside forces, anything was possible.

I sent a query through the gem Will had given me and was immediately hit with information culled from multiple open frequencies. The calming spells were the new hot topic around campus—slotting into a place of popularity after grief and trauma DIY fixes, gossip about the Origin Mage, and chitchatting on the combat competition.

The delinquents hearing my query, on the other hand, mentally chimed in that they were doing "mad business" in neutralizing spells, especially Lifen, who had served a stint on the Neutralizer Squad, and Loudon, who had some overlapping expertise with his dismantling skills.

My steps slowed as the live competition feed switched competitors. Axer was front and center of the magical projection on the dorm's wall. I released the armband and gem communications with an absent, "thanks."

He knocked an opponent down, but it wasn't as effortless as he usually made it look.

He was also protecting his midsection more than he had before Kaine had ripped him apart, and it hadn't gone unnoticed. The announcers were speculating that he had taken the injury in the "Bloody Tuesday Attack."

It hadn't stopped any of his opponents from trying to maim him there further.

Even tired, he was deadly, but these were the best fighters across the layers—and they were *far* better rested and at top form. As he climbed the heats, the matches became more grueling to watch.

A Third Layer mage got in a good swing.

"Damn thirdies. Shouldn't let them compete," someone grumbled.

"Especially *now*," someone agreed.

"*They* didn't do it," a far more reasonable person pointed out.

"But they *are* fighting for their layer. They condone the actions of their own terrorists."

"That's *not* true. Not everyone—"

"Yeah? You think Lorenzo isn't in league with the terrorists?"

Leonach Lorenzo was the leader of the Rebuilding Faction in the Third Layer. Their government was made up of about a dozen different factions,

Chapter Thirty-one

and currently the Rebuilding Faction headed them all.

Lorenzo had disassociated himself from the terrorists, but I had to admit, after seeing his visage a few times...he didn't seem *too* displeased.

But if he was involved, he was very good at covering his tracks. He was squeaky clean, and not even Bellacia's father could pin anything on him.

The Second Layer seemed to hate him for that even more.

The feed announcer made his presence known. "Due to the tragic events at Excelsine University, all competitors are a little off today. The Excelsine combat mages returned to campus to help secure it, and so did a good portion of the other combat mages at the competition—helping out their fellow young mages in need. As a result, there is a far more community-based feeling at today's events. But it should be noted, that the Excelsine competitors who answered the call, and stayed on campus for the night, are suffering."

Community-based feeling or not—and I could see how that worked, with the competing mages being the first ones to clasp their competitor back upright after a loss, manly bro-hug and all—no one was going easy on their opponents.

"In other news, Alexander Dare was retested for his ability as a Bridge Mage this morning before the competition restarted. He scored a fifteen on the ability test, not enough to register on the Bridge scale. However, it has been noted that fifteen is five points higher than his baseline, and people are talking about whether—"

I walked away.

I didn't want to see Axer lose. And I didn't want to hear about the people wanting to persecute him.

Chapter Thirty-two

TWO DEVILS AND A BAG OF POPCORN

THE REST OF the afternoon and evening passed in a flurry of magic gathering, checking in on the members of the group and their "assignments," mandatory justice rotations, peeks at the combat competition feeds, and check-in hours in Bellacia's room.

By the end of it, I was exhausted.

Constantine caught me as I was heading back to Bellacia's room for the night. He opened the door to their room before I even got close to approaching. He closed it and fell into step with me as I made my way the remaining five doors down the hall.

"I have to go beard the dragon for the night. Talk tomorrow," I said tiredly.

"Of course, darling."

The smile on his face should have concerned me more. With each step, his anticipation seemed to increase.

At Bellacia's door, however, his anticipation turned to anger.

"What is this?" Constantine sliced his hand through a spell on the door. Sparks shot to both sides as it fizzled.

"Another message?" I asked, not all that interested.

The door had experienced far too many messages and jinxes—all targeted at me—for me to care what this one said. I unlocked the door and opened it. Bellacia stood in the middle of the room, weirdly waiting.

Constantine's gaze narrowed on me. "*Another* message? Why haven't you been implementing the standard room spells? I don't care how temporary the roommate assignment is." He looked at Bellacia, gaze malicious. "You still get to implement protections."

I'd never needed them before, so I didn't know the spells. And, "I was, and am, too tired to care," I admitted.

"You can't let people put things like that on your space, Ren."

Chapter Thirty-two

It was rare that he called me by name. I wondered at his tone, and at what the message he had destroyed had said. There had been threats, thank you notes, slurs, and worshipful prose, along with a plethora of condolences to Bellacia for getting stuck with the devil's spawn. I might as well have posted an advertisement saying "Post your note about the *possible* Origin Mage in your midst right here!"

There had been some notes about Constantine too, since his stunt in the cafeteria. I wondered if that was it.

Olivia and I had barely had five notes pinned to our door in all the months I'd been at Excelsine. Mages had too many other ways to communicate, and so unless someone was overtly advertising a message—a declaration of love, celebratory news, death threats—then mages used other communication channels.

"It's fine," I said. It was easier to ignore the notes than the stares, and far preferable.

"It's a sign of weakness, and says that you aren't adequately protected," he said grimly. "That bitch knows this."

"Oh my, no, I'd *never*," Bellacia said, leaning one hip against the arm of a sofa. She looked smug and superior and so very *darkly* pleased. "Come, Ren, shut the door so the boy can return to his room. We have so many things to discuss before we sleep."

What she really meant was—I have so many awful things to make you witness or to taunt you with tonight. Yay!

"No, what she means is that she loves to hear herself talk," he said cuttingly, reading my mind.

Bellacia shot a vicious glance toward the room's threshold, as if waiting for him to try and cross it. Constantine hadn't yet, and I was starting to think that was because there was some terrible magic that Bellacia had placed there.

"What were you trying with that little stunt in the cafeteria, Connie?" She tutted, lifting her gaze back to meet his. "People are saying the *wildest* things."

"Are they? I wouldn't know. It's your domain to care what people say. However, Ren seems distressed by your little rumor mill, and we can't have that."

Eyes going wide, I motioned with my hand to him. *Not helping. Do **not** try and help.*

Her smile grew. I had never seen it so dark. "Is that so? Axer was a surprise, I'll admit. *You*, I expected," she said with a certain amount of relish, as if she was about to deliver a payback she had long planned.

"Did you?" Constantine's voice turned almost pleasant. The hairs at the back of my neck stood on end. "And did you expect this?"

* Two Devils and a Bag of Popcorn *

He gently pushed me to the right of where I *had* been holding open the door and walked inside the suite, then flipped the door closed.

"Wha—how did—get *out*," she hissed, jerking to stand straight. I could feel the temperature in the room drop, and the pressure from her Sirenic magic increase.

"No," he said languidly, and sauntered further into the room, as if he owned it. I could see magic rippling over him, Bellacia's magic, pulled violently from the *walls*, trying to *eject* him. I could see the smirk he couldn't hide behind a studied nonchalance as he continued walking, unhindered.

Bellacia looked angrier than I had ever seen her. "*Get out of my room.*"

The scarab around my neck *burned*, and I hissed, pulling the cord away from my skin.

She blasted magic from her palms at Constantine, but it slipped over him, like oil slicking over water.

Both horror and fury combined on her face.

"Ah, Bella, your magic just isn't enough to overcome darling Ren's." He fanned his fingers in a rolling wave and wards in the hues of violet, bronze, and ultramarine drew into view, pushing Bellacia's angry shades of crimson easily away. "Even when she's twelve spells to an ill wind."

Horrified, I looked between them. "I don't—"

"And dear Alexander made *such* a sacrifice to have this happen. Surely we owe it to our school champion—and likely two-time winner of the All-Layer Combat Competition with this little boost—to funnel our magic *appropriately.*"

Unlike me, Bellacia seemed to understand what he was saying *immediately*, because she blanched, skin going paper white. "The officials would never—"

"They already have," he mused, poking at something on the wall as if a listening fly device was more interesting than the girl with steam emerging from her perfect ears. "Stuart was beyond pleased to have me ask so *kindly*. It seems that the roommate reassignment magic wanted to put Ren in our room, and would have, if you hadn't opened yourself to the Root Magic. Tut, tut, Bella, what would Roald say?"

"He says that you will never work *anywhere* in the magical world again," she said viciously.

Constantine smiled. "Is he listening in? Right now? How delightful. Too bad that he doesn't control that choice."

"You will get *out* of my room," she hissed.

"Who would want to stay? Come, Ren."

I looked nervously at the clock. "I need to spend eight more hours here."

With the girl who was now looking to physically, verbally, and mentally

Chapter Thirty-two

annihilate someone. *Thanks.*

"See, now that's where you are wrong, darling. Look at the magic again."

The room magic was streaming in three different directions. At one point it had been in two—from my old dorm room to here and back. Now there was a third room added in, and from the context of the conversation, it was pretty obvious which room that was.

"So you can decide, *dear* Bella, in what room Ren will sleep tonight, and subsequently, where *I* will sleep. Will it be here? Or there?"

She looked like she might hyperventilate on the spot. I was vaguely concerned for her, truth be told.

"You can't take away all her hours here," she hissed.

"No, but I can cut them significantly." He smiled. It was a strange smile that was both unpleasant and exhilarated at the same time. "In fact, I was told they could be taken down by two-thirds. A third for each of the three of us Ren is currently attached to in the housing system."

"Axer's not—"

"Here, no, but he is still linked into the room. The officials were quite pleased when they thought they might increase his chances to win by giving him some extra juice. He is competing with a few injuries that are hindering him, poor boy."

"I will file an injunction."

"You do that." He leaned in. Her angry red magic slammed against his shields, and he smiled. "But in the meantime, what's it going to be?"

"Take her! Take her. Get *out.*"

I scrambled to grab everything, not even questioning it. There was no way Bellacia would have capitulated so furiously if Constantine wasn't right. Constantine and Axer had somehow gained permission so that I could spend eight of my hours in their room, and four with Bellacia.

I'd take it. I'd take it so hard. I grabbed everything—including Constantine's arm—and threw open the door.

A Justice Squad member blinked at me. "Er, Bellacia Bailey, Level Three?"

I nodded, pointed behind me, and shuffled around the squad member and into the hall—without letting go of Constantine.

I could hear Bellacia in icy tones accept her punishment for her overuse of Sirenic magic and violent use of spells with intent to harm.

I shoved my key into the lock of Room Sixty-nine. The key made *so much more sense* now.

"That was hardly a dignified exit, darling," he said as I unlocked the door. "I would have really enjoyed playing a last card or two. Just to watch the defeat fall over her face one shutter at a time."

"Ugh. How did the two of you ever think it was a good idea to hook

* Two Devils and a Bag of Popcorn *

up?" I pushed him inside and shut the door behind us, then slumped against the wood. I half expected the door to splinter behind me, and my last sight on Earth to be Bellacia shrieking as she murdered us.

"Beauty and madness are a delicious cocktail, darling."

"I hope you enjoyed the hangover." I wiped a hand along my eyes. I sure wasn't enjoying the aftereffects.

"It was quite unpleasant," he allowed. "I've switched to far better fare since."

I looked around the room. Sure enough, the wards had multiplied, little facets of Bellacia now running through.

"So...I'm really staying here?"

"Yes."

"Oh, thank God." I slid to the floor.

"I can have you saying that more than once tonight, if you wish." He leered.

"You. No." I pointed at him.

He laughed.

"But, seriously, I am going to bed."

"Perfect." He smiled.

"No." I pointed again, then motioned with my hands at the furniture.

The living room had long since retreated back to the standard layout Constantine employed with its expensive, but mismatched furniture—none of them sofa shaped.

He raised a brow.

"Couch me," I said, motioning again.

"Don't be an idiot, darling," Constantine said. "The whole point is to hook you into the wards."

He turned and walked briskly to their bedroom.

I pushed myself off the floor and followed at a much slower pace.

Their room was as small as Bellacia's. Just two beds, two armoires, and two nightstands. But whereas in Bellacia's room, everything was a little more interconnected, in here the room had two distinct sides. The two beds were against opposite walls, and a field separated the two halves of the room. Very likely it involved all sorts of evil enchantments I didn't want to know about.

Who was I kidding. I touched one of the wards. It sung with warning, but didn't shock me. Someone had spent a lot of time on these. They were a permanent addition instead of the quick curtain pull that Lifen and her roommate used.

All of the wards ran around the edges of the field, not interrupting any of the magic share. They simply prevented normal sensory things—like communication, viewing, and hearing, and so forth—from being shared.

Chapter Thirty-two

However, the magic had to be influenced by emotions, at least a little, and I wondered how that worked when Constantine invited his conquests inside.

Then again, maybe Constantine was just that detached. I'd seen him plenty of times with his number of the day, or week, during fall term. He had never actually seemed to emotionally engage with them. Not that they seemed to ever realize this. I wondered again at what my gender was thinking.

I shook my head and looked around again. Okay, it made a lot more sense now why Axer had pointed out where he slept. I stared at the bed.

This was a little weird. Okay, a lot weird. Not like sharing with Olivia or Neph. At all.

Constantine came up next to me and mimicked my posture. "I know. It's like the cooties are *real*."

I shoved him in the side, barely moving him, but making him laugh all the same.

He smirked down at the bed. "Here, let me help." He waved his hand and the bed became a princess setup, all pinks, tiaras, and silver.

I could feel the protest in the magic, in the permanent wards, but they allowed it, probably because Axer had allowed *me* to have a say.

I stared at the changes, aghast, Axer would *kill* him.

"No?" He waved his hand again, and it was dripping black and silver with gothic spikes and twisted posts. "Though, I think, that you would be far more likely to—"

I wrestled his hand down before he could change it again, as if his hands were what was responsible for the magic, instead of Constantine simply channeling the magic through the gesture.

"We could combine the two into one larger one," he said slyly. "Far more restful and easier for our magic."

"*Pass.*"

He laughed, and I shoved him through the field.

I changed quickly in the bathroom and brushed my teeth. Delia could look at my t-shirts and yoga pants in disdain all she wanted to, but this situation, here, was where they were a huge win.

Constantine was sitting cross-legged on his bed, in casual sleepwear, and thank god he had decided to be a normal human. Not like that show he had put on in the cafeteria.

"Hey," I said, punching the pillow and using the room's wards to remake the bed into what I was used to, trying to think of it as mine instead of...whose it was. "Your little exhibition in the cafeteria has caused me nothing but grief for the last twenty-four hours. And, now this? Ugh. Bellacia is going to spin the worst tales. Tomorrow is going to suck."

* Two Devils and a Bag of Popcorn *

I settled under the covers and blew a stray hair from my face. "And I have to figure out how to tell your *real* roommate that I'm leaving campus."

"Don't bother worrying over much. He knew what was going to happen when he left," Constantine said in disinterest.

"You told him?"

"*I* didn't know, did I."

"You're saying he anticipated it." I sighed. "Probably. He was packing for *inevitability*."

"Don't you think it interesting, darling?" Constantine tapped his finger on his bent knee as he examined me from the short space across the room. "That Alexander Dare knows all of your weaknesses? Exactly how you fight and how your magnificent brain works? Suspicious."

"You know those things too," I pointed out.

"And look how that always ends for you," he said.

I sighed.

He smiled. "I know how you *solve*. But Alexander knows exactly how you react in combat. It is his specialty, knowing what opponents are going to do before they do it. I could almost admire the forbearance he puts forth, if I could stand to contemplate the individual himself. How long do you think it would take for him to take you down, should he feel the need or *desire* to do so?"

There was no doubt of the answer. "I'd never even have the realization that it was about to happen. I know that. Everyone knows that when it comes to him. It's probably the best check to have in place on me."

"It is the worst check that the Second Layer governments could possibly contemplate."

I sighed again and tucked myself under the covers. "Yeah, the Department rats watch him with something akin to a nature documentary on modern, rampaging T. Rex's that they think might...rampage at any moment."

"And for you?" He hummed. "If he did display his mother's skills, have you thought what he might do to you with them?"

I put everything that I had clutched the previous night on the nightstand. Constantine wasn't going to mess with my things. "I've heard the warnings already."

And I didn't want to give away that I knew a *lot* more about what might happen than everyone guessed. That whole scenario Delia had described was a lot closer to the truth than anyone would be comfortable with.

"I worry for you."

"You do not," I retorted.

"Don't I?" he said lightly.

"Good night, Con," I said, turning off my light. "You were awesome to

Chapter Thirty-two

get me out of Bellacia's clutches, regardless of how painful it's going to turn out to be."

"Good night, darling, and it was my *pleasure*."

I touched the nearly empty paper balloon, then the orb, then let my fingers drift away. I fished the dragon figurine from my armband and gripped the dragon against my chest. Deep breaths.

It was disconcerting, trying to connect via a dream after the disastrous ones I'd had. It was also really, really weird to do it in the bed of the person I was trying to call. Even though it wasn't *really* his bed. I had changed it to look like mine in Room Twenty-five. But his magic was all over the space.

But sleep soon came, and with it so did a feeling of flying along on the back of a dragon made of clouds.

Axer was doing something in his mindscape. I couldn't quite see what it was behind the curtain that seemed to float in front. But he waved his dream away as soon as he sensed me, and opened the curtain. We were surrounded in white.

"What happened?" he asked, touching the clouds of white around us, as if each one held an answer.

"I'm in your room," I blurted.

He relaxed. "That's unfortunate for a number of reasons. But you seem fine." His fingers drifted through another cloud and he seemed to find the answer he was seeking. He nodded.

"Raphael has Marsgrove. And he issued an ultimatum on Olivia. He gave me three days to find them."

His expression sharpened and the white of the dream took on a darker cast. "There is no report that Phillip Marsgrove was captured. He didn't report in, but that isn't necessarily unusual given the circumstances. Julian said he registers as alive. Are you certain it wasn't just a dream?"

"I'm certain of very little. But...it felt real." The feel of Axer's mental scape had the same feel of my nightmare. It made me more certain that what I had experienced had been a reality. "It felt a lot like this. Kaine was there, too, on the outside, trying to get in."

"I'll find out. *Stay put.*"

"Three *days*."

"I know.

We talked of the competition and what was happening at school. And I calmed down enough, finally, to fall back into strangely dreamless sleep.

Chapter Thirty-three

PLANNING FOR FIRE

I WOKE UP and checked my magic levels. 75%. *Not bad*. I figured I had spent much of fall term at 75%, so, all things considered, I was doing okay. I touched the cocktail of wards on the walls. Two sets from Room Twenty-five, Bellacia's, Axer's and Constantine's, the combat competition boost, and Medical, which, strangely, hadn't been switched off yet.

I rolled out of bed and blinked to find Constantine gone. I would never have taken him for an early riser.

He had left me a note, though, with the word "vault" underlined twice.

Excellent.

It was Friday. I had today and tomorrow to find Olivia, and get the plan together.

I walked into Constantine's workroom to prepare.

The bag that he carried all our supplies in when going to the vault was hanging on its normal hook. All of our supplies were safely stored here between our normal thrice weekly sessions. I rifled through the bag until I found a tube of paint. It was one of our better mixes—a gorgeous foamy turquoise that conjured smells of the sea and surf and that imbued everything created with it with a sort of seaside quality.

I even had a very slim vial of Awakening paint that we had been modeling our mixes after. That was what I needed to find Olivia. The problem, as always, though, was *using* it. Under the Administration Magic, I still couldn't paint outside of the vault and the Midlands.

The Midlands were even more out of reach, at this point, and that left the vault. I thrummed with the knowledge that we'd locate Olivia today, as soon as we gained access to the building.

I touched Constantine's work desk where empty paint tubes littered a corner of the workspace. A drawing of our dodecaplex was beneath it.

I could hear Constantine entering through the suite's front door, and I

Chapter Thirty-three

stopped and took a good look at his workroom through clearer eyes. My things...were everywhere—interspersed in all of his. For every magical beaker of his, there was a stack of quality paper or a modified charcoal pencil of mine.

"I'm sorry," I blurted out as he entered the room.

He raised a brow and peeled off his long, expensive full-length coat. "I expect *favors* for my forgiveness. The more creative or *diverting*, the better."

I chewed on my lip and continued looking around.

He sighed, deep and full of ennui, though our connection told me he was amused, and feeling far better than yesterday. "And *what* are you languishing on about, Crown?"

"My stuff is *everywhere*."

"Your vision is keen. I now have this very positive feeling that we are going to win the day." He raised a sign of victory and stretched out in his work chair.

I replaced my lip with my thumb as my nervous chewing object. "I've taken over your workspace. Your hours. Your life."

"You've taken over the very heart of me. Blah, blah. What do you want to do about it?" He tilted his head and drew his ribbon through his fingers. "No, I'll tell you what *I* want. I wa—"

"I'm sorry!"

"Did you hear me complaining, Crown? Do you actually know me to do anything I don't want to do?"

"You room with Alexander Dare."

"Yes, okay, keenly spotted. Anything *normal* that I do not want to do?"

I already knew exactly what I was going to make him when we got back to campus.

"If you didn't solve it already, I think we could get Stevens to open the vault for us," I said, my brain switching to the next bullet point on its massive list now that I had a future apology labeled and sorted.

His ribbon paused. "You are terrible for my ego. Or tremendous. I assume which depends upon who is having the laugh."

"You are hot and brilliant and devious," I immediately ticked off on his asset list. "You are like a really pettable, but shitty cat." I motioned with my hand to go back to the other track of conversation. "Do you think Stevens would say yes?"

"I'll have you know that I've only bitten half the people who try, and most of those because they have no idea *how* to str—"

"Professor Stevens was friends with Raphael. I know it's a risk to even entertain her help."

That stopped him. He dropped his world-weary guise completely, and the air in the room grew charged as he leaned forward. "You didn't know

* Planning for Fire *

that before. When?"

"Tuesday was...quite an eventful day. I pieced a lot of things together, some with help. Things I should have realized before."

He tapped a knuckle against the table. He didn't look surprised.

"You knew?" I asked.

"Of course I knew," he said. "Why do you think I'm one of her students?"

"Because you..." My voice stuttered off. When one actually delved beneath his facade, it was impossible not to realize that Constantine was the best student at Excelsine in his field. Anyone would *rightly* think that was because it was his forte. "But you love materials."

"Yes. I learned to love them very much."

"What...?" I shook my head. "You became a materials student—the *best* materials student—to have access to Stevens because you thought you might get access to Raphael?"

He smiled at me like he thought my astonishment was cute.

"*Constantine.*"

He quirked a brow. "What reason does anyone have for following a path? Mine is better than most."

"What did you *want* to be?"

"A volcano grower. A plesiosaur handler. A mercenary." He counted off on his fingers, then tapped his chin. "There was that time with the harem thing too, but it sounded like so much *work.*" He shuddered. "And I was right."

I swore and threw up my hands.

He smiled.

"Fine." I pointed at him. "I'm glad that you ended up in materials, even if it was for dodgy reasons. You would have been wasted handling plesiosaurs."

"Some of them can fly in the Fourth Layer."

That made me pause for a moment. "No, you are not distracting me. Stevens."

He played with his ribbon, leaning back to look at the ceiling. "She doesn't have contact with Verisetti. Not a single letter that I've ever found. And I'm...somewhat persistent."

I frowned and drummed my fingers. "I'll bet every munit I've acquired that she used to make him his supplies." I dug out the first pencil that she'd given me. I had advanced in my abilities, but hers was still a work of art.

I twirled it slowly in the air. It glistened, opalescent. She had made that cryptic comment about it—how she had had a lot of practice making them years ago. Combined with all her staring at my shields... There was no way I was wrong about this.

Chapter Thirty-three

Constantine plucked it from my grip and examined it much in the same way. "She could have made this here. While they were at school. Or even later. Nostalgically."

I frowned. "Maybe. Probably, even."

He looked at me, eyes hooded and emotion edged. There was *anticipation* in it. "If you did your research... You do know who she is? Or was?"

My frown deepened. "What do you mean?"

He examined me for a long moment, teetering on some knife's edge decision, then waved a hand. A tablet flew into his palm. He set it down in front of me. A book popped up on top, dynamically produced from the electronic contents within.

The cover said it was an old Excelsine yearbook—or what passed for a copy of a magical yearbook, because it said in the footnote that you could find original copies in the library that would give the recorded feelings from hundreds of points of view at different times throughout the seasons in a calendar year. An entire, immersive experience—100% guaranteed nostalgia—from just opening the magical book of your desired year.

A flick of Constantine's wrist caused the pages to flip. As soon as the pages settled, magic filtered into the page, populating it dynamically. Olivia usually eschewed such magic for her tomes, but I loved this about Second Layer books—they could be both electronic and paper at the same time.

Constantine tapped a picture. A young Professor Stevens coolly stared at me from the page. She was as beautiful then as she was now, age doing nothing to dim her beauty in either direction.

But her face wasn't the thing Constantine wanted me to see.

Lucille Stevens wasn't the name listed under her picture. Lucille Stavros, however, was.

Chapter Thirty-four

DAUGHTER OF THE ENEMY

WE DECIDED to break into the vault after all.

Professor Stevens being friends with Raphael back when he was sane? Acceptable. Being Enton Stavros' daughter? Not so much. The combination of the two? Terrifying.

I had broken into the vault before. Of course, that had led to me burning down the entire complex surrounding it. But, the breaking in had still been accomplished.

It had taken me a few minutes to do it last time. Together with Constantine, though, we accomplished it in less than thirty seconds.

Constantine smirked at me as the large garage-styled door started to slide shut. "And now to the real villainy of the day. We'll find your friend, then we'll see what we can make to obliterate—"

The closing of the door halted, and Lucille Stevens smoothly ducked under and entered the room.

"That will be unnecessary, Mr. Leandred," she said coldly, heels clicking.

The wicked piece of magic that Constantine was forming smoothed out on the worktable with a tapped finger. Whatever he had created, it was still active and waiting.

She looked between the two of us, cool eyes taking us in. "Many things are explained by this," she said.

"Are you going to turn us in?" I asked, voice tight, magic tightening in my own fists. With seventy-five percent magic levels, I wasn't going to roll over.

"To whom? Provost Johnson? So he could assign you another two thousand hours?"

"To the...Department?" To your father.

Her head tilted to the side and cold eyes examined my face. "You are so intelligent, and at the same time so stupid, Miss Crown."

Chapter Thirty-four

My lips pressed together. "I deal with the lack of information that I have in the only way that I can."

"The answer to your question is no."

"Why?" I asked bitingly.

"You wonder why I won't turn you over to Enton Stavros?"

"He's your father."

"He supplied the genetic material required for my birth, correct," she said briskly.

That...was a far better answer than I had hoped for.

I relaxed a measure. "You saw Raphael's magic on me, and didn't report me. To anyone?"

"I don't get involved when I see his magic," she said, voice clipped.

Like Greyskull.

I relaxed a little more, in contrast to Constantine, who was growing tenser.

"But you saw his magic, and you took me on as a student anyway."

She hadn't *wanted* to give me that first tutoring session. She'd only done so because she'd wanted to quiz me to see if I was Raphael's minion—not that I'd understood that at the time. But she'd taken me on after that first session. Mentored me ever since.

She took me in, her gaze cool. "I saw more than just his magic."

"Was it for Raphael? All that talk about the schedule that I had to maintain and the path that I had to travel?"

"No. Nothing is for Rafi anymore." She smiled thinly. "I have long since resigned myself to being unable to help him. He does not want the aid." She looked at the top of my head, a brooding, unhappy quality to her gaze.

I cast a quick look at Constantine, who wasn't bothering to hide his emotions for once. His eyes were narrowed, our connections pulsing with strong, conflicting feelings.

I turned back to Stevens. "Did you try to help Raphael?" I was more curious than anything.

"Long, long ago. Before Salietrex." She cast her own glance at Constantine, who had turned into a living statue at that statement—stone still and silent. Salietrex was the town Raphael had destroyed years ago—his first big strike. Constantine's mother had been a casualty.

"I did everything I knew how to do," Stevens continued, gaze turning inward on distant memory. "But he couldn't trust me. That was stripped from him. Ripped away from me." She tightened her fingers into a fist.

"You didn't do enough," Constantine said, voice absent of all emotion.

"Do you know," she said, voice falsely amused. "How many times Phillip has castigated me for not snapping Rafi's neck in that singular moment in time when it was within my reach? For not giving him the peace he once deserved?"

"You should have," Constantine bit out.

"So easy, it is, to say what should or should not have been done. Would you have snapped your mother's neck while she tucked you into bed, had you known she might become a mass murderer? What about your father's? If you had known what was to come—what he would do—if you had known that intellectually while you were still a happy family, what would you have done?"

Constantine pivoted on his heel and ducked under the vault's door.

"All that can be changed is what *will* occur," Stevens said, as he disappeared from view.

"That wasn't kind," I said, woodenly.

Rooted in place, I stared at the place where Constantine had stood and sent a rush of comfort through our threads. He tried to slam the connection closed, but *couldn't*. I could feel his fury at that. *Viscerally*.

I shivered.

"He will betray you," Stevens said, almost idly.

"I've been informed," was all I could say to that.

"Leandred has one of the most brilliant minds I've come across. And it's tainted in a way that might be impossible to overcome."

I smiled tightly. "All that can be changed is what will occur, yes?"

She moved over to a cylinder where we'd once cooked up an enchantment that could lace paper. She gave the stir stick in it a whirl. It made a tinkling sound as it rounded the glass in an uneven motion.

"There are things I owe," she said. "Debts that I will pay. And then I can be done. I can *forget*."

I swallowed, hearing the pain she felt beneath the statement. "You feel guilty," I said, finally understanding. Conversations from the past fit together into a new pattern. "*You* brought Raphael to your fath—to Stavros's attention."

She drew herself up. "I'm like a magnet for all of you," she said mirthlessly. "Destined to have every interesting specimen of a mage cross my path. And you all die because of it. Or worse." Her lips twisted, gaze far away, taken by unpleasant memory. "It is a curse to be noticed by me. I spent years pushing anyone interesting away, and never taking on students outside of my field where such things would be noticed."

"Why did you decide to train me?"

"Because your potential outshines my caution." Her heels clicked closer, in a staccato march. "Because I'm as drawn to brilliance as it is to me."

She slammed her hands on top of the worktable. "Because I took one look at Rafi's magic on you and *knew*. I knew you would be the end game.

Chapter Thirty-four

The piece that saves or destroys us all."

She reached forward and gripped my chin. "And because if you don't destroy everything, you will be *great*. Greatness is within you." She let go abruptly, fingers bruising my chin. "And I won't accept any less from you."

I stared at her, heart hammering in my chest.

"The Third Layer must be fixed," she said. "Fixed or destroyed. These dangling, ruined pieces serve nothing but giving people a point on which to fixate, argue, and war. And it just gives Rafi something to use as a playing board in his war on my father."

She stabbed a finger onto the worktable. "And *you* are the one who will fix or destroy it."

I tried to form words, and couldn't.

She watched my mouth move soundlessly, and spoke in a detached voice when I didn't, couldn't, answer. "You do not get to have a normal life. You have a service and responsibility to your talents."

"I *want* a normal life," I whispered, voice finally free.

"Then *carve* one for yourself. Be *extraordinary*."

Chapter Thirty-five

APOLOGIES

I FOUND CONSTANTINE back in our room.

"Is it still?" I asked, taking a careful step inside. "Our room?"

He was lying back against a pile of pillows on his bed, ribbon pulling repeatedly through his fingers while broodingly staring out the window. It was my first room at Excelsine where I didn't have the window view.

"I'm very angry."

"I know."

"With you."

"I know that too."

I could feel it—the sharp edges of his emotions and the ragged edges of whatever magic he had done between the vault and the room. He had *ended* something or someone on the way here.

Since no Justice Squad member was in sight, he must have at least appropriately let loose the damaging magic.

I sat carefully on the edge of his bed.

"Did you paint with her?" His voice sounded too dull for the low thrum of anger that accompanied it.

"No. She said she can't be involved." We'd had a short discussion where Stevens had made that very clear, and, frankly, I was the happier for it. "She said she can't, and doesn't want, to know what we are doing. But she is letting us use the facilities. She'll open them for us at four, if you still want to do it?" I asked tentatively.

"Of course."

All sorts of conflicting emotions were vibrating through him. Ones he couldn't shut me out of.

I didn't know what I'd done, but part of Constantine's privacy, which he deeply, *deeply* valued, had been stripped away by my paint. Because of that, I chose not to ask him any questions about what Stevens had said.

Chapter Thirty-five

I curled up next to him, like he was Olivia or Neph. Or Christian, who had always run hot in the emotional category. Eventually, some of his tension released. A few minutes later, the remainder collapsed with a sigh.

He played with a lock of my hair. "I'm not angry with you, not really."

"It's okay. I didn't know. About a lot of what Stevens said. And...I'm sorry you can't shut me out fully. I don't know exactly what I did to you, with my Awakening paint."

My ultramarine Awakening paint created for fierce protection and patterned after the eyes of the boy who had saved me.

"Don't you?" he asked, too lightly.

"Do you?" I looked up at him, my head next to his shoulder.

He didn't answer.

Between squad calls and other things, I had been working on lotus flowers, like the one Greyskull had given Axer to help heal him. I had figured that I'd need more than a few healing tokens to take with me to rescue Olivia. Neph had been extremely helpful in the draft of my first two. And as with the roses, which I also continued to create, Greyskull always mysteriously strode by me in the halls of Medical, casually passing items to help me.

I called over the flower that I was most pleased with, letting it land softly in my palm.

I put it on Constantine's chest.

He picked it up and examined it, looking at all the details. "You are getting better. This one should be able to revive you, what, five percent?"

Five percent was a lot in a battle where every bit might count.

"Eight. To be used in special circumstances."

He handed it back to me carefully. I dropped it on his chest, and immediately pressed the fold in the center. The outer petals dropped down and the magic soaked into him.

He tensed, but said nothing as the magic worked, healing the ragged edges of whatever he had done between the visit to the vault and returning here.

"That was for you to use," he said. "It was specifically created to work with your magic."

"And I've given it to you instead," I said quietly.

We stayed in silence for a long period of time. I let Constantine break it.

"I don't think you fully appreciate the dirty lengths the people around you will go to for you," he said evenly.

"I don't want anyone to do bad things for me." I gnawed at my lip. "But I'm trying to rely on others more."

"That's a horrible plan, darling. You should only rely on yourself, and me."

* Apologies *

Tilting my head up, I gave him a look. "I don't want you to do bad things for me either."

"I'll do horrible, terrible things in your name," he murmured, fingertips dragging along my skin.

I sighed. "That doesn't work on me."

"I know. More's the pity." He smiled and lifted a lock of my hair against his lips.

It was the closest I'd ever felt Constantine experience contentment.

Chapter Thirty-six

SPELLS AND PLOTS

ARMED WITH A vial of lavender paint made during my Awakening, we arrived at the vault in time to see the back of Stevens's heels clicking away.

Constantine said nothing as we closed the door. The unnatural lighting illuminated the space, making everything crisp and bright.

We got everything set up like the well-oiled machine we were.

Constantine clipped the last spell card into place. "Excellent. Let's find your old roommate."

"Constantine..."

He smiled. "I'm kidding, of course." He rubbed a fingertip across the rune he had just drawn. "Unless, you want to get rid of both of them? I'm confident the Administration would put the two of us together, if they didn't return."

I grabbed his hand and pulled it toward the silver candle. "Not funny. Come on."

It was simple really, in the end. One of those Wizard of Oz things where I had the ability in me the whole time. Paint, the connection to Olivia, the remnants of the paper balloon, the ties from the leeches, the leash so lightly stretching between us, even now...

I would have failed at it on Tuesday, though. Without Marsgrove's fancy devices and someone else providing the horsepower, I had been too mangled to construct or find anything. But here, almost back to normal magically, the connection to my roommate popped up glittering and *alive*.

"He knew I'd do it," I murmured.

It had been a gift, really. A weird, *feral cat leaving a disemboweled bird at your door* kind of gift. These three days to get to Olivia had allowed me to get better and still function—to know that Olivia was still alive.

"What was that?" Constantine asked absently, his focus entirely taken

* Spells and Plots *

with the arithmetic, the data, and triangulating the location based on the plots we had created before beginning.

"Nothing," I said quickly, not wanting to bring up Raphael and see the darkness curl in Constantine's eyes. Because gift or no gift, Raphael *would* kill Olivia at midnight tomorrow. It was part of the rules in this tick-tocking game.

Constantine dragged his fingertip over the map, then tapped it on a small dot in a large surrounding area of brown. Brown meant Outlaw Territory.

"They are in Corpus Sun. A tiny Third Layer settlement with little value."

"Maybe it's a terrorist base of operations?"

"Maybe. Or maybe it is a very convenient spot on which to stage a production. Either way, we will be seeing it very soon."

I nodded grimly.

Constantine pulled his finger across the brown expanse. The very *large* brown expanse. "However, we can't have you blasting through layers and porting across surfaces to get there, not if we actually plan to return and not be on the run for the rest of *your* life. Which means, unfortunately, that we are going to need a little help getting there."

~*~

Which meant it was time to tell the team what I had been up to.

"I'm leaving. At dawn. To rescue Olivia."

No looks were exchanged. They all simply stared back at me.

"Yeah, Crown. We know," Loudon said finally.

I hesitated. "You do?"

"Well, not about the timing, but from the moment you started assigning us tasks yesterday, it became pretty clear what your goal was," Lifen said dryly. "You hooked us all together, you and Price. We talk now. We're a *group*." The last was delivered deliberately.

I slumped. "I didn't want anyone to—"

"We're a *group*. And all of the devices are going to have our marks on and in them."

"You're right," I said quietly.

"We are onboard, Crown. Chin up." Lifen smiled. "The Delinquents' Club doesn't do interventions."

"Thanks, Lifen," I said with a small smile. "Outlaw Territory is the thing that—"

"Wait, what? I thought we were leaving Price's rescue to Dean Marsgrove," Warden Wakes, a member of the Epsilon team, who wasn't quite as interconnected, said. His brows were furrowed. "I thought Jordan

Chapter Thirty-six

was joking about Crown's insanity the past two days."

I rubbed my sweating palms against my jeans. Time to lay it out there. "The, uh, the situation became worse Wednesday night."

Lifen looked dubious. "What could be worse?"

And I told them. About Raphael Verisetti having Olivia, about Kaine dogging their trail. About my plan to go after them.

I very carefully kept the knowledge of my own involvement with Raphael a secret between the few people who already knew.

"Verisetti wants something," I said, using his last name. "Maybe just to leash me up, I don't know. But this is a trade. He gets me showing up in person, I get Olivia. He lets us go."

They exchanged looks. "He's just going to let you go?"

"He will kill her, if I don't go," I said woodenly.

"It's a trap."

"Yes. Undoubtedly. I just don't know what kind. But Ra—Verisetti doesn't lie. If I go, if I show, he *will* release her." I held up my left hand and put it down on the tabletop. "That doesn't mean we'll make it *out*. Or even past whatever artificial boundary he has set in his mind. But we'll have a *chance*. We'll have *something*. Verisetti doesn't lie. He will kill her, if I don't go."

"Crown—"

"You don't get it. He *will* kill her. And he's...excited about something."

"Excited?" More than one look was exchanged.

"With him, that could mean that they are going to blow up the planet, or that they are being chased by demons who plan to eat them alive. I don't know. His reactions aren't normal. I'm not an expert," I said, trying to hide how much I *did* know.

"It isn't just that we are talking about *Raphael Verisetti*, which, hello? But the Department is going to be after you, full stop, Crown," someone said.

"Yeah, if Verisetti doesn't get you, the Department will," another agreed.

"I know. I have really cheerful options. Still, I'll take the *chance* over the alternative, which is certain."

Looks were exchanged around the table.

"We can't let it happen," Warden Wakes said, his voice full of regret.

Wakes was an older mage, months from graduating, who specialized in container magic and instrumentation. He was a voice of reason, and what he said was very reasonable. We couldn't let Olivia die.

"We can't let you go," Wakes said.

Warden Wakes was full of shit, and not in the least capable of reason.

"What?" I asked, sure that I heard him wrong.

"We can't let Verisetti control an Origin Mage, Crown. And, let's be

* Spells and Plots *

honest here about what you are." He gave me a look. "We all want to rescue Price, but, the cost?" He shook his head. "We can't let you go."

"What do you mean, *can't* let me?"

"I mean—" He looked very apologetic as his hand filled with green light. "That we have to keep you awa—"

His head hit the tabletop with a very loud thump.

Patrick smiled. "Anyone else?" He looked around the room. "No?"

I stared at him, then at the back of Wakes' unconscious head, then back to Patrick.

"You want me to get rid of him?" Patrick tipped his head to the side—a sure sign he was calling someone via frequency. "Right, then."

"No, that's not what—" I tried to say.

A knock on the door interrupted my protest. Patrick snapped his fingers, the door opened and two burly mages walked inside. They hefted Warden up, nodded at Patrick, and exited the room.

"We'll wipe Wakes and let him back in on the campus-only instrumentation section. Anyone else?" The last was asked in an extremely pleasant tone of voice.

No one responded. Utter silence permeated the room.

"Excellent. Now, back to what we were discussing. I thought I heard you say that the situation had changed and they would kill Olivia," Patrick prompted me.

He never referred to Olivia by name. It was always "the Queen" or "Her Majesty" or some other grandiose reference.

I stared at Patrick, pieces connecting sluggishly together.

Olivia had never wanted me to meet Patrick and Asafa alone. She had gone with me deliberately and specifically at the beginning. I hadn't thought anything more of it—I had just thought she was being protective.

"Ah, finally cluing in, Crown?" Patrick's smile was sharp. There was nothing fey about it.

Feck Jordan, who was friends with Wakes said, "And what do we do about Warden?"

"You are skipping subjects, ladboot," Patrick chided in a jovial manner, but his eyes were hard. I was reminded again of the interchange with Kaine on Top Circle—how he'd looked specifically at Patrick, Neph, and Delia ignoring all the others—and of the things Olivia had said about the O'Learys back when I'd first approached the boys about their game controller.

Looking at it from another perspective as I looked at the facial expressions around the table—and actually paying attention to social cues for once—it was *very likely* that Patrick was the son of some magical mobster in this world.

Chapter Thirty-six

Neph's hand drifted across my skin. *Youngest son*, came across the soft breeze of thought, *not part of the family business, but still part of the family.*

Jordan didn't look pleased at being reprimanded, but he also didn't speak against Patrick.

"We'll keep Wakes in on the campus plans—we need him for his expertise with containers—but we'll fix it so that he is left out of the Crown and Price tasks until too late," Patrick said.

"Yeah, and what? Are you going to do this to each of us, O'Leary?" Jordan asked. "Take us out one-by-one like your father and brothers?"

The people around the table were all poised. The group which had come together through our defense of campus was poised on a knife's edge. Poised to break apart in the shattered fall.

"When one of our lives is on the line, I'd like to think that wouldn't be necessary," Patrick said, twirling a rod that he had pulled from somewhere. A number of gazes followed the progress of the slim metal piece. "We were under the initial misconception that Price would get traded in a prisoner exchange, seeing who her mother is. However, that was becoming less and less likely as I watched that hag on the feeds."

Patrick caught the shift in my expression and something dark, but far more pleased, took over his. We were agreed on Helen Price.

With the additional information on Patrick, the past interactions with him took on a different tone. The puckish amusement, the general lack of seriousness, always full of confidence—the kind that came from *knowing* they were on top. More like...more like school was all a game Patrick was playing. One that he had every assurance he would win, no matter what he did.

I hadn't paid keen attention to Olivia's reaction to being in their room that first time, because I'd been so nervous of how she was going to skin me for the controller. But looking back...that first interaction had had a *lot* of undertones.

They were thick as thieves by the end, with Patrick calling Olivia "Queen" and "Her Majesty" and being delighted in everything. And it just made me wonder...what the devil was going on? I had missed a ton of subtext, very obviously.

You were slightly busy, Neph said, her mental voice droll, *And, quite frankly, more than anything else, your lack of reaction to all of it aided the good relations that developed. I doubt either Olivia or O'Leary are used to people just accepting them as is. A lot of preconceived notions come with their names.*

Patrick continued. "We were also under the impression that Dean Marsgrove had a chance. However, there again, we underestimated. Now, Crown is informing us of an end date, the last moves for whatever game is being played. How she has contact with Verisetti is not my concern. That she is telling the truth is."

He looked at Saf briefly, then Dagfinn, and finally Kita. They were a unit, the four of them, inside our larger group.

"My father had dealings with Verisetti," Patrick said. "After Salietrex, but before the rest. When it was not determined yet, what his plans were. We had nothing to do with Verisetti after his plans became clear. But Dominic O'Leary said much the same thing as Crown. Verisetti was slippery, sly, but not a liar. He kept the bargains he struck."

"Okay. So...should we discuss what is going to happen?" Will said, trying, and failing, to keep his voice upbeat.

"The details are hazy still," I prevaricated. Neph's fingers ghosted my skin again, giving me comfort.

"Well, let's break them down," Kita said, far too reasonably, in the continuing tension of the room.

I swallowed. "Sure, okay." I took a deep breath. "I have to escape Bellacia's notice, so I only have twenty hours to play with. During that time, I have to get past the Legion and Praetorian Tarei, who is tracking me continuously. Get through an off campus arch, none of which are active. Find and go through a port to the Third Layer. Trek through Outlaw Territory to their location. Rescue Olivia *and* Dean Marsgrove. Travel back doing all the steps in the reverse. All before Bellacia notices that I'm gone—let's call that *curfew*—and all without getting caught."

Every face staring back was blank. Neph was a reassuring presence, but even the rest of the Alpha team, who had already known, were tense as they thought those steps through.

"Mother of God," someone whispered.

"Right," I said shakily. "Why not, right?"

"Crown—"

I curled my hand into a fist. "It doesn't matter. I'm going, and I'll go down trying."

"If you get caught," Lifen said, and chanced a quick look at Patrick, as if making sure that her objection wasn't going to result in certain dismissal and memory loss. "The Department won't just punish you, they'll—"

"I know." My fingernails curled into my palms. "And that's why I started a lot of those tasks yesterday morning. Many of them are for all of *you*. For your protection here. Especially the ouroboros rings. I'm going to make sure they are *incredible*."

The knife-edged precipice held for another moment, then retreated. I could nearly *taste* it—the way the Community Magic in our group settled. Strengthened even.

I cleared my suddenly dry throat. "I'm going to do everything I can not to let the Department take over campus due to my actions. But I'm not

Chapter Thirty-six

weighing Olivia's life against what the Department will do. We'll—*you'll* figure out how to kick them back to the curb, if the worst happens."

Silence. Then a few solemn nods. Then a roomful.

"Any objections?" Patrick asked.

I looked at Wakes' empty chair, then Patrick. So did everyone else. Asafa waved his hand and the chair disappeared.

The Community Magic didn't bend.

Patrick smiled. "We'll give them more hell than they can handle, Crown."

I smiled. It felt wobbly.

"We'll need someone to replace Wakes," Kita said, all business once more. She was a large part of the reason the business ventures undertaken by a number of the mages at the table were flourishing. "Replace him completely. He's smart, and I don't think you want him knowing any part of the plan. He'll piece the rest together and we've seen that he will act on it."

Jordan reluctantly nodded. "She's right."

"We'll still protect Wakes too, though," I said. "He was part of our team. We'll just figure out a way to give him the protection where he won't question it."

The Community Magic strengthened even more. I blinked, and looked around. The expressions around the table looked more determined now, oddly enough.

"If Crown is going to the Third Layer, she's going to need Wakes' expertise."

"I can get her through Outlaw Territory and get her the cuff she needs for the Third Layer," Delia said, gaze daring anyone to say anything about *how*.

"Sounds great, Delia," Saf said, smiling gently.

"Crown will *need* containers, though. I know a few guys, but—" Dagfinn shrugged. "They aren't completely trustworthy."

Containers?

"I have someone who can handle that," I said. "Don't worry about that aspect."

Patrick lifted a brow.

"Constantine." I rubbed the inside of my left elbow. "He can do whatever is needed with them."

He was ideally suited for *any* task that involved our continued presence in the world of the living. But containers neatly fell under the materials banner, and at materials, Constantine was unequivocally the best.

"And, uh, he's going to be coming with me," I added poorly. There wasn't a great way to say it, really. I knew what people thought of Constantine, and he deserved most of it.

* Spells and Plots *

There were a flurry of immediate objections, unsurprisingly, but Patrick's expression barely shifted. He seemed to understand far more than I intended to share. The death of Constantine's mother had been huge news, I'd discovered over the past few days. That Constantine would want to hunt down the person responsible, Patrick seemed to implicitly understand.

The son of a mobster—I was beginning to see it more.

He tapped a finger on a device. "He hates Price."

I couldn't deny that, but I made a negative motion with my head. "He has sworn to help. He, too, will keep his promises."

Patrick continued to watch me, eyes taking in all of my nonverbal expressions. "Bring him by later."

I nodded, and we moved on to how to fool the Legion long enough to let me slip by.

"Might be time to start brushing up on on-campus terrorism, lads and lasses," Patrick said, rubbing his hands together. "The Department needs a little reminder of why they shouldn't be here. And, that, I have a lot of *family* experience at."

"If we do it, it will set back campus freedom," someone said, grimly. "They'll have more excuse to stay around."

The others joined in, each person at the table issuing a shot.

"We could make the terror *personal*."

"Make it so that anyone with a student ID is perfectly safe, and that only intruders are targeted."

"Make it seem like campus is fighting back."

"*Make* campus fight back. Show that we can defend ourselves."

"Can we change the identification spells?"

I thought of the Justice Squad meeting, and answered, "Someone from the Justice Squad did it. A mage named Travers. He formed a Justice Magic Negative Field?"

Dagfinn's eyes lit. Jordan nodded. "Yeah, we saw him do that outside the Magiaduct. He used the Administration cache. I think he might...be persuaded to point us in the right direction. From a purely academic standpoint."

"Funny thing, that." Patrick's gaze slid to me. "The Justice Squad has been particularly easy on us, the last few days." More than one gaze shifted my way. "All that business under the domes teaming up together through you has put them in a much more genial position. At least for the temporary present."

"The thing Travers did, he did say that the praetorians weren't affected," I warned.

"There's a difference between the Praetorian Guard and the Legion."

Chapter Thirty-six

Dagfinn pointed a finger at me. "The praetorians use spells that the Legion is not authorized to use, and only one praetorian remains."

"If we access the Administrative cache, we can focus the chaos to follow interlopers." Asafa looked thoughtful. "Not very friendly of Excelsine, but it would suit our purposes for a focused amount of time."

"And make it very personal." Patrick smiled, a bit maliciously.

Asafa exchanged a look with him, and a silent back-and-forth exchange occurred.

Asafa touched two fingers together. "I've got an idea for the praetorian too. But it'll only work once."

"Once is all we need."

Chapter Thirty-seven

IN BETWEEN

NEPH, WILL, MIKE, DELIA, and I were holed up in Constantine's living room going over a number of plans and magic when he walked through the door.

He stopped just inside the entrance and started undoing the closures of his expensive coat that wrapped around his throat. He examined each of them, then said, "Honey, I'm home," in a deadpan voice.

I rolled my eyes. Neph had been here more than once in the past few days, and I had been given direct permission to have people come by.

Mike gave a long-suffering sigh and gathered their materials. "We'll get the items and see you in thirty, Ren."

Constantine leaned against the wall as they left. Delia gave him a glare thickly drawn in kohl. Will gave him a cheerful greeting, because Will was just that awesome. Neph barely spared Constantine a glance as she gracefully walked from the room.

Mike pulled the door closed behind them, but not before giving me a pointed glance.

I sighed. "You are expected at a meeting in thirty minutes in Trick and Saf's room."

Constantine pushed away from the wall, and his gaze was back to its normal dichotomy of lazy and piercing. "Your little band of miscreants said they'd help?"

I pulled my ponytail over my shoulder and tugged on it. "Yes, and I told them you were coming with me. They want to have you come in for a chat."

"The ones with you at the Blarjack Swamp?"

"Yes. All of the ones that were there are in, along with a dozen others."

"Only you would buddy up with an O'Leary." He half-smiled. "Most of campus just participates in his betting, sporting, and gaming schemes and

Chapter Thirty-seven

leaves dealing with him to business transactions or ways to ingratiate themselves with the family."

"Patrick is nice."

"No, he is not. But that is not the argument at hand."

"Is it going to be a problem?"

"Between O'Leary and me? No. We know how to deal with each other. It is simply cleaner to stay far from each other's orbits. Like knows like." He smiled coldly.

"Great."

"How did your little muse take the news?"

"Don't call her that," I said tiredly.

"You chose well, all things considered," he said, eyes narrowed on the wall. "The Baus are powerful, and Nephthys Bau is said to be more powerful than most. You could still do better, on a general basis, with access to more muses. It would be far more in your control. You understand that, right? Da Vinci had nine in his rotation. And they were happy to have the smallest part of him."

"I'm pretty okay with my status quo." I didn't need nine muses. I liked my single one just fine.

Though, the thing about power was a little unsettling, and called to mind a larger fact that I usually tried to ignore. How did it happen that I had surrounded myself with, or put myself in the path of, the children of power players from all sides?

"Power speaks to power, darling, and draws it together for good or ill."

"Stop reading my mind, Con."

"And curtail my favorite pastime?" he said, unrepentant. "I think not. Your power is an all-consuming net that you drag around behind you, trapping each of us within it. Gathering us to you."

Stricken by his words, I could say nothing.

One dark brow rose. "This is the power of the gods, darling. Only you would think it a deficit." He leaned in. "With one little leech-leash to connect us...the responsibility can be out of your hands..."

I pushed at his chest and he smirked back at me as he allowed himself to be moved.

"I'm not giving up Neph," I said, returning to the previous conversation.

"Any fool can see that, darling." He looked at me through dark eyes. "You don't give up people, ever."

~*~

Constantine nodded at Saf, far more pleasantly than he did at Trick.

Asafa was as magically gifted as Patrick, but he used his power in far

* In Between *

different ways. Where Patrick was puckish, compelling, and, at times, mean, Asafa was strong and solid and trustworthy. They made a powerful combination.

Watching Constantine interact with the rest of the group was...interesting. Barbed, edged, but with enough respect to keep things from being militant. We were a pack of wild dogs. But as soon as the bite-snapping and butt-sniffing got sorted out, we got back to business.

Since the green flag had been waved on this mad plan, all forces had mobilized as only a bunch of crazy people who dealt with hundreds of their own mad plans could do.

Assignments and magic plans flew around the table, some of them shoring up what we'd brainstormed previously, and others offering new, better alternatives.

"Getting off campus and to the Third Layer is not a problem," Constantine said, bored. "Hiding the disturbance from the Legion is. They will know immediately something has happened."

Patrick's eyes glittered. "How are you getting off campus?"

"That's really not your concern, O'Leary," Constantine said lazily. "You have your tasks, I have mine."

When it came to how we would stay accounted for *on* campus is when things got tricky.

"They'll have the diversion magic fixed in fifteen minutes, tops. And after the diversion, they'll personally look for Crown," Loudon said. "She'll be on the shortlist of people they check physically to ensure she's still here."

"Bau will take care of Ren's *presence* on campus, and I will not be missed," Constantine said, in an almost bored fashion.

Neph stiffened. "I'm going *with* Ren."

"You can't," Saf said, not unkindly. "Not if we are to hold the Excelsine fort and not hand ourselves over to the Department."

I gave Neph's hand a squeeze, willing her to relax. I hadn't realized that her continuous calm in the face of dangerous plans might have come about because she thought she was coming too.

Safe. Protect everyone here. I'll return.

I carefully made sure not to make keeping everyone safe a direct order this time, though.

"The fewer people who go, the better," Loudon said frankly. "We just don't have the systems in place to trick the Administration Magic on a mass scale. Not with the Department watching."

Patrick nodded, eyes sharp. "And Leandred can slip out of anything. That's the perk of his father's position and status. You get caught, Crown, he'll go free. You won't. And none of the rest of us would either."

Constantine was smiling his bored smile, but it wasn't reflected

Chapter Thirty-seven

internally. Fury and bitterness waved through him, then were sharply contained.

"So how many hours does that give us?" Mike asked, bringing the conversation back.

"Ren has to spend twelve hours of a twenty-four period with Bailey, right?" Saf said. "So that gives us, twelve hours to work with, probably less due to timing constraints with the diversion."

"I, uh, um, I am actually rooming with Constantine and Alexander?"

I didn't know why Bellacia had chosen to keep it secret—whether she would suffer somehow socially or whether she was using it for other, more diabolical ends—but it was absolutely one of the best kept secrets on campus, something that no one outside of the Alpha team and Administration knew.

Silence met that pronouncement. A moment later, munits exchanged hands.

"Wait, you bet on, what exactly?" I asked, floored.

"Just on whether rumors were true," Trick said smoothly, obviously lying. "So, you'll be with Leandred on this little sojourn, that'll help. How many hours?"

"I don't know how the jacking between rooms works if we aren't in any of them, but I have to spend four hours at Bellacia's."

"Let's continue with twelve then, to be safe. A nice sturdy number. Crown?"

I smiled tightly. "I'll get it done."

"That's for getting back here too. Even if for some reason Bailey completely sat on her hands and wished you good luck, the system would alert Medical and the Administration. And we know the Department is monitoring those alerts."

"You can't be discovered," Dagfinn said.

"That would be an error, yes." Constantine's tone was bored again.

"Leandred..." There was warning in Patrick's tone.

"O'Leary, do you think I will fail at my task?" Constantine's ribbon was in his hand again, pulling slowly through his fingers.

Patrick's eyes narrowed. "The problem is, I'm not exactly sure what your task is."

Constantine smiled. It was cutting and sharp. "I will return Price and Crown safely and secretly back to campus. Price can be found aimlessly wandering the Midlands, cut off from getting back to the Magiaduct by the Department's spells. A number of students released from the battle field dome ran straight into the Midlands. Forces were dedicated just to rescuing them in the after-hours. The Legion cleared the Midlands. A nice hit for the Department in the media, especially if you spin it against her mother."

* In Between *

Looks were exchanged.

"We'll want assurance."

"Of course." Constantine dripped boredom. He slid something over to Patrick. I tried to get a look at it, but it was illegible, hidden by an enchantment.

Patrick's expression changed abruptly, the distrust falling away and his normal edge of brilliant mania returning.

He clapped his hands together. "Everything seems to be in order."

Patrick's pronouncement seemed to be the catalyst for everyone else accepting Constantine into our plans.

Everyone but the Alpha group, who still looked at Constantine with suspicion. But I was pretty sure that was due to other reasons.

Chapter Thirty-eight

FIGHTING IN TWO PLACES

IT WAS A little like planning for a mission to the First Layer. In both places, we couldn't use magic like we could in the Second. But unlike the First Layer, the Third Layer *did* have magic. On the flipside, using magic in the First Layer didn't cause the layer to attack *back*.

So, treating the Third Layer like it was the First gave me somewhat of an advantage. I had lived for seventeen years without magic. Putting magic into containers and devices felt remarkably similar to using computers and tablets to affect the world around me.

We were gearing up hard for Saturday. There were a few loose items I had still had to deal with, though.

First, I sent a message to Isaiah asking to be released from Community Service for a few days. Just until my "celebrity" was no longer affecting the Justice System. I cited a list of reasons why this was a good idea, backed up with solid evidence. The Justice Magic would trigger, if I was listed on rotation and didn't show.

The message back was all Isaiah — "You're a valuable member. We'll see you back on the squad on Monday, Crown."

I patted Justice Toad and set him on the chair's side table.

Second on my list, I visited Room Twenty-five, and took a moment to soak in the remnants of *home* and *Olivia*. I closed my eyes. The remnants were growing weaker, stale, like a room that hadn't been aired.

I grabbed a number of things from my secret stashes, including a few of my more powerful storage papers, and, with a silent vow, headed back to Dorm One.

Third, I sent a note to my parents. I rubbed my chest as I wrote about all the new things I was learning to do at school—protection wards, news spells, and healing magic. *Everything's great! See you soon!*

My chest hurt as I sent it, and I had to field an abrupt call from Neph

* Fighting in Two Places *

demanding to know if I was okay.

Number four on my agenda—I needed to figure out a way into the Battle Building.

That one, was strangely solved when I walked past Axer's workroom, and the door gave a click. I stared at it, then fished their room key from my pocket. I slowly pushed it toward the lock, and when nothing attacked me, I slotted the key into place.

The door opened, and the white room greeted me. I stared at it for a moment, then pulled the door slowly shut again. When the key exited the lock, the wards snapped back into place.

I tapped the key against my palm. *Interesting.*

With the knowledge that I could access Axer's workroom, I fished out Draeger's cartridge from deep within my duffel bag. Tapping it against my thigh, I opened the door to his workroom again and stepped inside. Surrounded by white walls, I pulled the cartridge slowly along the walls of the room, *hoping*. A slot appeared.

Yes!

The Eighth and Ninth Circles were still closed to students, and I'd been itching to get into the Battle Building to practice Third Layer tactics.

When Draeger appeared with his shaved head, barrel chest, and knee-high athletic socks, I threw myself in his holographic direction.

"What's this, Cadet? Why is it so thin in here? And what the hog's tendons have you been doing?" He asked as he glowered, paging through my magic and stats as only a construct magically designed to read me could do.

"Giving those squirrels *hell*," I said.

He gruffly allowed me to hug him, but the magic here wasn't as strong as in the Battle Building. My arms passed right through.

"Come on, Cadet," he said gruffly, but not without affection. "Let's see what we can do to get you back in working shape."

~*~

Two hours later, I was prone on the floor. Again. But anticipation was buzzing through me. I was almost *back*.

"Not bad, but you keep ignoring the way magic can betray you, if you pin it as something constant."

I scrambled upright and blinked at Axer, standing before me with his arms crossed.

"I'm in your workroom," I blurted.

"I know," he said, like I was being particularly slow.

I frowned. "Where are you?"

Maybe this was a construct?

Chapter Thirty-eight

"At the competition. Did you hit your head?" He frowned at said body part.

"What, no! Maybe. A little. How are you *here?*"

"You're in my room with the dragon I gave you."

"Oh." I fished it out of my armband. "Well, this saves me having to update you later. Great!" I said, completely flustered. I had been fighting with Draeger for hours, working out the last of my magic's kinks, and I was both sweaty *and* intruding.

He looked to the side and there was almost a twitch to his movements. He returned his attention to me. "What's wrong?"

"Nothing. Nothing. Why would you think anything was wrong?" I babbled, then drew myself together. "Fine. We are leaving in the morning."

He narrowed his eyes, and a moment later he flinched, as if he'd taken a blow. "Tell me."

I gave him the full rundown on what we'd been doing and what we were planning.

At the end, he just smiled.

I narrowed my eyes. "You wanted me to get all of the delinquents on campus working together to protect it instead of pranking it, right from the beginning of term, didn't you?"

He smiled and leaned back on his heels, hands in his pockets. "It was a possibility. You present so many of them, it is sometimes hard to choose."

"I saw you, in the library talking to your friends at the beginning of winter term. You meant to use me then," I said, narrowing my eyes further.

"Yes." He smirked. "With a book clamped to your hand, and your eyes impossibly wide and unshuttered as you eavesdropped."

Okay, that was a little embarrassing.

But I rallied. "You seemed too smug about Plan Fifty-two's formation for it to have been anything other than intentional."

It wasn't a bad thing, but it did make me wonder, in an insidious voice that sounded horribly like Constantine, what else I'd been led to do.

Axer leaned forward, eyes oddly intent. "I didn't form the group. Only you could have formed it."

"Oh, please. You could have half this campus following you, even if you declared a field trip through hell." I might be fielding my own share of awed (and terrified) expressions from others these days, but he'd been dealing with them for *years*. He'd been a *hero* on campus since he'd stepped foot here.

He tilted his head. "I have carefully cultivated a role. And still, most of them would only be following to see if they could use it for their own gains."

"You could be friendlier," I pointed out.

* Fighting in Two Places *

He smiled. "That's a different family member's task."

"Not your family sniper's?"

His eyes narrowed for a second before he laughed, gaze never leaving me. "No, not Nicholas's. Did you see the audience reaction to his performance so far at the games?"

"People are unnerved."

Unnerved that someone could shoot magic so far and so precisely with so little setup time. Anyone semi-competent could do the intricate calculations involved in setting up a target somewhere, setting up shields around the target and each magic bolt to account for the small variables always in flux in a world where outside magic use was sometimes unpredictable.

Long and tedious motions could be made to accomplish this. Nicholas Dare could do it in seconds.

"He does tend to make himself more affable so that people forget what he is capable of." He looked at me as if he were making a statement about more than just Nicholas.

"No one forgets what you are capable of."

"Me? No. It would be wasted energy to try." He shrugged, then looked to the side again, body twitching again just the smallest bit. "And I dislike most people who try to gain favor anyway."

"Why do you save them, then? As a feint for some larger plan?"

"I save them because they need saving. Plans are worthless if the end goal isn't a positive one."

A positive one for whom, was the question. Most people thought it was for the Dares.

I examined him. "What are you going to do with my team?"

He smiled. "The same thing you are doing now. Use them."

"You always have two or three plans in the works, don't you?" I said, voice trailing off as I thought about it.

"Always."

I opened my mouth, but watched his eyes shift left again and his body twitch. There was something familiar about those twitches...like the start of a movement I had seen many times...

"Are you...are you *fighting?* Right *now?*"

"Yes," he said, as if I should have known this.

I stared for a moment, then reached toward the dragon. "You are insane."

He nodded, distracted now that he was pulling his attention back elsewhere, but said, "Ren, don't forget to take the vine when you go."

Chapter Thirty-nine

DEPARTMENT OF JUSTICE

STANDING AS close to the Midlands as I could come—two mountain circles up—I gave a whistle.

Nothing.

Why I had thought that might work, I didn't know. It wasn't a dog.

But Axer had said that it wouldn't stay in the Midlands long. That was both a blessing and a curse. Which, speaking of the Midlands, they looked *way* better. Maybe the vine had been helping out in there?

Actually, the mist almost looked *too* thin—like the chaos was being normalized.

I gave another whistle, just in case it would answer. Nothing.

I contemplated what I knew of the vine. It wasn't much. I had a feeling that I could call it with paint, but it would have to be good paint, and the tube would get taken away. But...there *was* something else.

I made a small cut on my arm, just enough that a drop of blood welled up, then dripped onto the ground. I gave another whistle, because, well, I didn't know why.

A rupture sounded as the vine broke through the ground, bursting from under the Midlands' border. Shaking itself, it headed my way, dolphining into and out of the ground lazily. It was *way* fatter—like a six foot boa constrictor now, in girth and length.

"Hey, so, I was thinking, how does a nice excursion to—" I started to say as it approached.

It lunged forward and clamped around my arm, sinking its thorny teeth into my skin.

"Argh. No." I tried to pull it off, but it remained firmly attached, thorns curving painfully inward like the fangs they resembled.

Great. I let it finish, gritting my teeth at the pain. It released me moments later and plopped its bottom quarter down on the grass, the rest

* Department of Justice *

of it undulated in the air hypnotically, waiting.

I sighed. "That's really unpleasant."

I got a mental flash containing images of dozens of thin vines biting a girl, then injecting magic into the ground. It was a mishmash of half-formed images, but the same girl was featured heavily in most of them.

"Yeah, okay, that's...weird. Listen, I have a little task for—"

It hopped upward, folded into a jackknife, and dove into the ground.

Great.

I ran a finger over the puncture wounds. If I had to bleed again, I was going to be really irritated. And I had no idea why it needed to come with us. Though, now that I was thinking about it, I could totally use its recycling capabilities in the harsh Third Layer landscape.

I scanned the mountain, trying to determine the vine's direction, so I could chase after it. But it wasn't surfacing, and only the shadows from the clouds and sun were changing shape on the grass. Stupid, rotten—

A hand grabbed me on top of the wound and jerked me around.

Tarei smiled down at me.

I hadn't heard him coming.

That thought was followed by the sure knowledge that those shifting shadows hadn't been from the sun.

On someone else, I would have labeled his smile as smug, but on Tarei, combined with the coldness of his gaze, it looked far more sinister. Almost like I could see a different face overlaying his.

"Ah. I knew you wouldn't be able to resist. Criminal types can't, you know." And there was that voice again, a blend of two different people.

"Let go of me."

Tarei wrapped his hand more tightly around my arm. The same power —though weaker—that Kaine had had was present in Tarei's grip. "Now, Miss Crown, I think you will answer a few questions about your Blood Magic offense, and then we will be making a *short* trip off this bloody campus."

Coldness gathered in my limbs. I had forgotten about Blood Magic offenses. Blood Magic was used in a lot of things—I'd used it extensively when trying to bring Christian back—but, like with anything, certain usages were off limits. It was the first Justice call I had ever made to Constantine.

Whatever the vine did when it bit me, obviously provoked the Justice Magic to respond.

And I hadn't been thinking of that at all. When the vine had bitten me before, we'd been in the Midlands—one of the only places where Justice Magic didn't register. The place where I'd always done most of my tests.

Shadows shifted in Tarei's eyes, hiding a second presence, and he smiled in triumph as ice froze me in place. "Finally."

Chapter Thirty-nine

"Ren Crown, you have registered a Level Three offense," a familiar, pinched voice said.

Tarei, who was painfully holding onto to me, stiffened. Peters was standing behind us, canary yellow tablet in hand, expression resolute.

"Go away, boy," Tarei bit out, dismissing him just as quickly, as he looked down at me. "Or, better yet, report to your Provost that I am escorting this student off campus." His vicious, triumphant smile started to curve again.

"I cannot do that, sir."

"Excuse me?" Tarei said coldly, turning back to Peters again.

"This student has registered a Level Three offense, sir, and needs to be dealt with."

"I have the student in my custody." Every word was clipped and icy. Threatening.

"Absolutely, sir. I thank you for holding her. I will take it from here."

Tarei gave him a contemptuous glance. "You will leave."

"My apologies, sir, but I cannot. Campus Justice Magic needs to be satisfied. Rulebook section 192.453.2 states that once a Level Three has occurred I must detain the perpetrator, then issue a punishment to be served within a reasonable timeframe. No detainment can be made following that punishment. I *do* have ten minutes to issue said punishment, so you may still ask any questions of the offender that you might have. Rulebook section 35.24.5 states that a recording device is to be used in these matters, however, and that all parties must be made aware of that."

He tapped the small blinking blue light on his yellow tablet. "I have informed both of you and activated the record. You may commence your questioning."

He maintained a solid gaze with Tarei, perfectly respectable and respectful in attitude, but I could see moisture sliding down the back of Peters' neck.

Peters wasn't doing anything extraordinary, per se, as Tarei couldn't say that he was being belligerent or standing in his way—Peters was following the letter of the law. Several laws.

And that was a very Peters thing to do.

What *wasn't* a very Peters thing to do, was helping *me* in any way. And by standing there, issuing a blatant statement to a very powerful Department member concerning how long he could speak to me before he had to let me go, was helping *me* remain on campus.

Peters didn't have to be recording. The rulebook stated it was *preferred*. Since I almost always let miscreants off with lesser punishments, I generally chose to be on the "it is not mandated" side of that rule.

If he wanted, Peters could defer to the Department and stand to the

* Department of Justice *

side for eight minutes, recording device nowhere in existence.

Instead, Peters was standing witness, and *recording*, and there was nothing subversive Tarei could do while he was.

This time.

Tarei smiled unpleasantly and something in his eyes shifted, taking hold of him and changing his actions into something far more controlled. His voice took on that same odd tone. *Stavros.* "Following your protocols, are you, boy? What is your name?"

That voice issuing from Tarei's mouth was far more clinical and removed from emotion. The kind that stepped on people like ants in one's path, thinking no more on the actions than that.

"Joseph Aldwin Peters, of the Seddenbury Peters', sir. It is a pleasure to make your acquaintance."

In any other circumstance, I would say that Peters was being sycophantic. But with another sweat drop rolling down his neck—and the absolute assurance that Peters hated me—that was not what this was.

Peters had always been ballsy. Defiant in his rule following, even. And I was going to need to dial back my scoffing for his rule following tendencies from this point forward.

"I never forget a meeting, Mr. Peters." Tarei abruptly let go of my arm. "We will meet again, I'm certain."

"I do so hope so, Praetorian Tarei." Peters sounded absolutely sincere.

Tarei disappeared into a shadow, and I massaged the muscles and bones he had been crushing.

I stared at Peters.

He met my gaze head on. He always had. Joseph Aldwin Peters was a rule following prick, but he *believed*. He believed in his path.

"Why?" I asked.

He required no specification. "Because you saved campus. And after, you helped people and made things better. There's an entire club now dedicated to duplicating those roses you've been handing out. And I might think a lot of things about you, most of them negative, but that action— those actions—require a boon."

Like Camille and Bellacia and my "dispensation" and "grace period."

He continued—"I thought it was an absolute disgrace when you were paired with Mr. Dare at the beginning of term." Never Axer, not for Peters. "I reported you," he said frankly.

I hoped my expression conveyed how *not* surprised I was.

"But then..." His expression took on a sort of constipated cast. "You worked hard. You were combing campus all of the time, *far* outside of what was expected. And shadowing Mr. Dare into the worst places."

As fantastic as I found the Midlands, the levels deserved their

Chapter Thirty-nine

reputation.

Peters examined me in a dissecting manner. "We aren't cut out for campus protection in that way on the Justice Squad. We follow the letter of the law. We help society stay even and on the right track by focusing on mage related crime inside of the system, not monsters or war."

I remembered Peters' reaction to being in the Midlands that first day. As a shadow to Lox, who was one of Dare's teammates, Peters had been in there more times than he'd desired this term, a few of them with me.

"You...you were a part of the *solution* to a number of things that the combat mages alone should have handled. Mr. Dare actually had the two of you solving things together instead of deferring to his team. And you *did* them."

Peters and I had rarely talked during group patrols, and those group outings had barely registered on my continuously sleep-deprived and Dare-driven days. But Peters had obviously registered those outings.

I rubbed at my arms, uncomfortable with any words approaching kind from Peters. "It was expected. You...you shouldn't have helped me with Tarei. You are going to be punished for it."

"I am following the letter of the law," he said. "If the makers of those laws have trouble with that fact, then I'm going to need to rethink my path in life, won't I?"

He said it as if it was that simple. Maybe for Peters it was.

"This is a pass, Miss Crown, do you understand? If you bring additional trouble to Excelsine, we are going to have to deal with you as a community does." He looked at me through narrowed eyes.

I nodded. I did understand. "Thanks, Peters."

He dealt with my Level Three—adding on service hours—and walked away.

I stared after him for long moments.

"His older brother was waylaid in an Outlaw Territory years ago," Delia said, materializing behind me, as she was wont to do. "Didn't survive. Peters took up the Justice Magic mantle the next day. Justice is important to him."

I swallowed and clenched my fingers into fists. Peters and I didn't like each other, but respect wasn't out of the question.

"How do you know these things?" I asked her.

Delia shrugged. She always knew everything and she always seemed to pop up where I least expected. "Knowledge is social power, Crown."

"Did I bat signal an alert or something?"

She smiled, kohl drawing itself on her eyelids underneath her black bangs. "Let's just say that we might have put a small addition into your armband in order to keep track of you."

* Department of Justice *

I sighed. "Great."

"It only registers if someone from the Department touches you. I was waiting to see if I was going to need to call in the Omega plan," she said lightly.

"What plan?" I said suspiciously.

She waved it away. "So what were you doing? Blood Magic only registers if you are doing something egregious."

"Yeah." I sighed again. "Listen, do you have some time?"

She spread her hands, palms down. "I'm all yours. What are we doing?"

"I need you to help me hunt down a killer vine."

Chapter Forty

FRIDAY NIGHT LIGHTS

THE REST of Friday evening was a last minute mass of gathering and gatherings.

We met up for a final group dinner at Patrick and Asafa's. The meeting had a "last meeting" vibe to it—in more ways than one. We all huddled around the round table, going over final plans. Who would be where, doing what.

Our plan would start at precisely noon on Saturday, but I was going to need to spend most of my time between midnight and noon in the two rooms that I was expected to be in, filling up on whatever magic rejuvenation and renewal spells I needed.

"Before you turn in for the night, Crown." Saf pulled a tiny orb from a box and held it out to me.

It was a container for magic. Tiny and powerful and already filled.

There was a warm, living vibe to it. Comforting and exhilarating at the same time. I looked at the others in question.

"We all gave some," Saf said.

My stomach dropped in a heart-wrenching form of shock and gratitude. I clutched the tiny marble against my chest, protecting it.

"In case of need," he said solemnly.

Loudon motioned to me, and I looked down at the ouroboros ring hanging from a cord around my neck. The orb fit exactly inside. I secured it there and it warmed my chest.

"And here." Delia held out two bands. "You need to cover your cuffs the second before you leave. These will dim them. In the Third Layer, especially in Outlaw Territory, they tag anyone with a Second Layer cuff, and there are groups who will hunt you down for them."

The hatred went both ways between the layers.

Constantine would be able to remove his cuff, but mine was an absolute

* Friday Night Lights *

cuff. Marsgrove always made sure that I couldn't remove mine.

I nodded.

"Guides will meet you at the point we talked about. Say as little as possible to them, just give them the half-payment and the town name of where you are going," Delia stressed. "I had to call in a lot of favors for this."

I nodded more slowly. Delia seemed nervous, agitated. "I will."

Dagfinn's gaze narrowed on me—whatever he was thinking was sharp and serious. "You have a lot of protectors already, Crown. But know that if you get sucked into the system, you *will* be found."

Trick raised a dubious brow at him.

"You might not get rescued," Dagfinn allowed. "But there will be an entire frequency dedicated to the injustice and effort at getting you released."

Like a prisoner of the state.

I smiled softly. "Thanks, Dagfinn."

~*~

I walked back from Patrick and Asafa's with Delia and the others. We stopped at Mike and Will's to do the last fittings on the cloaks.

"As camouflage, the cloak will work for a week or until it takes a few specifically targeted hits," Delia warned. "The magic starts to ebb and be called in different directions."

I examined the material, which flowed around my fingers. "Battle cloaks must have different properties then?"

With the way the combat mages took hits, there was no way the cloaks could stop working like that.

"Battle cloaks use magic that has been partitioned *just* for that use. It's not permanent, but it's not temporary either. You have to get special permits." She looked up at me through her bangs, magical pin held between her lips. "There's no way we could have gotten permission for creating one for this mission. And with the Legion staring in our windows, we can't have you breaking the layer in order to enact permanent space."

Delia patted the folds of the cloak and made an adjustment. "But this will work perfectly with your shields as long as you wear it *judiciously*." She cocked her head. "Your shields really are better than most I've seen. During the battle, you took more hits than anyone around us."

I knew by now that I'd probably have been dead a thousand times over without the shields Raphael had given me, and that Marsgrove had made stronger. After doing a little more fact finding, I'd discovered that while Raphael had been considered a shoe-in as a Protection Prodigy, he'd made very few things for the marketplace in the time before he'd "disappeared."

Chapter Forty

All of the things he *had* made, had been given to friends.

He'd had all the time in the world to become a market sensation. Only, he hadn't.

And after he'd broken out of captivity—after that long stay in the Department's Basement? Raphael hadn't been interested in protecting people any longer.

Most people didn't have access to a Raphael Verisetti shield.

I cleared my throat. "Thanks. Where do you usually secure shields?"

I had no idea where mine were attached, but it seemed like a good idea to find out. Just that everyone who knew, looked at the top of my head. I'd just assumed my shields were some...layer that went around my body. Like a lotion that never washed off.

I had looked into protection wards extensively, but not shields. Wards were what I had needed to secure my parents. And later, what I had used for Olivia. Wards, especially those that could be drawn, were directly in my skillset, which, for the distinctly small amount of time I had been in the magical world relative to everyone else, was a bonus. Shields required a different sort of engineering. One that I would like to tackle at some point in the future.

Since I'd been gifted with a stunning set, I'd put it on my list of things to examine later.

Delia examined my expression and said, "Undergarments work really well, but I'm guessing that's not what you have."

I looked down at my arms. So where were mine? I wasn't wearing any jewelry that I'd had at my Awakening.

"True masters can embed shield sets into skin—so deep that they never shed. I've even heard of prodigies being able to concentrate them in hair follicles, so that they always renew." She shrugged.

And...there was my answer.

"That is outside of my expertise. But I'll make you lots of things when you get back. You can thread all sorts of things in the fibers of a bland, innocuous shirt."

That made sense. I had seen Bellacia's shirt *glitter* as her shields shifted into place against Constantine.

"Thanks, Delia."

She smiled wanly. "Buck up, Crown. Tomorrow you get Brittle Britches back. It is going to be an *adventure*."

Will and Neph joined us, and we all took a moment to strengthen our ties before we turned in for the night. The twilight before battle.

Chapter Forty-one

TATTOOS AND MEMORIES

I DID HAVE one more stop to make, before turning in for the night.

Greyskull wasn't in his office. But there was a little spell that started ticking a countdown saying he'd be back in eight minutes.

The wards had let me in, so I walked further inside and poked around his office. There were a number of pieces of art and some fun posters that I thought were probably magical medical jokes—stick figure mages running around and getting into scrapes, then being treated in all sorts of horrifyingly amusing ways.

Surprisingly, there weren't any personal pictures in the room or on his desk.

A small magical bookshelf was bolted to the wall. Inside, a number of medical texts were taking bites out of each other, then healing their neighbors. Small chains connected them to the case.

Five tomes stood together at the left side, steady and slightly glowing. I recognized them as Excelsine's yearbook equivalent.

Impulsively, I reached for one and pulled it free. It was a different year than Constantine had shown me. Even better, this one was like a book in the library, complete with its own spells.

Not knowing what I was looking for, I paged through the book, letting the spells attach.

The spells read me and flipped through to show me the hundreds of pages I was looking for. The taste of memory and the smell of emotion curled around me with each new page experienced.

It was...mind-bending.

From an artistic perspective, Raphael was one of the best looking men I'd ever seen with his golden skin, symmetrical features, and laughing, intelligent eyes. I knew that already, though. He had been my very respectable teacher for a month, and he had been just as good looking at

Chapter Forty-one

thirtysomething as he was at early-twenty-something, even when he had finally let the insanity bleed into his gold eyes at my Awakening.

What *wasn't* expected was how he was portrayed in the memories preserved on the pages—memories that remained unaltered—freshly bestowed a little over a decade ago.

Mind-bending.

Raphael had been a mischievous, well-liked mage who people had thought of as *kind*. And though he'd been friendly with everyone—people staring after him longingly or fondly in every captured memory—his overt affection for his close set of friends—Greyskull, Marsgrove, Stevens, and a man named Lassiter—was obvious. His magic draped every one of them in the memories—the flutters of feeling on the pages.

Marsgrove and *Greyskull* had been the ones who everyone stepped softly around in the memories. And the three of them were thick as thieves, all over each of Raphael's pages. There wasn't any statement of it on the page, but the notes of caution whenever the other two came into frame were easy to interpret.

I mean, I had always been actively terrified of Marsgrove, but that was because he held my fate in his fists. His classmates had been afraid of him for other reasons. And Greyskull? My mind boggled.

Stevens was much the same as I was used to—active, driven, and icy. She frequently looked irritated or exasperated with the boys, but a fond affection always softened her eyes. And Raphael was frequently tweaking her in memories given by outsiders to the group, pulling unwilling smiles to her face when she thought no one was looking.

Lassiter was a wild card. A crafter. Weapons and devices. He was in the background of a lot of the pictures I flipped through, my mind not seeking information on him, and therefore, the pages not flipping to memories that had him in the foreground. He was still a decided part of their group, though.

Looking through the pages and experiencing the captured emotions of friendship and love—was *painful*.

There was a wild aspect to young Raphael that he still retained—like he lived in a world of endless possibilities and just couldn't be bothered to come back to reality, but the overall feeling in young Raphael was far more *fey*. The jagged lines, vast canyons of insanity, and cliffs of emotion, were missing.

Instead, there was a huge well of protection and love lacing each picture.

No wonder all his classmates stared longingly after him. He was a small sun that made sure to never burn those around him.

I could see aspects of current Raphael in the pictures of young Raphael —the mischievousness, the cleverness and brilliance—but it was all doused

* Tattoos and Memories *

now in insanity and revenge. The well of positive emotion had turned into the jagged cliffs, the protection of those around him had turned into a complete disregard for the safety of others, and the feyness had turned into psychopathy.

"What did they *do* to him?" I whispered.

"No one knows."

I jerked my head up to see Greyskull leaning against the wall next to the door, arms crossed. Greyskull was watching me carefully, and I quickly reined in my emotion and expression.

I closed the book and slid it carefully into its spot. "Sorry. I...I shouldn't have been nosing around your office."

"I wouldn't have allowed the wards to let you in, if I'd been afraid of that result, Miss Crown."

He pushed away from the wall and walked to his desk. "May I help you with something?"

"Yes. I need your help with," I cleared my throat, "Raphael."

He stopped his movements, and I could see his tattoos growing restless. "Miss Crown. I know I wasn't being explicit before, but I thought you understood—"

"It's not just that he has Olivia, my roommate. He has Marsgrove."

The skin at the edges of Greyskull's eyes and mouth pinched. He pushed his medical implements around the desk. "I told Phillip I would not get involved. He knows that and he knew that when he left."

"Raphael will kill him," I said.

Greyskull stopped his motions. "I know," he said quietly. "That hasn't been in doubt for years."

It was more painful to hear the emotion in his voice now that I had experienced the emotion on the pages. The emotions of *all* of them. They had each freely given their emotions to the pages that held their own memories.

"Listen, I don't like Marsgrove and he doesn't like me," I said. "But I'm not leaving him with Raphael. And I will be getting my roommate back."

Greyskull looked at me from the sides of his eyes and he smiled, just a bit. "You are a lot like him, you know. Raphael. From before. There wasn't anything he wouldn't do for a friend."

I swallowed. "Well, he's not like that now."

I didn't want to be unnecessarily cruel, but the man Greyskull knew was not the same man running around killing people. If anything, the yearbook had highlighted that completely.

"I know." Greyskull said it simply. "But I won't aid in his capture."

I jumped on it. "Not his capture. He can go free." That would kind of suck, and Constantine would be *pissed*, but I could make it the truth. It

Chapter Forty-one

would be *easier* to make it the truth. "I have to meet him, in order to get Olivia back. I just want to be able to return from that with Olivia and Marsgrove alive and in tow."

Greyskull tapped a scope and looked off into the distance, in some memory I couldn't know. "Just you?"

I cleared my throat. "There will be others...possibly...maybe." Greyskull *was* still staff. "But I don't want them to engage with Raphael anyway. And we'll have Kaine and the praetorians to deal with. So if I have something that puts him out of commission...?"

After experiencing the yearbook memories, I was even more convinced that Greyskull could help. Marsgrove had been chasing Raphael for years—they knew all of each other's old *and* new moves. Greyskull had been silently carrying out whatever penance he had claimed for his own on Excelsine's campus for the last however many years.

I could see him wavering.

"Please?" I put my hands together and held them forward in a mage gesture for binding trust. "I will promise almost anything."

Greyskull sighed and stepped toward me. He motioned for my hand and I held it out. "He'll know I helped you," he said reluctantly. A tattooed snake slithered down the back of his hand, then his finger, then stopped at the tip of mine. It sniffed at my skin, then slithered up onto my ring finger and wrapped around. It settled in, camouflaging itself to my skin tone.

"Is it...will you be in trouble?"

He smiled. It was a very sad smile. "I've watched you here for the last few days and you remind me so much of him. I hope you make it back, Miss Crown. If he does decide not to let you go, and you are close enough, touch him with that finger. It will give you a few seconds." He closed his eyes. "Don't waste them."

Chapter Forty-two

THE ENEMY OF MY ENEMY

WITH OUT timetable moved to noon, in order to take into account the twelve hours needed to get back before Bellacia reported me, I spent eight hours in the boys' room, trying not to listen as Constantine didn't sleep either. I finally fell asleep sometime in the middle of the morning.

I woke, went over last minute plans with Constantine, then spent the last hours at Bellacia's in order to "fill up" on time with her before the clock started ticking.

She was strangely subdued, and the news tickers scrolling the room seemed to reflect this.

I picked up my things from Constantine's room and headed out of the Magiaduct thirty minutes before our countdown, in order to meet him at the vault. He said he would have everything set up there by the time I arrived. I made a quick stop at the small copse of trees where Delia had helped me trap the vine—"I'm from a long line of nature, fiber, and timber mages, Crown"—though she'd given the carnivore a *very* long look and had stayed well out of its range.

I scooped up the vine—placed a small, spelled bag over its head before it could bite—and tucked it into my oversized jacket with a few minutes to go. It wrapped around my waist like a pet boa.

A small explosion occurred somewhere on the mountain.

"Tarei engaged. Two minutes and counting," Trick's voice said through the armbands. *"Hold on to your butts!"*

Butterflies in flight flew against each other in my chest. The vault was just around the next copse of trees.

Suddenly, all of my communications went down. I tapped my armband. "Hello, hello?"

"I don't think they are going to answer."

I stiffened and turned around.

Chapter Forty-two

We had planned for Tarei. Planned for making sure that he was nowhere near our position.

Keiren Oakley hadn't been a blip on our radar.

Oakley emerged, a device outstretched in his hands. I didn't know what it did, but Oakley seemed entirely too confident for me to be anything other than wary.

"This is too good. Really, Crown? A conveniently timed explosion somewhere on the mountain, and that against your chest?" He pointed at the green leaves that had started poking above my collar. "And, *strangely*, you seem to be packed for a trip."

He said it as if he didn't find it strange at all. Judging by the smirk, he knew I was attempting to leave campus, he just didn't quite know *how*.

"I found it," I said quickly. "Thought the green mages might know where it goes. And I'm on my way to see one of the professors." Sort of. Professor Stevens was sometimes at the vault.

Oakley laughed. "Carrying that beast against your chest? I'll bet we'll find your magic inside of it too. You holding it is all the evidence we need, no less whatever else you are carrying."

I was literally *covered* in evidence. Most of it was in my storage papers, but they *alone* were enough to convict me at this point.

"Evidence that I'm helping to rehabilitate campus one plant at a time?" I asked.

I inched toward the vault. It was just around the copse of trees, but also *slightly* too far for Constantine to hear us. And Oakley seemed to have some sort of communication jammer.

The real threat of Oakley's detainment was that I couldn't afford to use magic indiscriminately—I couldn't raise *any* type of alert—and all he needed to do was throw up a flare or give a shout via frequency, killing all our plans before they even began.

Or he could depress the red button on his device and have it do whatever he was threatening.

I edged to the side.

Oakley moved a step closer. "Now, now, Crown. I'm liable to get touchy and blast a much higher setting, if you go making me nervous."

I eyed the device. My shields would probably be up to the task. For pranks, they could care less. But mortal peril tended to be one hundred percent in their purview. And I didn't think Oakley was here looking to spray paint or make me go streaking.

"You don't belong on campus," Oakley said with a tight smile. "You *should* have been taken care of in the carnage."

That sounded suspiciously...suspicious.

"Taken care of...while you were gone," I said, narrowing my eyes. "What

* The Enemy of My Enemy *

exactly do you know about Bloody Tuesday, Oakley?"

He gave a mirthless laugh. "Not as much as you do, I'd say. But a lot more than Bailey and the others, who wish they had half of my knowledge, contacts, and plans. Stop moving, Crown, or I depress this." He finger tapped the red button. "And believe me, you don't want me to do that."

I eyed it. My internal clock said I had forty five more seconds to take advantage of the group's first diversion. Not a lot, but enough to try and talk my way into a better position.

"Come on, now." Oakley motioned me forward with his free hand, then thrust his hand into his pocket. He pulled out a cuff. A nullifying cuff.

I narrowed my eyes at it. "There's no way you are getting that on me, Oakley." I had magic to defend myself with now, and I *would* use it, if needed. I hadn't been shadowing Alexander Dare for weeks learning nothing. Magic gathered under my skin.

"Now, now, don't be hasty. See, that's where you are wrong. This," he shook the device, "is a one-way ticket to your muse's brains getting liquefied. So you have a choice to make."

Alarm rang through me. "What?"

"Here, I'll even let you contact her to find out." He smirked.

I immediately checked my communications. *"Neph, are you there?"*

"Yes?" Her voice reflected my alarm. *"Why didn't you answer a second ago? What is wrong?"*

"Did someone put something on you?"

"What? No. Just the control spells at my sanctioning." There was something off in her voice. *"But those are only accessible by the head of the community."*

Oakley smiled as horror overtook me. "I think you've figured it out, haven't you? Excellent. Let's turn her back off, now. There we go. That's what deal making begets, Crown. Not that you know, feral mongrel that you are," he said viciously. "Come now. Your muse is waiting. The Department wants you and the Department is going to get you."

He took a careful step forward reaching out toward me with the cuff while I stood, frozen.

"This will take care of two problems," he said. "Then the real fun will begin when the terr—"

Oakley hit the ground in a spray of striped black-and-green ropes and chains. I didn't wait to see who had cast the magic, I stepped on his outstretched wrist and ripped the device from his hand. I clutched it against my chest and backed away as striped snakes of magic lashed out and tightened around him, slamming him repeatedly into the ground. Blood spurted from his broken nose, but that too was soon covered up in a burlap hood magicked over his head.

Stunned, my head jerked up to see Bellacia striding over, hips swaying.

Chapter Forty-two

She kicked Oakley in the stomach.

"What—" I started. The vine had flattened against me, tucked out of sight, as if it found *Bellacia* a threat, where it had found Oakley merely boring.

"Oh, please." Bellacia stood, back straight, one leg out, posed like the high society model she was, one finger casually making figure eight motions in the air. Her magic followed the paths she drew, trussing up Oakley like a holiday turkey with the magical rope that I had seen law enforcement on the feeds use—a measure just shy of a nullifying cuff.

The nullifying cuff, she left curled in his fist.

"I've had my eyes on him for weeks," she said with disdain. "With his precious double dealing. Thinking we didn't notice. Giving information to the Thirdies."

I stared down at Oakley. "But he wants to turn me in to the Department."

"Yes. He does. Interesting, isn't it?" She hummed as she worked.

"The Department is working with the Third Layer?"

Bellacia sighed. "You ask that as if it is so simplistic. Certain elements in the Department are working with the Third Layer terrorists. All in the pursuit of their own goals, of course. As we all do."

"Goals to what?"

"To get the populace more under control. To increase weapons production, all in the name of a continuing war. To rise from the ashes of the old and form the new. To justify a new experiment. Or to keep certain members of the population in their direct control. Name it, and there is someone pressing forward on their agenda."

"And Stavros?"

"Ah." Bellacia smiled, eyes cold. "Now there *is* the question. What is the head of the Department's goal? That, my dear...that is what is shrouded by all of the underlings and minions who each fall beneath him. Which ones took the fall for their superiors, and which ones did he weed out himself? What is his ultimate goal?"

I thought of what Olivia and Marsgrove had discussed at the end of last term as they'd been drawing up the terms of my remaining on campus. Olivia had held "Omega Genesis" over Marsgrove's head to get Marsgrove to capitulate.

Bellacia would probably love to have me mention such a thing.

"What are you going to do with Oakley?" I asked instead.

She smiled beautifully. "Traitors to the cause are...dealt with."

"Dealt with how?" I asked, looking uncomfortably at Oakley with the burlap hood over his head. The hoods were used to mute magic and normal senses, like sound, from reaching a prisoner. But it looked far too much like

* The Enemy of My Enemy *

the preface to a First Layer torture scene.

"Why use your imagination, dear. In the most horrifying fashion imaginable—stretched across the front page of every major feed in the most grotesque and terrible positions. University stress is so all consuming." She shook her head. "It just got to poor dear Keiren and now he will be humiliated in such a fashion that he will never again be able to work in Magicist circles."

"You are going to...embarrass him? But, he'll be alive?"

Bellacia's brow delicately lifted. "Complete social estrangement is a fate far worse than death."

I had the device that was hooked to Neph in my hand, where no one else could use it—I could afford to be merciful. I started to inch back along the path that lead around the bend and into the vault. "So...we're good here?"

"I'm not going to stop you," Bellacia said, eyes glittering.

I swallowed and put another foot of ground between us. "Great, thanks."

I didn't get Bellacia. Like, at all. But as long as she didn't follow me—

"No, dear. You misunderstand my intent. You are going to *do* something for me." She held up a small recording device.

Okay, maybe I got her just fine. "Or?"

"Or...let's say, or else." She held up another recording device. This one was inactive, but her threat seemed to be that whatever was on it was something I would pay to hide.

"Okay." I nodded. "Sure. Let's try option #1."

She looked amused. "Yes, let's." She threw the first recording device to me and I caught it in the hand that was not holding the precious device linked to Neph. "When you activate it, it backs up to retrieve the ten previous seconds of data as well, so that the reporter doesn't miss the best parts. Get me something good."

"No promises." I stared down at the slim black square.

"Oh, you'll want to rethink that. Now, go." Her eyes narrowed as she looked toward the trees in the opposite direction. "I need to pay the Justice penalty for this, and Oakley needs to pay for many other things." She dropped two things to the ground and toed them beneath him, planting whatever it was she had decided to frame him for.

I backed away, then turned and hurried around the corner. Behind me I could hear people gaining ground. Another explosion sounded farther off.

Diversion number two.

I looked nervously over my shoulder and knocked on the door of the vault. The door rose a space of three feet, and not an inch more. I glanced again at the empty area behind me, ducked underneath the door, then

Chapter Forty-two

nervously hit the switch that would seal us in. The door closed *theatrically* slowly as I waited for Tarei, or a member of the Legion, to burst into the clearing and roll beneath it.

The door sealed shut.

"You were almost late," Constantine said in a clipped voice that almost startled me as I was still staring at the seal.

"Traffic."

He raised a brow. I shook my head and walked toward him. The vine shimmied up from my collar and slithered out, plopping on the floor of the workshop. I grabbed it before it could consume everything.

"And...*what* is that?" He cast a disdainful, almost uninterested, glance at the vine, but our connection said he was anything but uninterested, and more than a little disturbed.

"Er...? Axer told me to bring it."

"He *didn't*." Anger suffused his feelings.

"No, he really...oh, I see. Yeah, Marsgrove was pretty ticked too."

Constantine licked his lips. "Well, we can't leave it here. Perhaps he is planning that we set it loose in the Third Layer?" He smiled dangerously. "See what havoc we can wreak?"

"Maybe." I looked at the vine, which was now rubbing its cheek against my hand. It was like a really disturbing pet.

I fished out a storage paper—one of my best ones. "What do you say to traveling in style?"

The vine cocked its head, then dove neatly into the paper. "Huh," I said picking it up and seeing it curled up inside. "It did it on its own."

Usually I had to use my own magic to sink things inside.

"Don't trust it," Constantine said darkly. "Get rid of it as quickly as you can once we find a spot."

That seemed...unkind. "I'll find you somewhere nice," I whispered to it, and folded the sheet, sticking it in a secured pocket along with the cloaks, the containers, and everything else I was carrying like a mad art mercenary.

"So, how...?" My question faltered as I rounded the main worktable in the center of the room.

Constantine hadn't said exactly how we were getting off campus, but now...now I knew.

A vortex projected upward from a single dot on the floor, swirling in controlled rotations.

He'd been making vortexes in his room—in an *ottoman*—over two terms, maybe more. He'd let me observe some of his progress after we'd become daily business acquaintances. I'd *helped* him hide some of the Justice Magic infractions. I hadn't known what the vortexes had been for.

Until Tuesday.

* The Enemy of My Enemy *

It was simple really, as Constantine had said it would be, to get off campus and into the Third Layer. Constantine had held the solution in his room the whole time.

I crossed my arms. "This is one of the vortexes you built for Godfrey."

"Never. I had to make this one again from scratch," he said idly.

"Constantine."

"All of the others started in the Third Layer and ended at Excelsine. This one goes in quite the opposite direction."

"Will it take us to the spot where the others originated?"

Constantine smiled, but it was without humor. "The origination points were designed to be used at the moment of activation. They never did get a chance to use the vortexes for human transport, though. They tested them only, sending small things through to my room. *Emrys* was the one who opened the school's wards from the inside—using Telgent and pawns in the Administration."

And Constantine. Raphael had used Constantine to dissolve the wards. Constantine had left the mixture in a designated spot on the mountain. Axer was right—oh, how that must have *stung* when Constantine realized who he had been talking to that whole time. Even if Raphael had been in golem form, he had been *right there*.

"Verisetti set it all up, every last piece of Tuesday, except for you."

"Oh, he planned for me too. But I don't think he minded how everything shook out. He was playing multiple games, trying to get me discovered, trying to hide me. He had plenty of plans for if I was taken by the Department."

Could still have those plans. It was obvious to everyone, even me, that this was some sort of a trap. It was just a trap the mouse was hoping to conquer.

I looked at the vortex. Time was ticking. "You programmed in a destination?"

"Yes, the same one given to us by Peoples."

I nodded. Delia had been working her contacts.

"So, how do we do this?"

I didn't know enough about vortexes to even chance a guess. And it looked uncomfortably like the one that had almost eaten me in the Library of Alexandria.

This was Will's field, not mine. Will was going to be *crushed* he missed this.

"You jump in," Constantine said as if I was being dense.

"You are crushing Will's heart right now by not having him help."

"Tasky is addicted to portal pads," Constantine said dismissively.

It was a little true—Will and I had met because Raphael and I had

Chapter Forty-two

created a portal pad that worked in all layers during my Awakening. Will and I had tried to dredge up the memory of that process *several* times with no success.

"Will loves everything interesting. Especially when it has to do with travel."

"You are stalling, Ren." Constantine hummed.

I looked at the vortex. It was a one-way trip down that supernatural whirlpool. And I was going, but Constantine... "Are you sure you want to do this?" I asked him.

"Don't be silly, darling." His voice was light, but the undertone was not.

"We are likely to get expelled or jailed, even if Patrick says you have a 'Get Out of Jail Free Card.'"

"Those are but trifling concerns."

Trifling concerns, in contrast to the revenge that he had been seeking for years. It was glittering in his eyes. Truth.

Looking at him in this moment, even with his promise and my belief in him, I wasn't so certain that his revenge *would* come second.

He abruptly stepped toward me, gaze entirely focused, and his fingers wrapped around my elbow—the one that held so many of the threads connecting us. "I swear that I will rescue your roommate first and foremost after making sure that you survive."

My breath hitched as the magic wrapped around us, securing the vow. Everything in me relaxed.

"You didn't have to—"

"You are at ease now," he said, as if unaffected by the magic I could still see rippling over his fingers. He slowly released my elbow. "And your trust is critical."

I frowned. "Critical to what?"

"To me, of course," he said lightly.

I sighed. "Right. Why do you make everything sound so shady? We could have had a nice moment there, you know."

He smiled, though he tried to hide it. "It's one of my many skills. We can still have a nice moment. Come here."

I held up a hand, palm out toward his descending face. "Not a chance."

He laughed and walked closer to the vortex. "Come, darling. Destiny awaits. And your troublemakers have just set off diversion number three. There will be no more to be had."

The vortex swirled in a mesmerizing mass of white and purple.

He flashed a hand toward it. "Beauty before gorgeousness."

I sighed again. "Stupidity before supervillainery?"

"Yes. Also, because I need to close the vortex behind us, unless you want Praetorian Tarei diving in when they come to search the room in—"

* The Enemy of My Enemy *

He tapped his arm. "—three point five minutes."

I stared at him, anxiety rising again. "Constantine, what—"

"Jump in."

I carefully examined his resolute expression, then nodded. Above everyone, Constantine knew what he was getting into.

"So, I just..." I looked at the small white and purple tornado. "Jump in?"

"Enter the vortex," he said, voice low, while unnecessary smoke rose around him in a parody of some hoary, mystical moment.

"Very funny. Glad to see your humor is still intact." I examined the swirls of the vortex. I was again reminded of the Library of Alexandria. "If my leg goes in, but the rest of me is still out here for too long, will it swallow my leg somewhere?"

"I can drop you in." That wasn't an answer, and he seemed amused. Which *likely* meant that I was going to be fine. Constantine's amusements were sometimes quite dark and vicious, but I hadn't yet been the victim of anything cruel. And on a mission of such importance to him, he'd have told me up front if there was something to fear here.

I pulled over a chair and stood on top, staring down. Olivia was on the other side. And, in the end, that was what made the choice easy.

I jumped and the room disappeared as I was sucked into a space too small.

Swirls of white and purple pulsed over and around me as if I was being forced down a tube at great speed. I could feel added magic—Constantine—as he jumped in after me.

We disappeared from campus, from the Second Layer, and into the Third.

Chapter Forty-three

THE THIRD LAYER

ALL THE PRACTICE in the world wouldn't have prepared me for the *feeling* of it. We landed on an endless expanse of amber colored dirt.

My first impression of the Third Layer was so disjointed from reality that I couldn't process it mentally for a moment.

A slim, audible stutter of air escaped my throat.

Constantine kicked a small rock with his foot and it propelled itself with too great a force into the *finite* sky, then just as suddenly altered its course and slammed back to the ground, creating a five-foot crater that rocked the ground beneath us

"Welcome to the Third Layer, darling."

A dusty, wasteland of magic swirled uncontrollably around us. The atmosphere was *pinched* in places, the sky meeting the ground in a foreign, Daliesque way—as if magic couldn't sustain the pillars of the world, and had melted plastic pieces of sky and earth together in the collapse.

I had seen pictures. Eight weeks of Layer Politics classes three times a week plus homework hadn't kept me ignorant of what had happened to the Third Layer. But most of our classes had to do with the politics between the layers and the political efforts made between. And we'd been saving the "ways to go forward using everything we've learned" discussions for the last few weeks of term, which we hadn't yet fulfilled.

Seeing the devastation firsthand—*feeling* it—was a lot different than reading about it and abstractedly observing pictures.

"It—" I reached out a hand as if I could unhook the sky from the ground where it was pinched, then curled my fingers back in. My breath stuttered and my magic tried to reach forward. To connect to all the broken paths.

It would be visually fascinating if it didn't feel so *wrong*.

"Darling?"

"It's horrible," I breathed.

"It's the Third Layer." His lips curled distastefully. "It's akin to hell. Or a vacation in Tus Onus," he said pensively. "Horrible place. All tourists and pr—"

"The magic here. It's broken."

He looked around, cocking his head as if to try and see it from a new view. He held out his hand to me without looking back, and I put mine within his grip. I sent the vision of it—the grid of broken connections and strings with torn ends.

"Ah. I could swim in your brain, darling."

"Yeah, I've heard that before." I sighed and dropped his hand, concentrating on what I *could* do.

"You can't fix it," he said sharply. "And you *can't* do magic out here without drawing on a container hooked to your recycler. We went over what happens if you use magic here outside of a safe zone, Ren."

It was always serious when he was addressing me by name.

"Yes, I know, layer shift, blah, blah. What if we just *fixed* the layer shifts?"

"And world hunger. Peace. We could go for a trifecta."

"You heard Stevens," I said softly. I had shared the memory of what had happened after he left.

"Yes. And I'm quite *put out* that she pinned you with any such feeling of *duty* like that," he bit out.

"I could do it. She's right. Technically right." I swallowed the dry—no, *sterile*—air and looked carefully around. "It's not like I'm going to say abracadabra and fix anything. But I have the correct...skill set, or whatever. I could fix it. And because I *can*, I do have an inherent responsibility."

"Or you could let them all *burn*. It's what they will do to you."

I crossed my arms, tucking my hands beneath my armpits. "Let's just find Olivia."

"Yes, let's find your wayward roommate," he said. "Who will tell you what such ridiculous notions these are."

He wasn't wrong about that.

A strange animal, half-cat, half-lizard screeched as it appeared around a pinch in the world—jumping from around its bend and taking us completely by surprise.

Enough of a surprise that I formed my mental pyramid and blasted magic to encase it—magic that I pulled from the air. The magic rippled out, then up, then out again—the layer shifting almost audibly around us. Wow, well *named*.

Next to me, Constantine closed his eyes.

"Sorry," I said, cringing. And here I'd thought I'd be all "First Layer cool" and not even think to use magic—but no, when magic attacked, my first response was to respond with magic, apparently. I blamed Alexander Dare for this.

The gathering mushroom cloud of magic spread over us. The earth rumbled beneath our feet and a hundred bolts of green lightning fragmented the sky.

In the Second Layer, the backlash from every magic use was contained and distributed, safely dealt with over an intricate system of ever-expanding technology and research.

In the Third Layer, this system was...not present.

"Run, Crown."

To where? I wanted to say. But instead I grabbed his arm. "We aren't going to make it."

"One of us will." He sounded resigned, even though he nearly had to shout over the howling winds. He pushed me. "Go."

His fingers were already glowing, drawing magic, and he was staring upward, preparing. The magic cloud had finished gathering, and it shot down toward the one who was drawing more magic, completely uninterested in me.

I launched myself at Constantine, shoved him to the ground, and arced the containment field I had strapped to my shoe over the top of us just as the blast hit.

Pain. Darkness. Blinding light. The backlash swept over the field and upward in a long arc, then made a rapid swirl and hammered down.

Lightning—completely unnatural lightning—howling winds, and grinding cracks struck and shifted and *broke* upon us.

Over and over. Until finally, the hammering grew less and less, and the tendrils dissipated outward in almost caressing wisps.

The black spots slowly, painfully cleared from my vision. Tinnitus still rang my ears. Mineral dust clogged my nose. And my body...

"Ow," I said into the unyielding rock my shoulder was pressed against. My shoulder ached, I had a fractured rib, and something was bruised in my midsection. No stranger to pain, the sensations running through my body were still extremely unpleasant.

I turned my head to see Constantine staring at me blankly, as if a soul-sucking wind had swept through him and left nothing behind. But a quick—passive magic!—check through our connection indicated he was physically fine. I had taken the brunt of it all as the person connecting with the field.

I put that on the list of fixes to make.

"So...the Third Layer sucks," I said, my words clenching a little, as I looked up at the too-close, warped sky that was now a strange vermillion and sulfur-yellow mix.

"An understatement," he said in a clipped voice.

He was angry with me. I didn't know if it was from me unthinkingly grabbing magic in the first place, or for not running when he told me to. Probably a little of both.

"I can kinda see why the people who live here might want it fixed."

Something wriggled out from underneath me and I shifted to see the animal that had started the whole thing bristle its back fur, hiss at me, then dart away on four short, scaly legs.

"Well, the lizardcat made it, and so did we, so we can just count this as a small oops, right?" I said, and turned to look at Constantine.

He ignored the fleeing animal and continued to look at me, gaze intense. "What was that you used?"

I painfully sat up and looked at the remnants of the field. "Well, it *was* a prototype of Professor Mbozi's that I tweaked yesterday, then again this morning while I was stuck at Bellacia's. I have a duplicate in my other shoe, but it is a copy with just my magic. I'm not sure we want to try that again before I fine-tune it. I already know three things that need to be adjusted, so don't start," I grumbled.

I looked back at Constantine, and for a moment, his expression held a look of longing so fierce that it made me blink. It was gone in that slim, bantam beat of time, a fleeting moment of my imagination.

"We will be making more as soon as we get home," he said, brushing himself off as he stood up.

"Mbozi is going to sigh at me again," I said, poking at the debris, then pushing painfully to my feet and brushing myself off as well. "This one was mostly his."

"He is going to do anything but sigh."

I cocked my head at flashes of light bending around the pinches of earth and sky. There were vehicles coming toward us from the distance. "We have company."

Constantine followed my gaze and stepped an inch in front of me. "Give me the device."

I handed him what Delia had given to me. It was blinking.

"That is our ride then?" I asked.

Or our *rides*, to be exact. A group of vehicles sped toward us, around pinches and strange-looking spots. Rocks kicked up from the tires and flew out in all directions, pinging wildly in the abnormal physics.

Constantine looked at the group of approaching vehicles as they drew closer, and said, flatly, "You have to be kidding."

"What?"

"Peoples set you up with the Ophidians?"

"Delia set us up with whom?"

Constantine looked up at the too-low sky, as if seeking guidance from a...lower power.

"Does it matter?" I asked, as they drew closer. They wore thick goggles and protective gear that covered most of their skin. They looked like extras from an insane version of a magical Mad Max movie. Small serpents covered their vehicles. "Should I be concerned?"

"Are you ever?"

"I feel like you are poking fun at me during a high-stress situation."

"I'm stating the obvious. However, if they don't kill us outright and strip us of our things, we *should* make it to our destination in their company."

I'd been in a constant state of panic for a week, and we'd just nearly died. Seeing what looked like cannibal outlaws headed our way wasn't the worst thing I could imagine.

Constantine's hand pulsed with magic. Safe *container* magic. I touched the ouroboros's cord at my throat to keep a focal point and I hooked into one of the containers secured in my armband. I felt how the magic leaked through it into the ouroboros field, then slid back around. I closed my eyes, feeling the circulation around my body instead of inside, then firmly told my body to use *this* in a startle response instead.

The vehicles soon surrounded us. Their wheels did something in the last twenty-five yards to throw debris away from us.

They stopped. The most intimidating of our new compatriots sat on the largest of the single person vehicles. He-she-it held up a device similar to ours, then nodded at someone behind us.

I'd been assured that the translator spell would still work with my containers and the magic field generated by the ouroboros ring.

"Hi," said the person on the left, in a decidedly female voice, confirming that the translator spell worked just fine. She hopped off her two-seat bike. "Regan, right?"

"Yes." I stepped forward, answering to the fake name. "Thank you for helping us."

She shrugged. "Getting paid for it. Said it would be a quick trip, though they didn't say where."

"Corpus Sun," I said. "Not too far, I hope?"

Silence greeted that pronouncement. I shifted on my feet and forced myself to keep looking at the fully-covered person in front of me, instead of checking Constantine's expression. He'd been on edge since we stepped into the Third Layer—but the edge of boredom that was ever present outside of a lab setting or real two-person conversation, was in full effect.

"Listen, kid," the girl said—who didn't sound all that much older than me. "You might want to reconsider that. Some heavies in that territory right now."

I nodded. "That's why we are going there."

Looks and gestures were exchanged. Frequencies—like any active magic—weren't used in Outlaw Territory, but they obviously had some form of communication.

"Going to need some extra munits for that, then," she finally said.

Constantine held out his hand. A magical bomb ticked on his palm. "Or you can do it before I kill all of you and everything around us."

The group shifted backward.

"What are you doing?" I hissed.

"Making sure they realize that getting us to Corpus Sun, *quickly*, is really their best option."

"You're bluffing," the girl said flatly.

"And you, obviously, don't realize who you are dealing with. All I have to do is activate this and watch all of you burn around us. Then, perhaps, I will reassemble the remains of your vehicles and find the place myself."

There was a short communication with the large person—man?—who'd had the device, then the girl shrugged. "Fine. Get in. I'm far happier dropping you off there now."

She motioned to me. "You, with me." To Constantine, she said, "You, in the middle of that one." She pointed to an oddly-shaped vehicle that held three people already.

Constantine narrowed his eyes.

"You can be pissed all you like, Privilege, but you're getting on that bike, or you're walking."

~*~

The girl who wouldn't give us a name said the ride would take three hours. Once we had been riding for about forty minutes, and I felt like we might survive the *insanity* of the trip around holes of death, other bandits, and places where the earth *attacked*, I dug a lotus out of my bag.

Making sure to hook the magic of it under the ouroboros field, I let the healing magic settle into my skin, fixing my fracture and soothing my aches.

"How are you doing that?" the girl asked, with an askance motion of her head.

"We hooked up a small, portable system. Personal magic recycler. It's not infinite in its use, but at least it doesn't shift the layer," I said with a cringe at the end.

The Ophidian nodded. "We use something like that too. But a littler rougher around the edges. It's hard to test things here without...consequences. You Second Layer folks have a lot more options."

It was said without rancor. Just a statement of fact. The Third Layer was a half-gutted world of hardship. But even the harshest deserts contained life.

At Excelsine, at the pinnacle of scholarly pursuit, I was used to being surrounded by overwhelming magic. Little was impossible at Excelsine.

Far less was possible here.

I touched my pocket, where I had the extra set of containers and ouroboros for Olivia. I needed both sets for us to escape. But...

But these people were doing *incredible* things with the little that they had. We would have died at least fifty times if we'd tried to walk to our destination. What could they do with *more*?

"How could I get something to you, after we get home?"

The girl cocked her head, but still stared straight ahead, concentrating, and dodging, the numerous pitfalls that Outlaw Territory provided. "Do you think you will get home?"

"I have to believe that, don't I?"

"Hope is for fools."

"Hope is sometimes the last thing we have," I said quietly.

"Hmmm... Well, hope is something that your friend Privilege over there is dearly wishing he had right about now."

I looked over to see what she was talking about and nearly laughed at the narrowed look on Constantine's face whose ride wasn't going nearly as well in the larger vehicle as mine was. Also, my driver was way more awesome.

"Tell you what, kid. You get home, you go through the same contact that got you to us, whoever it was. Then maybe we can talk."

I left her a lotus flower, tucked under her seat.

Chapter Forty-four

APPROACHING DOOM

AFTER AN EVENTFUL ride that I was sure Constantine *never* planned to repeat, the Ophidians stated that "for everyone's protection" we would be dropped off about a ten minutes' walk from Corpus Sun. Without a wave, they took off at high speed into the distance.

"Well, that was fun," I said cheerfully.

"I will make you bleed, darling."

I didn't bother trying to hide my smile. I couldn't *wait* to tell Neph the story when we returned.

"You will not," he warned as we started our trek.

"Oh, I will," I said. "And, seriously, how do you always know what I'm thinking?"

"Anyone could have read that from your face."

"What about the other times?" I asked.

He hesitated, oddly, and I zeroed in on it. "Yes?"

"Practicing Mind Magic is illegal, so let's say that your auditory deficiency affects you in ways other than just making you susceptible to mages with high levels of skill in audition."

I thought crazy, secret things all the time. I'd have been taken by some shady government agency long ago, if that were true. *Bellacia* would have made it happen. And Constantine and Axer could only read me sometimes.

"Listen, Ren—" he began.

"I can't. I'm obviously terrible at it."

That got a reluctant smile from him, which I thought he sorely needed. "When we get back—"

"*Praetorian Tarei has disappeared.*" Dagfinn's voice suddenly came through on the only channel that we had connected for the Third Layer—the emergency channel. "*I repeat. Tarei has disappeared from campus. He has taken at least three dozen Legion soldiers with him. Do you copy?*"

"Yes," I said immediately, exchanging a grim look with Constantine. The praetorians knew we were coming.

~*~

We slipped on our cloaks, pulling them securely around us. We had mimicked the shadow cloaks and connected the three cloaks into a network of magic, so that we could still see the people under the others. We'd give the third to Olivia as soon as we found her.

Delia, Mike, and I had constructed Constantine's and Olivia's off the same pattern as mine, and I took a moment to take pleasure at how well they worked.

There was a rippling sort of illusion to them—the weather, fiber, and misdirection charms on them tricking the eye. I hadn't used Origin Magic, per se, but I'd used what I remembered of seeing the layers, connecting that vision to reflect in the fabric. We *lived* in the layer system and were surrounded by it, by definition. Duplicating the qualities visually, so far, had succeeded in tricking everyone's eyes that we tested it upon.

But tension coiled in me as the town came into view. Olivia was somewhere inside.

"Corpus Sun," Constantine said, in a low voice, looking at the small, barren town surrounded by a thin dome. "A less apt name, I couldn't choose."

We carefully made our way down the small slope toward the town. From our higher vantage point, I could see inside the clear barrier reasonably well. Two trenches stretched the length of the dome's interior, forming a cross at the center. A clear glass material covered the trenches, allowing roads to cross over the top. I could see magic flowing through the trench and out into the dome. It appeared to be similar to Ganymede Circus in that respect, funneling magic use into strengthening the dome around it as it simultaneously dissipated each magic use into something less dangerous.

There weren't any visible openings or arches in the dome. "Do we just walk through?"

Constantine pulled a hand over the material that Delia had given him to cover his cuff. "The magic will absorb your intent and form a contract." His lips tightened. "Depending on what the founders set the magic to do, we will be at its mercy. We will break the contract after finding Price. We will need to in order to fight and escape. Our exit won't work with it in place."

I nodded slowly. I was still hoping that we could get out of this with Olivia, Marsgrove, and zero bloodshed. "Maybe we shouldn't be thinking about how we are going to subvert the Justice Magic before it scans us and binds us to it, though?"

Constantine took my face in his hands and pressed his fingertips to my temples.

A moment later, I blinked at him. "You just took a thought from me." I couldn't remember what it was; just that we'd been speaking of whatever it was moments ago.

"I temporarily subverted it. You'll regain it in five minutes' time."

He closed his eyes, and a moment later his gaze was glassy as well. "Let's go."

I pointed at the dome. "Do we just walk through?" A weird sense of Deja Vu gripped me.

"Yes," he said. "We are only here to reunite you with your lost loved one. Keep that *firmly* in mind. You'll...need to pull me through with you. Once inside, you can use magic sparingly—the dome will process it without backlash. But our presence will be noted—two additional ticks in the population ledger—and we don't know *who* might be watching for it. We have the cloaks, but we need to be quick."

No pressure.

Shadows stretched along the walls of the dome, making me eye the landscape around us. Somewhere, Kaine lay in wait.

Never one to delay, I thrust my left hand forward.

Touching the dome was like touching a liquid just viscous enough not to attach to my palm. Trusting Constantine's words, I projected calm, peaceful thoughts—I wanted to be reunited with Olivia, it *was* what I desired—and pushed the feelings out through my fingers. My hand sunk through, magic parting around my fingers, allowing me to pass as if through a waterfall of beads. I gripped Constantine's hand tightly in my other hand and pulled him through behind me.

No alarms sounded. But a gripping tension took hold of my body—a slowing of sound and movement.

The streets of Corpus Sun were desolate and lifeless. They were so dusty and empty, I expected a tumbleweed and crooked sheriff to greet us at any moment.

A neighborhood of Tudor and Colonial houses elevated the dusty and dreary atmosphere slightly. Small gardens were brown and wild. At one time, this must have been a beautiful place.

There was *still* a sort of wild beauty. A sense of survival permeated the air. *We have seen worse and we are still here*, the wind of the town seemed to whisper.

But the shadowy presence grew larger in my mind, and I tugged Constantine closer.

Mentally following the connection at my chest that had *abruptly* strengthened, I sent slim tendrils of magic to look for corresponding connections.

Points popped up in my mind, spreading a sensory grid through the town, pinpointing areas where Olivia might have *been*. There was a vague sense of darkness surrounding all of them, but she'd walked that path there, then turned that corner, and—

A vibrant rose glow pulsed to life from a point a few streets over, connecting to my magic so suddenly that I stumbled. Tart strawberry and sweetened wine.

Constantine neatly caught my stumble and tugged me into a spot behind a fence.

"What is it?"

"She's there," I whispered, pointing.

"In the building that looks like the Grim Reaper's summer home?"

"Yes," I said, looking at the half-Gothic, half-broken building that towered above everything else.

Used to a lot of decrepit buildings in the Midlands, there was still something especially concerning about this one. "Let's go."

Constantine held me back, gaze fiercely serious all of a sudden. He slipped something circular into my armband, under my cloak. "That is your exit, if I don't..."

If I don't survive.

"All of us are getting out of here. We *will* be making it out of here together," I vowed.

"Ren..." His eyes were distant.

I squeezed his hand. "You think you will die and take Raphael with you. And I'm telling you that is not going to happen."

A small smile slipped over his lips. "I suppose your wish is my command?"

"The only differences between the evil witch and the fairy godmother are the decisions they make and the actions they take," I said pointedly. "They can both be clever."

He let out a low laugh. "My wardrobe is already fixed, though."

I cast a look around the corner in both directions down the street. We were still alone in an abandoned town. "You, of anyone, can figure out how to carry off white and pink in style."

He smiled and we slipped back out onto the street.

Our cloaks were well-suited to magical camouflage as we edged around buildings and darted between alleys, and I had practiced maneuvers like this plenty of times in the Midlands where there were always man-eating beasts to avoid.

But as we continued on without encountering anyone, our stealth was more for our own satisfaction than anything else.

The best thing that could be said about Raphael was that he worked *alone*. Godfrey had mentioned that both he and Raphael had *superiors*—but Raphael seemed a free agent, more than anything else.

A vicious pet that the terrorists let have its way.

The target building was as eerie on the inside as it was on the out. It reminded me of the upper level of Okai in that way—creepy, like there was something *specifically* scary about the building that I hadn't yet put my finger upon.

Constantine paused in the middle of a huge, empty atrium decorated with columns at the edges and composed entirely of what looked like marble and sorrow. He cocked his head at me in question. I put up four fingers then mimicked climbing stairs with them. Olivia was four floors up.

So was Raphael.

Constantine dropped to one knee on the black marble floor.

"What are you doing?" I whispered, darting sharp glances around the large open hall. "We need to go."

The gold that emanated from my skin when I focused my sight had started pulsing. Raphael was doing active magic four floors above us.

"Fulfilling a bargain." Constantine's lips curled unpleasantly, as he sketched out a rune, then carefully placed a single emerald on top of the design.

"If you are calling a demon here, so help me—"

He looked up at me with surprise. "How did you know?"

A very *fake* look of surprise. This close to his goal, the feelings in him were bordering on manic.

Not good. Not any of it.

He rose and in one fluid move stepped forward into my space. "Do you trust me to be your fairy godmother?"

His eyes were direct and fierce, his gaze slightly unhinged. There was something balanced precariously there, despite the joking we'd been doing in order to keep our anxiety under control.

I thought of the betrayal that everyone was positive Constantine was going to enact. Then I thought of what I knew and *felt*. I grabbed his wrist. His pulse point was beating wildly beneath my fingers. "Yes."

He pulled his free hand down a lock of my hair, smiling at it as he captured it in his fingers, then released it, leaned down to the floor and touched the top of the gem, activating whatever it was. "Let's go."

At the top of the stairs, we secured our cloaks more tightly before rounding the last corner.

Raphael stood alone in a large, broken solarium at the end of the decrepit hall. Constantine's focus sharpened. By silent agreement, we split to each side of the hallway.

I couldn't count on Constantine not to attack him, but if we could slip past...

We were almost level with Raphael's position, one to each side of him in the large room, when he smiled.

"You came, Butterfly." His smile was almost real in his golden face as he looked directly at me, through all the concealing spells we'd laboriously threaded into the cloak. "I knew you would."

Chapter Forty-five

GOLDEN STORM

HE WAS STARING right into my eyes.

"You are wearing something truly exquisite, Butterfly. But you can't hide from me. Not this way. Your magic, your presence is too rich. I've been saturated by it before." He smiled. "I know you are there."

I pushed the hood from my head. There was no reason to hide anymore.

Over Raphael's shoulder, I could see Constantine grit his teeth, *deeply* displeased at my action. Even with my hood off and his still on, the cloaks were still linked together, allowing me to see him. He stayed back, silent and hidden.

"I'm here. Under your deadline," I said to Raphael.

He motioned to the door at my right. His movements were a little strange—almost wooden. I was used to slinking grace from him. "She's just where you were heading, and as alive as she was when you saw her last. Take her and go."

I frowned and shifted. "That's it? No tricks?"

He looked at me innocently as he raised his palm. "Tricks?"

Constantine was already in motion, striding up behind him, magic glowing in his hand. The shadows shifted, and for a moment I saw the old Raphael—the one from his classmates' memories—as unshaded light hit his face. I mourned for that boy as Constantine's hand rose.

But Constantine's hand never fell.

Constantine made an abrupt quarter turn, defensive instincts reacting lightning fast, and thrust his hand into the massive shadow that appeared from nowhere.

Right into Kaine's chest.

Kaine shrieked, but whatever offensive magic Constantine had conjured had been for direct use against Raphael, not Kaine, and dark pleasure fell over the praetorian's expression as his form seemed to sharpen and a shadowed hand thrust Constantine's hood back, exposing him.

I threw magic at Kaine, but a force slammed into my chest and I was slammed against the wall. Breath knocked from me, I blinked through blurry eyes to see Tarei standing over me, smirking maliciously. Among other things, he'd re-fractured the rib I had fixed on the ride over.

I saw a phantom spring up and envelop Raphael. Then there were three, then nine of them. Praetorians appeared out of nearly thin air. They gripped Raphael, trying to force something around his neck.

"Come precious boy," a voice cooed as Stavros' face spiraled into view on one of them, then appeared on another body when Raphael whipped a blade through the first. "Time to return."

Behind them, black shade dripped from Kaine as his razor-sharp shadow fingers pierced Constantine's chest. Blood arced everywhere.

Blood bubbled up from Constantine's mouth as he smiled. "But at least you won't be able to have *her*." He ripped something from his belt and slammed it into Kaine's throat.

Kaine's hands wrapped around his own throat and he gurgled, then burst into a thousand shadows that dropped to the floor in writhing, black curlicues.

The individual parts immediately started pulling together—Kaine regenerating quickly at Constantine's feet. Tarei, gaze still focused on me, drew back his hand.

I released the magic from an *entire* container directly into Tarei's chest, and thrust my free hand into my pocket and *pulled*. A boom exploded from the area where the praetorians held Raphael, but I couldn't afford the distraction to look. The vine leaped free of my hand as soon as it hit the air, dove at Kaine's fragmented shadows, and *devoured* them as they were reconnecting on the floor.

Tarei hit the floor from my blast in the midst of Kaine's pieces, and the vine leaped on Tarei, devouring him too.

My breath came in pants as I looked frantically around the space. Raphael and the other praetorians were nowhere to be seen. I would have thought them figments of the imagination, if not for the debris littering the space where they'd stood. The whole series of events after Raphael's last spoken word had taken about fifteen seconds.

Crimson lips parted, Constantine stared at the spot where Kaine and Tarei had been. The fattened vine lay on the ground, absently grooming itself with engorged lethargy. "That was morbid, darling."

"I don't think they are dead," I said shakily as I rose.

Alarm peels were ringing in the air outside and lights were flashing through the broken windows. A persistent pain in my right leg was growing, trying to hobble me. The Justice Magic had definitely registered our fight.

"Not dead, though being digested alive seems quite dire."

Constantine coughed up blood, a red mist spewing from his lips. I shoved one hand against his cheek and pushed a tiny lotus flower on his tongue. This one had been made with the help of Greyskull, specifically with Kaine's magic in mind.

"You aren't going to die for me," I said fiercely, shaking him a little, using up half a container of magic to heal everything in him faster.

His smile was red. "Don't worry so, darling. I'm far too pretty to die." He swallowed, then shuddered as the concentrated magic immediately went to work. "Paper, Ren, really?"

I shoved him back a step, relief making me angry. "You can help concoct something better when we get home. Don't *die*. And, watch the vine."

Not knowing how long we had or what might happen next, I wasted no time in pushing open the door where Olivia's life force pulsed.

Like the rest of the Spartan, creepy building, this room was devoid of furniture.

But not of people.

I stumbled on my pain-magicked leg, almost unable to *believe*.

"*Liv*."

Olivia was trussed up in one corner, Marsgrove in another. Her eyes were closed, and spells laced patterns over her.

But I could see the rise and fall of her chest. *Alive*.

I wanted to *grab* her, but caution prevailed. It would be a mistake to touch her yet. The spells were all linked to a small box a few feet away from her. I fell to my knees in front of the box, and as soon as I neared it, it was like a switch flipped and she jolted upright. Upon seeing me, her eyes went wide.

"*Liv*," I repeated.

She didn't respond verbally, but she was frantically tracking my movements with her eyes, and she glanced pointedly at the lock.

The lock had an embellished design, and inside the box I was sure I'd find the spell's initiation point. A lock made by Raphael. I plucked two hairs from my head and pulled magic into my fingertips—magic supplied by my shield and the spells Raphael had placed upon me long ago. I coated the plucked hairs with the magic in order to use the hairs as a focal point and a key shield—the last one quite literally.

Kneeling, I pulled out my lock picks—the magical ones I had gotten after being locked up by Marsgrove—and wrapped a single hair around my favorite pick and best wrench. My gaze flitted to Marsgrove in the corner. He was watching silently as well, but with something infinitely strange in his gaze.

He was personally getting to witness how I'd escaped from him.

Constantine cast a glance over all of us, but didn't move to help. He braced himself painfully against the doorway, keeping watch.

I got one spell free and Olivia's voice escaped. "*Ren.*"

She looked at me as if I was an apparition, face drained of color and shock painted across her features. "It was really... You really..."

"Of course." Automatically reacting to her distress, I tried to pick the other spells free faster, fingers slipping. "Did you think you were talking to a figment?" I asked lightly—my voice only shaking a little despite my crushing relief mixing into a terrible cocktail of terror, panic, and liberation.

"What are you doing here? You can't *be* here," she hissed. "You need to be at Excelsine."

"*We*. We need to be at Excelsine."

"*Who let you out?*" She demanded in a way that sounded like a death threat. Warmth and further relief rushed through me.

"Psh. Like anyone *let* me."

I finally got the lock free and the box clicked open. I pressed the button inside, and the shield fell. It was almost too simple.

She looked at the box and the origination of the spell. Then she looked at me. I shifted on my knees, unable to read her for a moment.

She launched herself at me.

"You *idiot*," Olivia said, as she sobbed into my neck, holding me tighter. "You absolute moron."

I hugged her tighter, burying my face in her hair. "I missed you too."

She sobbed.

"*Red Colonel?*" came a familiar voice through the emergency line.

"I've got the package," I said, face in her hair. I had her. I had saved her. I had failed with Christian. But I had saved Olivia. "And we will initiate the return sequence in five."

Kaine and Tarei were temporarily contained, and as far as I was concerned, we could *leave* them. Raphael and the rest of the praetorians were...gone. I had no idea where they were. And, we were in a *ghost* town, because, thankfully, Raphael worked *alone*. Things were looking *up*.

"*Intercepted Legion communications. Troops moving your way. Three minutes. Hurry.*"

Or maybe not.

"We have to go," I said, manhandling Olivia to her feet as I painfully rose. The Justice Magic was trying to work its way through my second leg. I hobbled over to Marsgrove and made quick work of his bonds. His were a lot less complicated than hers, oddly. Maybe Raphael had thought I wouldn't save him?

Marsgrove was up and out the door almost before I got the last spell free.

Olivia, however, was unmoving, looking out the broken window at the Legion pounding down the hill and toward the dome.

Three minutes? We had forty seconds. I pushed her into motion. "We have to go."

Her skin was the color of chalk.

"I can't leave." The skin around Olivia's eyes tightened in pain. "I *can't*."

"What? No. Did you develop some magic psychosis?" I demanded, physically hauling her taller frame toward the door, shooting pains in my legs be damned. When she stuttered to a stop, I put my arm through hers and *dragged* her.

"You don't understand, Ren, there are things implan—"

"*Red Colonel*," the voice was far more tense this time. "*Correction! Thirty seconds. And two terrorist cells coming in from the north, intercepting the same transmissions. You need to move.*"

"We have to *hurry*, Liv," I said, dragging her into the solarium where Constantine and Marsgrove were looking out windows with varying degrees of grimness. The vine was still fat and full in the middle of the floor.

"No! Ren—there are—"

"Seriously doesn't matter. Tell me at *home*." I headed for the vine. I didn't know *what* we were going to do with it. I turned to Marsgrove to ask while trying to ignore Olivia frantically shaking her head.

"No, Ren, home is too lat—"

The entire building rocked, making all of us lurch.

Marsgrove had an intense look on his face, and his head was cocked as if he was waiting for something.

He turned to me. "What's the plan?"

Olivia looked at him, brows furrowed like she was wondering what he was doing here. I was killing Raphael myself if he had whammied her permanently.

Constantine answered him. "We need the Justice Magic extinguished and thirty seconds to get everything set, but we have to be closer to the earth. Any height between the disk and the earth gets multiplied by the vortex on the other end," Constantine said grimly. Combat troops were streaming into the building at all access points four floors below.

We weren't getting to the ground floor without fighting the Legion. And the praetorians were likely still lurking *somewhere*. Marsgrove might be able to hold his own against a good number of them, but with all of them focused on the four of us in the halls or stairwells? Our odds were really bad.

The smell of ozone and wood permeated the space for a strange instant, almost seeming to come through the floor. It was a familiar smell, but one I couldn't immediately pinpoint.

"We have—"

Constantine's eyes went wide, and he threw himself at me, magic flashing.

He didn't make it to me before the floor dropped out from beneath our feet.

Chapter Forty-six

CHAOS

WHEN THE DUST cleared, we were four floors down, surrounded by rubble in the marble atrium and in the midst of a battle that had already begun without us. Olivia was lying on top of me, but I couldn't see the others.

Spells were impacting and being shielded, and impacting again. Colored lights and percussive blasts were ricocheting back-and-forth like a psychotic pinball game where the ball had become stuck between two obstacles. Only, there were a hundred balls.

I crawled behind a pile of debris, pulling Olivia with me. Magic whizzed everywhere and three bolts got me before I managed to activate my small chaos field and pull it over us, hunching beneath it and making sure Olivia was completely covered. Magic battered against it, ricocheting from the *ceiling*, like fireworks that had misfired on the launcher.

God, where was Constantine? Marsgrove?

I had no idea how we'd survived the fall. Someone had to have done magic to cushion us before we'd hit the floor. Very likely Constantine, as he'd been calling magic.

Olivia was alive next to me. I closed my eyes and hoped for the other two.

On the positive side of things, whatever had happened with the explosion had destroyed the Justice Magic, I could move freely again, and we were on the ground floor. On the negative side, we were separated, and in the midst of all-out warfare.

The field protected Olivia and me from stray blows, but didn't allow us to shoot off our own magic. We were bystanders, and if we remained as such, in this conflict we would be taken—or killed—by whoever was the last one standing.

We were in the atrium, and though debris was semi-hiding us, we needed to get out of here before anyone noticed us as anything other than cannon fodder troops.

But something was wrong with Olivia. Her eyes were closed tightly and she was whispering something to herself over and over. It sounded terrifyingly like, "I *won't* kill, I *won't* kill."

I framed her cheeks in my hands. "Less *Shining*, more *Mary Poppins*. We have to get out of here."

She nodded frenetically at me. In one of her hands, the butterfly I had given her was clutched tight.

I touched it, then looked back at her and cupped the back of her neck like Axer sometimes did to me when he wanted to stress a point or strengthen fellowship. "It's going to be fine. Remember? Breathe. There you go."

I channeled everything I had learned through the panic attacks on Tuesday and sent the feelings into her—with one of my hands wrapped around her clutching the butterfly and the other against the skin of her neck.

Eventually she nodded. She even managed a shaky smile. "No blonde to resurrect."

"I'm sure we can find one," I said, only half joking. Bodies littered the debris around us.

I quickly withdrew the containers and ouroboros I had brought for her. She ran a finger along the metal of the infinite snake, then attached it around her neck. "You've been busy."

"Trick has all the reports. It looks like all current business ventures are in the black. The *deep* black," I said. "Lots of business for the suppliers of paranoia right now."

She faintly smiled.

When I tried to hand her the containers, though, she shook her head. "Better not."

"Ren," a very familiar voice shouted.

Mouth dropping, I looked over a massive chunk of broken marble to see Axer motioning with his hand.

"In five," he said.

Without waiting to second guess it, I shoved the containers into Olivia's hands on the count of five, grabbed her and ran. The field didn't fully cover us, and I took two shots to the leg.

But, in military precision, cover fire took down five targets shooting at us. Maybe it was Nicholas Dare, somewhere far away at the top of the hill.

Axer reached out and pulled us both around the wall as something exploded where we had just stood.

I stared at him, heart racing from adrenaline, and not quite believing my eyes. He was supposed to be at the competition. Right now. "You are missing Freespar."

He raised a brow and shot off another bolt of charcoal, making it curve around the corner. "I wouldn't say I'm missing it."

Constantine and Marsgrove, thank God, were further down the hall. We made eye contact. They both were sending their own spells into the atrium. Olivia and I quickly joined in.

But again, there was something wrong with Olivia. I could see it on her face whenever I could catch a glimpse. There was a strain there, and strangely, she was attacking the Legion with far more fervor and precision than the terrorists.

And it looked like she was trying to close her eyes whenever she didn't feel the three of us to be in immediate mortal peril.

Down the hall, Marsgrove seemed to be taking special delight in killing Legion troops as well. But whereas Olivia flinched each time she threw a spell, Marsgrove was fiercely invested.

It was...not right. Yes, the Legion was actively against us, but they were the security force for the Second Layer, and Marsgrove and Olivia, while they didn't wear a magicist hat, were *darn* close.

In the middle of the chaos, the praetorians appeared. Kaine and Tarei looked far worse for wear, but still functional. I wondered if in the fall, the vine had hit the ground and barfed them out.

All we needed was for Raphael to appear and we'd have the whole band back together.

The vine, looking far more raggedy, shot through the atrium, launching itself from the piles of debris and from the walls and flying like a deadly arrow through the air. I tried not to pay attention as it swallowed people. Nope, nope, nope.

"What *happened*?" I asked Axer. "How did you get here?"

Axer flinched. "When we exited the port, one of the people with me targeted the Justice Magic immediately, to give us an advantage. It worked, but there was a failsafe in the Justice Magic and the port exploded with all of you *directly above it*."

He said it like we had positioned ourselves that way on purpose.

But...porting explained a *lot*.

Port magic was singular, smelling like ozone and minerals and freshly cut wood, as magic split two places at the same time, then joined the two together.

"*How* did you port here," I demanded.

"Constantine set it up. Illegal vortex."

That explained the gem and his reply to the demon bargain.

Grimly, I looked around. "You shouldn't be here."

"None of us should. But you aren't surprised that I am."

I wasn't. Though we had left his attendance in the "dire circumstances only" category, I had figured he would pop up if we got into massive trouble.

I chanced another glance down the hall. Constantine was a bundle of emotion and rage. Normal.

"There's an opening. Go." Axer pushed Olivia and me down the corridor of columns toward Constantine and Marsgrove.

We were all edging toward a broken window that was large enough to exit when someone, somewhere, decided to end it all.

An explosion rocked the world and a gaping hole appeared in the ground, then rapidly expanded outward. It was like a sinkhole that reached to *hell*.

Marsgrove grabbed me by the back of my cloak, plucking me out of range, and magically sending us sliding back across the marble that was crumbling in front of our backsliding feet.

Constantine pitched himself forward and grabbed a long cord hanging from the ceiling, when the ground gave way beneath his feet. It was a long mass of braided wire that had probably extended up multiple levels, until the first explosion had occurred and ripped it from its moorings. He twirled wildly, gripping the cord about halfway up, dangling over a vast expanse of nothing.

Axer pushed Olivia to the side with a thrust of magic that shot her twenty feet, past the rim of the gaping hole, saving her, but the rocks beneath his feet gave way, and he pitched forward toward the center.

I threw my hands forward to call up *the earth*, but Marsgrove yanked me back, some foreign magic clamping down on me.

Constantine released the cord, letting it slide in one palm as he reached out into space, fingertips hooking into Axer's at the last possible moment. I could see him using magic, attempting to get a better grip, but the slipping shriek of world-ending magic—the maelstrom someone had unleashed that had caused the sinkhole—had a grip on everything and was *pulling downward*. Bodies were falling, being *dragged* inside.

"Let go of me," I said to Marsgrove, who was staring at them as they swung and slipped, with only a faintly strange smile on his lips. He was doing *nothing*.

"Magic will kill them faster," he said, like he was watching a semi-interesting sport.

"Are you that angry with Axer for the Midlands' visit and the vine?" I said furiously.

Marsgrove said nothing, but he was right about one thing—all magic in the room seemed to be sucking into the gaping hole, causing it to increase its pull.

Bolts of offensive and defensive magic were still shooting everywhere. Olivia was still fighting, working her way back toward us, still shooting magic at Legion members like she had been *made* to.

The hole was growing increasingly larger with every shot. I yelled at her to stop, but she just shook her head, looking as if she might cry.

A jet of black from a praetorian hit Constantine in the leg. Another struck Axer in the back. Their shields held, but the hits caused them to spin wildly on the line. They slipped again.

"I *hate* you," Constantine spit, fingernails clawing into Axer's hands.

"It's shiving mutual," Axer yelled back.

They slid down another inch, and Constantine's expression grew more pained. His blood was slicked along the cord, a visual representation of the length of their slide.

I tried to yank free from Marsgrove.

"You're going to have to let go," Axer said, in a voice that was eerily calm. "Get them out of here."

Constantine's gaze met mine, just for the moment the violently twisting spin allowed. Something darted across his face, and he looked down at his roommate. "If you let go, I'll kill you myself," Constantine said, and I could hear the strain.

I ripped free of Marsgrove, and swiped my hand downward, ripping a piece of my cloak away, yelling at the magic within it to give me *wind*.

"*Hold*," I yelled and flung the magic like a Frisbee toward them. It hit them solidly, sending them careening to the other side of the room on the pendulum, then back toward us. The magic of the sinkhole increased, pulling them downward with the swing—like a string pulled past its elasticity.

But the cord held *just* enough to make it over our edge. They let go and tumbled at our feet.

Constantine's palms were ripped and bloody, the slices from the cord deep.

Our gazes met for an instant in silent communication, then we all ran.

The five of us emerged into the light, and immediately ducked into a narrow alley where Axer quickly took down two terrorists. The alley opened into an overgrown field. The Legion, terrorist cells, praetorians, and unknown hooded figures were engaged in open combat. We needed a secured spot and thirty seconds of time.

"That way." Axer pointed.

I glanced at Marsgrove again as we hurried toward the indicated spot, trying to figure out why he hadn't let me help the boys immediately and *what* was nagging at me. I saw the slight curl of his lips, and I turned suddenly and blasted Marsgrove against the wall of a building.

"Ren," Axer demanded. "What are you—?"

"That's not Marsgrove," I spit. No, I wasn't going to be fooled by this again.

To his credit, Axer immediately turned and stepped between all of us and Marsgrove, ultramarine magic gathering in his palm.

Marsgrove laughed, slumped against the wall, then his body *rippled*. A moment later, Raphael was standing in his place, shaking free of the remnants of magic like a dog shaking after a bath. He deflected Axer's magic, then Constantine's, pulling a shield between us out of thin air and pulling me neatly next to him. Their magic pinged against his shield, until Axer held out a ceasefire hand to Constantine.

Once again, I was on Raphael's side of a barrier. Just as I had been under the dome. I moved my fingertips, just an inch, signaling the others. *Wait*.

"Such a shame this didn't work out," Raphael said, mischievous smile curling his lips. It looked far more natural on him than on Marsgrove's face. "It was going to be a delightful excursion too. To live in Philly's shoes for a bit."

"You would have sucked at it," I said, tight-lipped. "Where is Marsgrove?"

"The praetorians have him. *Such* a shame." His smile didn't dim, but his eyes darkened savagely. "Though maybe dear Phillip will have a change of heart after a few months in their care. Perhaps even join the side of glory."

"How long have they had him?"

"Since the night you set Kaine upon us," he said, smiling at my reaction.

I flinched. "But *why*?"

"He's too dangerous to them if he's free," Axer answered. "He showed that politically Tuesday. And it will be easy to lay his ruin at his old roommate's feet."

"What your little friend said," Raphael said, eyes cold. As my golem wearing Emrys Norr's face, Raphael had *not* gotten along well with Axer.

"Was it *you* in the hall upstairs when the praetorians attacked?" I demanded.

"One of your lovely lifelike dolls, Butterfly. With a very handy bomb stitched inside. *So* useful."

I flinched. Thank god I had never put life into the dolls. They had been empty husks waiting to be filled. The golem had been something far more and it had *hurt* when it was destroyed.

"Fine," I said, lifting my chin. "This has been a fantastic reunion, but we are at a stalemate and all of us need to disappear. We go our way, you go yours."

"I *did* let you go, Butterfly. For a moment there. I fulfilled our bargain through the eyes of the doll." His fingers curled up and around, a completed slip of a contract fluttering around his fingers. "So, now, we can speak of *new* games to be had."

I could see Axer moving, and I could see Constantine holding up his palm. All of Constantine's container magic was sweeping into Axer's hand.

Everything in my vision slowed as, behind them, Kaine and Tarei leaped —one moment shadows on the wall, the next corporeal machines of death.

I didn't think. With one palm I shot the entire contents of the container given to me by the members of Plan Fifty-two into Kaine and Tarei's faces, and with the other hand, I thrust a single finger at Raphael. The tattoo shot from my finger as if it had been attached to a hair trigger the whole time. It zipped into Raphael's skin, and shock painted his features.

His shield dropped, as if staring at the tattoo required the entirety of his being and he couldn't handle performing a second task.

Axer grabbed me, Constantine grabbed Olivia, and then we were *hauling* down the street.

That Constantine hadn't tried to end Raphael when he'd finally been standing *open* on the field of battle was just one more shock in a street full of them.

Raphael was *never* surprised. He was always so far ahead of the games he played, that it was almost as if he was playing on a different board than the rest of his competitors. Of anyone I knew, only Axer seemed to plan so far in advance.

That I would get help from Stevens was something Raphael would have planned for.

That I would get help from Greyskull, was *not*.

I looked over my shoulder as we ran.

Raphael smiled, a *real* smile that transformed his features into something almost ethereal—he'd always been very much a devil in an angel's guise, but for once it nearly seemed the opposite—and I was caught for a moment staring at him, jaw hanging. But I also remembered Greyskull's words, and as Raphael started to glow, I yelled at my friends.

"*Take cover!*"

They did—all in opposite directions. I chanced a single look back.

Raphael was still looking down at his skin and Tarei and Kaine were closing in on him, seeing his shield down, seeing *opportunity*. The euphoria on Raphael's face morphed suddenly into sadistic glee.

The tattoo shot from his finger and hit Kaine. Kaine bellowed and shadows shot from him.

The shockwave sent everyone in a five block radius sprawling. Except Raphael, who remained on his feet.

Raphael looked at me from far down the road, and smiled, then dropped a wide, round, black circle to the ground. It stuck like a suction cup thrown with great force.

I knew what that was.

"See you soon, Butterfly." He stepped onto the portal pad, and immediately, sunk down as the edges of the pad pulled in toward center. There was a streak of darkness, then the dredges of Kaine were launching at Raphael just as his head was about to be covered. The edges sealed over the top of them, sealing them fighting inside as they disappeared into the earth.

I gaped at the scorch mark—the only evidence that they'd been there at all.

A bolt hit me in the shoulder, jerking me left, and I blindly threw a combination that Axer had taught me.

Tarei morphed in front of me with a horrible, sadistic look on his face.

Panting, I raised a hand. "We couldn't resist, right? I've been told criminal types can't."

The rage on Tarei's face lasted only for the moment it took for my magic to knock him back again.

The praetorians were suddenly surrounding the two of us. Not slowly and creeping, but absent one instant, and *there* the next. I forgot how to breathe.

I *didn't* forget how to yank the chaos field over me. Shaking, I looked around; only the thin field a protection. Surrounded. Beaten. Outnumbered. Friendless. Exactly as they'd wanted me on Tuesday.

Wanting, *hoping,* that I would show myself as an Origin Mage. I could see the device they'd had on Top Circle—the one that captured the magic of an Origin Dome. And in Tarei's other hand was a gold cuff.

Tarei smiled at me, cracking his neck to the side. "We're going to strip you apart. I love to watch the master at work. We'll remake you so that you only work for the master. In the basement, where all hope is lost."

Tarei's purple eyes glinted suddenly. "Shhh..." he said, his voice changing tone and sound. "Save the best of the surprises for when she visits us."

Stavros.

Terrified calm descended over me. I touched my armband, then clenched my fingers around it. I slowly rose to my feet.

"Your basement? I don't choose to accept your invitation."

"It's less an invitation...and more a demand." Stavros smiled, image flickering between Tarei's insanity and Stavros' cold regard. "You *will* accompany us, Miss Crown."

"It is illegal to just take students."

"How tiresome." He sighed. "Are we really going to go through this again? Here? And, you without your support?"

I smiled tightly. "Are you going to throw me in with Marsgrove? You have Phillip Marsgrove, the Dean of Special Projects at Excelsine, *illegally* in your custody," I bit out. "How do you plan to justify *that* to the public?"

Tarei's face flipped back into view, as if he'd wrestled for control. He smiled sadistically. "We aren't. And I'm going to cut into him while you watch me, then I'm going to turn the scalpel on y—"

His face flipped and Stavros was there again instead. "Now, now. Let's not get ahead of our agenda, Tarei." Tarei's whole body flinched, as if Stavros had done something to him from whatever remote hole in the earth Stavros inhabited.

"Now, if you would, Miss Crown." He motioned toward the surrounding praetorians. "We have a schedule to keep."

Still holding the field, I sidestepped the first attempt to grab for me. The field sparked about me and they carefully eyed me, obviously trying to decide if it was some Origin Magic trickery.

"Release Marsgrove. I'm betting that the public doesn't even know you have him. Were you going to blame that on the terrorists too?"

"I find that there is little that the public cares to know as long as their safety is secured. And I do that quite well." Stavros smiled coldly.

"The public won't stand for it."

"After they discover you in the Third Layer performing *Origin Magic*, no one will care about other matters."

They were going to try and force my hand. My heart picked up speed, but I kept hold of it.

"How do you plan to get me off campus? And to frame me—trying to pretend I'm an Origin Mage so you can scare the public more? You tried on Top Circle already with that bogus test."

His eyes narrowed.

"Just like you got me here to the Midlands. Invited me here, telling me that you had finally found Olivia Price after your men mistakenly sealed her inside a building that was inaccessible to scrying attempts. She barely survived. Constantine and I brought a hologram of Axer along so that he could help us search, because he knows the Midlands best. Are you going to go after him now, too?"

Stavros stilled, image flickering once, twice, then becoming *harder*. He knew what I was doing. And his gaze promised *death*.

Tarei's puzzlement—his master might have figured it out, but Tarei had not—started to flutter through the unnatural facade.

I pushed two fingers into my armband, then pulled out Bellacia's recording device that had been running since I squeezed my fingers over it. "Smile." I clicked a button and the device whirled. The last thirty seconds replayed in the air, Tarei's voice speaking his threatening words again, followed by Stavros's.

If I knew Bellacia, she was downloading and cutting the news into headlines already—*Dean Illegally Taken! Department Basement Real!* or maybe a clickbait, *Praetorian Says All Hope Is Lost.* And the club would already be spreading rumors that the Department had taken me from campus—salting and burning the path behind me. If we got the information out there first, the Department would have a more difficult time convincing the public that I'd left campus on my own recognizance.

Tarei immediately shot a spell at Bellacia's device, and I was only able to half-deflect it, as my shields absorbed the rest of the force of the blow. I stumbled back.

Blinding light exploded—Axer, Constantine, and Olivia finally taking their opportunity—and the praetorians around us fell, but Tarei, in the center with me, continued forward.

Spell after spell flew from him. Half of them would have obliterated me without my shield set.

"Get it," said Stavros's voice over his. "There is still time. I am blocking the transmission."

"Give that to me!" Tarei yelled, firing another blast. "Where did you get that?"

Blocking it? I grimly dodged a spell, tucking the device firmly into my armband now that I had clicked it and its use was complete. I could only hope Bellacia retrieved the footage at some point.

Tarei didn't allow me time to recover, and I was thrown against the wall of a building.

Tarei raised his palm to end the fight, and Axer stepped calmly behind him and snapped his neck. Tarei dropped, strings cut. His purple eyes moved in his lifeless face, showing someone still alive behind the scenes. With an absent wave of Axer's hands, and Tarei's lids slid closed.

I shuddered. "Will someone revive him?"

There was something dark in Axer's eyes as he looked down at him. He looked up at me and smiled. "Who can say, on the field of battle?" One hand hooked behind my back and he urged me forward. "We have to go."

The praetorians were already fighting again, but the terrorists had also revived many of their own numbers and were attacking them from behind. The Legion had done the same, and they also joined the fight.

It was a bloodbath.

The unidentified hooded mages that I had seen briefly, flitting from one dark cranny to another, seemed to be on our side. Or on Axer's side, more specifically.

One of the hooded figures opened his cloak and the carnivorous vine dove inside. The figure turned and disappeared around the corner. Gone. I silently thanked the vine, then turned my attention back to surviving.

Axer, Constantine, Olivia, and I fought together. Well, Olivia was trying to obliterate anyone Department related, while the two boys and I were trying to get all of us to a better position so we could activate the vortexes and *leave*.

It was easy fighting with them. I was very used to working separately with all three of them, even with Olivia's out-of-character beserking. And it was easy to pass magic between us using me as a focal point. Axer and Constantine fought with an easy awareness of each other. As with the other combat mages in Axer's unit—they had a keen knowledge of the moves the other would make. They had fought together, some time, long ago.

We were vastly outnumbered still. And even with the transmission to Bellacia, Stavros still had plenty of heads to hop and plenty of damage to deal, and he was getting closer to us.

However, active magic was waning. *Quickly*.

Corpus Sun had a recycling unit, so the magic inside the dome wasn't shifting and attacking us yet, but it wasn't *regenerating* either. The recycler wasn't instantaneous. Loudon had given us the rundown on it. It took hours to pump clean magic back out. The active magic in Corpus Sun had been drained almost as soon as the fighting had broken out—in the initial bloodbath. Everyone had used as much as they could, not waiting to let the other side do so.

With the active magic gone, everyone was now fighting with containers.

And, of course, with every additional use of magic, the recycler became more overloaded, and the extended magic use had started creating cracks in the magic of the dome. Soon, it would splinter out, like Ganymede Circus, and collapse, leaving those who survived completely exposed to the Third Layer at its most base level—where magic was precious, but its origins and environment were hostile.

Another crack appeared in the dome.

Each strike had to be well-aimed. Every piece of magic had a cost.

Instead of bolts flying everywhere and resurrections occurring continuously, each magic use had to be weighed and given now.

I looked up at the dome and palmed the ouroboros. Somewhere, Loudon was rubbing his hands together in anticipation.

"Are we ready?" I asked.

Axer looked at me, then gave a hand signal. The hooded figures started to disperse, still fighting, but clearly in retreat.

"Constantine?" he barked.

"I need thirty seconds." He pointed to the building behind us. "I can do both at the same time."

"Price, go with him."

Olivia strangely obeyed.

Then it was just the two of us defending the street. Axer looked at me. Our gazes held for a moment.

"Do it," he said.

I looked around the town of Corpus Sun. The thinly magicked town and the decrepit wasteland surrounding it. I snapped the ouroboros from my neck and held it in my palm. I disengaged the empty container marble and held it up to the sun. It was empty, waiting to be refilled.

When the dome collapsed... Well, might as well give it a try while I was destroying things.

I shrugged at Axer's questioning look, then activated Loudon's spell.

Chapter Forty-seven

EXCELSINE UNITED

CONSTANTINE, OLIVIA, and I fell into the Midlands.

The vortex fizzled out, gave a crack of chaos magic, and a troll appeared.

I let a single hysterical laugh escape, then pulled myself together and knocked it out.

"Oh my god, I'd never thought I would say this, but even sleeping at Bellacia's sounds awesome right now. Let's go *home*."

Axer and a portion of his hooded friends—who had sprinted into the room as Corpus Sun broke around us—had taken the other vortex back to the competition. However he had gotten away from the competition, he had to have devised a way to return and not to be missed.

Not all of the hooded figures had accompanied him—some of them had melted away into the Third Layer landscape.

The three of us had taken the other vortex. The one to *home*.

I brushed myself off and started moving energetically forward through a section of Roman ruins, arm hooked with Olivia's. Constantine rolled his eyes next to us. But there was a focused sense of satisfaction thrumming in him that was new.

"Ren, I can't go back on campus," Olivia said.

"We already have all our excuses lined up and ready. And I got Stavros on *tape*."

Hopefully "tape" translated to whatever the correct word was here.

"No, you don't understand," Olivia said. "If I see my mother, I'll kill her."

I nodded. "Yeah, I feel that way too."

"No. I'll actually kill her."

I nodded again and shrugged. "I'll help you hide the body."

Constantine snorted next to me.

"Ren." She yanked my arm and stopped. "Look at me."

I did. There was something black zipping along one of her veins. Horror abruptly filled me. "What is that?" My gaze jerked to hers, as three things that Raphael had said in the dreams and in the past coalesced.

"He turned *you* into the assassin instead of me."

"*Yes.*"

The idea that Helen Price might not see another sunrise...? Not really top of my concern list. That Olivia would be forced to make it happen? That etched itself into the top five.

Because all joking aside, murder outside of regulated combat was still illegal in the Second Layer. And Justice Magic was in play in almost every community here.

There had to be some devious exceptions that occurred in homes—now that I knew Raphael had been used by Helen, Olivia had probably been abused with *protection* magic growing up, in order to subvert the Justice Magic in some way.

But Olivia committing outright murder? Probably on some public street?

I didn't know what the legal system was like outside of Excelsine, but the outcome of that action couldn't be good.

"Okay," I said, taking two deep breaths, then pulling us back into motion. "Avoid your mom, got it."

"*Anyone* in the Department."

I stumbled and turned to her. "Anyone?"

She nodded grimly.

"That...makes all your actions in the past hour make a lot more sense," I said slowly.

I rubbed my lip, thinking. Constantine stayed silent at my side.

"We could go to ground," I said finally.

The Third Layer, with its large swaths of Outlaw Territory, would work for a number of purposes.

"We can't go to ground," she said. "I know what's been going on. We have to go back to the dorms. *You* have to go back."

"I'm not going without you. And the Legion is all over campus. Give it five or ten minutes, and their numbers will probably include some of the same men we *just* fought. I won't—"

"Don't abandon me, then." She cut me off, knowing exactly what I was going to say. "But we need to get back to the dorms, and we need alternatives fast."

"I will never abandon you."

Her hand wrapped around the back of my neck and she pulled my forehead against hers. "Ren, I *know.*"

~*~

We exited the Midlands to great fanfare.

Bellacia's broadcast had played *everywhere*.

And even if some gazes were narrowed dangerously on us, many looked happy to see any students returned. *One of us*.

I wasn't sure what it meant, but many of the students in the front of the crowd had paper roses in their hands.

The only negative aspect was when the first member of the Legion pushed past the students in order to take us for questioning.

Olivia whipped back her hand to cast, but Constantine was faster with the spells, and I was faster with physically wrapping myself around her. I tucked her head into my shoulder so that she couldn't *see*.

"She is delirious. She needs to be taken to Medical," I heard Constantine say in his normal, dismissive tones to the crowd around us.

Olivia panted into my shoulder, trying to get hold of herself, but one member of the Legion, then another stepped closer, and she grew tenser and tenser.

Then she went abruptly limp, and I caught her as she slipped to the ground. Tendrils of clear magic simmered on Constantine's fingers.

We exchanged grim looks over her fallen form.

Much to Constantine's dismay and ever-simmering rage, Stuart Leandred cleared a path and the professors rushed in—Mbozi, Wellington, Greyskull, and others. Even Stevens clicked her way to stand in the path of the head of the Legion.

"I do not believe we need your assistance. In fact, I believe there is a Senate review at this very moment that you are required to attend, Legatus Shike."

The adults argued and Greyskull bent over Olivia.

"Phillip was released," Greyskull murmured as he scanned the worst of our wounds and touched fingers to Olivia's temples. "They are calling it a *clerical* error. I don't know how long they would have kept him. *Thank* you."

I closed my eyes. "It was my fault he was taken."

"No," Greyskull murmured. "Our actions are each our own." In a louder voice, he declared, "These three students need immediate attention in Medical after fighting a fleet of trolls and two dozen zombies."

He lifted Olivia and I stopped him before he moved away. "Don't let anyone question her. Not yet. Healing coma, *please?*"

Greyskull examined my expression, then nodded. He carried her toward the closest arch that connected near the Magiaduct.

As Constantine and I followed in his wake, through the gauntlet of students, I was greeted with more of the same. The weaving, waving bodies of the crowd—those who wanted to reach out, and those who shied away.

Peters handed us our Justice punishments—Level Fours—for going into the Midlands against regulations. It was the nicest Peters had ever been when giving me a Level Four. On a disdain scale of one to five, it was a weak two point three.

We neared the arch, and I withdrew the container that had held the group's combined magic, and that now contained a tiny amount of the Third Layer.

The magic within the marble reached out broken tendrils to me. It vainly tugged its fused tendrils, from where they had once more become stuck on the glass. A broken plasma ball.

Constantine looked down at me.

"What? No." He swore under his breath, while trying to keep a bored look on his face as we navigated the last of the crowd. "I know that look," he said in a low voice. "What are you thinking?"

I looked around our beautiful campus and the healthy magic zipping everywhere. I thought of the devastation and despair we had left behind.

"That after we deal with this, and get Olivia back to rights, we can—"

"No. Don't say it."

I looked thoughtfully at the marble, tilting my head as the magic tried to touch a fused tendril to where my thumb touched the glass, and smiled.

About the Author

Anne Zoelle is the pseudonym of a USA Today Bestselling author. Anne is currently working on the next book in the Ren Crown series.

Find Anne online at http://www.annezoelle.com.

If you'd like to contact Anne directly, you can reach her at anne.zoelle@gmail.com.

Made in the USA
San Bernardino, CA
13 January 2017